THE SPREAD

Lamont R. Chatman

PAGE PUBLISHING, INC.
New York, NY

First originally published by Page Publishing, Inc. 2018

ISBN 978-1-64214-161-0 (Paperback)
ISBN 978-1-64214-162-7 (Digital)

Printed in the United States of America

PROLOGUE

Thomas stood atop the high-rise building at the edge of the city. It was burning; it was on fire, the entire city destroyed. He watched as it burned, and wondered, Did it work? Was it worth it? He'd lost so much, sacrificed so many. It was all so chaotic, choices so *impossible*. He was tired.

The city was so still after all that had happened. Calmness and quiet, as if the city decided to die in peace and go quietly into the night.

The placidity of his surroundings gave him a brief moment of solace that had been foreign to him in what had become his world now. Before, stillness meant death.

The surreal, almost-tranquil state of the city made him relax too much. There was movement behind him. He reached for his weapon. Too late. It hit him with the force of a small truck. Pain, darkness. His mistake.

Stillness meant death. That hadn't changed.

CHAPTER 1

Nine Months Earlier...

It had been an uneventful day for Sheriff Thomas Pratt, even by the standards of the small town he patrolled. Ghostwood, West Virginia, population 8,231, was appropriately named. It was near Petersburg, along the Appalachian Mountains, and about two hundred miles northeast from the capital, Charleston. It was a place where everyone knew everyone and deals were sealed with a handshake, not a contract. Wedding invitations weren't sent; it was assumed you were invited. Sometimes, the one-horse town located on a mountainside in West Virginia seemed barren.

Thomas sat in his patrol car across the street from the school, waiting for Jessica. He had always picked his kids up from school. Maybe Jessica was getting too old for this, but he just wanted to keep her his little girl as long as he could. Jessie hated the fact that her dad was the town sheriff; what seventeen-year-old kid wouldn't? Thomas was six feet one and a strong, well-built man. Years with special operations while in the Navy played a part, but his dark-blue eyes and short blond hair gave him a natural Adonis look, even at forty years old.

As Jessie came out of the school, Thomas spotted her immediately. Her short red hair and pallid, freckled face stood out, a gift from her mother's Irish origin. She shared her mother's green eyes and beauty. At the moment, she was attached to the arm of who looked to Thomas like the local captain of the team. Rolling his eyes and breathing out a sigh, Thomas mumbled, "Oh, baby, you're so much better than this."

"Hey, Mr. Pratt!" the *captain* called out.

"Hey, Douglas," Thomas replied with restraint. Quickly turning to Jessie, he said, "Hey, baby, how was school today?"

"School," she replied with a quick shrug.

Happy to at least get a response, the sheriff took what he could get these days.

"Hop in, Jessie. Let's go. We gotta get your brother before he escapes the schoolyard."

"Yeah, Dad, about that… Think you could pick up James by yourself today? Doug and some friends are going to the lake, and I really wanna go. Please don't mess this up for me."

"Can't do it, Jessie. Not today," said Thomas. He didn't want ole El Capitán adding another notch to his already notoriously infamous belt. *This guy's a tool, Jessie. Why can't you see that?* he thought.

She stood there, not moving, not talking, hardly breathing, it seemed.

After a few seconds of deafening silence, Doug said, "Hey, sweetie, that's cool. I'll just catch you at school Monday." He hugged her goodbye and slipped a note into her hand.

> *Sneak out at ten. We'll pick you up around the corner. Knew your dad would trip out. Already made the arrangements. Tonight's our night, baby.*

"Yeah, see you then," she said as she got in the car.

Jessica and Doug exchanged smiles as Thomas drove toward the school to get Jimmy. Awkward silence filled the car as Thomas searched for a middle ground conversation, but he came up short. Jessica turned on the radio, and they rode the remainder of the drive pretending to listen to the music.

Jimmy came out of the junior high school still dressed in his track practice uniform. Like his dad, he had natural athletic ability. Jimmy was tall for thirteen—almost five feet seven inches, and mostly legs, which he used well when running. Both of Thomas's kids were gifted athletes. Whereas Jimmy had natural athleticism, Jessie was a dead-shot bow master.

She had won the state championship as a junior. The competition wasn't close. As a senior, she was favored to repeat and win state again. Many colleges were very interested in adding her to their archery roster. She'd even been approached by an assistant coach for the team USA archery. She was that good, and Thomas had great pride in her.

Jimmy jumped in the car, excited. "Dad, I just broke the school record for the mile! I ran a 5:15, and I got the second best two-mile record."

"That's great, Jimmy. You have some serious skills, son."

"Well, James, better hope you can get into college with those legs, 'cause it sure won't be your brains," Jessica snapped.

"Whatever, Jessica! And how many times do I have to tell you my name's Jimmy, NOT James?"

"Same thing. Besides, Mom called you James, and she had you, so… you're James."

Thomas saw where this was going, so a quick change of subject was in order.

"So," Thomas said, "how do we celebrate this triumphant achievement of yours, my son? Ice cream?"

"Can't, Dad. In training," Jimmy replied.

"Can't, Dad. Not seven," Jessie said.

"Well," Thomas said, ignoring them both, "ice cream it is."

As they drove off to the local ice cream parlor, he could not have possibly known the horrors that were just hours from changing not only their lives but also life as it had ever been known.

They sat in the park eating ice cream, laughing and talking, with Jimmy forgetting all about his training and Jess about how she was too cool for ice cream. This was their way: they would really enjoy one another's company until, usually, Jessica would remember to be mad at her dad. Thomas would enjoy this accidental good time for as long as he could. He knew with a heavy heart that soon Jessie would remember to hate him. It wasn't his fault that Sue got sick and that he'd been deployed when he found out. There had been a rash of deaths in Ghostwood from the illness that had taken his Sue. Many families had lost loved ones before they attempted to isolate the disease. He'd gotten home as soon as he could, leaving the teams to take care of his family.

He'd tried any and every possible thing he could for his wife, but their mom still died. Jessie needed to blame someone, and he'd let his family down by not being there.

It was his job to give his little girl whatever she needed, even if that *whatever* was at his expense. He just hoped she'd overcome it. It'd been three years; he guessed his sentence wasn't gonna be over anytime soon.

"Hey, neighbor!" shouted Tim from a nearby bench as he and his family came over to visit with their friends. Tim, Claire, and their son, Carl, lived down the road from Thomas.

Thomas really liked the Winters, especially Carl. They met ten years earlier when some backwoods, small-minded racist decided to send a message to Tim and his family with an old-fashioned cross-burning on the front lawn of the Winters home to scare them.

Well, the intended effect was not achieved. Tim was not a big man at five feet seven inches, but the 12-gauge Winchester Defender loaded with hollow-point slugs seemed to add a few inches to his stature. He'd blown a hole in their engine block, then the next one blew the cross right out of the ground. Tim then proceeded to chase the cowards down the hill.

By the time Thomas had grabbed his Glock and ran down the street to help, there were rednecks running down the hill as fast as their little racist legs could carry them. Shortly after, Tim Winters had introduced himself to Thomas. "Hi. Dr. Tim Winters. I'm your new town doctor."

Thomas appreciated the irony.

They'd been close since.

"Hey, loser," Carl joked as he gave Jessica a playful push.

"Hey, you going to the lake tonight?" Jessica asked.

"Maybe. You?" Carl said.

"Not if my dad has anything to say about it," said Jess.

"Well, doesn't he?" asked Carl. Jessica simply rolled her eyes and shrugged. "I like your dad, and you should really give your ole man a break, Jess. You're really hard on him."

"You don't know my life, Carl! He's such a great American hero, saving lives around the world. But maybe he should've been home, saving lives here! Maybe my mom would've still... forget it, Carl. You goin' tonight or what?"

Not wanting to push her away, Carl surrendered the point. "You go, I go, Ke-mo sah-bee."

"Key-who?"

"What, you never watched *The Lone Ranger*? It means... never mind. Just sayin' I got your back, Jess."

* * * * *

Caleb watched from the tree line in the shadows. He was dressed in black slacks and a gray button-down shirt, with a long black trench coat. Even though he had a hat and sunglasses on, the light from the setting sun hurt his eyes and irradiated his wrinkled skin. He held a little box tucked safely under his arm. He'd thought the park would be the best place to start what had to be done, but after hearing the children talking, he thought this event at the lake would offer a much better chance to start the process. The children there would make much better hosts. Once the spread began, there would be no stopping it. There would be pain, there would be great suffering and great death, but in the end, the end results would far outweigh the means. There was no remorse, only anticipation.

Their end meant such a glorious beginning.

* * * * *

The drive home was strangely quiet. Jessica was trapped in her dilemma of sneaking out—things were bad with her and her dad, but she'd never really lied to him. Jimmy was lost in his dreams of Olympic gold. Thomas couldn't help but notice Jessie had once again become distant. How could he reach her? It seemed like such an impossible task, but one he'd never abandon.

Finally, Thomas decided to break the silence.

"So… what were you and Carl talking about, Jessie?"

"Nothing, Dad. Just stuff."

If she was going to date someone, Carl was definitely Thomas's first choice.

At home, dinner was quiet, and Jessica soon excused herself to her room. Just as she'd closed the bedroom door, her cell phone lit up with a text from Doug.

So you're in…right ;-)??
Be at the corner at ten, we're gonna have
the time of our lives baby.

Jessica replied:

See you then.

Meanwhile, Thomas settled in his favorite chair, with Jax, the family German shepherd, at his feet. They'd had Jax since he was born, and now the hundred-pound shepherd was a part of their family. Thomas swore that dog understood English. He had to be the smartest dog he'd ever seen or heard about.

"Dad, I'm going for a run!" Jimmy shouted on his way out the door.

"Not too late, Jimmy," said Thomas. With Jessie in self-imposed isolation and Jimmy's roadwork, Thomas sank into his chair and began channel-surfing.

* * * * *

Carl finished dinner and excused himself; he wanted to finish a few chapters of his bio studies before he headed out to the lake. Carl was wanting to follow in his father's footsteps and become a doctor. He had a plan. He always wanted to make his way on his own and not rely on his parents' money. He was in line to get a full-ride wrestling scholarship to Howard University in Washington DC. It wasn't that his parents weren't willing or able to provide him with the education, but he was a very spirited young man. The pride his father had when he looked at him inspired him.

"Mom, Dad, I'm going out."

"Slow down, young man," Tim said. "Where ya headed?"

"I told you earlier I was going to hang with some kids from school at the lake."

"Some kids, or Jessica Pratt?" Tim teased.

"We're just friends, Pop!" Carl said.

"I don't know why you don't just ask that girl out," Claire added.

"Mom, Dad, please give me a break."

"Might just be the boy's got no game, Claire."

This made Carl laugh. "What do you guys know about game? Y'all been watching *Real World* on MTV again? Told you, old folks, act ya age."

"Well, I know I got enough game to have married the most beautiful woman I've ever met," Tim said.

"Mr. Winters, you trying to get lucky tonight?" Claire said with a mischievous smile.

"Okay, this is becoming traumatic. I'm out!" said Carl.

"Might wanna knock before you come in the house tonight, son," Tim said. He and Claire laughed, very much out loud.

I just threw up in my mouth a bit, Carl thought to himself as he walked out the door.

Carl met up with Jessica down the street, and they began to walk to the corner.

"Your pops okay with you going to the lake this late?" asked Carl.

Jessica said, "What he doesn't know—"

"Your funeral."

Deciding to change the subject, Jessica stated, not expecting her request to be granted, "I gotta tell you something. I'm going to hang out with Doug at the lake tonight. Please don't lecture me, all right?"

"You're a big girl, Jessie. You can make your own decisions."

"Okay, well, seeing that I've known you since we were in third grade and the only times you've called me Jessie were when I sat on your precious project in Mrs. Zimmerly's eighth-grade science fair and the time I broke Mr. Steven's window with that baseball and blamed you, I'll consider myself *lectured* after all."

"Well," Carl said, "I did work hard on that ant farm and took the blame for the window. So yeah, guess you can consider yourself lectured." They both smiled. "Besides, I'm pretty sure you sat on my project on purpose. Funny how you got first place after I had to withdraw."

"Guess we'll never know," Jessica said as she smiled, sliding her arm into Carl's, and they continued down the street.

They got to the corner and were met by Doug driving his over-size pickup truck. When Doug saw Carl, he could barely contain his antipathy. He couldn't be obvious with his prejudice and disgust, or any chance with Jessica would end before it got started, so he'd wait.

"Hey, guys, jump on in." Doug opened the door for Jessica but held his hand up as Carl tried to get in. Doug barely looked at Carl as he shot out a quick "Sorry, bro, front's full. You'll have to ride in the back, buddy."

"Whatever," Carl said.

"That's cool. I'll keep him company back there," Jessica said, giving Carl a wink.

Tightening his grip on the steering wheel, Doug smiled through clenched teeth. Jessica then slammed the door to the truck, and she and Carl climbed in the back, and they drove to the lake.

* * * * *

Following behind the kids, Caleb went completely unnoticed. He stayed close by, waiting for his chance to do what he'd come to do.

He parked far enough away to not be noticed, waiting until the kids had cleared out of the truck and walked down to the lake. He walked over to Doug's truck and opened a box. Inside was a hideous *bug*. Caleb placed the bug in the cab of the truck with the care of a mother placing her baby in a crib. It looked like an ant, about four inches long, with a spiky stinger on its backside. It had long very sharp teeth, twice as big as that of any ant ever known. Its back was deformed into an oversize hairy hump that dripped an oozy substance that, if you were close enough, had a horrific odor. It was an ugly creature, but to Caleb, it was beautiful, like a child he'd raised from birth. He placed it in the back of the truck. Easy enough, he thought. Soon it would begin its cleansing cycle. It was only a matter of time now.

He went back to his vehicle and waited and watched.

* * * * *

Thomas and Jimmy had settled on a movie to watch on TV together, Thomas only half-watching after knowing Jessica had sneaked out of the house a little earlier. He'd decided stopping her would have only made the situation worse. He had to give her space to grow up.

After Jimmy had fallen asleep on the couch, Thomas went to his laptop to get some work done. He opened his documents and came across an old file marked FAMILY. Now distracted, he clicked on it and looked at the old photos of him, Sue, and the kids. This wasn't the way he'd ever thought it would go. He never figured in a million years she'd leave him so alone so suddenly.

Thomas thought back to a time when they were barely newlyweds. Seemed like such a lifetime ago.

"Hey," Sue asked as they lay in bed, *"where are you?"*

"I'm here, babe, with you," he answered.

"Liar." She smiled. *"Thoughts?"*

"Just wondering how I'll manage, I guess, with the baby on the way. Work keeps me always on the move. It's not the most family-friendly job—things happen, baby," he said.

"I knew what you did before I married you, Lieutenant Pratt. I'm very proud of you, Tommy, and your guys. I know the situation and the possibilities, baby. I know how hard it's going to be. I accept that. It's just a good thing you married such a kick-ass chick, huh?"

"Yes, it is, and that you are, Sue. I love you."

"You better," she said.

"So... what have we come up with? I'm thinking Jimmy for a boy and Tina for a girl," Thomas said.

"Mmm, James, not Jimmy, and for a girl... Jessica," she said.

"Fine. Jessie, not Jessica," he responded.

"Deal! Kiss on it," she said.

"Dad… Dad!" Jimmy shouted, bringing Thomas back. "Dad, I'm going to bed, okay? Love you!"

"Love you too, champ. Bring it in. Give your ole man a hug," Thomas said.

"Jess back yet?" Jimmy asked.

"No, not yet."

"Is she in trouble?" Jimmy asked.

"Probably," Thomas answered.

"Yeah, well, she is a butthead most of the time. Even though, you ought to go kinda easy on her. She's sad a lot since Mom, but today at the park, she did a lot of laughing. If you yell at her, she's going to sink right back to being sad, and I guess butthead is better than sad, right, Dad?"

"Yeah, son, *butthead* is definitely better. Maybe we give her a break. Just this once." Thomas had already decided to give her a pass, but it was good hearing Jimmy say it. "Goodnight, son. Love you."

"Night, Dad."

Thomas responded to a few emails. He fought the incredible urge to get in his patrol car and take a little drive by the lake. He finally settled on a cold beer and some easy reading in bed. He had to at least act like he was asleep when Jessie "sneaked" back in. It was almost midnight; he'd give her till two, then he was going to get her. He knew Carl was with her, and that gave him some peace of mind. At the park, Tim had mentioned Carl was going to the lake and asked if Jessica was going. Thomas had explained the whole Doug situation to him and Claire.

"Oh, I wouldn't worry too much about him," Claire had said. "Carl isn't going to let anything happen, Thomas, not to that girl." She had smiled. Thomas had smiled too.

Thomas had changed his mind about letting Jessie go to the lake as long as he knew Carl wouldn't let things get out of hand. When he had gone to Jessie's room to tell her, she'd already taken it upon herself to make that decision. He was disappointed. She would have never done this to her mom. She had been closer to Sue than him; after all, he was gone a lot with work in those early years. It wasn't until later, when Sue had gotten sick, that he came home. He started with the sheriff's department and was able to stay home full-time and be a father to Jessica and Jimmy. Thomas lived with guilt and regret, not for the service he'd given his country, but just for the time he'd lost with his kids. He was willing to do anything to make that up to them. He felt like *anything* just wasn't enough, but giving up wasn't in his blood. Thomas wasn't sure he was capable of it, not in life, and most definitely not with his kids.

* * * * *

Jessica walked with Doug along the shoreline as Carl and some of the others set up for a campfire. They unloaded the beer they'd managed to get from the local gas station, which wasn't too hard, considering one of Doug's teammates worked the counter. A couple of the girls were getting ready to hit the lake for a late-night swim, and the guys had grabbed the football off the truck and were getting ready for a nighttime lakeside football game. Carl stood by, keeping a very watchful eye on Jessica.

"Yo, Carl, come on, bro!" one of the guys yelled out.

"You playin' or what?"

"Yeah, man, I'm coming." *Like I said, she's a big girl able to make her own choices,* Carl thought as he ran off to join his friends by the lake.

"Hey, Jess, want a beer?" Doug offered from the six-pack he'd grabbed before they began their walk.

"Sure," she said. "Doug, what do you want to do when we graduate this summer?"

"Play ball somewhere, I guess," he answered. "Town university is as good as anywhere, though. Then if I don't go pro, maybe I'll join the police department and give your old man an early retirement."

"I don't know how well that'd work out—he's not exactly your biggest fan," she said.

"Yeah, well, things work out with you and me, and he'll come around," Doug said. He leaned in and kissed her; it was their first kiss.

Honestly, Jessica wasn't really sure she wanted it, but it was happening now, so she decided to just go with it.

"Hey, let's go back to my truck. I need to grab something. Are you babysitting that beer or what? You're still on your first one, and I'm on, like, my fourth. Don't make me drink alone, babe."

"You're doing just fine. I'm a lightweight, Doug. Thanks, anyway. Besides, I'm sure you wouldn't be trying to get the sheriff's daughter drunk, right?" she said.

"I wouldn't dream of it," said Doug. They got back to the truck, and Doug rolled a blanket out in the bed. "Wanna lie back and watch the stars with me?" he asked.

"Sounds nice," Jessica answered. As they lay in the back of the truck, Jessica asked, "Why don't you like Carl? He's, like, my best friend, you know."

"Maybe I wanna be your best friend, Jess." He leaned in and kissed her.

At that moment, the bug, sensing a target close by, crawled next to Jessica's neck. She had no idea what was about to happen to her. Relying on instinct, the bug raised its head and spread its large mandibles as it prepared to bite its intended prey. It lunged forward just as Jessica sat up to push Doug off her, barely missing its victim.

"No, seriously, Doug, what's your problem with him? He's real easygoing, and I think you're kinda a jerk to him."

"Hey, who are you here with, him or me? I really don't wanna talk about him. He's just some guy that always seems to be with my girl," Doug said.

"First, not *your* girl. Second, he and I have known each other, like, forever. Show some respect, or keep clear of both of us!" Jessica said.

"Both of you? What are you, some kinda tease? What did you come up here for? Is this some kinda getting-even-with-your-ole-man deal? Dating the guy Daddy hates, does that get you off or something?" The smell of alcohol was heavy on his breath, and his agitated state concerned Jessica. He grabbed her and held her down.

"How about we give your daddy a real reason to hate me?" Doug ripped open Jessica's shirt, popping several buttons. Just then,

Doug yelled out, "Ow, WHAT THE HELL!" He lifted his arm to see the biggest, ugliest thing biting him, its teeth still locked onto his arm. The sight of the bug horrified him, causing Doug to yell again. He came out of his shock and grabbed it, threw it down in the back of his truck, and smashed it.

The yelling brought everyone up from the lake.

"What's going on?" Carl asked.

Before anyone could say a word, Carl saw Jessica in the back of the truck with her shirt torn. Words were no longer necessary; Carl's right hook knocked Doug out of the truck and onto the ground.

"Get up, punk!" Carl yelled.

Doug got up, eyes full of rage. "This has been a long time comin', boy. Now Imma put you in your place!"

"Stop, Carl, let's just go home," Jessica pleaded.

Doug looked at her. "Not happening, girl. Now, shut your mouth, or you're next."

Doug was a big guy, six four and 240 pounds—much bigger than Carl's five feet ten inches and 180 pounds. But they don't just give away wrestling scholarships to Howard.

Doug charged right at Carl, though a quick sidestep then double-leg takedown had Doug on his back so fast that if you had blinked, you would have missed it. Not that a single eye was blinking during this.

Two quick punches from Carl and a choke-out later, Doug had had enough. Doug and Carl's friends broke it up.

When they picked up Doug, he was very slow to get up and seemed very disorientated.

"I didn't think I hit him that hard," Carl said.

"He's been drinking, so that plus a hardy ass-whoopin's what he's feeling. He'll be all right in the morning, at least physically," one of the boys joked.

"I'll get him home, Carl. Don't worry about it. Sorry, I would say Doug's a good guy once you get to know 'em, but he ain't," Doug's friend said, only half-joking.

Carl, noticing Jessica holding her blouse close as best as she could, took off his shirt and gave it to her. She put it on over her ruined one.

"Come on, guys, I'll give you a ride home!" one of the other kids yelled over to them.

Carl sat in the back with Jessica. "I'm so sorry, Jess. I should have been there."

"You were there," Jessica said.

"I won't leave you alone again, Jess, okay?"

She kissed his cheek, putting her head on his shoulder. "Nice right cross, by the way." She smiled.

"Yeah, yeah. Me Tarzan, you Jane," he joked, and they both laughed.

* * * * *

Caleb watched the whole episode unfold. It was disheartening for him to watch as his beautiful creation was crushed by that dolt. She had served her purpose, though, and now so would the boy. It had begun, and dawn would only bring the light of a new world. The end of this world had been ushered in with the bite of his creation, his child. He would be revered in history as the great savior. He watched as the children departed. He saw a car leave with a load of kids, but his attention was on the truck and the boy. He pulled out and followed behind them.

Ten minutes later, as Caleb drove around a bend, he saw that the truck had run off the road and crashed into the railing. He approached the truck and looked in the truck bed to where the bug had been crushed and still lay.

There were five new smaller bugs.

That's not even the best part, he thought. *Soon they'll see, those who doubted me, just how genius I am. Even if they can't appreciate or understand it.*

He walked to the cab of the truck. Doug was gone, and his friend lay over the steering wheel, not moving. One of the bugs had bitten him on his neck. Caleb called 911 on a cell phone, not because the kids needed help, but because his babies would need more carriers.

* * * * *

It was around 2:00 a.m. when Sheriff Pratt got the call that a truck registered to Douglas Tanner had been involved in an accident, with one fatality. Thomas, half-dressed already, was out of the house in minutes. All he could think of was how it might be Jessica found dead with that halfwit and how he had allowed it to happen by not going to get her fast enough.

He was getting in his patrol car when Jessica and Carl arrived. "Dad, where are you going?" Jessica asked, half-panicked, sensing something was wrong.

"OH, THANK GOD!" Thomas exclaimed. Seeing her made him forget the call and everything else around him for one minute. He grabbed her and hugged her, almost crying. "I have to go," he said, returning to his senses. It wasn't his child dead, but it was some-one's—he had to go. "Go inside, take care of your brother. Carl, you ought to get home, son."

"Yes, sir," Carl said.

Thomas got into his car and sped down the road, lights and sirens blazing.

Carl's cell rang as he walked Jessica inside her house. "Yes, Mom, I'm okay. I'll be home when the sheriff comes home. I'm going to stay with Jess and Jimmy. Something's wrong, and I don't think they should be alone right now," he explained to his mother over the phone. "Love you too. Bye," Carl said as he hung up.

"Welp, I'm grounded till I'm thirty," he joked.

"What do you think happened, Carl?"

"I don't know, but I'm sure your pops can handle it."

"That's not what I mean. It was something with Doug, I just know it," Jessica said.

"I know, Jess. I was thinking the same thing. I just didn't want to say anything. We'll just have to wait and pray, Jess, 'kay?"

The sound of glass breaking in the back of the house startled them.

"What was that?" asked Jess.

"Stay put. I'll check it out," Carl said.

"I'm going to check on James," Jessica said.

Carl went into the kitchen and found glass from the back door on the floor and the back door open. He turned around and went back into the living room and found Jessica and Jimmy.

"What was it?" Jessica asked.

"Probably just a raccoon. Hey, Jimmy."

"Hey, Carl, what's going on? Who's that?" Jimmy asked.

Carl and Jessica looked up to see Doug standing in the doorway behind Carl.

"Doug, are you all right?" Jessica asked. "My dad said there was an accident, and I was so worried," she added.

They could barely make Doug out because he was standing in the doorway in the dark.

"Get behind me, guys," Carl said, feeling something was wrong.

Doug walked into the lit living room. His eyes were completely void of color—they looked iced over. His skin was moist and wrinkled, like he'd been in the bathtub too long.

"What the hell?" Carl said.

"Oh my goodness, Doug, what happened to you?" Jessica asked, almost in shock.

Doug came at them.

"Stay back!" Carl warned Doug.

He grabbed Doug and attempted to push him back from Jessica and Jimmy, but this time was different from their earlier encounter. Doug was much stronger. Carl struggled just to stop him from taking a step, then Doug grabbed Carl and threw him up and across the couch as if he were tossing a throw pillow.

Jessica and Jimmy screamed.

"James, run! Doug, please stop, please!" Jessica begged.

Doug came at her, but before he could take a second step, Carl was back to his feet. He jumped on Doug from behind, trying to choke him out.

Doug grabbed Carl's arm and broke free from his grip as if he were a small child.

"Jess, he's too strong. Take Jimmy and get the hell out of here now!" Carl yelled.

Jimmy was on the phone, trying desperately to call his dad.

Thomas was on the scene of the crash, his cell phone ringing on the dash of his patrol car as he was examining the crashed truck. The EMTs had already loaded the body into the ambulance and were on the way to the hospital. As Thomas examined the truck, he found evidence of alcohol and was prepared to wrap this up as a tragic drinking-and-driving-teenage accident.

Suddenly, he noticed what looked like the remains of a very strange insect. Maybe an ant, but if so, the biggest and craziest-looking ant he'd ever seen. Thomas went to his trunk to retrieve his crime scene kit. He put on a pair of gloves and used a little metal stick to collect the remains of the bug and put it in an evidence container. As Thomas was gathering the bug, he was so occupied that he failed to notice the offspring crawling along the truck bed toward him.

Thomas leaned against the truck, his back against the bed, as the tow truck arrived and the driver got out. "Hey, Sheriff, you ready for me to take this in?" the driver asked.

"Sure, Ralph, take it into the station impound. I wanna check it out some more this afternoon, when I can see better."

The offspring had made its way to Thomas. It was midway up his back when it pulled its head up and prepared to strike. He turned and gathered some more things from the truck bed when the offspring struck. It bit deep, injecting the venom into its prey.

* * * * *

The ambulance arrived at the hospital, and the EMTs took the body down to the morgue after a quick examination from a doctor. The body was placed on the examination table, where they left it till the medical examiner could do the autopsy in the morning. As it lay there alone, the body jerked, then jerked again. It sat up on the table. Eyes iced over, it began to sweat. It got off the table and fell to its knees, buckling over, with its mouth open. It began dry-heaving, like it wanted to throw up. But it wasn't vomit that came out; instead, offspring rushed out of its mouth. Two, then two more, finally another. The offspring scurried away, and the body got to its feet and walked out the room.

* * * * *

Jessica took Jimmy and ran out of the house. Carl grabbed Doug and pushed him against the wall, trying desperately to create enough space to get clear and make a run for the door, knowing this wasn't a fight he was going to win. Doug grabbed Carl and again threw him with little effort, this time six feet through the air into a wall. Carl yelled out, and he was down. *I think he might have cracked my ribs,* he thought, *but I have to get up. Can't let him get close again.* Carl made his way to his feet as Doug closed in. Carl grabbed a lamp off the end table and hit him across the head with it.

The blow caught Doug off balance, and he fell back, but not enough. Carl tried to run past him, but Doug was faster than Carl guessed and grabbed him. This time, Doug didn't throw Carl; he pinned him to the ground.

Doug sat over Carl and opened his mouth, making a dry-heaving motion, as if he had to vomit. Carl fiercely tried to get up, but it was no use; Doug was too strong. As Carl struggled to get away, he looked up and saw Doug attempting to regurgitate, but it was not vomit or food. Carl watched in horror as he saw a large ant-like insect poke its head out of Doug's mouth and begin crawling out. Carl yelled and began to panic. He knew that thing was bad news and whatever had happened to Doug was about to happen to him.

God, please help me, he thought.

Jessica ran back in the house with Jax on a leash. She then dropped the leash and commanded, "Jax, GET HIM!"

Understanding his master's command completely, there was no hesitation, and Jax leaped forward and was on Doug fast and hard, knocking him to the ground.

Carl was on his feet and heading for the door. He grabbed Jessica, and they took off together.

"Come on, Jax! Come, boy, let's go!" Jessica yelled.

Jax and Doug were in a fierce fight, Jax ripping into Doug's leg. Doug showed no sign of fatigue or pain, no fear or any emotions whatsoever. Doug got a grip on Jax and finally threw him out a window. Jessica, Carl, and Jimmy took off down the street, followed by a limping but otherwise okay Jax. Doug came out the door, his leg too mangled for him to follow. Jax stop for a minute, giving Doug a look and growling. He was tempted to go back and give him a rematch. The sound of Jessica's voice in sent him running down the street with them.

"Jax, come on, boy."

CHAPTER 2

Thomas was finishing gathering the evidence from the truck.

"Holy crap, Sheriff, what the hell is that on your back?" Ralph exclaimed. "Hold still, let me get it." Ralph grabbed the offspring by the head, careful not to let it bite him. "I don't know what this thing is, but it's big and it's ugly. Look at the size of those teeth—they must be almost half an inch long!"

"Here, put it in this," Thomas said, opening the evidence container.

"Turn around, Sheriff. Let me see something. Oh my goodness, it ripped right through your shirt and cut deep into your body armor. If you hadn't been wearing that, I believe that thing woulda bitten a chunk right outta you, man. Count your blessings," said Ralph, not knowing just how right he was.

Thomas secured the offspring into an evidence container. The container was glass, so that should hold it, he thought. He then saw he had a missed message on his phone. He checked it, heard Jimmy's voice, and was again on the move, blazing with lights and sirens.

* * * * *

The hospital was quiet, though it usually was. Jackie was about halfway through her shift. She really just wanted the second half to go by so she could go home and sleep. She was ready to go meet Billy at the diner for her dinner break when she noticed a mess in the hallway. A medical tray was overturned, and a bed in the hallway had been pushed over.

"Johnny?" she called, looking for the orderly who worked the midshift with her. "Hey, Johnny!" she called again.

Jackie went over to clean up the mess but then heard the sound of a tray crashing to the floor in the next room. She opened the door and saw Johnny being held down by the guy they had brought to the morgue earlier.

"Help me! Get this guy off me!" Johnny yelled, and immediately, Jackie ran over to help.

She tried grabbing him but was pushed down, sliding across the floor and hitting her head on a bedpost. Stunned and a bit groggy, Jackie looked on in horror as she saw the previously dead man choke up a large bug. It moved to bite Johnny, causing him to convulse and lose consciousness. The man then got up and walked over to Jackie. She screamed but was helpless to stop him from delivering her to the same fate as Johnny.

* * * * *

Carl, Jessica, Jimmy, and Jax made it to Carl's house and ran inside to find his parents. "Dad, Mom!" Carl yelled.

"What's going on?" Tim asked as he came rushing from the back room.

"Dad, something really crazy is going on," Carl said.

"Baby, call your dad right now and tell him where you're at," Claire said, handing Jessica the phone.

Jessica called her dad, and he told her he was already close by and would be there in a few minutes. The sheriff's patrol car pulled up the Winters driveway, and Thomas ran into the house, grabbing and holding his children close. Jessica gave no resistance—she had never been so happy to see her father. Jax had been lying quietly on the floor and came over to greet his master. Thomas felt like he never wanted to leave them alone again. The kids sat down and explained what happened. When it was all over, the kids couldn't help but notice the very unconvinced looks on the faces of their parents.

"You don't believe us? You think we'd make something like this up?" Jessica asked angrily.

"It's not that," Tim said. "There are explanations for what happened, I'm sure. The fact this kid was throwing Carl around the room and that he is an athlete gives the probability of some kind of steroid or human growth hormone. As a doctor, I can tell you I've seen it in kids more than once. I've seen Douglas. He is a very big guy."

"You didn't see him—his eyes, the way he was moving, it wasn't natural. If it was drugs, then that's one thing, but how do you explain the bug thing coming out of his mouth?" Carl said.

"You hit your head pretty hard during the fight, didn't you, son? Is it possible that you somehow didn't see what you thought you saw because of the blow to your head?"

"Bug?" Thomas asked. "Tell me more about this bug, Carl. Can you describe it for me?"

"Not really, sorry. I didn't get a good look. I only really saw its head. It looked like a really big ant," Carl said.

Thomas didn't want to cause panic by showing them what he'd found at the crash site, but now he felt he had no choice. "Carl, come with me," Thomas said.

They went out to his patrol car, where he had put the container with the offspring.

"Is this what you saw, Carl?"

"Yeah, I think it is, Sheriff. It was crawling out from inside him. What do you think is going on? Sheriff, I don't think Doug was just hopped up on something. We had a fight at the lake tonight, and he was nowhere near as strong as he was at your house. This was different. He didn't seem angry or looking for payback. He didn't seem like himself at all. Like there was nobody home upstairs," Carl said.

"I'm going back to the house, Carl. Look out for Jessica and Jimmy while I'm gone."

Again, he was leaving his children, but it couldn't be helped; he had to get to the bottom of what was going on. Thomas radioed for one of his deputies to meet him at his house.

* * * * *

Billy Hall was a young man, only twenty-eight, but with a good head on his shoulders. He was from Ghostwood and had returned

26

from his tours overseas, his black hair still cut high and tight from his days in the army. He'd married Jackie, his high school sweetheart, and joined the sheriff's department.

Deputy Hall arrived at the house shortly after Thomas did.

Thomas wasn't sure how to explain what was happening, mainly because he didn't know himself. "Billy, we got a teenager possibly on a narcotic like PCP or even some kind of HGH, but whatever it is, the kid is really strong and dangerous. He came here looking for my daughter while I was at the crash site. Luckily, Dr. Winters's boy, Carl, was here, but he took a bit of a beating saving Jessica. Extreme caution here, Billy, okay? No extra chances, kid."

"Copy that, Sheriff," Billy said.

They searched Thomas's house and found it in disarray. There was no other evidence to support the children's claims. Doug was nowhere to be found.

"Okay, Billy, put out an APB on Douglas Tanner. Also, his parents are still out of town—we couldn't contact them earlier. Go to his house and see if he's there before your shift is over."

"Roger that, Sheriff. I'll check things out, call you if I find anything. Otherwise, I'll just check in with you tomorrow. Go take care of the kids. I'll take care of the paperwork," Billy said.

"Thanks, Billy. I know Jackie gets off shift soon. Don't be late and blame me," Thomas joked.

"It's okay, Sheriff. We could use the overtime," Billy said.

Thomas went back to the Winters house. The kids we're sleeping already, Jessie and Jimmy were lying on the couch together. Jax lay on the floor next to them. Thomas had been going full throttle for over twenty-four hours, so he settled in a chair in the living room. Exhaustion and fatigue had begun to bear down on him. Claire gave him a blanket, and before long, he was asleep.

Thomas awoke a few hours later to the welcoming smell of bacon and coffee. Jimmy and Jax were playing in the next room. He looked at his watch: 8:00 a.m. "Where's Jessie?" he asked.

"She and Carl went for a walk. She is still a little shaky, I think. She wanted to get some fresh air and clear her head," Tim said, handing Thomas some coffee.

"Thanks. I have to check in. I'm going to the department. Is it okay if the kids stay here for a while?" Thomas asked.

"That's fine, of course. What did you find out yesterday?"

"Honestly, I don't really know. I never thanked you for taking care of the kids for me. How's Carl? He okay?"

"It was our pleasure. I examined Carl—couple of bruised ribs, but he's fine otherwise."

Just then, Thomas's radio chirped. "Sheriff, come in," Shirley, the radio dispatcher, called.

Shirley was a kind woman, sixty-five, but with no intention of retiring. She had been a constant fixture in the Ghostwood PD. She wasn't only Thomas's predecessor's dispatcher, but also of the one before him.

"Go ahead, Shirley," he replied.

"Sheriff, Christine Wagner called. Said her husband didn't come home last night. She'd like you to go check it out. I'd ask Billy, but he just left to go home. Are you available, Sheriff?"

"Sure, Shirley," he said. *Johnny Wagner isn't exactly husband of the year, so I'll check the bar,* Thomas thought. "Oh, 8:00 a.m. is five o'clock somewhere" was pretty much Johnny's motto. Thomas picked up his cell phone to call Billy. Billy answered, sounding anxious. "Billy, are you all right?"

"Sheriff, Jackie didn't come home from the hospital last night. I'm on my way there now."

"Stay calm, okay, son? I'm on my way. I'll meet you there."

This was a very different situation. Both Johnny and Jackie worked there. Johnny not coming home was not really a big shock, but Jackie, no.

Thomas told Tim what was happening at the hospital with his people. Tim got dressed so he could ride with Thomas to the hospital.

Then Thomas's radio chirped again.

"Sheriff, come in," Shirley called.

"Yes, go ahead, Shirley."

"Sheriff, I'm getting a call from the staff at the hospital. They say someone came in and vandalized a couple of the rooms. Can you go by and check on that too? I've already called Billy and Wayne in.

Billy was already on his way to the hospital. Wayne is on his way in, and he'll be standing by at the station. It's all hands on deck, Sheriff, and we're standing by."

"Thanks, Shirley. I don't know what we'd do without you. I've got Dr. Winters with me, and we are en route to the hospital now."

Something was really wrong. Thomas felt it. There was something dark coming.

Jessica and Carl walked in the door as Thomas and Tim were walking out. "Jessie, stay with Jimmy and don't go anywhere. Stay here with the Winters," Thomas said. He pulled Carl to the side. "Carl, I can never thank you enough for what you did for my family last night. I need you to look out for them, okay, son? Don't say anything about what I showed you last night—it'd just cause panic. I'm going to show your dad as soon as I get a chance, but for now, keep it between us."

"Yes, sir. Don't worry about Jess and Jimmy. They'll be okay with us, Sheriff."

Thomas shook Carl's hand and gave his kids a hug. Tim blew a kiss to Claire as she watched from the kitchen window. Carl, Jessica, and Jimmy stood outside and watched as Thomas and Tim got into the car and drove down the road and out of sight.

* * * * *

Thomas and Tim arrived at the hospital and were met by Billy.

"Sheriff, Jackie didn't come home last night. Something is wrong, Thomas. She would never do something like this," Billy said.

"I know, Billy, but I need you calm. We'll find out what happened. We just have to keep it together," Thomas said.

Tim asked then, "What do you need from me, Thomas?"

"Surveillance videos and clock-in and clock-out records. We'll start there after I look at the scene."

Thomas investigated the room and the hallway. There was evidence of a struggle, but no sign of who was involved. Thomas found what looked like a husk; it resembled one of the bugs he had in the evidence container. It was fragile, so he took pictures of it before touching it. It was a good thing he did, because when he attempted to collect it, it crumbled into dust. It was definitely time to bring Tim into this, he decided then. Tim had a minor in bioengineering, and his experience would prove invaluable. First, though, Thomas wanted to check the hospital tapes and records. The records showed neither Johnny nor Jackie had clocked out, and the hospital surveillance videos showed Jackie in the hallways and Johnny periodically walking the halls. Whatever happened here unfortunately hadn't been captured on the tapes.

Thomas called Billy over to him.

"I know this is especially hard on you, but I need you at the station. Stay there, and you and Wayne be ready to deploy, okay?"

"Okay, Sheriff, I'm holding it together here. I need answers, though," Billy shot back.

"We're on it, Billy. You have my word that I won't rest till we get to the bottom of it. Please, son, trust me," he said, placing his hand on Billy's shoulder.

Billy met the sheriff's sympathetic yet firm gaze and understood this was more than a request. Reluctantly, Billy turned and walked out to his car.

Tim asked, "You sent him away?"

"Yeah. He's too close to this."

"You made the right call."

"I gave him my word we'd find his wife," Thomas said. "Tim, I have to show you something. Brace yourself."

Thomas led Tim outside. They stood by Thomas's vehicle, from which he had retrieved the container and given it to Tim. Tim was captivated by the sample. He finally recovered his thought processes to give Thomas his ideas, limited as they might be.

"I don't know what this is, Thomas, but I know it wasn't born—it was bred. It looks like something grown, most likely in a lab or something. I need to go into Charleston and use the university lab equipment at UC. I know a really good entomologist in Atlanta. She used to work for the CDC, so she should have some answers for us."

"Okay, take it. I'll send you pictures I took of the one in the room too. Whatever you can do. I think I'm going to need some help on this," Thomas said.

"Feds?" Tim asked.

"Yeah. Things are getting out of hand. Maybe they can shed some light on things. I'm really feeling out of my depth here."

* * * * *

As evening fell on the town, Tim was home, preparing for his trip to Charleston. Thomas called the local FBI branch to request assistance, and Agent Graham Keen assured Thomas that help was on the way. Tim hugged Claire and gave her a kiss. Mouthing an "I love you" to her, he turned to his son. "Take care of your mother. I love you both. It should only be a few days. You got this. I wouldn't leave otherwise," Tim said. He hugged Carl then playfully rubbed his head.

"We'll stay together while you're gone, Tim. Strength in numbers," Thomas said with an uneasy smile.

"Call you as soon as I have something."

The two friends shook hands, and Tim was off.

* * * * *

Caleb watched closely. He saw how beautifully the spread had begun. All he had to do was wait. It couldn't be stopped. There would be no mercy or compassion. *They think this is a punishment, but it's not, it's just necessary. Does the cow feel it's cruel when it's slaughtered? It's just the food chain.* Caleb knew what the night would bring. Although this was necessary, he couldn't help but feel excitement, or even joy. The night would come, and his children would come and continue the spread.

* * * * *

As nightfall came to Ghostwood, Christine Wagner still waited for Johnny to come home. She poured herself another drink. Their house seemed so dark without him. Christine knew Johnny wasn't a good man—he drank too much and hit her most nights when he did. She was pretty sure he was sleeping around. All in all, she was better off without him. None of that mattered, though. The days were unbearable without him. She knew it was codependence and not love, but she just didn't care.

The crashing of the lamp in the back room startled her. "Johnny?" she called out. "Is that you, baby?

It was him.

"Where the hell have you been?" she yelled, her concern becoming anger now.

His fluctuant figure stood in the doorway, not moving, still barely out of sight. Christine's feelings of having her husband home swayed her, and she ran to him and hugged him.

She felt everything that was wrong all at once. The wetness, coldness, and smell of rotten produce.

He grabbed her, and she looked up and screamed as the off-spring crawled out of Johnny's mouth and bit her. The bite would bring convulsions, spasms, unconsciousness, death, and finally, the undead.

He dropped her and waited for her to become part of the spread.

* * * * *

Billy hadn't been home all day. Every ounce of stress weighed on him like a wet, heavy blanket. He was tired but couldn't find rest without Jackie. He came home and tried his best to relax, to take a moment to catch his breath, then a shower to help wash the day off. The sheriff had sent him home. He trusted Thomas, but he knew he was being sidelined. He also understood why.

Billy had to shower; it had felt like days since he had.

The water felt like such a relief. It ran hot and rinsed his stress off like it was the grime that ran down the drain. Billy was so relaxed it took him a minute to realize someone was standing on the other side of the shower curtain. He pulled back the curtain to see Jackie standing there. The surge of relief rushed through him like a wave of electricity.

"Baby! Are you okay? What's wrong? Are you okay? Talk to me!"

Billy jumped out of the shower and hugged his wife.

The coldness was the first thing he felt.

He pulled away and saw what used to be his wife. He knew it was all wrong. Relief quickly turned to horror as she grabbed him. Billy resisted—he tried to pull away, but she was strong, unnaturally strong.

"Let me go, Jackie, NOW!"

Billy had seen action in Iraq, but never in a million years did he think he'd have to put any of that to use here, and never with her. He couldn't tear free.

Jackie opened her mouth, and the offspring began crawling out. Billy grabbed a towel and wrapped it around her mouth. He used the towel as leverage and spun her, slamming her head into the sink. He ran into the bedroom. Jackie was surprisingly fast—she had recovered and was right behind him. Billy reached his service weapon, drew it, and fired a shot into Jackie's shoulder. It didn't slow her down at all, as if she didn't even notice she'd been shot. She slapped the weapon out of Billy's hand and continued to press forward. He fell over the bed and hit the floor. Jackie was on top of him before he could recover. She wrapped her hands around his neck. It felt like a vise grip around his throat. He began to black out.

He saw the offspring again, crawling out of Jackie's mouth.

Then darkness began to set in.

* * * * *

Thomas sat wondering what his next move would be. It came quickly.

"Sheriff, come in, over!"

He picked up his radio. "Go ahead."

"Sheriff, we have a report of shots fired at the Hall residence. Billy isn't answering his radio or his phone!"

Thomas was running for his patrol car before the dispatcher finished her sentence. What the hell was going on? Why was this happening? There was no way this was all some big coincidence, he thought.

Thomas tried to put all that was happening together in his head. The accident, the fight at his house, the bugs, the hospital. The missing-people reports. They still had no idea where Douglas Tanner was.

Thomas was still trying to piece things together when he got to Billy's house. He got out of his patrol car and drew his weapon, making his way to the house and looking in the window. He couldn't see any sign of trouble from there.

His other deputy arrived and exited his vehicle.

Thomas signaled for him to go around back. Wayne grabbed his shotgun from his patrol car and took up position at the back door, while Thomas went to the front. He signaled Wayne by clicking his radio twice, and they made simultaneous entry. Thomas cleared the front of the house, and Wayne the rear.

They found Billy in the bedroom. He was sitting, holding his weapon, his face in his hands, crying. At his feet was a body, Jackie's.

"I killed her, Sheriff. I shot Jackie in the head."

Thomas took Billy's weapon and helped him to his feet. "Tell me what happened."

"I don't really know for sure. She was so strong. I tried to get away. I fought my way to my weapon. She was choking me so hard. I was blacking out. Then they started coming at me. I had to fire!" Billy stated, still in shock.

"Who, Billy? Who came at you?"

"Bugs… the bugs," said Billy.

Thomas stood there a moment, terror sweeping over him. This was the second time he'd heard this. Whatever was happening, one thing he knew was that this was real, and it was terrible.

"Sheriff, come in."

"Yes?" Thomas said into his radio.

"We have multiple calls coming in from all around town. People are reporting that they're being attacked."

Thomas snapped out of his momentary shock and began to take control of the situation. "Give me locations, Shirley. Then call the state police. Tell them we have a situation and need their assistance immediately."

"God help us, Sheriff, there are too many calls to sort." It was apparent Shirley was beginning to panic.

"Hey now, pretty lady, you calm down, or I'm gonna have to tell Charley about those Milky Way bars you keep hidden in your top desk drawer. Bet those aren't on the diet list. Now give me two locations. Wayne and I will take it from there."

Hearing her husband's name and the calmness in Thomas's voice calmed her down enough to function. "Sorry, Sheriff, I'm okay. The worst calls seem to be coming from the bowling alley. Then from the movie theater. I'd start there, sir," she said.

"Three locations, Sheriff," Billy said. "I'm okay, and I've got a job to do," he added.

Billy had just done the unthinkable. His grief was choking him harder than the grip that had just been around his throat. He reverted into his ranger training. It was the only way he could imagine maintaining his sanity for now.

Thomas started, "You sure, son? We understand—"

Billy cut him off. "We're wasting time here! I'm good."

"Dispatch, give Deputy Hall a third location," Thomas said into his radio.

"Yes, sir."

The officers rode off to the locations they'd been given. Thomas radioed Shirley and advised her about Billy's wife. He told her to get the medical examiner out to Billy's house to collect her body. Thomas hated putting Billy back in service after what he'd been through, but Thomas had known him most of his life. Billy was tough and an airborne ranger. If anyone could bounce back, Thomas hoped it was him. There was just no choice. Thomas knew that until the state police got here, he and his deputies were all Ghostwood had.

* * * * *

Deputy Wayne Hicks wasn't from around there. He was a former Charleston police detective. He was a solid man, about six feet tall, and in good shape for a man of almost fifty. He had a little gray in his dusty blond hair and some crow's feet around his brown eyes, but otherwise, he had aged very well. He'd come to Ghostwood and applied with the sheriff's department when his now ex-wife had moved there to take care of her mother. His mother-in-law passed, and his ex rekindled a flame with her high school boyfriend. They moved away, but he stayed. It turned out quiet, small-town life suited him just fine—till now, anyway.

Wayne was on his way to the movie theater. The parking lot was in a frenzy. People everywhere. It was chaos! People were running, bleeding, and what looked like fighting for their lives.

Wayne felt panicked. He'd seen his share of bad scenes, but nothing like this. He saw a man grabbing a woman and pinning her to the ground. Wayne gathered himself together and got out of the car. He took out his intermediate weapon, which, in this case, was a department-issued Taser gun, a fifty-thousand-volt contact weapon with projection prongs that would cause neuromuscular incapacitation and drop a four-hundred-pound man with ease. He yelled what he intended to be his only verbal warning to the man on top of the woman. Once ignored by the assailant, Wayne let the Taser take over the discussion.

Both prongs entered the man's chest.

As the man stood up, seemingly not affected by the Taser, Wayne thought the weapon must have malfunctioned. That was okay—the weapon came with a backup tactic. Wayne used the Taser's contact function and pressed it into the man's neck. This fired the full fifty thousand volts through the man's body.

The man reached out and grabbed Wayne by the wrist, squeezing until Wayne dropped the Taser.

That's impossible, Wayne thought. *Even on drugs, that isn't possible.*

The man came at Wayne, who stepped back and tripped over what turned out to be a body. The man closed in on Wayne as he lay on the ground, and desperately, Wayne drew his firearm.

* * * * *

Thomas pulled up to the bowling alley to find the carnage everywhere. He quickly got out of his vehicle to try to help, but then his radio came to life. *Blam blam.*

"This is Deputy Hicks. I need backup at the theater!" Wayne yelled in between discharging his firearm.

"Wayne, this is Thomas, sit-rep!" He was asking for a situation report.

"Thomas, these things aren't human. Forget using any kind of nonlethal force—Tasers are ineffective. Shots to center mass are also ineffective. Headshots drop them and they stay down!" Wayne yelled loudly, trying to talk over the chaos and his own gunshots.

Thomas looked around; there were people running, bleeding, fighting, and dying everywhere. He saw a big rig truck driving erratically down the road. There were people hanging outside, attacking the driver of the truck. The truck swerved and ran into a gas station, exploding and causing the ground to shake. The explosion sent Thomas and those around him down hard. A fireball rose in the air, followed by several other smaller explosions.

Thomas had to regroup. "Billy, where are you?" he yelled into his radio.

"Still en route to the location," Billy responded.

Thomas swallowed hard. "All units, gather whom you can and fall back to the station!"

Wayne attempted to say on the radio, "Sheriff, we can't leave all these people out here, they—"

But Thomas cut off his transmission. "That's an order, Deputy!"

Thomas knew he'd signed people's death warrants with that order, but he had to save whom he could—he and his deputies wouldn't do anyone any good dead.

Thomas picked up his cell phone and dialed Carl's number. "Carl, gather everyone and get to the sheriff's office NOW!"

Carl knew from Thomas's tone this was not the time for questions. "On our way, Sheriff."

Thomas drove toward the sheriff's office, announcing on the patrol car's PA system to stay inside behind locked doors. Get to any storm shelter or protected area. At the moment, that was all he could do, and it killed him inside.

He arrived at the sheriff's station with four people he'd picked up. Wayne was there with four more. As Thomas and Wayne began to gather and organize the people who were brought in, they noticed a city bus come speeding down the main road, heading for the station's front doors.

"It doesn't look like it's gonna stop!" screamed one of the people.

"Get to the back now!" Wayne shouted.

At the last moment, the bus came to a hard stop a couple of dozen feet short of the front steps. The door of the bus came open, and Billy stepped out with a half-busload full of people. "This is all I could find, Sheriff," Billy said.

"You did good, Billy," Thomas said with a smile.

"Dad! What's going on?" Jimmy asked as he came running around the service desk. Carl, Claire, Jessica, and Jax followed.

"Thank you, Carl. Thank you for my family," Thomas said as he hugged them before turning to Claire. "Claire, have you talked to Tim since he left?"

"Yes. Just before all this craziness started. He's still on the road. He should be at the university by morning. I don't think he knows what's happening. There's no signal, and the landlines are so packed I couldn't get a line out to call him."

The people were starting to get impatient.

"Sheriff, what's going on? What are these things? I think I knew some of them!" people shouted out.

Thomas knew he had to get control of this situation fast. "People, please calm down. We have to get everyone downstairs. It's fortified and should provide us with adequate protection. Let's stay together and organized. Form a line and start moving to the back. Follow Shirley, everyone."

Just then, Wayne exclaimed, "Sheriff, you gotta see this!"

Thomas came over to the window Wayne was looking out of. There were infected people coming toward the station. "There must be close to fifty of those things out there. They're strong, Thomas, and hard to put down. We gotta get the people into the holding cells and lock them in, keep these things from them."

"We will, but if these things get in, everyone will be trapped. We still need to be able to hold them off, keep them out as long as possible. Shirley, put everyone in the holding facility. Wayne, lock down the station."

Luckily, federal grant money had updated the sheriff's station a few years back. Part of that update included a riot-control system. Metal shutters covered the windows, and Wayne locked a metal gate across the glass doors. Many of the townspeople called the update a complete waste of time and taxpayer money due to the low and infrequent high crimes. There were many complaints filed with the state to try to redirect those funds. They had fallen on deaf ears, and the articles of the post-9/11 Patriot Act were cited.

No one was complaining now.

Then Wayne activated the emergency help beacon that sent an officer distress call to the state police. It was a dedicated hard line, so no cell signal or phone line was required. The building was single-story with a subbasement that contained holding cells and the evidence storage room. The lower level was reinforced, and Thomas hoped it would provide sufficient protection.

Thomas went to the weapons locker, retrieving three Remington 870 tactical shotguns with extra ammunition, an AR-15 equipped with an A-cog scope, and three extra magazines. The officers grabbed the weapons and extra magazines for their handguns.

Thomas called for Jessie. He'd been teaching her how to shoot since she was thirteen. "Here, Jessie, take this," he said, handing her a Glock .40-caliber handgun.

"Dad, you're scaring me. Why do I need this? What's happening? Please talk to me."

"Baby, I love you guys. I have to stay up here and make sure nothing gets past us. You and your brother stay with Carl, Jax, and Claire. I'll be down as soon as I can."

"Dad, please come now. You can protect us down there, okay?"

"Soon, Jessie, I'll be down soon."

A loud banging noise startled Jessica.

"They're trying to get in, Sheriff!" shouted Billy.

"Jessie, go now!" Thomas yelled.

"Be careful, Dad. I love you," Jessie said as she went down the stairs to the holding cells and joined the others.

"Okay, guys, everyone focus on one area. Wayne, you take the east wall. Billy, you got the west wall. I'll take the front door," Thomas ordered.

The station sat on the north side of the lake.

"Unless these bastards can swim, at least, we don't have to worry about them coming in from the south," Wayne said.

Billy went to the camera surveillance monitors.

"Sheriff, they're all around us. There are more than fifty now, for sure."

The surveillance system had also been upgraded.

"Billy, set the counter on the monitors and sweep them around the station," Thomas said.

Billy did as he was told and began panning the cameras around the station, which then counted all the surrounding infected people. Ten, thirty, forty-two, ninety-one, one hundred and thirty-seven. Billy's heart sunk.

"Over a hundred and thirty, Sheriff! There are too many. We can't fight that. Jackie almost killed me by herself. No way we fight that many."

"Billy, I need you to calm down and focus. We have to keep them out till help comes. The state police are on the way, and so are the feds. It's gonna be okay. Those things probably can't get in. If they do, though, we'll be ready."

The power went out, and a backup generator kicked in. Emergency power only kept essential systems operational. They had lights, air, and security systems.

"What's happening out there, Billy?" Wayne asked.

"They pulled the box right out of the wall. They intentionally cut the power!"

They're not mindless drones, Thomas thought.

They were laying siege to the station. Cutting the power was the first step to a breach. Thomas began to think that maybe he'd underestimated these things.

The infected smashed through the glass doors and began to pull on the metal gate.

"We have to hold the front doors!" Thomas yelled.

He engaged the intruders, dropping two of them with his shotgun. Two well-placed shots made their heads explode. The rest moved away from the door before he could get any more shots off. They were fast, much faster than Thomas had ever seen anyone move.

Each window in the station was wired with alarm sensors and motion detectors. A window alarm went off.

"Where is the alarm coming from, Billy? Which window?" Wayne asked.

"Oh no! It's the evidence room window. How could they have gotten in there? There are bars on the inside of the window."

Billy pulled up the camera outside the evidence room window. Three of the infected were slowly ripping the bars out of the wall.

"They'll be inside soon. Someone's gotta get down there," Billy said.

If they get in the evidence room, they'll be able to get to the holding facility and to the people downstairs, and to my family, Thomas thought.

"I got it. Stay here and hold this perimeter, no matter what," he said.

With that, he headed downstairs.

CHAPTER 3

"Those were gunshots!" Jessica exclaimed.

"Shotgun shots," Paul said after hearing the blasts from upstairs.

"What's going on, Carl?" Jessica asked, nearly in tears.

"I'm not sure, Jess. I am sure, though, that those guys upstairs are tough and well-trained, your dad most of all. I know they're okay. They're just doing what they have to do to protect us."

Paul had lived in Ghostwood all his life and had very little to show for it. He mainly knew Thomas because of the numerous times the sheriff had arrested him. Being drunk and disorderly came quite naturally to him.

"If they do get past them, we'll all be fish in a barrel for those things," Paul said, with the sound of panic in his voice and the smell of last night's alcohol still fresh on his breath.

"Calm down, Paul. No one needs to hear your rhetoric. It's not helping," Carl said.

"I'm just saying what everyone is thinking, man," Paul replied.

"Well, damn, Paul. I wasn't thinkin' it," another one of the men said. "I sure as hell am now, though! Thanks! You're an ass."

"Blame me all you want. I didn't lead us all down here to die. You all's big-time war hero did that," Paul said.

"If it weren't for my dad and the other deputies, you'd already be dead, jerk!" Jimmy shouted.

Paul started to yell at Jimmy while walking toward him, "Watch your mouth, little boy, or I'll—"

A firm, deep warning growl from Jax changed that real quick.

"That damn dog shouldn't even be here," Paul whined.

"You go before the pooch," Jessica said.

"Yeah. Those things do get here, that hundred-pound shepherd's going to be more useful than your sorry, scrawny butt, Paul," someone said from the crowd.

"Plus, he acts and smells better than you do, you ole drunk," another said.

This brought some small but much-needed laughter from everybody. Even Paul gave a small smile.

"Whatever."

"It's okay, James. Calm down, okay? Carl's right, everything's going to be fine. Dad's goin' to be here soon," Jessica said with a smile.

She hoped she sold the smile, for her heart was in turmoil over her father. She'd been hard on him, and he'd let her to. She had used him for a punching bag since their mom died, and he returned all her aggression with love. She couldn't lose him. *Please, God*, she silently prayed, *not him too!*

Shirley addressed the crowd. "Pardon me, folks, can I have your attention? Did anyone see my husband, Charley, Charley Sheffield? I couldn't get through to him before the lines went down. Did anyone see him?" she asked, starting to cry a little bit.

No one answered. No one had seen Charley.

"I'm sure he's okay," Jessica said, hugging her.

* * * * *

Thomas got downstairs to the evidence room and found the door still secured. That was good, at least. He went in, noticing first that the window to the outside was broken and the bars bent back. They were in!

"Sheriff, come in," Billy called.

"Go ahead, Billy."

"Sheriff, they know the window's down. They're all breaking off the assault. I can see them on the monitors. They are all heading your way." Billy's voice was panicked, and with very good reason. Once they got in, there was no stopping them. The counter on the monitor was well past two hundred now.

"Sheriff!" Billy shouted into the radio with a newfound confidence. "Locker 214, Sheriff, 214!"

Thomas immediately understood. Why didn't he think of this before?

"Billy, you're a genius!" Thomas said into the radio as he ran for the locker.

A year or so back, Thomas had gotten information on a little backwoods meth lab. The information also said the men running it had set booby traps throughout the hills surrounding the lab. Thomas had gone in at night alone and disarmed all the traps he could find, creating a safe trail for him and his deputies to cross the next morning. The bust went without incident. They took three suspects and their equipment into custody. The men took a plea bargain, so there was no trial. ATF was slow with the recovery of the equipment, despite several administrative requests from the sheriff's office. For once, slow, dragged-out red tape bureaucracy was good for something.

Thomas reached the locker and punched in the code. He took out four M18 antipersonnel Claymore mines, a small block of C-4 with blasting caps, and a detonation cord. Thank goodness for paranoid, drug-dealing meth heads, he thought, only half-kidding. Thomas was EOD (explosive ordnance disposal) for two years before joining his special operations unit in the Navy, so this was right up his alley.

Thomas set up four kill zones with the mines, quickly placing the C-4 above the broken window. The C-4 was set with a proximity fuse—first thing through that window would trigger the explosives and be buried under the whole wall. The mines should take care of any stragglers. Thomas began to search the evidence room for the creatures that had made it in already. They had to be in here, since the door was still locked when he arrived.

"Billy, come in. Over," Thomas said into his radio.

"Go ahead, Sheriff."

"Billy, what's going on up there? Any activity?"

"Nothing. They are gathering at the evidence window, but they haven't moved in yet. What are they waiting for?" Billy said.

"Billy, did you see how many came in?"

"Three, Sheriff. Three crawled in. Do you think the others are waiting for some kind of signal from them?"

Thomas started, "I don't really kn—"

One of the infected came around the corner. Without hesitating, Thomas fired his weapon, hitting it square in the head. Another came out from Thomas's blind side. His peripheral vision caught the movement just as it lunged at him. Thomas didn't have time to turn his weapon toward his assailant. He used the butt of the gun, striking it in the head. The blow sent it to the ground, but not out of the fight. Turning the shotgun at the infected's head, he pulled the trigger. Sensing another behind him, he turned, and there a third infected stood. Before a shot was fired, it grabbed the shotgun, tearing it out of Thomas's grip and flinging it across the room. Thomas was still far from defenseless, striking the creature twice, once to the side of the head, at the temple, with a palm thrust; then the other, a closed-fist hard hit to the thyroid cartilage of the larynx. The execution of both strikes with speed and precision showed his SEAL training. The first blow delivered was meant to stun, the second to incapacitate or even kill. Thomas had successfully implemented this maneuver several times in the field.

Yet the infected stood unaffected.

It swung at him with a powerful back-fist punch. Thomas barely ducked the forceful blow. The infected grabbed him by the arm and launched him hard against the wall. As the infected stepped forward, Thomas saw the face of Douglas Tanner. Then the thought hit him. *We're fighting and killing our neighbors. We know these people! These are our friends and family! Shake it off, Pratt, get back in this fight,* he told himself.

Doug came at him clumsily, his leg still mauled from his fight with Jax. Thomas rolled over and was on his feet. A straightforward fight would produce an outcome he wouldn't live to regret. These things were strong, but they still needed legs to stand. Thomas circled wide, causing Doug to turn and cross his feet. The moment Doug's feet crossed each other, Thomas struck, launching the heel of his boot to the side of Doug's knees. Doug went down like a brick, falling backward into one of Thomas's mines. The explosion rocked the room, and Thomas fell back. He got to his feet and saw what was left of Doug. There was no love lost between him and Doug, but the weight of what had been done was not lost on Thomas.

"Sheriff, they're coming in! Get out of there!" Billy yelled into the radio.

Thomas was too close, so he ran for the door. He had to get clear of the room before they set off the C-4. He was almost out the door when *boom!* The C-4 detonated, bringing down the wall, the roof, and half the room. Thomas felt the weight of the rubble on top of him, then he blacked out.

* * * * *

Caleb drove through the night and was just a couple of hours from his destination. He was part of the US East Coast team that was responsible for spreading the infection. As he drove alone with his thoughts, his mind began to drift to his creation. He'd chosen the queen driver ant as a base for his creation for several reasons. Its size and brutal nature, for starters—no ant was bigger or fiercer. The ants are natural lords of order and structure; they would follow orders better and more precisely than any human ever could.

He'd created the perfect carrier system.

The oversize mandibles he'd constructed were hollowed but hard and were the injector of the larva. The larva was in a liquid base that, once joined with a human host, would begin its rapid metamorphosis to form three to five parasitic offspring inside the host. The host would, at that point, no longer be cognizant of its former self and completely under his control. The host would have greatly increased strength, speed, and agility. They would no longer become fatigued or require sleep. They would no longer feel cold, get hot, or feel fear or pain. The host would expel new offspring so they might find new hosts. The process would repeat itself until the host was rendered defunct or, after a period of time, became debilitated.

Music from the radio brought Caleb back from his thoughts. Johann Sebastian Bach, *No. 1 in C major.* There were few things he could bear about this place, but he couldn't get enough of Bach.

Caleb continued to enjoy his music. Next stop, Washington, DC.

* * * * *

The explosion shook the holding facility. Dust and small pieces of plaster fell from the ceiling, and the crowd began to panic.

"What's going on?"

"We have to get out of here!" they shouted.

Carl knew that if this panic continued, there would be pandemonium. "Wait, everyone calm down. Please, this isn't helping. Something very real is happening out there! We are in a dangerous situation. The only way we're getting out of this alive is, one, together, and, two, calmly."

"Good boy," Claire said quietly, almost to herself, beaming with pride in her son.

"Okay, fearless leader. What now?" Paul said, only half in sarcasm, the other half truly wanting to know what to do.

"You all wait here. I'll go see what's going on," Carl said.

"I'm coming with you," Jessica said.

"No, you're not, Jess. I need you here to keep the peace. Jimmy needs you here."

"Well," Jessica asked, holding up the weapon her father had given her, "do you know how to use this?"

"Sure. Point with the hole facing away from you, pull the trigger," Carl said.

"Not quite, Carl. I'm going."

"Henry, please keep everyone calm," Carl said, knowing he wasn't winning this argument. "Jimmy, look out for my mom, okay?" he added.

"We'll look out for each other," Claire said.

"Don't worry, Carl. Nothing will happen to them," Henry said.

He was an older man, but hard work casting and moving steel all his life had given him size and strength. That gave Carl some assurance.

"Thank you, Henry," Carl said before he and Jessica ran to the front of the holding cell.

Through the bars, they could see Thomas lying unconscious, half in the hallway and half in the evidence room. The door was electrically locked. They were sealed in the holding facility.

"Dad!" Jessie yelled. "Dad, wake up. Dad!" Jessie yelled, with no effect.

Billy and Wayne came running down the hallway.

Thank you, God, Jessica prayed to herself.

"Billy, help me get Thomas clear of this debris!" Wayne shouted.

Wayne and Billy pulled Thomas out of the rubble, and Wayne carried Thomas down the hall to the holding facility. Billy ran ahead and opened the door. "Get to the back of the room now, guys. They broke through upstairs. They're inside. We have to hold up back here and try to keep them out and away from everyone," Wayne said.

They ran to the rear with the rest of the people. Wayne laid Thomas down and went to address the crowd.

"People, listen to me. Those things have broken into the station. We've locked down the holding facility, and we hope that will hold them out. In case it doesn't... Billy." Billy came forward with a large bag and placed it on the ground. "We were able to clear out the weapons locker after we heard the explosions. This is everything we have. We're going to have to work together here, people."

Billy opened the bag. There were three shotguns, one assault rifle, and four handguns, plus various ammunition.

"Does anyone know how to use any of these weapons?" Wayne asked.

"Son, this is Ghostwood, West Virginia. We were shooting guns before you were an inch in your daddy's pants," Henry said with a half-smile.

"Guess we gotta do your job for you, huh, Deputy?" Paul said, grabbing a shotgun.

"No, Paul," Billy said. "You could just sit here and die."

"No big loss," Henry said.

"Say what you will, but let them damn things come in here and watch me work this shotgun like a surgeon uses a scalpel," said Paul.

"He ain't lying. I been hunting with the man. He hits what he aims at," Henry said quietly to Wayne.

Billy rolled the riot door down; it was heavily fortified with built-in gun ports. He'd seen these things pull apart metal bars, so he hoped and prayed it would hold.

The infected were right outside. They tore, hit, and ripped at the door.

The crowd inside screamed and jumped with every bang.

"We gotta thin them out!" Wayne said.

"Pick a port and blast some of these bastards back to hell!" Wayne shouted.

The armed men all ran to the door and started firing into the swarm of infected.

"They don't stay down, Wayne. What the hell are these things?" Paul yelled.

"Headshots, guys. You have to hit them in the head!" Wayne yelled.

Carl stood in the crowd, holding Claire and Jessica. "Keep your ears covered, guys. These gun blasts will deafen you!" Carl shouted, trying to be heard over the onslaught of gunfire.

Jimmy sat next to them in the corner by his still-unconscious father. He was trying his best to keep Jax as calm as possible.

"We can't get clear headshots through these ports. We're wasting ammo," Billy said.

"Hold your fire, hold your fire!" Wayne shouted.

The men stopped shooting.

"Guys, we're not making a difference if we can't put them down and keep them down. Conserve your ammunition till you can get a clean headshot," Wayne said.

The banging stopped.

"Hey, maybe they gave up," Paul said.

"Doubtful," Billy replied as he went to look out one of the gun ports. The infected were standing there in a group, as if in a trance. All at once they awoke, and together, they rushed and slammed into the barrier with such force that the ones at the front of the herd were smashed against the door.

The blow sent Billy falling back and knocked one of the support bolts out of the hinges.

"What the hell?" Paul shouted.

Another coordinated blow to the door had a similar effect, only this time the door was knocked off-center.

"They're coming in here!" Paul shouted in a panic.

The crowd began to scream and panic also.

"Form a firing line, men. Blast anything that comes through that door. Do not break formation. We can do this," Wayne said.

Another hit. The door creaked hard, metal twisting and ripping. The stress was too great; another few hits, and the door would surrender to the strain.

"We go out fighting. Don't stop shooting! Make these bastards work for any lives they take," Billy said quietly to the men on the line.

"Get behind me, guys," Carl told Jessica, Claire, and Jimmy.

"I love you, Jimmy," Jessica said.

"James, you always call me James, Jessica. It's going to be okay. We just have to wake Dad up. He'll know what to do. Dad! Dad, wake up," Jimmy begged.

The desperation of the situation began to close in around Jimmy. He felt Jessica giving up, and he knew the key to this was simple: *Just wake up, Dad.* Jessica knew she had put a black cloud over Jimmy, and regardless of the outcome, she would be his rock and protect him in every way.

"It's okay, James. You're right, it's going to be okay. Dad's okay. Just let him rest," Jessica said as she hugged him.

Jessica looked at the gun in her hand as she held her little brother. Allowing these things to rip into him or her father was not an option. She would end it quickly for them when and if the time came. She said a silent prayer as a tear escaped her eye. She quickly wiped it away, but not before Carl saw her and understood what she intended to do.

Jessica looked up and caught Carl's stare. He reached over as more tears came down her face and wiped the tears from her eyes. Carl nodded at Jessica to acknowledge that if it came to it, he'd rather the same quick, merciful end for him and his mother. Taking Carl's hand, the three of them held one another.

Another hit—a very hard hit that broke the concrete frame around the door. That was it; the door was finished. The first of the infected crawled over the smashed bodies of the others and through the top of the opening created by the smashed doorframe. He was met with a quick shot to the head from Paul's shotgun.

"One down, 'bout a million to go!" Paul shouted as he fired another shot, which dropped another infected that had followed the first.

Thomas began to stir in his unconsciousness.

"Where am I?" he asked, not fully aware.

"Dad!" Jessie and Jimmy shouted out.

"We're trapped, Dad. They're coming through the door," Jessie said.

Thomas looked around, got his bearings, and saw what was going on. He reached into the bag he had slung across his back and took out the grenade he'd taken from the evidence locker.

"Carl, give this to Billy," he said.

Carl ran up to the line and gave Billy the grenade.

"What the heck! Where the hell did you get—never mind." Billy stopped short, realizing it didn't really matter.

The infected were starting to tear a bigger hole in the door. They were coming in more frequently now, two and three at a time. The men were barely able to get the headshots they needed.

Billy ran to the door, pulled the pin, released the spoon (safety lever), and tossed the grenade over the door to the other side. Three seconds later, the explosion sent pieces of infected through the opening in the wall.

Billy looked over the broken door. There were bodies of infected scattered across the floor. At the end of the hallway, he could still see more infected. There were too many to count, standing there once again in a trancelike state. Billy jumped back down to the ground and readied his weapon. He looked at Wayne and the others and shook his head. They understood that the grenade hadn't been enough. Thomas joined the men on the line and picked up the rifle. The men prepared themselves for what they knew was their last stand.

"What the hell are they waiting for?" Paul said.

"I don't know what your hurry is, Paul. I still got a warrant for your arrest. All you're doing after this is cooling your heels in your usual cell," Thomas joked.

"Well, consider this me turning myself in, Sheriff," Paul said with an uneasy smile.

Thomas put his hand on Paul's shoulder as an unspoken truce.

"Okay, what the hell are they waiting for? Unlike *Cool Hand Luke* over there, I do have dinner plans tonight," Wayne said.

They actually managed a laugh.

Thomas went to the broken wall and looked over it. The hallway was empty.

"Wayne, with me. Billy, stay here… in case," Thomas said.

Wayne and Thomas went through the hallway and up the stairs. There was no sign of any live infected. The station was utterly destroyed.

It was morning now.

"What the hell, Wayne? They had us. Why pull back?"

"Maybe the grenade Billy tossed out there ran them off," Wayne suggested.

"I guess," Thomas answered, unconvinced. "Let's clear the outer perimeter before we bring everyone up."

Arriving outside, Thomas pointed for Wayne to go left; he'd take the right, and they'd meet in the middle.

"Sheriff, you'd better come see this. I know why they left in such a hurry," Wayne said into his radio.

Thomas came around the building. The C-4 blast from the evidence room window had trapped one of the infected halfway in, with its upper body exposed to the outside. It was still alive, and as the sun rose, the infected's veins became thick and black. Its skin became brittle. Black fluid started coming from its eyes and ears. After a few minutes, the infected withered away and died.

"The sun. These things can't take the sun," Thomas said.

"Good to know," Wayne replied.

Thomas brought the others up, and Shirley ran immediately for her car. "Shirley, wait, where are you going? Don't go alone!" Thomas yelled.

"I have to find Charley," she said.

"I'll go with her," Henry said.

"Okay, be safe," Thomas said.

The town was devastated as far as anyone could see. There were fires burning and bodies in the street.

"We can bet those things will be back as soon as the sun goes down. We have to find and help whomever we can and gather supplies in the meantime," Thomas said.

"Supplies for what, Sheriff?" one in the crowd yelled out.

"We can't be here when they come back. We won't survive another night like last night. We have to get out of town and to the city. We need help," Thomas said.

"I'm not leaving my home, Sheriff. I can hold up there till the army or someone gets here," Paul said.

"Okay, then. Anyone who wants to go with me and my family, meet us here by one o'clock. We're going to move while the sun is high in the sky."

As the crowd broke up and went their separate ways, Billy came up to Thomas. "Sheriff, Henry and Shirley don't know the plan. I'll go catch up with them and meet you here by one."

"Okay, Billy. Don't be late, son."

Thomas took Carl, Claire, and his family, and they left. As they drove out, they saw two all-black Chevy Tahoes with tinted windows. One was overturned on its side, and the other was crashed up on the sidewalk against the side of a building. Thomas had never seen the vehicles in town before. Cautiously and with his weapon at the ready, he approached the vehicles to check them out. The doors on the upright vehicle were all open. The driver was dead—it appeared he'd smashed his head on the steering wheel. He was dressed in a black suit. Looked like a fed. Thomas reached in the driver's inside jacket pocket and retrieved his ID. Federal Agent Taylor Gilman. There were no other bodies in or around the truck. Thomas knew how these guys traveled, so he went to the back of the SUV and forced open the trunk. He gathered four Heckler-Koch MP5 .40-caliber submachine guns with extra magazines and ammunition. Thomas also cleared out the other vehicle.

Guess the feds were on their way to help and got caught in the middle of all that madness. God rest their souls, Thomas prayed.

He then quickly gave Carl, Jessie, and even Jimmy and Claire a crash course in the use of the MP5.

"Guys, we have to get food, water, and more weapons. We're going to go by Sam's sporting goods store and see what we can find," Thomas said. He knew they could get dry foods and hunting apparel there.

As he drove, Thomas tried to get a grip on what was happening. These things were the townspeople—he knew that. They had somehow become infected and were now these *things.* The bug that he'd collected was somehow responsible—he knew that too. He'd heard from more than one person that the people infected had choked up the bugs. He figured that was how it was being spread. The infected people were carriers or hosts to these bugs. He couldn't figure out the how or why, but the what was clear to him. Get his family and as many people as he could to safety.

As they approached the store, they saw a crowd already gathered there. As Thomas got out of his vehicle, he was met with a mob of frantic people looking to him for answers he didn't have. Through the crowd, Thomas spotted Sam, the owner of the store.

"Sam, what's going on?" Thomas asked.

"Sheriff, I got here and there were people inside. There's no power—the power plant is offline. Whole town's got no power. I know some crazy stuff is happening. Me and my boy were up in the hills hunting, and we had to shoot some crazy idiot that came running up on us. Hit him three times, and he kept coming. Finally put a round in his head, and he stayed down. I was coming straight to your office just before daybreak to report it when I saw a couple hundred of 'em all on your station. We sunk back in the tree line. There was too many to help you, Sheriff, honest. I ain't no coward but me and my boy just wasn't fitted for that, ya understand?"

"Completely, Sam. I would have done the exact same thing. Now, what's going on here?" Thomas asked.

"Well, Sheriff, I got here and some people had broken the doors. I thought people need supplies, so I wasn't gonna try to stop them, considering what's going on. I heard some screaming from inside, Thomas. Real bad like. I stopped the rest of these people from going in. I figured there must be some of those damn things in there."

"They can't take the sun, Sam. It's dark in there, so there might be a bunch of them gathered inside to avoid the sunlight," Thomas said.

There were too many supplies in there to just abandon, Thomas thought. What was it about the sun that killed them? he wondered. It could be the intense light or the heat or, more than likely, the UV radiation.

When he'd seen the infected die outside the station, it wasn't that hot or bright yet. It had to be the UV.

"Sam, do you have any UV type of lightning in there?" Thomas asked.

"No, Sheriff. The lamps are regular kerosene and a few electric lamps. That's it," Sam replied.

"How about the roof? How much sunlight can we get into the building? We need to flood as much sunlight as possible inside," Thomas said.

"Yeah, I use a lot of natural light to keep the place lit during the summer months. Saves a ton on my electricity bill. I got about thirty sunroof openings up there. Problem is, they're still covered. I don't start using them till next month. You have to roll back the metal shutters from the office. It's manual, so you don't need power, just turn the hand crank."

Thomas didn't like the idea of going in the store in the dark. "We can't force the shutters back from the roof?" he asked.

"Not a chance. I had them reinforced after I had that break-in back in September, remember?" Sam said.

"Yeah, I do. How about power? Don't you have a generator?"

"Yeah, but it's in the back storeroom, Sheriff. The office is a lot closer."

"Well, the office it is. Do me a favor and draw me a map—the shortest route to the office, Sam."

"No can do, Sheriff. You just follow me, and I'll show you myself," Sam said.

"I can't let you do that, Sam. These things are more dangerous than you know. I'll get it done. Just tell me the way," Thomas said.

"Not happening, Thomas. There's no way I'm letting you go in there alone. Now, I may not be one of them fancy Navy SEALs you're used to working with, but it's my store, and you ain't going in there without me," Sam said with a wink.

"You would have made a great frogman, Sam." Thomas smiled.

"I'm going too," Jessie said.

Thomas started, "Now, that is not happ—"

"Actually," Carl interrupted, "I need you to watch out for my mom, Jess. You can't let anything happen to her. I wouldn't normally call in a chit like this, but you owe me."

Carl knew this was the only way to keep Jessica out of that store. Thomas understood just what Carl was doing, and so did Jessica, but she was bound to take care of Jimmy in her dad's absence. Now she was also bound to take care of Claire.

"Take care of my boy, Thomas," Claire said, close to tears.

"Always, Claire."

Thomas, Sam, and Carl loaded up and moved toward the store.

* * * * *

Billy drove to Shirley's house, where he saw Shirley and Henry outside in the driveway. "Billy, he's not here," Shirley said.

"Have you tried work? Or maybe he took shelter in the church?" Billy tried.

"Come on, guys, let's try the church," said Henry.

"Okay, let's ride together. I'll drive," Billy said. They got into Billy's patrol car and set off for the church.

The ride through town was disturbing for them. There were bodies in the street. Cars and trucks crashed and overturned. Complete chaos.

Seems like there would have been more dead bodies, Billy thought to himself. *It's like these things aren't really killing people, more like infecting others to spread this virus. It's like it's more about the spread than the kill.*

Viruses that take ten years to kill the host are deadlier than a virus that kills in just days or even months. The carrier infects ten times as many people.

This kind of thing ends species. It's like a self-aware virus that is aggressively and intentionally spreading itself.

Billy saw three state trooper patrol vehicles in the middle of the street with their emergency lights on. There were about a dozen dead infected around the cruisers. They went out fighting, Billy thought. *Rest in peace, brothers.*

They approached the church, driving up to the door. Billy got out.

"You two stay here. I'm going to go check it out. Henry, watch out for Shirley. I'll be back. If I'm not back in twenty minutes, then go back to the station and meet up with Sheriff Pratt."

They did not like the idea of leaving him behind, but they nodded just the same.

Billy went to the window of the church and looked inside. It was too dark to see anything. He went to the door; it was locked. Billy knocked and announced himself, but there was no answer. Finally, he tried forcing the door. It must have been barricaded from the inside. Billy made his way to the back of the church and found a side door that had been broken open. He drew his weapon and went inside. The church was dark.

"Anyone in here?" he called out softly.

Billy used his flashlight to search the room. He was almost to the rear of the building when he heard something fall in one of the side rooms. Billy remembered there was an attic in the church somewhere. He went toward the noise and opened the door on the side of the main chapel. He saw a sign on the wall: a picture of a stickman walking upstairs and an arrow pointing to a door. The attic, he thought. It was still dark, and he was having trouble navigating the room. Billy approached the door, and as he reached for the handle, he heard a noise behind him. Something had come behind him, and he'd missed it. He turned swiftly, weapon ready, and a big red blur came at his head. Then he was out.

Billy came to in the attic of the church, surrounded by the pastor and half a dozen people. Billy started out, "What the hell—"

"Easy, son. Language. You're in God's house," Pastor Ray Daniels said.

"Yeah, well," Billy said, "I hope He's home, 'cause we're gonna need Him." He looked around. "Who and what hit me? And why?" Billy asked.

"Sorry, Deputy, I thought you might be one of them things. We've been up here all night, hiding, listening to the evil outside. I felt so helpless. Then I heard something downstairs. I didn't want one of them things getting up here, so I grabbed a fire extinguisher off the wall and went to check it out. I didn't know it was you," Michael said.

Michael had been a deacon at the church for over a decade.

"Michael, normally, you'd be under arrest for assault on a peace officer. Seeing how I got sloppy and you sneaked up on me, though, you don't tell and I won't," Billy said.

Charley came out of the crowd and asked, "Deputy, my wife, Shirley, she works with you. Please, is she all right?"

Billy took a few seconds to smile. We needed this win, he thought. "She's fine. How long have I been out?"

"Nearly an hour," Ray said.

"She and Henry were outside, waiting for me. She came looking for you, Charley, but I told them to meet me at the sheriff's office if I wasn't out in twenty minutes."

Billy gathered everyone and took them outside, briefing them on the night's events. When they stepped outside, Shirley and Henry were still there, to his surprise.

"She wouldn't leave you, Deputy. I wanted to go in after you, but I didn't want to leave her out here by herself," Henry said.

"It's ok, Henry. Shirley, got someone here who wants to know if you'd be interested in dinner and drinks when this is all over," Billy said.

Charley walked out of the church, and Shirley ran to him. They held each other and cried. Billy, seeing them, remembered Jackie. He felt the bittersweet feeling of loss and reunion.

"Okay, everyone, gather around. We have to meet the sheriff at one o'clock at the sheriff's station. We're going to move out from there. Get what you need and be there if you're going with us. Stay safe, and Godspeed," Billy announced.

"Sheriff, come in. Over," Billy said into his radio.

"Go ahead, Billy."

"I'm clear here. Where do you need me now?"

"I could use you here at Sam's," Thomas said.

"On my way." Billy took Henry, and they drove off.

* * * * *

Thomas met his deputies at the sporting goods store. Wayne arrived shortly after Billy, and they convened for a briefing. Thomas began explaining the situation. "There are too many supplies in there to leave behind. It's almost ten, so we got three hours to get this done and be at the station. Billy, stay here for crowd control. Wayne, you're with me, Carl, and Sam. We stay grouped. Carl, you're by the door. Stay in the sunlight," Thomas said. "Keep our exit clear in case we need to get out of there fast. We're counting on you. You're good with the weapons training I gave you, right?" Thomas added.

"I got it, Sheriff," Carl said.

"Wayne, you and I provide cover for Sam. He's leading the way to his office. We don't have any idea how many of those things are in there, so silence is our friend, guys. Here, Wayne, found these on some federal agents that were coming to help. They didn't make it," Thomas said as he handed Wayne one of the MP5s.

"Okay, guys, let's move out."

They came to the doors, and Carl posted up right inside as the rest of the group moved in quietly. "The office is to the right, up at the end of the fishing aisle," Sam whispered.

The store was fifteen thousand square feet. The shelving was as high as fifteen feet, with merchandise stacked up another four or five feet up. They made their way down the aisle. Thomas signaled for Wayne to stay at the end of the aisle and keep watch while he and Sam moved on. Thomas grabbed Sam by the shoulder and pointed to the next aisle over. Two infected were wandering up ahead in the other aisle. They seemed completely oblivious. Thomas had seen firsthand what these things were capable of, so he wasn't taking any chances. He and Sam stayed low and out of sight until the infected wandered by. Thomas signaled Sam to move on, that it was clear.

They made it to the office.

Sam went to the crank right away, and Thomas watched as Sam began opening the metal shutters on the sun windows. Sam's first turn made a very loud creaking noise.

"Sam, stop! It's too loud," Thomas whispered.

But it was too late—the infected were now fully aware.

Thomas saw two of the infected moving fast toward the office, but Thomas was in a good position. The infected, no doubt, had seen Sam, as he was standing in plain sight.

"Sam, trust me. Don't move. Stay right where you are."

"Sheriff, they're coming right at me!"

"Sam, I've got you covered, trust me!" Thomas pleaded.

The infected smashed through the office window. Their only focus was on Sam; Thomas was completely overlooked, hiding in the corner. When they jumped through the window, the infected leaped straight past him; he was now behind them. Sam involuntarily yelled out as the infected charged him. Thomas rose up and leveled his weapon. Two quick bursts, and the infected were down, two rounds to the head each.

"Now, Sam, go for the shutters!" Thomas yelled.

Wayne came running into the office.

"We got company coming," Wayne said.

"How many, Wayne?" Thomas asked.

Wayne didn't answer; he just looked at Thomas and quickly shook his head. Thomas understood.

"Hey, Wayne, ever have that Butch and Sundance kind of day?" Thomas joked. Wayne didn't laugh. "Too soon?" Thomas said, attempting one last shot of calming humor.

"They're coming. Sam, get those shutters open. Wayne, short controlled bursts. We don't have to kill them all, just hold them back till Sam opens the shutters."

The infected were coming toward the office quickly now. They were gathering, preparing to crash down on them. Thomas and Wayne readied their weapons and rose up from cover. But they were not prepared for what they saw. There must have been fifty infected outside the office. They opened fire and prayed. All they had now was God and their guns, and they'd need both to walk out of there alive.

CHAPTER 4

The gunshots rang out loud to the group outside. Billy ran up to the entrance of the store. "Sheriff, come in. If you can report in, let us know what we can do from this end."

Carl and Billy stood outside, waiting for word from inside.

"Should we go in and try to help out, Billy?" Carl asked.

"No. They're depending on us to make sure they have a clear exit."

From where they were standing, they could see numerous infected running through the store toward the office. "They'll never get through them," Carl said.

"Yeah, they will. I've got an idea. Wait here, Carl."

Inside, Thomas and Wayne were holding their own against the horde. These things were fast and incredibly agile. It wasn't easy getting the headshots that they needed to put them down. All at once, the infected stopped coming.

"What the hell? These things had enough?" Wayne asked.

"Don't count on it, Wayne. Stay ready. Sam, how's it going?"

"I've always used the electric opener. This crank is stiff and hard to turn. The panels are starting to open, though," Sam said.

"Over there," Thomas said, pointing to one of the infected standing just outside Thomas's gun range.

Wayne and Thomas watched as the infected bent over and released the offspring he was carrying inside of him.

"What the hell just happened?" Wayne exclaimed.

"I've seen these things before, Wayne. They're bad news. Don't let them near you. I think their bite is what turns people into these things," Thomas warned.

Just as they were preparing for the offspring's attack, the sun windows began to open.

Outside, Billy ran to the propane tank cage and used his asp baton to break the padlock open. He grabbed two propane tanks and ran back to the front door. Placing the tanks in front of the doors, he ran to his patrol car to retrieve two road flares and some duct tape. Taping the flares to the tanks made for a potent makeshift bomb.

Inside, Thomas and Wayne were firing at the offspring, which were harder to hit than the infected. At least you didn't need a headshot.

"We have to move now!" Thomas yelled out.

"I'm almost done," Sam said.

One of the offspring climbed along the wall. They hadn't seen it. It crawled down the wall toward the hand crank, opening its mandibles wide, preparing for its attack, as Sam was making the final turns.

"Ah! Something bit me!" Sam yelled out.

The offspring bit deep into Sam's hand, latching on and injecting its fluid and larva. Sam finished the last turn and fell to the floor.

"Sam!" Wayne cried out.

"Come on, Wayne, we have to go!" Thomas said.

"We can't just leave him, Sheriff."

"He's gone, Wayne, and we have to go."

Wayne ran over and picked Sam up in a fireman's carry and headed for the door. By then, the building was streaked with rays of sunlight. But it wasn't enough. The infected were able to avoid most of the rays of light.

"We have to get out of here. There is not enough light to kill these things, but we should be able to navigate through the store back to the front door. We just have to stay in the light, Wayne. I'll do my best to cover you. Let's move!"

As they moved through the store, the infected and the offspring moved in close to them but avoided the sun as best as they could. The ones that tried to brave the sunlight were met with rounds from Thomas's weapon. Thomas and Wayne moved as swiftly as they could to the door.

"We're almost there, Wayne. Keep moving!"

Fifty yards from the door, Thomas's heart sank. It was darkness. No beams of sunlight to protect them. The infected were gathered in front of the door. There was no getting past them. To make matters worse, it looked like rain—clouds closing in, taking what little sunlight they had for protection away.

"Okay, what now, Sheriff?"

Thomas stood in silence for a moment then spoke. "We fight them till we can't, Wayne, fight them till we can't."

The room was loud with the sound of the infected and the offspring. There were still too many of them. This plan was a complete failure. They'd lost Sam and had not recovered any supplies, and now it looked as though he and Wayne wouldn't make it out either.

"Sheriff! Sheriff, can you hear me? Sheriff, get to cover, get to cover!"

The sound was barely audible.

"Wayne, did you hear that?"

Thomas could not see very well past the infected, but he could see the exit, and he was sure that Carl and mostly likely Billy were still by the door.

Once again, he heard, "Get down, guys, get down!"

The infected began to close in—the sun was behind the clouds, and they moved in while they had the opportunity. Thomas and Wayne raised their weapons. They had nothing but ill-willed intentions for their final stand. Then Thomas saw a flare come rolling in their direction. All of a sudden, it all made sense. Thomas grabbed Wayne and threw him to the ground, then using his own body, he fell on Wayne to shield him.

"Down!" Thomas shouted.

The propane tank stopped in the middle of the infected. Billy got the tank square in the A-cog sights mounted on his rifle's top assembly. Billy squeezed the trigger, followed by a loud bang, and then *boom!* The infected were blown back, some in pieces.

"Up, let's move!" Thomas commanded.

Wayne went to grab Sam, but he had already become infected. Sam's body lay in a beam of sunlight that had broken through the sunroof. His skin was full of thick black veins, and his eyes and ears were streaming with black fluid from the exposure. He was already dead.

"They're giving us an opening, but we have to move now!"

Thomas and Wayne ran for the door, the infected and the offspring in pursuit. The infected moved with so much speed; they leaped thirty feet in the air, grabbing on to shelving units and propelling themselves forward. Their agility was only matched by their speed. As the infected moved closer and closer, Thomas didn't think they would make it—the infected were too fast. Thomas and Wayne saw another flared propane tank rolling at them. It was the chance they needed in order to get clear. They jumped over it and continued running. Billy had the tank in his sights. He had to give his friends a few more seconds, and then he could fire.

The infected were on Thomas and Wayne. Another few seconds, and it'd be over; they would be overwhelmed.

Billy fired the weapon with perfect precision. The round flew true straight at the tank. At the last possible moment, one of the offspring happened to move in the path of the bullet. The offspring was shredded into mush, but the tank stood untouched.

"No!" Billy yelled.

Billy raised his weapon for a last desperate attempt. Before he could level the weapon, a shot from behind him fired, and the propane tank exploded. The offspring and infected behind Thomas and Wayne were scattered. They now had a clear path out. Billy turned to see Paul standing behind him, his hunting rifle still smoking.

"Still doing your job for you, huh, Deputy?" Paul teased with a wink.

"Damn! Nice shot, Paul," Billy replied.

The cloud cover had passed, and it was sunny again. The fire from the tanks spread and began consuming the store and the infected. Thomas and Wayne ran from the store, barely avoiding the flames.

The group outside looked at them with disbelief and disappointment. While bent over and holding his knees, Thomas spotted Danny, Sam's son. Thomas took another second to catch his breath before approaching him. He was just fifteen years old and went to school with Jessica, but the grade difference kept them from much socializing. Danny had been with Sam through the night and witnessed the infected firsthand. The flames now shooting high into the sky danced through the building, bringing it down. The infected, now exposed to the sun, fell and died.

Thomas solemnly made his way over to Danny. The look on Thomas's face as he approached the teen told Danny everything he needed to know. "He's dead, isn't he, Sheriff?"

"Yes, he is, Danny. I'm so sorry. He saved us—Wayne and I both would have died in there if your father hadn't opened those shutters. Even after getting wounded, he still saved us," Thomas said.

Jessica put her arms around Danny. Carl and Jimmy placed their hands on his shoulder, and they comforted their friend as he cried. It was almost noon now.

"People, can I have your attention?" Thomas shouted out. "As you can see, there are no supplies here for us. If you need help getting out of town, meet us at the sheriff's station in one hour."

"Sheriff!" Danny called out to Thomas. "If you take me to my house, my dad kept some stuff there. Maybe it'll help."

"I'll take him, Sheriff," Billy said.

Thomas took his group and headed to the sheriff's station. He wanted to be there to start organizing the move.

* * * * *

Thomas and Wayne waited outside the sheriff's station, arranging the weapons and supplies they had. Billy and Danny drove up.

"Any problems, Billy?" Wayne asked.

"None. Sam had some good stuff, though. Not a lot, but it'll help," Billy replied.

They unloaded the bags Billy and Danny had brought back, and Thomas inspected the inventory. There were two 12-gauge shotguns and two .30-06 Springfield hunting rifles with various ammunition, an M1911 .45 handgun, gallons of water, and multiple packs of dehydrated food and beef strips. Also, maybe most importantly of all, a short-range radio.

"Good job, guys. This stuff is a lifesaver," Thomas told Billy and Danny. "Danny, you'll ride with me and my group, okay?"

"Okay, but the 1911 was my dad's service pistol when he was in Vietnam. I'd like to have it, please. I know how to use it," Danny said.

"Of course, Danny," Thomas said, handing the pistol over to Danny.

It was one o'clock now, and very few people had come to the sheriff's station.

"Guess people decided to venture out on their own," Wayne said.

Thomas replied, "Do you blame them after the fiasco at Sam's? That was a cluster. A good man died, and it's all on me. I don't blame them for losing confidence in me."

"Okay, well," Wayne said, "if the pity party is over, I'm still banking on your ass to get me out of this mess, so… shall we?" Wayne added.

"You're a jerk, Wayne, and you can forget all about your annual pay raise too."

"Yeah, Thomas, and you're the best chance we have, whether these people realize it or not. You can keep your raise—at this point, I'd love to just see the annual."

They laughed.

Thomas gathered everyone together. There were Wayne, Billy, Jessica, Jimmy, Jax, Claire, Danny, Henry, Paul, Shirley and Charley Sheffield, Pastor Ray, and the church deacon, Michael. Two families that had decided Thomas was the best way out of there. Pete and Mary Smith and their thirteen-year-old son, Phillip. James and Pauline Crest had been married for twenty years. James wanted to go out on their own, but Pauline had convinced him to go with the sheriff. They divided into four vehicles: three Chevy Suburban four-wheel drive V8 LTs and one Ford F350 superduty pickup truck, all of which Thomas, Wayne, and Carl had acquired throughout town. Paul and Henry rode with the Crests, while Wayne rode with the Smiths, Ray, and Michael. Billy drove the pickup with Shirley and Charley and the supplies in the back. They had planned to head for the city. First, the university. Thomas wanted to meet with Tim and learn everything he had found out, and Carl and Claire were more than good with that plan. Once they hit the city limit, the convoy would split up. Thomas and his group would go to the university, and the rest would head to the local law enforcement station.

They headed out hopeful, driving out of Ghostwood's city limits and leaving behind the worst night they'd ever had, a lifetime of the best memories most of them ever made.

Everyone in Thomas's truck had fallen asleep except Thomas, who was driving, Carl, and Jessica.

"I'm glad Danny fell asleep. Poor guy," Jessica said.

"Yeah, I know. I can't imagine losing my dad like that," Carl added.

"Yeah, well, I almost did lose my dad last night, more than once."

"I know. He was pretty amazing, they all were. They saved us, Jess."

Jessica said. "Who knew *Mayberry* PD were such badasses?"

"I heard that," Thomas said. "Language, Jessie," he added.

Carl and Jessica sank low in their seats, laughing softly.

"Seriously, though, guys, get some sleep," Thomas said.

"Okay, Dad," Jessica said. "Hey, Carl, you mind if I stretch out?" she asked, patting his lap.

"Go ahead, Jess. I've been your throw rug since we were twelve. I may as well be your pillow too."

"Good boy. Isn't it better when we agree?" Jessica said with a wink as she lay her head in Carl's lap.

They were asleep in minutes.

Throughout the drive, Thomas tried calling Tim and multiple law enforcement agencies, but his cell still had no signal, and his radio wasn't receiving. Even the police emergency broadcast channel was down.

* * * * *

James and Paul knew each other from late nights at the local bar and struck up a conversation.

"What's this guy's deal, Paul?"

"What are you talking about, James?"

"The sheriff. He sure likes to be in charge, doesn't he?" James said.

"Well," Henry jumped in, "he is the sheriff, James."

"Don't mean nothing to me," James said.

Paul said, "He kept me alive last night, James. As long as he follows that pattern, he's okay with me."

"I heard he got ole Sam Collins killed while trying to take stuff from his store," James said.

"Oh, don't believe everything you hear, James. We were there, and it was nothing like that. Sam died protecting those boys, and the sheriff and Wayne were trying to help all of us!" Henry said.

James said, "Well, damn, Hank, join the man's fan club, why don't ya?"

"Shoot! Truth be told, I didn't even vote for the guy during the election. He's just doing okay, that's all I'm saying. Give him a chance, James," Henry said.

"I voted for Sutters in the election," James said.

"Vote? I didn't even know we had an election," Paul said.

"Maybe you outta stop drinking so much, or at least stop drinking earlier than dawn," Henry said.

They laughed.

"Wish I had a drink now," Paul mumbled.

The convoy had been on the road for hours when they came to the next viable town, Huntersville.

"Okay, guys, we'll stop here for gas and stretch our legs," Thomas said into his radio.

They rode into town, and it was as if the nightmare had followed them. They had driven through a few other towns on the way here, but they were too damaged from the infected's attack for the group to stop. This town didn't look much better. The streets were littered with vehicles and a few bodies. It was eerily similar to Ghostwood, but they had no choice but to stop.

"It happened here too," Jimmy said.

Thomas responded, "Looks that way, champ."

"What's going on, Dad? Is this happening everywhere?" Jessie asked.

"I'm not sure exactly what's happening, Jessie. Same plan, though. This town still has power. We gas up, and we keep moving."

They pulled over at a gas station, and everyone got out of the vehicles. Wayne, Thomas, and Billy walked over to the gas pumps for a quick parley.

"What are you thinking here, Thomas?" Wayne asked.

"Well, it definitely looks bad. We don't have time to figure this out either. We got maybe three hours of daylight left. We have to get into the city."

"What do we do if it's the same there?" Billy asked.

But Thomas had already entertained that thought. "We'll work it out, Billy," he said with an uneasy smile.

"Dad, we're going to get some stuff to eat out of the station," Jessie said.

Jessica and Carl took Danny, Jimmy, Phillip, and Jax into the gas station to fill up on junk food and let the adults talk. The rest of the group gathered around the officers.

James said, "What's the plan here, Sheriff? This looks like whatever happened in Ghostwood is bigger than we thought."

"You're right, James. To be honest, I'm not getting a good feeling about Charleston. I've tried multiple channels, and I haven't been able to reach a soul. It's going to be dark soon. If we go to the city and it's like this, we'll be exposed and we will not survive the night. These things are, or *were*, people. We need to be where there wasn't a lot of people, like the woods. We can drive about a hundred miles outside of town and set up an overnight camp. We can then head into the city at first light, with plenty of sun to protect us from them."

"I don't know, Sheriff. That seems risky. Why don't we find a bank and hide in the vault?" Paul asked.

"Well, Paul, if we find a vault, how do we open it? If it is open and we go inside and close it, then how do we get out in the morning?" Thomas said. "I think we should just camp out for the night."

"You want us out in the open? That's a death sentence!" James said. "Look, I know this town. I used to be an armored car driver here for ten years before I moved to Ghostwood. The bay where we stored the money for delivery is basically a bank vault. We can hole up there and then, in the morning, figure out what's best," James added.

"Listen to me," Thomas said. "Some of you weren't in the police station last night and didn't see what these things did to a heavily fortified structure. That station was designed to withstand a full riot assault. Those things went through our walls and steel doors—only daylight saved us. You won't be safe there, James. Please trust me."

"Sam trusted you, and where did that get him?" James taunted.

"Sam's dead, James. If the death of a good man gives you sanctification, then by all means, rise above and lead us. My family and I are headed north. We'll camp out for the night then head into the city at first light. Anyone who wants to is free to join us," Thomas said.

Wayne, Billy, Henry, and Claire walked behind Thomas.

"Sorry, James, I saw what these things do to big doors and walls. I'm sticking with the sheriff," Paul said.

"I don't know. The vault sounds good, sounds safe," said Pete.

Pete and Mary went to James.

"Michael, I think we should go with the sheriff, but you have to decide for yourself. Either way, God bless us all," Ray said.

Ray went with Thomas.

Michael went with James.

Charley went toward James, but Shirley pulled his arm.

"Charles, do you trust me?" she asked.

"More than anything, my love, you know that," he said.

With no more words, she gently led him to Thomas's side. Thomas and James split the weapons and supplies between them, and Thomas gave him one of the SUVs.

"Good luck, James. Be careful."

"Sheriff, you're going to get these people killed. Don't you think you've got enough blood on your hands?"

Thomas looked James in the eye. "Just try to keep these people's blood off yours."

The two groups separated, James and his followers heading to the armored car facility after getting the supplies and gas. Thomas and his group gathered together and prepared to be on their way.

"Hey, Dad," Jimmy said, "I want to show you something." He led Thomas around the corner. "Do you think we could use any of those?" he asked, pointing to a Honda motorcycle and dirt bike dealership.

"Most definitely, son."

Thomas and Billy hitched a trailer with three Honda CRF450R dirt bikes to the pickup truck. They would be invaluable in a wooded area. Thomas, Jimmy, and Jessica had ridden a lot when Sue was alive. It was a regular weekend thing for the family.

The group loaded up and set out.

* * * *

"James, you're sure about this, right?" Pauline asked.

"Paulie, trust me, baby. I won't let anything happen to you. The sheriff's wrong, and he's going to get more people killed."

"Just out of curiosity, James, how did you guys get through last night?" Pete asked.

"We stayed in my rig. I was supposed to haul a load to Charleston today. I was already hooked up, so when things started getting crazy, I grabbed Paulie and my shotgun and we hid out in the back of the 18-wheeler. We could hear a lot of crazy stuff going on out there. We finally fell asleep, and when we got out of the truck in the morning, we headed for the sheriff," James said.

"Yeah, well, Mary, Phil, and I made it to the church. We hid there with Pastor Ray and a group of others. It was a nightmare. We heard people yelling and fighting and dying. We just hid," Pete said, lowering his head.

Michael put his hand on Pete's shoulder.

"Okay, guys, the facility is close. We have about two hours before dusk," James said.

He pulled up to the building, went to the door, and rang the access button.

A voice blared through the intercom system. "Yes, what do you need?"

"Hey, my name is James Crest. I'm here with my family and some good people that need shelter before those damn things come back out. I used to work here for a while, and we need help, please."

"Jimmy, Jimmy boy," a voice called out through the intercom.

The door clicked, and they went in. They were met by a group of four men, all armed. One of the men came over to James.

"Jimmy, how's it going, man? Besides the whole end-of-the-world thing," he said.

"Brian, Brian Walker! Man, it's good to see you! Thank you for helping us out. You gotta have at least ten years here by now. I remember training you on your first day," James said.

"Yeah. Twelve years, actually. I'm the branch manager now, or rather, I *was*. Let's get you guys inside. Can you tell us what's going on?"

They walked into the vault area. The trucks were loaded with stacks of money.

"You guys planning to run your routes, Brian? I see you got the trucks loaded up," James said.

"We consider it severance pay. Is there a problem?"

"None here, man. We're just looking for a safe place to lay our heads till the sun comes back up."

"Good. Now, James, how about you shed some light on what's going on? We were on a two-day run the day before yesterday. We rode back into town this morning, and we found this. Last night, we heard about some kind of attack. We got here, and the four of us couldn't find anyone. The town was turned upside down. We figured it was some kind of al-Qaeda attack, so we figured this is the best place to be. We have weapons and hard walls and transportation if we need," Brian said. "Now you're talking about them coming back."

"This ain't no terrorist attack, Brian, at least none I ever heard of. These things ain't even people, not anymore, anyway. You shoot 'em, they just get back up. You gotta get them in the head, just like in the movies."

"You messin' with me, James? These things ain't human? Come on, man."

"Look, I'm just telling you what I know."

"Okay, okay, you say they're coming back tonight? All right then," Brian said before gathering the men who were with him.

"Listen up, guys, Jimmy boy here tells me that whatever did all this is coming back tonight. Robert, take that 12-gauge and go up on the roof. Let me know if you see anything. Matt, you watch the monitors, and, Gary, you go check and make sure everything is all locked up nice and tight, now, you hear? Nothing's getting in here, folks. Don't worry about a thing."

Michael stepped forward. "Um, sir, Brian, is it? I haven't seen these things—none of us have—but we were with a group that did. They said they're really strong and fast. Our sheriff said they ripped apart a heavily fortified building. I just want to tell you what we might be up against."

"This right, Jimmy?" Brian said.

"Maybe. It's what the sheriff said. His answer is to lie out in the open. That plan didn't sit well with me. We'll take our chances with you, man," James said.

"Fair enough. We'll watch your back. Just stay clear of my and the boys' loot, huh?"

James and the others went to a corner of the facility and set up a place to rest.

"They got a break room in the back, and there are probably still vending machines in there. Anyone want anything?" James asked.

No one replied; they just wanted sleep. As they lay in a small circle, they did just that.

A couple of hours later, the sounds of shotgun blasts woke James from his slumber. He got to his feet and found Brian.

"What the hell's going on, Brian? Who's shooting?"

"It's Robert on the roof!" Brian shouted as he and Gary ran for the stairway to the roof.

James jumped up and ran up with them. They emerged onto the roof, and Robert stood on the edge, firing down at the street.

"What the hell are you doing, man?" James yelled.

"I saw a couple of them things walking around down there, so I decided to take them out. What's your problem?" Robert responded.

"My problem is that you just announced to every one of those things where we are, you moron!"

"Oh, man! Oh, man! Oh, man, look!" Gary exclaimed.

Where there were only two or three infected moments ago were now fifty to sixty, and growing. They were coming out of the buildings and flowing down the street toward the facility.

"So what? They can't get in here," Robert said, his hands starting to tremble.

"You better hope they don't, or you just killed us all!" James said.

* * * * *

Thomas rode out about a hundred miles, with another hundred and fifty miles to the Charleston city limits.

"This should be good," he said.

The convoy pulled off the road to find and set up camp. They found a spot close to a stream, where they could set up a close perimeter. It was the middle of May, so a campfire would not be necessary to stay warm. Thomas had Wayne, Billy, and Paul set up a first shift for the watch. Thomas, Henry, and Ray would take the second watch.

Thomas gathered the group together. "Okay, guys, the key here is stealth and silence. We can't afford for those things to find us. The good news is, they seem to assemble together to go after groups, and they seem to stay within a town. We should be okay out here. If there was no one to turn, then there shouldn't be any of them out here," Thomas said.

"Can I ask you something?" Ray asked. Thomas nodded to him. "How do they infect other people? Is it a bite or something like that?"

"No, Ray. They spew out some kind of bug, and then the bugs crawl around and bite people. That infects others, somehow," Thomas said.

"Okay, so these *Spewers* vomit up these *Crawlers*, and they spread this infection? Is that about right, Thomas?" Ray asked.

75

"Yes, sir, that about sums it up," Thomas answered.

"How do we beat something like that? Better yet, how do we even survive it?" Ray asked.

Thomas really didn't have an answer for him. "Okay, first watch, post up. Everyone else, get some sleep," he said.

It was dark now, and Thomas knew this was the time to be on high alert. He also knew that he needed to rest; it had been almost three days since he'd had any real sleep. He lay down with Jessie, Jimmy, and Jax. It wasn't long before he slipped off.

"Thomas… Thomas, wake up. Time to change watch," Wayne said.

Thomas asked, "How long have I been out?"

"It's 3:00 a.m.," Wayne answered.

"What the hell, Wayne, you were supposed to wake me at eleven!" Thomas replied.

"Yeah, well, fire me. You needed the sleep, Sheriff," Wayne said.

"Thanks," Thomas said.

"Henry and Ray are on watch. They got the north and south point, you got the east point. It's been very quiet—no Spewers or Crawlers all night. You made the right call coming out here. Good night," Wayne said.

"Get some rest, Wayne. Good night."

* * * * *

James ran to his group.

"Come on, guys, we're going into the vault," James said.

"Wait!" Pete exclaimed. "Look around—there're no windows in this building. I know there are none in the vault. If we close ourselves in there, even if the sheriff is wrong and they can't get in, they'll just wait in this nice, dark building for us to have to come out for food or water or… air."

James stood stunned. He had been wrong. If they got into the bay, where they were now, the vault was a death trap. He'd been so eager to show the sheriff up that he never even considered the fact that the vault was more of a tomb than a sanctuary.

A loud slam on the metal bay doors made the group jump.

"That was a hard hit," Michael said. "It's not gonna hold."

"Brian! Get over here and look at this!" Matt yelled out, pointing to the monitors.

Brian ran to the monitors. The infected were all over the building.

"Okay, guys, time to break out everything we got," Brian ordered.

Gary went into the next room and returned shortly with a bag marked POLICE on it. It was full of guns and ammunition.

"While we were out trying to find everyone, we went to the police station. There wasn't anyone around, but we found these."

He handed James a shotgun and some shells. He offered one to Michael, who refused. Pete, despite being raised in hunter's country, had no idea how to fire a weapon, but he took one anyway. *I'll figure it out,* he thought to himself.

The banging and slamming on the huge bay truck doors became heavier and more frequent.

"Look at them all out there," Matt said, continuing to look at the monitor feed.

"We don't have enough guns or bullets for this," James said. "Forgive me," he added, taking Pauline by the hand and looking into her eyes.

"James Crest! We're not dead, so snap to and stop acting like we are! I trust you, baby. I'm just not ready to die, so can you please get me the hell out of here?" she replied with a half-smile and eyes starting to surrender their tears.

Get me the hell out of here! Her words rang in his head. That was exactly what he planned to do. *The trucks,* he thought. *They're powerful, mobile, and most importantly, armored.* Brian had them loaded with cash, so chances were, the keys were in them already.

James was putting his thoughts together when the power went out.

"Hit the emergency lights, Matt!" Brian yelled out.

There was another big slam, and this time, the bay doors came off the frame. They were still holding the infected out, but there were minutes left at best.

"Okay, everyone into the vault," Brian said.

"That's a death sentence, Brian. We have to get into those trucks and barrel our way through them and out of here," James said.

"First, we don't know how many of those things are out there. We may not be able to plow through them. Second, those trucks are full of my and my boys' retirement, and you ain't taking it!" Brian said.

"I don't care about money you ain't ever gonna get a chance to spend! Give me an empty one," James pleaded.

"There ain't no more. That's why we filled them three. That's all there was, James, now back off! Or someone's bound to get hurt," Brian said, leveling his weapon at James.

"Damn fool," James said as he stepped between the gun and Pauline. He grabbed Brian's gun and punched Brian so hard the gun fell to the floor.

"Run for the truck! Go now!" James shouted.

James's group ran for the truck as the doors came crashing to the floor. The infected were in and moving fast. Brian had recovered, and he and his group were firing into the infected. This gave James and his group precious moments to get to the trucks. The lighting was bad. The shutdown had caused the lighting system to reboot, and the warm-up time made the lights extremely dim.

"That one over there!" James yelled, pointing to the nearest truck, which Michael, Pete, Mary, Phil, and Pauline ran toward.

They never saw the infected coming. They just looked over, and Phillip was gone. The lights were so low they could barely see the truck.

"Phillip... Phillip! Where are you?" Mary called out.

"We have to keep moving, I'm sorry," James said.

"I'm not leaving my son!" Pete said.

Mary screamed as an infected grabbed her and held her down, the offspring already almost out of its mouth.

"No!" Pete yelled, pointing the shotgun in his hands at the infected. He pulled the trigger, but the weapon did not fire.

James started, "The safety, Pete! Pete, you have to take off the—"

But he was stopped short as he saw another infected jump out of nowhere and grab Pete. It took Pete down so hard James doubted he survived the hit. James grabbed Pauline by the arm, and they continued to the truck.

Michael jumped in through the open back doors, followed by Pauline. James got in and went for the driver's seat. He'd gotten it right—the keys were in the ignition.

"Guys, pull those doors closed! We're out of here!" James said.

Michael grabbed one of the truck doors to close it, and Pauline grabbed the other as James began the drive out of the truck bay. With one door already secured, Pauline pulled her door as an offspring crawled inside the truck just before the door closed. Crawling on her arm, the offspring spread its jaws apart and delivered its deadly bite into her wrist. She screamed. Michael grabbed it and threw it down on the floor of the truck, smashing it with the heel of his boot till he felt the floor through the mush of the offspring's head.

"Baby! Pauline! What's happening back there?" James called out, still trying to get the truck clear of the parking bay.

"I got her, James! Just drive!" Michael said.

Pauline lay in Michael's arms. "Tell him… it's not… it's not his faul…," she whispered to Michael.

He held her as she breathed her last, and said a prayer, asking God to welcome home all the people who died that night.

The infected were mainly focused on the building as James flew by them in the truck. Two or three attempted to jump onto the vehicle but were easily discarded. He checked his rearview mirrors—there were no other vehicles behind him, and the now hundreds of infected swarmed all over the building. None of the others had made it out.

"We're clear, baby. We made it out of the building. Ain't exactly smooth sailing, but we're moving. Babe, Pauline!" James yelled.

"She's unconscious, James. I got her, though," Michael lied, tears streaming down his face. Michael hated lying to him but knew the truth right now would only cause more harm than anything.

"We'll pull over first chance I get so I can take a look at her. We just have to keep moving. These damn things are still all over the place."

"Sure thing, James. Whatever you need, brother."

They drove, not staying still long enough for the infected to grab onto the truck. James was heading out of town. If he could get to an area isolated enough, they could hold the few that were still with them off long enough for the sun to come up. He'd failed horribly. The sheriff was right. James had gotten blood on his hands, after all. He was guilt-ridden. They'd all died listening to him, following him. He'd need Pauline so much to get through this; he wasn't sure what he would do if anything ever happened to her.

CHAPTER 5

Thomas sat on the ridge, keeping watch as the sun broke through the trees. He had always appreciated a beautiful sunrise, but this life-saving daybreak had taken on a whole new meaning to him. Thomas knew he couldn't figure this out alone. He had to keep things in prospective, keep his people safe, find Tim, get help. Things had to be done in big block movements and kept simple.

"Sheriff, check this out. We have an incoming vehicle," Billy said.

"Why aren't you sleeping, Billy?" Thomas asked as he walked over.

Through the trees, Thomas saw a truck coming down the road—a big one.

"It's an armored truck. Must be James's group," Billy said.

"Go to the main road and bring them in."

"Copy that," Billy replied.

"Everyone, time to get up. We have to move. Wasting daylight could literally get us killed," Thomas said.

The group snapped into motion. Ray, Carl, and Claire began to roll up the sleeping bags. Danny and Jimmy got their things together and then helped Shirley and Charles gather up their gear. Jessica helped her dad gather their bags as Henry and Paul cleaned the pots and got the leftover food together. Nothing would be wasted.

Billy drove back into the camp, followed by James driving the armored truck. The vehicles came to a stop, and James and Michael got out. Thomas saw that they were the only two, and it wasn't difficult to put the pieces together.

"James, I'm so sorry… Pauline?"

James lowered and slowly shook his head. "We had to put her down, Sheriff. She got bitten. She was gonna turn into one of those freaks, and I couldn't have that," James said.

Michael came forward and hugged Ray. "Sheriff, we knew you'd be on this road, so we headed north, hoping to catch up with you before dawn," Michael said.

"Thank God you did," Ray said.

Claire hugged James as he wept softly. Ray placed his hand on James's shoulder and said a prayer for James, Pauline, Pete, Mary, and Phillip as well as the rest of the fallen. The group prepared to move out.

"What are we going to do with the armored truck?" Billy asked.

"Keep it with us. It'll come in handy," Wayne said.

Ray asked, "Thomas, do you mind if I ride with you?"

"Not at all, pastor," Thomas said.

The group loaded up and moved on. Next stop, the city university.

"Thomas, I asked to ride with you 'cause I'd like to have a word with you," Ray said. He unbuttoned the top few buttons of his shirt. There was a large scar down the middle of his chest.

"Open-heart surgery," Thomas asked.

"Pacemaker," Ray said. "The reason I'm telling you this is, there'll likely come a time when I won't be able to keep up. If that happens, I don't want anyone risking themselves for me. My soul is ready for whatever God's will is for me. I won't allow anyone to die for me, especially you—the group relies on you for so much. I hope we understand each other, Thomas."

"Yes, sir," he simply replied.

As they approached the Charleston city limits, what they found was disheartening. It looked like there had been a war there. There were abandoned vehicles everywhere—police, fire, ambulance, even National Guard vehicles. There were buildings and vehicles on fire. There wasn't anyone in sight. This had been the answer, they'd thought. How could this be? And what now? The capital had been their best hope. The hollowness of the city filled them all with anguish, the possibility of it all being over suddenly a reality.

Thomas pulled over; his original plan of sending the rest of the group off to the local law enforcement was forfeit, so they needed to improvise. Thomas and the group gathered together to outline a plan. Thomas still felt that getting to the university was critical.

"We need to get information. Dr. Winters came here with a sample a few days ago. It's likely whatever answers he got, we'll find at the university. It's eight thirty, so we've got plenty of daylight. I say we go see what we can find," Thomas said.

"I agree," Carl answered quickly, wanting more to find his dad than the information.

"I think that, from what we've seen, going to the school is a waste of time, but I'll do whatever the group decides," James said.

"I vote university," Billy said.

Wayne nodded in agreement.

"Whatever," Paul said.

Henry just shrugged. Ray and Michael smiled and nodded.

"Thank you, Thomas," Claire said.

"Okay, people, stay close and gather whatever you can. Stay outside in the sun only. No going indoors unless there's plenty of sunlight," Thomas said.

They gathered supplies from nearby vehicles and gas stations. Thomas, Wayne, and Billy got what weapons and ammunition they could from the National Guard vehicles. There were very few bodies, likely because the majority of people were turned into Spewers rather than killed.

The group loaded up and continued to the university. They reached the bioengineering building and parked in front of it.

"This is where he would have been," Thomas said.

"That's a lot of dark building to look through. You think that's a good idea, Sheriff?" James said.

"Not particularly. That's why I'm going to check it out myself," Thomas said.

Carl exclaimed, "No way! It's my dad, I'm going with you!"

"What would your dad say if I took you somewhere that could get you killed, Carl? I move much better and faster alone. I can take care of myself by myself much easier. You being there actually makes this a much more dangerous mission, son, please."

Carl nodded. Claire hugged her son and gave Thomas a soft smile of gratitude. Thomas went to get together some things he'd need.

"Kids, huh?" Billy said as he walked up behind Thomas.

"You're five minutes older than he is, Billy," Thomas said.

"Maybe, but I'm a hard-charging, ass-kicking Seventy-Fifth US Army Ranger. We lead the way, all the way, and… I'm going with you. Don't give me that *frogman*-I-work-alone crap you fed Carl either."

"I'm still your boss, Billy, with all due respect to you and the ranger creed. You're. Not. Coming."

"Fine. Then I quit, Thomas, and I'm still coming!"

Wayne came over. "Either him or me, Sheriff. I know you military types like to work together, but if you don't let him come, then I'm going instead. You're not going alone."

"Fine. Billy, gear up. You do as I say in there, copy? And it's *Sheriff*, by the way," Thomas said with a half-smile. They began to walk toward the building.

"So I'm rehired, right?" Billy joked.

"Yeah, you're rehired."

"Good, so are we still on the clock? 'Cause technically, I never clocked out," Billy said.

"Yeah, that's 'cause someone destroyed the time clock, and most of the station."

"Fair point, Sheriff. So what's the plan?"

"Get in, find Tim, or whatever information we can gather, then get the hell out alive. Search, retrieve, and escape. Simple."

"Hey, guys, hold up!" Wayne shouted. "Look at those structures around the bio building. Paul and I can provide over-watch for you from there. Give Paul one of the high-powered rifles we got from the guardsman's trucks, and I'll spot for him with the binoculars. You guys just let us know where you are, and we'll use those little windows around the top of the buildings to cover you."

"Those are really small windows," Thomas said.

"I'm a really good shot," Paul replied.

"He is," Billy confirmed.

"Okay, good. We'll be on channel 3," Thomas said.

They tuned their radios and set off to the door. They would use a standard clearing formation and go quickly and quietly from room to room till they found what they were looking for.

"We're going south along the first-floor corridor," Billy whispered into his radio.

"Roger that. We have you," Wayne replied.

The university was in ruins, and there was no power. There had been a massive firefight there. There was blood on the walls and floors and bullet holes from small-arms fire everywhere. They moved along the hallway till they came to room marked LABS 1A THROUGH 1E.

"As good a place to start as any," Thomas whispered.

Billy gave Wayne their location, and he and Thomas went in. The room had big windows and lots of sunlight in it. Not much chance of any infected in here, so they relaxed a bit and searched the room.

"Anything, Billy?"

"Nothing here, Sheriff."

"This is more like a classroom. We need a place where they do testing, not teach students," Thomas said.

"We need to find a directory," Billy said.

They left the room. As they approached the middle corridor, Thomas saw a directory posted on the wall by the elevator. TEST LABS B-1, BASEMENT. Thomas thought, *Of course, they'd be in the basement.*

They made their way to the stairwell.

"Wayne, come in," Thomas whispered into his radio. "We're moving into the basement. We may lose radio contact."

"Sheriff, there are no windows in the basement," he replied.

"Copy that," Thomas replied. "Okay, Billy, listen up. When we get down there, you're going to stay by the stairwell. You keep our exit clear."

"What! That's no good, Sheriff. I should go with you and watch your back. Besides, we may not even be able to come back this way. You know I'm right."

Billy was right. Thomas figured the safest place for Billy would be the stairwell, but he had to trust him. Billy was a good man and a good soldier, and it was time Thomas treated him as such.

"Okay, Billy. On me, stay close, stay quiet."

"Copy that, Sheriff."

They made their way down the stairs. Thomas figured that since the infected operated only at night, they must be able to see in the dark, while Thomas and Billy couldn't. They reached the basement, which had emergency fluorescent lighting. Fluorescent lighting used less power, and the freezers in the labs were the priority. Thomas held up a closed fist, indicating for Billy to stop. Thomas pointed ahead to his left. There stood an infected, wandering around obliviously. Any stimulus, and it would jump into action and probably attract others—then they'd be in trouble. The best plan of action would be to wait for it to pass, but that wasn't going to happen.

Billy tapped Thomas on his shoulder and pointed behind them. Two more infected wandering toward them from around the corner. They were trapped! They hadn't been seen yet, but it would be only moments now. Thomas knew he had to act. Two behind, one in front, and who knew how many more wandering around down there. Thomas had to go with the odds. He signaled for Billy to stay put and slid out his Ka-Bar combat knife. The infected were strong and fast; he would only get one shot at this. One mistake would likely be his last. This had to be perfect.

Thomas quietly moved into position, hiding behind the corner of a desk right behind the infected. Time was running out. The other two infected would be on Billy in seconds, a minute at most, and Thomas had to move now. With the silence, swiftness, and grace of a dandelion caught on a breeze, he rose from behind the desk. Grabbing the infected around the neck, he pushed the blade of the Ka-Bar into its head, breaking through the bone of the skull into the brain. Thomas pushed deep and twisted the blade to ensure the damage needed to finish his target. He lowered the infected to the ground without a sound. Billy moved up, and they took cover from the other infected as they wandered by.

Thomas and Billy moved down the hall, and they came to a room marked TESTING FACILITY. They entered the room, where Thomas saw the evidence container he'd given Tim on one of the examination tables. This was the room they'd been looking for. The disarray told Thomas the others had left in a hurry. They stayed low and quiet, searching for any clue to what had happened. There was a load of paperwork inside a satchel on the table with the container. Thomas grabbed the satchel and the container. They looked around for any other information. Thomas signaled for Billy to move out. It was time to go. There was nothing else there for them.

They made their way to the door and re-entered the hallway. There were three infected blocking the way back to the stairway. Thomas signaled Billy to move to cover and wait for the infected to move on. They reached their position and posted up, but suddenly, Billy's radio picked up a broken signal.

"Sherif… illy… ome n… over."

The sound of Wayne's voice set the infected into motion. They were on Thomas and Billy fast.

"Go hot, Billy, now!" Thomas yelled.

Thomas began firing his weapon, hitting one of the infected in the head, another in the chest. Billy began moving back, trying to get a better angle on the infected. Taking aim, he held his breath and fired two shots. The first shot hit the infected in the neck; the other hit it in the head, dropping it. Thomas could see infected coming at them from the direction of the stairwell.

"Back, Billy. We have to go back. There are too many!"

They ran back deeper into the basement. Then as they ran around a corner, they saw a stairway exit sign.

"Over there, go!" Thomas shouted.

They hit the stairs running, having no idea where they were going, just that it was away from the infected, and that was good enough for now.

"Do you have any idea where we're headed, Sheriff?"

"Yeah, up," he shot back.

"Let it be to the sundeck, let it be to the sundeck," Billy mumbled.

The infected were close behind them, and closing fast, as Thomas and Billy moved up the stairwell. Thomas burst through a door and saw a candy vending machine.

"Give me a hand."

Thomas and Billy pushed the machine down in front of the door, blocking it and buying a few precious moments.

"Wayne, come in. We've turned around and on the run. We got infected on our tail. I see a sign, stand by one. North quad, we're on the north quad, heading to the nearest exit!" Thomas said.

"Copy that, Sheriff. We're changing position now."

The door broke free, and the infected were through it and pursuing their intended prey. There was little sunlight in the hallway to offer any sufficient protection. The windows were small and high on the walls. The gymnasium was up ahead, so there had to be an emergency exit somewhere in there. Thomas grabbed the door; it was chained from the other side. He pulled the door open as much as he could—if he could just get a clean shot at the padlock, they could get through.

"Billy, I need a minute. Cover me."

Billy began firing into the infected. He was dropping them, but they either recovered or were replaced.

"Hurry, Sheriff. I mean fast!"

One of the infected jumped through the rest of them, pushed off the wall, and was lunging toward Billy. It was too late—Billy didn't have a chance to raise his weapon toward it. It was over, he thought. The echo of a distant crack, the sound of a window shattering, and the infected's head splitting open as Paul's high-powered round hit home gave Billy a much-needed second breath. Then the sound of Thomas's 12-gauge as the lock blew apart meant it was time to move. They ran into the gym, closed the doors behind them, and jammed a metal flagpole into the push bars. Thomas saw the exit sign on the other side of the gym, just past the basketball goal. The wood panel floor normally used for layups and jump shots would now become a ninety-four-foot race for their lives.

As they prepared for the mad dash, Thomas picked up his radio.

"Wayne, we're on the west side of the gym. I see an exit on the north side. We're heading that way now."

Halfway there, Thomas saw infected coming out of the doors in front of the exit he and Billy were heading to.

"Head back, Billy, that way's no good!"

As they were running back toward the doors, the pole broke loose and the doors holding back the other infected busted open. They ran toward the wall. The windows were high up. Paul continued firing and killing infected as best as he could to provide cover from his over-watch position outside. But there were just too many. Now Paul's cover fire was becoming more and more ineffective. Thomas and Billy stood with their backs to the wall, firing, trying to create a path to run through.

"Look out!" Billy yelled as he blasted an offspring that was creeping toward Thomas. "You hear that? Sounds like an air horn," Billy said.

Wayne's voice yelled over the radio, "Move away from the wall now! Move NOW!"

Thomas and Billy ran and dived almost right in front of the infected as the back end of the armored truck blasted through the wall. Dust, debris, and most importantly, sunlight filled the area. The infected and offspring scattered and ran for the cover of darkness. The back doors flew open, and Henry jumped out, helping Thomas and Billy into the back.

"Go, they're in!" Henry shouted to James.

The truck took off as Thomas held tight to the satchel. *Hope this is worth it,* he thought.

"Thomas, come in. Are you guys all right?" Wayne called through the radio.

"All good," Billy replied.

"You know, Sheriff, you almost went a full twenty-four hours without almost getting killed," Billy said.

"Color me lucky, then," Thomas said, still trying to catch his breath.

Thomas arrived back at the group. Jessie and Jimmy rushed their dad, and the three stood together and hugged.

"We've hugged more in the last three days than the last three years," Jimmy said, wiping tears from his face.

Jessica responded, "Yeah, and all it took was the end of the world."

"I love you guys," Thomas said.

"We know, Dad. I also think one day soon we'll be orphans," Jessie said and walked back over to Carl.

Thomas took a deep breath. He didn't blame her for being upset. The last few days, he'd come so close to death so many times, and he knew it was only a matter of time before he didn't come back from the brink. There was just absolutely no choice now.

Wayne walked over to Thomas. "Give her a bit of space. She understands what you're doing and why you're doing it, but that doesn't mean she likes it. James really came through. He and Henry were listening on the spare radio," Wayne said.

"Yeah, I owe him for that one. I'll catch up with him later. For now, I need to go through this satchel. We need answers, and I'm praying they're here," Thomas said as he emptied the satchel.

There were papers, some files, and two Zip drives. After a quick scan of the papers and files, Thomas didn't get much out of them. He walked back to the truck and got his laptop, plugging in the first Zip drive. He was surprised and happy to see Tim's face on a video recording. The time stamp was dated for Saturday afternoon. Tim had gotten here before the infected had hit; he'd had no idea what was coming. Thomas needed to watch the footage before letting the group see it. If there was bad news to see, he didn't want anyone, especially Claire and Carl, to see it this way. Thomas put his earphones on and watched.

"My name is Dr. Timothy Carlton Winters. I'm a medical doctor with a PhD in bioengineering."

A stunningly beautiful woman then also entered the screen. Chocolate-brown skin, sharp hazel eyes, and a smile that almost made Thomas forget all about the impending apocalypse.

"This is my colleague, Professor Julia Anderson. She is the foremost bioengineer on the planet. She is an entomologist that specializes in myr-

mecology. In layman's terms, she knows everything possible about insects, especially ants."

"Thank you, Doctor Winters." Julia picked up the sample that Thomas had provided. *"First, I'd like to point out that this specimen was not born like this. It appears to have been spliced and infused with another organism, though what kind has me completely stumped. We have run tests and sent samples via electric data transfer to Dr. Chris Riley at the CDC in Atlanta. We should receive his results by the end of the day. This specimen has extremely close characteristics to the* Dorylus gribodoi, *or queen driver ant. It's about three times bigger than I've ever seen or even heard of."*

For the next forty minutes, Thomas watched Julia talk about ants. Who knew such a beautiful woman could be so boring? he thought. His interest was pinged once more when Tim announced that they had gotten the report from Dr. Riley. Tim seemed very upset.

"We've just received a very disturbing message from Chris. There has been some sort of attacks in Atlanta. There have been fatalities, Julie." Tim took the camera and centered it on himself. *"I have information on a situation escalating on the East Coast."* Tim proceeded to talk about the infected's attack in Atlanta. The attacks were similar to the attacks Thomas and his group had endured. This was a national, if not global, disaster.

"We have decided to call in local and federal law enforcement as a precaution. Communication has become extremely limited, and I haven't been able to contact my family. Cell towers are all but gone. We will continue to research and record for as long as we can until the agents get here, and then we'll make a decision on movement."

Tim focused the camera back on Julia as she had the offspring now pinned to an observation tray, and he began talking again.

"For our safety, we have had to terminate the subject in order to properly study it. What we've gathered besides the insect's basic anatomy, which we described as best as we could earlier, is very limited. The most interesting part of this parasite is its venom. I've studied it earnestly. This toxin is filled with so many different complex hormones in the venom. It is filled with protein, amino acids, and adrenaline all tied together

with a completely foreign bonding agent. If this toxin didn't kill you, it'd make you a regular superman. I can't identify the bonding agent. It is like nothing I've ever seen, read, or even heard a rumor about. The venom also carries multiple eggs, which hatch embryos. The embryos are definitely fatal to humans—they seem to have been deliberately designed for just that purpose. The parasite impregnates others asexually through its bite. Its reproduction rate will bypass rats, chickens, and even rabbits by leaps and bounds. This parasite is a weapon designed to kill people, of this I have no doubt."

Thomas continued to watch the video; they didn't even know about the Spewers yet, he thought. She was exactly on point when she called this a weapon, because this was nothing short of war. Thomas had seen war, but he'd never had the feeling that he was in a fight he couldn't win before. That wasn't a habit he was planning on breaking, not now, not ever.

It was nearly 1:00 p.m. now, and Thomas had no plan for shelter after sundown. The woods had been safe, but if they were to get caught in the open like that, completely exposed, at night, that would be the end. Thomas didn't see much choice for now. They would spend the rest of the day gathering what supplies they could then head back into the woods. Hiding was the best way to make it right now. Thomas needed to see the rest of the Zip drive, but first, he had to organize the group.

Thomas gathered Wayne and Billy.

"Wayne, I need you and Billy to get everyone together. Gather what you can and meet here by four, not a minute later. We'll get deep into the woods and set up a perimeter before dark. I need to finish watching these files. Hopefully, they'll help us make our next move."

Wayne then gathered everyone, put them into groups, and gave them assignments. It was just as important to keep them busy as it was to get supplies. They were tired and scared, and he had to try to keep their minds busy.

Thomas settled back in to watch the video and clicked on the next file. The scene was chaotic, and Tim was trying to record. There were people moving all around behind him in a very big hurry. It looked like they were packing everything to move fast. Tim begin to talk.

"Okay, we've had a situation here. This facility has come under attack from... from... I honestly don't know what they are. The National Guard is here and doing what they can, but it's a regular war zone up there. We've been instructed that we are moving to a secure facility in Washington, DC."

Gunshots rang out in the background of the video. Tim was gathering all the materials he could as he continued.

"They said they have a secure area in DC. Whatever is happening is nationwide, possibly worldwide. If you're watching this, get to DC. Good luck. God bless."

Tim switched off the feed.

DC, Thomas thought, *that's a six-hour drive.* It was too late for that today, but Thomas knew their next move now.

Jessica, Carl, Jimmy, Jax, and Billy made up one search team, searching anywhere with open and exposed areas. They gathered food from gas stations and mini-marts and weapons from National Guard and police vehicles. Billy walked ahead of the group. Jessica realized she hadn't had a chance to talk to him since all this had started happening, so she approached Billy.

"I'm sorry about your wife, Billy. I met Jackie at the school blood drive. She was really nice."

"Yeah, thanks, Jess," Billy said, not really ready to talk about that yet. "You should stay close to Carl and your brother, though. I got point. You guys stay together back there, okay?"

"I didn't mean to upset you, Billy. Sorry. It's just, I know what you're going through. I lost my mom, and it was hard. I'm here if you wanna talk."

"It's okay, Jess, just stay back. We don't need any surprises. Your dad would kill me if anything happened to any of you."

Realizing she was causing more harm than good, Jessica went back with Carl and Jimmy.

"You okay, Jess?" Carl asked, noticing the defeated look on her face.

"Yeah, but I think I upset him."

"You were just trying to help."

"Poor guy lost his wife and the world ended all in the same day," Jessica said.

Carl said, "Billy's a strong dude. He'll be okay."

Two hours later, Carl, Jimmy, and Jessica gathered to see what they'd picked up. Pickings had been slim. They had been through three gas stations and one corner store. Those had been the only places with big-enough windows to ensure ample sunlight to keep any infected away. The end tally was two trash bags full of beef jerky, bottled waters, batteries, toiletries, and moon pies. Everything else was either looted, rotten, or useless.

"Come on, guys, time to head back," Billy announced.

They made their way back to Thomas and the others. Once everyone had arrived, Thomas gathered the group.

"We have a plan. Tonight, we'll find cover in the woods. Tomorrow, we will make our way to DC to try to catch up with Tim and his group. The Zip drives I watched told me a lot. Load up, and let's move out. I want to get as deep as possible into the woods before nightfall."

"Sheriff, is my dad okay?" Carl asked.

"It looked a little crazy, but it also looked like he made it out okay," Thomas replied.

He gave Claire and Carl the laptop and Zip drives so they could see for themselves. Carl eagerly grabbed the laptop and Zip drive from Thomas. He and Claire sat together in the back of the SUV and watched the video.

The group then drove back into the woods to prepare for one more night before they began their way to DC.

* * * * *

Caleb watched as the nation's capital fought against the infected and the offspring. He was satisfied with the results. There was no defense to what he had created. The others in his group had reported in; the results were equivalently effective throughout the rest of their intended targets. Although he felt no personal ill will toward anyone, he couldn't help but swell with pride over the perfect execution of his project. Within two years, the world would be molded into a productive realm where he and his group could complete their work.

* * * * *

Thomas set up twenty-four-hour watch schedules and advised those who could to get some rest. Carl and some of the others watched the videos, while others distributed the newly acquired weapons, ammo, and food supplies. Thomas mapped out their movements to and around Washington, while Wayne and Billy finished passing out supplies and pulled Henry, Paul, and James aside to assign watches.

"Guys, we're hoping and praying for another quiet night. No shots unless absolutely necessary. There weren't many people out here when this thing hit, so the number of Spewers out here should be low. Loud noises will bring any other stragglers in, and that's the last thing we need," Wayne said.

Wayne took Paul and Henry. Billy, James, and Thomas made up the second team.

Carl put aside the laptop and approached Wayne. "Deputy Hicks, I want to help. I can take a watch shift also. I'm not a child."

"Carl, in case you haven't noticed, you have a watch shift. It's your mom, Jessica, and Jimmy. You make damn sure nothing happens to them. That's not a job the sheriff or I would give a child. You good?"

"Yes, sir," Carl said.

The sun set as the group settled into their makeshift camp. Wayne and his team took first shift. The group lay awake until fatigue took them into an uneasy slumber.

Thomas's nightmarish sleep was interrupted by Wayne.

"Shh," Wayne warned, holding his finger up to his lips.

Thomas immediately understood that danger was close. He got up, grabbed his weapon, and silently followed Wayne. Wayne led him to a clearing in the woods, careful to stay hidden in the tree line. Wayne placed his hand on Thomas's shoulder and quietly pointed out an infected. It hadn't seen them. This one was different from any of the others they'd seen; it seemed frustrated and angry. The infected were normally void of emotions, completely indifferent. They didn't even show much facial expression. This one definitely had expression on its face, not just anger, but more like rage. It didn't wander around aimlessly, waiting for stimuli, like the rest; it was looking for something. The infected were dangerous, but Thomas knew right away that this one was a whole new kind of threat. It seemed to be moving away from the camp.

"Where are Paul and Henry?" Thomas whispered.

"Paul is on the other side of the camp, but Henry is somewhere on the east end. That thing is heading into his area. If it sees him before he sees it…"

The thought made Thomas flush with fear.

"We can't risk radio communication," Wayne said.

"I'm going to circle around and get to Henry before it's too late," Thomas said.

He moved quickly and quietly through the woods.

Henry sat against a tree, watching the camp, but deep in thought. He felt himself getting sleepy, so he thought it best for him to get up and walk around a bit. Henry was walking his designated perimeter, his thoughts wandering with all the recent events. The infected walked a parallel path just a few dozen feet behind him on the other side of the tree line. Henry had no idea the danger he was in. He continued walking, the infected heading on a collision course with him. A couple dozen feet behind Henry, the infected sensed or heard prey close by. Henry turned around to return to his post. The infected moved in, preparing to close in on its prey. An arm silently reached in behind Henry. It wrapped around his chest, dragging him to the ground. A hand then closed around his mouth.

"Spewer. Don't move or make a sound," Thomas whispered into Henry's ear.

Thomas and Henry lay perfectly still on the ground, using a tree for whatever cover they could. Thomas leveled his pistol up toward the infected, who was now looking in the area for prey it was certain was close by. Nearby twigs broke under the weight of a deer. The infected became aggressively alert. The deer also noticed the infected and darted off into the woods. The infected howled an earsplitting screech and gave chase with a speed and quickness that seemed to match that of a cheetah.

Thomas and Henry got up and moved quickly back to the camp.

"Thank you, Sheriff. You saved my life."

"We're all we got, Henry. Besides, just a few hours ago, you were pulling me and Billy out of that gym and back to my family. This is what we do now, we take care of each other."

Back at camp, the others were now awake.

"I thought it best to wake everyone. No snoring or coughing while sleeping seemed best with that thing out there," Wayne said.

"Good thinking," Thomas replied.

"What was that? Is it just my imagination, or was that thing different from the others?" Wayne asked.

"No, it was definitely different. You should have seen it move. And I thought the others were fast! This thing is faster, maybe stronger. The scariest thing is that it seemed aware. The others just wander around, waiting to attack. This one was looking, even hunting. That screech, it sounded like it was in pain or something. Also, Wayne, did you notice it was alone? They are usually in groups."

"Maybe the others are afraid of it," Wayne said.

"I doubt they're afraid of it. They most likely don't register fear or any other emotions, but it may be some kind of survival instinct telling them to stay clear of it."

"Yeah, well, that's one thing we have in common with these bastards," Wayne said.

The rest of the night went quietly.

As the sun rose, the group began gathering their belongings. The group loaded the trucks, getting ready for what they hoped was a trip toward salvation. They ate breakfast together, and then they would begin the trip shortly after daybreak. The meal was unusually quiet, with everyone's thoughts on DC. As everybody finished up, they began to load up and move out.

Michael made it a point to ride with Thomas. He sat in the front and waited for Ray to fall asleep.

"Thomas, I need to speak to you. Ray told me not to say anything, but I cannot, in good conscience, keep quiet. Ray needs angiotensin. It's a heart medication he needs to keep blood flowing to his heart. He'll die without it. I know you have so much on your plate, so if you can just get me to a hospital, I'll get it. You've risked so much for us. Let me do this for him."

"Michael, we need meds for the group, anyway. We'll take care of it." One more thing to add to the list. But like he'd said before, "This is what we do now."

CHAPTER 6

Washington was in ruins. Thomas had hoped it would be different there somehow. But seeing the carnage there of all places had dashed their hope. The most powerful and most protected city in the world taken down in a day. Thomas brought the convoy to a stop so they could put together the plan for the day. They pulled into a side alley between two large buildings and stepped out of the vehicles. Wayne and Billy did an immediate check of the surrounding area while Thomas gathered everyone together.

"Where do you think my dad is, Sheriff?" Carl asked.

"I'm not sure. His group more than likely would have sought cover in a secure area. I'm sure he's okay," Thomas said, trying to sound hopeful.

"Thomas, may I speak to you, please?" Claire asked.

"Yes, ma'am."

Claire took Thomas by the arm. "Walk with me, will you?" she said. "Thomas, I love my boys more than anything on this earth. Are you looking for Tim so he can help us or because you feel some kind of misguided obligation to my family? I don't want you putting the group at risk for Carl and me."

"I understand, Claire. I do want Tim with us, but he and his colleagues are the best chance we have of turning this thing around. Plus, if we have one agenda, it's gotta be saving one another. Otherwise, what's the point? I don't just want us to survive, I want us to live!"

Wayne called out, "Sheriff, come look at this."

Thomas gave Claire a small hug then went over to Wayne. There were two bodies lying on the sidewalk.

"What do you have, Wayne?"

"Look at these bodies, Sheriff. They've been shot. They weren't Spewers, they were human, and someone shot them."

Thomas examined the bodies. They were two young black males, both wearing gang colors. They'd been shot execution-style.

"We have a situation here and have to take more precautions. These guys weren't killed by Spewers—this is old-fashioned murder. We've been so careful to protect ourselves at night we've forgotten the monsters that still run around in the daylight," Thomas said.

He gathered the others.

"Okay, we don't have a location on Tim's group, and we can't sit around here in the open and wait for them. It's only a matter of time before someone gets hurt or sick. We need medical supplies. We'll go to the local hospital and salvage what we can. I'll lead a team inside to get supplies while the rest of you stay together and be ready to move as soon as we come out. Tonight, we head back to the woods and away from the city. James, I need you to map out a location for us and find a secluded area where we can rest for the night. Billy, Michael, you're with me. Wayne, Henry, and Paul, come with me for a second. You've got a different assignment."

Thomas led the men away and explained their assignments. Ray, Claire, and the kids did a supply check. Claire then prepared lunch for the group. After lunch, Thomas and his team moved out to the hospital.

"Michael, I'm bringing you so you can get Ray's heart meds. Also, I need you to pick out medications that we might need for the group, okay? You stay in between Billy and me, and you'll be fine. Move when we move and stop when we stop. Stay quiet in there and listen to me."

Michael nodded; he understood.

The hospital lobby was deserted and demolished. The power was out, the hospital running on emergency power only. Thomas, Billy, and Michael moved through it into the hallway, staying tight against the wall and moving as quietly as possible. They came to a corner, and Thomas signaled for them to stop as he peered around it. The hallway was filled with so many infected that he could not even see to the end of the hall. He signaled for them to move back.

Thomas took a brochure off one of the waiting room tables. It had a map in it they would surely need. They moved back outside and saw Claire, Jessica, Jimmy, Carl, and Ray sitting together in a small group. Jax was in the truck, barking like a crazy dog. Terror and rage filled Thomas as he witnessed two men standing over them, holding guns, with the barrels aimed at their heads. Another man came from Thomas's right, and another stood over by the truck. They were armed as well. The men were wearing what appeared to be gang colors, with colored bandannas around their heads and in their pockets. Thomas could disarm and take out one of them, maybe two. With Billy, he was pretty sure they'd get the other two also, but with his family in the middle of this mess, *pretty sure* wasn't enough.

"Drop them guns right there, cabrón, or we gonna start poppin' off your people esa," the man standing over Jessica said. He was a large man, about six feet tall, Hispanic, and heavily tattooed.

"Okay, relax man. You got it," Thomas said, lowering his weapon. "We don't want any trouble. We're just trying to survive like everyone else. We need medical supplies, then we're moving on, that's it."

"This is our territory, and you ain't welcome here. Now you got to pay tax, white boy. Things changed. We run it 'round here now," the man said.

Thomas slid his hand down and switched his radio to open transmit; now he knew Wayne would be able to hear him without him having to push and hold the talk button on his radio.

"You got it. Take the trucks and whatever else, just don't hurt anyone. There are plenty of supplies for everyone, there's no need for this. What's your name, man? I'm Thomas. That's my family you're pointing your guns at."

"Man, don't worry about my name, and I don't want your damn trucks. We got so much crap we ain't even got places to put it. Naw, tell you what I want. I likes this li'l sweet chica right here," he said, bending down and rubbing his hand down Jessica's cheek.

This set Carl off. "Don't touch her!" he shouted, attempting to protect her.

The man smacked his pistol across Carl's head, knocking him to the ground. The other armed men refocused their guns on Billy and Thomas. Thomas had to end this.

"Okay, stop. Enough! Everyone calm down. Claire, check on Carl. I've had enough. Hey, banger, you see that car window you're standing next to? We tried the carrot, meet the stick!"

As Thomas finished the last word, there was a small distant crack, and the car window exploded into pieces.

"Team 1, is everyone in position?" Thomas asked into his radio.

"Copy that, Sheriff. Standing by on your order," Wayne replied.

"I've got multiple snipers stationed all around this area. Drop your guns and put your hands over your heads, *now*!" Thomas shouted.

"He's bluffing, he got one foo hiding somewhere with a rifle. He can't take all of us especially if we start poppin' off his family here." The man lowered his gun toward Jessica.

Thomas knew he would shoot her; there would be no reasoning with this man.

"Take him," he said into his radio.

Paul held his breath and squeezed the trigger. The bullet went through the man's chest and burst its way out of his back. He dropped to the ground and was dead before he hit it. Convinced, the other men dropped their guns and raised their hands. Thomas wasted no time and ran to his family.

In shock, Jessica and Jimmy hugged their dad; they had never seen a dead body before, much less someone killed in front of them. Thomas checked on Carl; he was okay.

"Everyone, rendezvous back at the vehicles," Thomas said into his radio. "Everyone okay?" Thomas asked.

"We're fine, Sheriff. How did you have Wayne and the others set up for that?" Ray asked.

"We found some bodies shot down when we got to town. They were humans, not Spewers. I decided to put the others up as over-watches in case something like this happened," Thomas said.

"Sheriff, if there was danger, then we should have moved on. Now a man's lost his life and someone has had to take it. We look for you to save lives, not set us up to take them."

"Ray, we need those medical supplies, and we don't know when we'll get another chance, so I did what I had to."

"And put your children and us in danger in the process."

"Pastor, with all due respect, do you think there will ever be a day when we're not in danger now?"

Wayne, Paul, and Henry regrouped and headed back to the group.

"I never killed anyone before," Paul said as they walked. "Them things, yeah, but they ain't people anymore. That guy was human. A scumbag gangbanger, but still."

"You did what you had to do, Paul. He was going to kill Jess. He had a choice, and you didn't, brother," Wayne said, putting his hand on Paul's shoulder.

Wayne and the others got back to the group. "We wait for James to get back, then we have to figure a way into that hospital," Thomas said.

"What do we do with the other men?" Ray asked.

"We'll cut them loose right before we head out," Thomas said.

It was almost eleven o'clock now. The morning was gone, and they were no closer to getting what they needed. Thomas was trying to plan a way into the hospital when Billy called to him.

"Vehicle incoming, Sheriff!"

What now? Thomas thought.

There wasn't just one vehicle, but five, incoming. They were coming; there wasn't much time.

"Billy, take Paul and get to high ground. Henry, get everyone else out of sight. Wayne, you're with me. Bring our new friends—I have a feeling they're coming for them," Thomas said.

"You want me to gag them, Sheriff?"

"No. We'll let them do the hard part for us," Thomas replied.

Thomas and Wayne stood over the kneeling, handcuffed men as the vehicles pulled up. A very large man got out of the lead truck. He must have been about six feet four inches tall, 250 pounds easy, and not more than 18 percent of it body fat either. He wore the same colors as all the heavily armed men that got out of the vehicles after he did. Thomas counted eighteen men; there was no way they could take them if this went bad. He hoped this man was more reasonable than the last. Thomas didn't have much information about local gangs in this area, but he did notice the front man was wearing different colors from one of the men he was holding.

The man approached them. "You got my boys there. I think we need to talk," he said.

Thomas stepped forward.

"Careful, Devon, they got snipers all over!" one of the cuffed men shouted.

This was the very reason Thomas didn't want them gagged. Now he had a name. *Devon.* The threat of Thomas's sniper was much more effective being delivered by one of Devon's own men.

"Yes, sir, we, without a doubt, need to talk."

Devon approached Thomas. "What you got here, cop? Looks like you shot one of my guys."

"They killed Dino, man," one of the cuffed men said.

"He didn't give me any choice. He was unreasonable and threatening my group," Thomas said.

"He was a dick, true enough," Devon said. "I think maybe I got something to level our playing field," he added.

Devon signaled one of his men, who pulled James out of one of the trucks. "This your man, right? How about we trade? Your man for my men. You come out on top. Three for one, huh?" Devon said.

"Sounds right, Devon. I have a proposal, though. You don't know me, but I can help you. I have certain training and skill sets that, in our current environment, could greatly benefit you. You and your men lend a hand in clearing out that hospital, and we'll both have medical supplies that, if you don't need now, you will eventually," Thomas said.

Devon seemed to realize Thomas was a man worth knowing. "Okay, supercop, give me a plan, and I'll let you know."

A nod from Devon, and his man let James go. Thomas signaled Wayne, and he released the men that he had handcuffed. But the situation required one last casualty. Taking the Glock semiautomatic pistol from his waist, Devon walked over and put a bullet in the head of one of the men.

"What the hell?" Thomas shouted.

"Listen, man. Look at his colors," Devon said. "He was Fourth Street, part of a huge neighborhood crew. The man you killed was their head man. I had to truce with him when all this shit hit the fan. The dude you killed was a true psycho, though, for real. You did me a favor getting rid of him, but his crew back at camp would want blood for blood no matter what happened. Now you and my crew say he got done by them damn things running around. No score to settle. Get me? We Eighth Street, and we got your back long as you earn it, cop. Things real different now—no more you, no more us. You got plans, let's hear it."

Thomas saw Devon was a man who did what he had to do. It was extreme, to be sure, but like he said, things were different now.

The hospital was completely infested, and even with Devon's crew, they wouldn't last long in a head-on confrontation. According to the map Thomas had retrieved, the medical supply room was located on the first floor. It would be impossible to get in unnoticed.

They'd need a distraction, and that was where Devon and his people would come in.

"So if the hospital is full of these… what you call 'em? Spewers? Then how the hell you think we gonna pull this off without getting a whole bunch of people killed? I seen these things in action—they don't stay down no matter how many times you pop 'em," Devon said.

"First, you have to put one in their head. That puts them down for good. As for how we're getting in, we're not… I am. I'm going to use the ventilation system," Thomas said.

"You crazy, man? You think you can move through the vents without them hearing you up there? One sound of you hitting something or your weight causes the vent to bend, and they'll be on you like white on rice. You'll be dead before you could get a shot off."

"We won't have to worry about me getting any shots off, 'cause I won't be carrying a gun or anything else. I'll be wearing pants, a

T-shirt, and socks. It'll be too tight for anything else. As for noise, that's what I'm counting on to keep me alive, and lots of it." He paused, as if thinking. "Come on, let's go back to my camp. Devon, my family is back there, my children. I'm trusting you, and if you're gonna try something, then you better kill me now. Try something with my children, and I promise you blood," Thomas said without blinking and with complete conviction.

"Understood, cop. Let's make this happen. When this is done, I need something from you, if, by some miracle, you still alive and not one of them Spewers, that is."

"Cross that bridge when we come to it, Devon."

"Coo'. By the way, call me Dev, or just D. Only my mama and my cousin, who you already met, call me Devon."

Thomas recalled Billy and Paul then led them back to the others. It was time to lay out his plan. He would make entry into the hospital and access the vents in the lobby. He'd need the others to make enough noise to pull the infected to the west wing of the hospital. The infected wouldn't come near sunlight, so that meant Devon and his men would actually have to go into the west wing and draw them out. They had to stay close enough to the exits to make it back out but in far enough to draw the infected to the wing.

"How far in we talking?" Devon's cousin asked.

"Well, I'm not exactly sure, man. What's your name?" Thomas replied.

"I'm Marcus, and this seems like some kinda suicide mission or something. Running right up in there with them things… I don't know if I'm down for this. Devon, we seriously gon' do this, cuz?"

"I am. You know the deal. You do what you gotta do, cuz."

"You know I got yo back. I'm just saying I don't like it, but screw it, it's whatever."

"We good here?" Thomas asked.

"Yeah, we'll hold it down, cop. Don't worry, Marcus gon' be all right. He might bitch up from time to time, but he's been down with me since his first breath. Ain't no one I trust more."

Carl had been listening closely. "Sheriff, I need to talk to you. I should be the one going in. I'm smaller than you, and I'll fit easier, which means I can move faster and more quietly."

"This ain't no spelling bee, li'l nigga. Let grown folks take care of this," Marcus interrupted.

"Naw," Devon said, "he got a point, cop. What he say makes sense. Smaller, quicker, quieter."

Thomas knew there would come a time when Carl and the others would have to place themselves in danger, but he'd hold off and keep trying to push that day back as far as he could. He also knew he could not treat Carl like a child.

"Okay, listen, Carl. I know you want to help, but say you do get through. What happens if you come across one of them? Your mother needs you here, and so do Jessie and Jimmy."

"Stop throwing them in my face, Sheriff! I'm not a babysitter, and I don't need a babysitter. You know Jess can take care of herself, and so can my mom. I need to help, I gotta do something."

"Let the li'l nigga go, then. He feels like a badass, let him go," Marcus taunted.

"Stay out of this, Marcus," Thomas warned.

"Who you think you talkin' to, cop? I ain't your li'l token Negro like ya boy there," Marcus said, standing up over Thomas.

"Sit down, Marcus!" Thomas warned again.

"My name is Carl, not li'l nigga. Don't call me out of my name again, banger," Carl snapped, standing up also.

Thomas was about to get to his feet when Devon put his hand on his arm. "Let Carl get his respect, Sheriff. We'll stop it before it gets outta hand. If you keep babying him, he'll never last five minutes without you."

This made too much sense for Thomas to argue against, so he looked over at Claire. She nodded, knowing Devon was right; she also knew her boy could take care of himself.

Marcus took the first move—he was fast and had lots of scrapes and scars that came from holding his own in many street fights. He caught Carl with a straight right punch that sent him stumbling back and almost to the ground. Carl recovered and relied on his extensive wrestling background. He went low, grabbing Marcus around the waist and placing his head against Marcus's chest to avoid being placed in a headlock. Then he shifted his weight and pulled, picking Marcus off the ground and slamming him hard into the side of a dirt hill. Devon and the rest of his crew seemed impressed with this. Carl got on top of Marcus and landed a few punches—this was a mistake, and Thomas knew it. He attempted to yell instructions to Carl, but before he could react, Marcus recovered and threw him to the side, shifted his own weight, gained top position, then landed a few punches of his own. Marcus's experience and power were too much for Carl, and Thomas and Devon knew this was enough. Carl had made his point. They quickly moved in and separated the two brawlers. Carl was still irate and had to be restrained. Marcus, on the other hand, went on as if business as usual. He was a good street soldier. When Devon said enough, that was all it took.

"Hey, calm down, *Carl*. You made your point. You got heart for a young buck," Marcus said as he extended his hand to Carl.

"Take it," Thomas said quietly to Carl.

But Carl shook his head. "I still say it needs to be me to go, Sheriff. We all have family here, and you can't protect everyone all the time. Let me help."

"Not this time, Carl. I just need to make sure you're ready. Be patient a little longer, please."

Carl walked away, and Claire went to him. "Let me look at that eye. It's going to swell if we don't get a compress on it."

It was almost two o'clock now, and they had to move fast. Thomas made last-minute confirmations with Devon, and they got ready to move out.

"Dad, Dad!" Jessie called out. "Dad, Carl's gone. I think he might have gone to the hospital. He was irate and talking about being tired of being treated like some dumb kid. I've never seen him like this. We have to stop him!"

Thomas knew exactly where Carl was going. "Dev, we have to move now. Go to your setup point. We're going ahead according to plan. I'll get Carl then get inside. Stick to the same timetable."

"You sure? We move in and he's not set up and hidden in them vents, and we might just bring them things down right on top of him," Devon said.

"We got no choice. We have one shot at this, and we can't get caught out here after dark. If he is in those vents already and we don't move, he'll be left hanging, surrounded and alone," Thomas said.

Carl made his way to the hospital lobby. He knew by now that Thomas would be there soon. A street fight brought him no closer to earning the respect Carl felt he needed, not from Thomas, anyway. The only way for him to be seen and treated like something other than the kid next door was to get this done.

Arriving at the hospital, Thomas found a note taped to the door.

Sheriff,

I know you're mad but it's no use coming in after me. That will just increase the chances of us getting caught. The best way is for you to trust me. I can do this. I know what to do. I won't move until I hear the signal. I'll be in and out before they know I'm here. I even know about Ray's heart meds. I heard you and Michael talking, so I looked it up in one of my dad's medical books I brought. I know exactly what it is. If something does go wrong, tell my mom I love her and I'm sorry. Please take care of her. Tell Jess I love her too. She'll always be my best friend.

Thomas stood by the hospital door, holding the letter. He looked through the door at the vent cover lying on the ground and Carl nowhere in sight. Carl was right; going in behind him was not an option. Carl was in play, and all Thomas could do was be ready when he came back. There was no turning back now.

* * * * *

Caleb watched the hospital from the building across the street, their futile struggle amusing him. He had to meet Sera soon, but there was time for observation. Sera was his tactical adviser, a bit soft for his liking, but necessary. She had little vision of the grand picture but had been an integral part of his plans. For now, he would take solace in watching these small simple people and their small simple schemes.

* * * * *

Thomas hurried around to the west wall of the hospital, the explosives he'd wired in place and set to go. These were the last of the explosives he'd taken from the evidence locker, and he intended to make them count. After one last check, he joined Devon on the east side of the building.

"Okay, Dev, we're a go."

Devon signaled his men, whom Thomas had divided into three teams of five. Team 1 moved into the hospital and set off multiple flash-bang stun grenades. This got the attention of every infected in the area.

Carl heard the flash-bangs go off and knew that was his cue to move. He moved through the vents with good speed. Truth be told, he moved much more quickly than Thomas could have. As Carl crawled through the vents, he was careful whenever the infected were close by and would stop and wait for them to pass. He followed the map Thomas had taken off the hospital wall. The medication storage room was straight ahead, and he was almost there. Carl came to the opening, pushed through, and jumped down into the room.

Team 1 cleared out of the building and back outside into the protective sunlight. Team 2 was set up to provide cover fire should team 1 have any unexpected problems. Team 3 entered the southwest wing of the hospital just close enough to Carl that if there was trouble, they could provide assistance.

The infected rushed through the wings with a fierce velocity, fully stimulated and in search of prey. They reached the east wing and found it empty. Their stimuli seemed to dull, and they went back into a dormant mode. Thomas's plan was working impeccably.

* * * * *

Caleb saw the group's progress, and although he was impartial to the event's outcome, he decided to, as they say, up the ante.

* * * * *

Thomas and Devon watched as the plan unfolded without flaw. "Dev, have your guys keep the Spewers' attention steady. Fire a shot into them from time to time to keep them interested."

Feeling very much in his element, Devon gave a broad grin and radioed his guys, relaying Thomas's instructions. Thomas watched closely, but things were going just as planned. The infected, all at once, began to start clearing out of the east wing. Thomas saw the progress but knew better than to relax. This was far from finished.

"Dev, have your men fire into them, full force. We have to keep them here!" Thomas shouted. The infected ignored the group completely and began to move back toward the west wing of the hospital.

"Tell your men in the southwest end to expect company," Thomas said.

Devon informed his men as Thomas ran the length of the hospital toward the west end.

Meanwhile, Carl had gathered the medications and was walking out the door toward the exit when he heard the infected tearing toward him through the hallway. If they found him, he wouldn't have a chance. Exiting the room, he ran down the hallway away from the sound of the incoming infected.

Thomas ran to the wall that he'd wired with the explosives. Getting Carl into the supply room was paramount. He couldn't blow it till he knew Carl was inside. Carefully placed charges on the outside of the building had rigged the wall to collapse downward so there would be no blowback into the room. Detonating the wall too early would be disastrous—it'd only bring the infected here before Carl had a chance to get into the room.

In Carl's rashness, he didn't get this part of the contingency plan. He had no idea he needed to get to this room.

Thomas became desperate; he was tempted to run into the hospital to retrieve Carl, but his chances of getting in and out with him were not slim but none. He couldn't let Carl just die, but what about

Jessie and Jimmy? He couldn't leave them either. This decision was impossible.

Thomas grabbed his weapon and ran for the door to the hospital, making up his mind as he prepared to make entry into the wing.

"Sheriff, it's Carl. Please come in. Over."

Carl might have acted rashly, but he was smart enough to have grabbed one of the camp's radios.

"Carl! Thank God! Listen, you have to get to room 212 on the west end of the building. It's a supply room. There is an exit prepared for you. Can you make it, son?"

"I'm hiding in a storage closet. They're outside of it. I can't get clear, Sheriff—they have me trapped."

"Stay put, Carl, and turn your radio down as low as you can. I'm coming for you." Then he said, "Dev, this is Thomas. Where is your team in the west wing?"

"We got a problem, Sheriff. Meet me at the main entrance," Devon replied.

Thomas ran around the corner, where Devon was waiting. Devon's somber expression told Thomas what was coming wouldn't be good.

"Sheriff, my boys say there's too many in there. No offense— you a cool dude and all—but I ain't sending my boys into a slaughter for ya boy. I like you, but not that much. I pulled them out."

"That wasn't the deal, Dev, but I get it."

Thomas keyed his radio. This turn of events was unfortunate, but Thomas would improvise as always and as needed.

"Wayne, come in. I need you, Billy, and Paul down here ASAP."

Thomas briefed Wayne and the others about Carl's situation.

"I need Billy to come with me. Wayne, you and Paul find some high ground on the west side of the hospital—you know what to do from there. If we don't make it out by five o'clock, take the group back into the woods and wait for us there. If we're not back by morning, keep the group together and take care of Jessie and Jimmy."

Wayne nodded. "Sheriff, you'll make it out. You always do."

Billy and Thomas did a last weapons check and got ready to move in.

"Just you two alone?" Devon asked. "You two crazy white boys!"

"We don't leave our people behind. We're all we've got now," Thomas said.

"I can't send my boys in there, Sheriff. I'm sorry, man. That don't mean I can't go with you myself," Devon said.

"Hold up!" Marcus said. "Hell no! You ain't goin' in there to save some dude you don't know. That ain't cool, cousin, not even a little bit."

Devon took Marcus aside.

"I gotta do this, fam. If something happens to me, you get our crew and do what you gotta do to take care of them. This cop is solid, man, something about him. We get out of this in one piece, and he gon' do good things for us, for a lot of people. The world gone mad. We need some of what he got, we jus' do, Marcus."

"Okay, I feel you." Marcus walked over and grabbed a rifle from one of Devon's men. "You go, I go. I kinda like the li'l scrappy homie, anyway," Marcus said.

Two of Devon's men, Antony and Kevin, stepped forward. "We got y'all too."

Thomas stepped up. "Okay, thanks, all of you. We need you. Let me run through a brief QRC with everyone—that means 'quick reaction combat.'" Thomas gave a quick rundown to the men. The two were now six.

Thomas led the men through the main entrance. The goal was to clear the hallway so Carl could make it to the room they'd designated for egress. They loaded up with flash-bangs, which Thomas knew would have little or no effect on the infected, but he would use them to herd the infected where he needed them to be. He hoped the grenades would move the infected as planned. The infected had broken their pattern when they moved back to the west end of the hospital, and that worried Thomas.

Moving to the narrowest part of the hallway, Thomas and his group were still undetected. There was a corner there.

"We are going to use this corner as a choke point to thin their numbers. They can only come around the corner a few at a time. We will fire in groups of two. When the front two need to reload, the next two will move up and continue to lay down suppressing fire. We're going to draw them here and away from Carl so he can get clear. Then, using the maneuvers I taught you, we move back and out two by two," Thomas whispered to the group.

Thomas threw the flash-bang, and the response was instantaneous. The infected roared around the corner. Thomas and Billy began firing the second the first target presented itself, and infected fell one right after another.

"Reloading!" Billy yelled out.

Devon and Marcus stepped in between them and took up position, immediately firing into the infected. Thomas and Billy reloaded quickly. Thomas was impressed by Marcus's, and especially Devon's, poise and accuracy.

As the infected continued to come, Thomas radioed Carl.

"Carl, come in! Can you move yet?"

"They're moving away, Sheriff. They're almost gone. I should be able to move in a few minutes if they keep moving at this rate."

"We have to keep firing!" Thomas yelled to the men over the gunfire.

"Reloading!" Devon yelled out.

Antony and Kevin moved up, firing into the infected. Their fire was wild and undisciplined. They weren't getting the headshots necessary to put the infected down, and because of this, the infected were closing in on the group.

"They're getting too close!" Billy hollered out.

Thomas and Billy had to break rotation and begin firing out of turn while Devon and Marcus were still reloading.

"I'm out!" Antony yelled out, way too early.

Thomas and Billy moved up, already halfway out of ammunition. "We're out of rotation! We're not going to have our weapons reloaded in time to get clear!" Billy shouted.

Thomas knew he was right; they had to move and pray that Carl was clear and in position.

"Reloading!" Billy called out.

Devon and Marcus had barely reloaded but moved up and began firing. Antony and Kevin had not finished reloading and were clumsy and panicked.

"We have to move. Devon, Marcus, move out on your next rotation, reload, and cover our fallback!" Thomas said.

Devon and Marcus finished the volley and moved back down the hall about fifty feet before beginning to reload.

Antony and Kevin moved up and began their brave yet ineffective assault on the incoming infected. Once again, Thomas and Billy were forced to fire out of turn to keep the infected from overtaking their position.

"Reloaded, move!" Devon shouted.

"Go!" Thomas yelled to Antony and Kevin.

"No, you go!" Antony shouted back, pulling a grenade out of his pocket. "I told you, cuz, we got you."

"Give me your gun, cuz. Imma stay and watch my boy's back long as I can," Kevin said.

There was just no time to argue. Billy handed his fully loaded rifle to Kevin, and he and Thomas ran back to Devon and Marcus.

"New plan. Run!" Thomas shouted.

They ran right for the exit. As they bolted down the hallway, they heard laughter. A blast cleared the pursuing infected and off-spring and brought down enough of the roof and wall to cover their escape.

"Sheriff, this is Carl. I'm in the room. Now what?"

"Get down, Carl, now!"

Reaching into his pocket, Thomas pressed the detonator button. The force of the blast threw Carl to the floor as the wall crumbled and fell in front of him. He ran outside just as Thomas and his group ran out the main entrance. Exhausted and excited with the feeling of a job well done, Carl ran to Thomas with a backpack full of meds. Thomas stopped him short and grabbed his shoulder.

"Are you okay?" Thomas asked.

"Yeah, I'm good, and I got what we needed."

After he had seen Carl safe and sound, the relief of his safe return was soon washed over with disdain.

"That's great, and you only cost two men their lives! You want to be treated like a man? Then try growing up and acting like an adult! Real life has started, boy!"

Thomas then stalked off toward the vehicles. Carl stood there shocked as Marcus came up to him.

"Those were my homies that died getting you out. They names was Antony Williams, a.k.a. Big Tony, and Kevin Hall, a.k.a. K-dog. Remember them. The homies knew what was up, though, and they went out like some straight-up Gs. No regrets, li'l homie. You got some stones. Your man right, though, get with the program."

With that, Marcus went back with his cousin.

* * * * *

Caleb watched from a building across the street, astonished. How was it possible that this man was able to escape what should have been a death trap? Caleb had underestimated this *sheriff.* That wouldn't happen twice, he decided. He was intrigued by this man. His scientific curiosity had gotten the better of his sound judgement, and Caleb decided that he would meet him. Caleb wanted to see what exactly made this man function; he'd never seen or met any person like him. This would be a very enlightening opportunity, to say the least.

CHAPTER 7

Thomas and Wayne were the last from the group to head back to camp and were loading the truck when Caleb approached them.

"Excuse me, gentlemen. I need a word with you, Sheriff. If you'll come with me, please," Caleb said.

The newcomer was a man of average height, about five feet ten inches, Thomas estimated. Dress hat worn low, sunglasses, long coat in May, long-sleeve button-down shirt, long pants, with dress shoes. Thomas didn't like the fact he couldn't properly make out the man talking to him. He seemed to be purposely hiding.

"Who are you? And what do you need, friend?" Thomas asked.

"I'll explain much to you, Sheriff. Now, come with me. I won't ask again."

Wayne stepped forward. "Buddy, that sounds suspiciously like a threat. If you need help, we can help you, but you need to relax."

"Enough of this," Caleb said as he grabbed Wayne and threw him into the side of the truck with enough force that it knocked him unconscious.

Thomas reacted fast, delivering a quick blow to the side of Caleb's head and then another to his ribs. Caleb walked through the punches, barely even noticing the blows. He hit Thomas with a back-fist punch that sent him to his knees. Thomas had never been hit so hard before—it stirred a primal survival instinct in him. Thomas took a knife he kept in his boot, thrust it forward into Caleb's thigh, and twisted the blade. Caleb responded with a knee to Thomas's face, knocking him five feet into a pole. Thomas, barely conscious, watched Caleb pull the blade out of his leg, toss it to the side, and walk toward him without so much as even a limp. Thomas struggled to his feet, prepared to attempt to fend off his attacker.

"I'm losing my patience," Caleb warned. "Know when you're beaten, and you may survive this conversation."

Thomas didn't know how much longer he could stand or even stay conscious, but he knew giving up wasn't an option. He gathered the last of his strength and mustered a breath.

"Not happening."

Grinding his teeth and clenching his fist, Caleb lunged at Thomas, bringing a blow down across his face and knocking him back against a car. Caleb had had enough of this bravado. He followed up his attack with multiple blows to Thomas's midsection. Blood splattered from Thomas's mouth, causing Caleb to regain his senses and calm down. The point wasn't to kill him, after all. Caleb picked up the unconscious sheriff as if snatching a pillow off the floor and threw him over his shoulder.

"I did ask nicely," he said, smiling as he walked away to his vehicle and drove toward his refuge.

* * * * *

Wayne staggered to his feet as he grabbed his radio. "Billy, come in! We got trouble! Meet me back at the truck now!"

Billy and the group, who were still at the staging area half a mile away, responded to Wayne's call immediately and were there in minutes. He quickly explained to Billy, Devon, and the others what happened.

"So this guy just knocked you cold with one hit?" Marcus asked.

Paul interrupted him. "This blood is fresh. Looks like there was a fight—bad one too, judging from the amount of blood. Blood on that car and across the street over here... someone was carried over there. Trail of blood ends there. There was a car. Them tire tracks in the dirt lead to the road. They could have gone anywhere from there."

"What the hell is going on? Why would he take the sheriff? He must have something to do with all this madness," Billy said.

"We have to get back to camp now. It's gonna be dark soon," Wayne said.

"We can't just leave him out there. He'd never leave one of us!" Billy shouted.

"I know that, Billy, but I have to think of the group. I gave him my word I'd look out for everyone and take care of his kids. Now, we move. We don't have a choice."

"He's right. Come on, Billy," Paul said.

Devon shook Wayne's hand. "We gotta move too, man. I hope you find him. If you need us, you can find us here." He handed Wayne a piece of folded paper.

"You guys go back, Wayne. I'll find cover tonight, but I'm not leaving him out here," Billy said.

"Billy, we have to stay together. Don't do this," Wayne said.

"No time to argue, Wayne. I'll take the other truck and meet you guys as soon as possible. Get our people safe. I'll be okay." Billy walked to the truck.

"Let him go, Wayne. We have to go now. He'll be okay. He can take care of himself," Paul offered.

Heavyhearted and torn, Wayne turned and loaded the truck. The ride back to camp was thick with silence, everyone's head full of thoughts that no one could put into words. So they sat and rode in stillness and concern. Wayne knew this would be a painful conversation with the camp. He had to hold it together, but God help him, he didn't know if he could.

* * * * *

Thomas faded in and out of consciousness. He woke to see two people, his attacker and what looked like a female. He could hardly make them out or what they were saying.

"He's going to die if you just leave him like this. Why did you even bother bringing him here?" the female said.

"I did lose my composure a bit. If he does live, I wanted to talk with and maybe observe him. He is a fascinating specimen, to be sure. I saw him coordinate and escape a trap I set into motion myself.

He has insight like I haven't seen since I've been here. His fortitude is immense."

"How long has he been here?" she asked.

"A couple of days," Caleb said.

"He needs to drink," Sera said as she came over with a cup of water, which she gave to Thomas. He was badly beaten. She pitied him. She pitied them all.

"Caleb, this is wrong. I didn't sign up for this. I understand what's at stake here better than most, but there has to be a better way."

"Sera, we're not only saving a planet, but we're also making history. Don't lose your way now, not when we are so close! Look, if it'll make you feel better, you can take him after I've had a chance to talk to him. He'll more than likely die, anyway. You can save me the trouble of getting rid of the body."

"Why bother wasting time talking to him? Their minds are completely open to us. Read his thoughts, take what you want, and let us move on," she protested.

"No, Sera, you don't understand. It's not his thoughts that interest me but his thought process."

"Well, you better talk fast. He doesn't have much time left," she conceded.

"Very well, then," Caleb said. He took a chair over to Thomas, set it in front of him, and sat down. "Hello, Sheriff, my name is Caleb. I'm so sorry that I got so carried away earlier. If you knew me better, you'd know I hate getting my hands dirty. So now, tell me, how did you get by my children earlier in the hospital?"

"Ch-children? I don't... understand... what are... you?" Thomas struggled to say.

"Oh, now, Sheriff, I could explain it, but let's just say your simple human mind will always assume we're little green men or wanting you to *take us to your leader*," Caleb mocked.

"A-a-aliens," Thomas managed.

Caleb started, "Yes, Sheriff. Now, tell me, how did you manage to..."

But Thomas was out again.

"This is a waste of time. Sera, take one of the offspring and let's get the sheriff on the workforce. We may as well get some use out of him."

Sera picked Thomas out of the chair one-handed, with little effort, and carried him down the hall. Thomas was helpless. His semiconscious state of mind drifted between his kids and the memories of Sue. If today was his day to die, he wanted his thoughts to be of them.

* * * * *

Wayne, Jimmy, Jessica, Paul, and Jax made up one search team. The other team was looking in another section of town. It had been four days since Thomas was taken. The group's morale was low, and they were beginning to think the worst. Wayne felt responsible since he'd been with Thomas when it happened; he couldn't help feeling he could have done more.

"Jess, Jimmy, we won't stop looking for your dad. He'll be okay, guys," Wayne said.

"Deputy Hicks, I know you're trying to make us feel better, but you don't have to," Jessica said. "You never knew our dad before, when he used to be with the SEALs. He left us a lot, always running off to fight someone else's war. After my mom died, I kind of blamed him for not being there. Thing is, as many times as he left, he always came home. He always came back then, he'll come back now."

Wayne prayed she was right. He wasn't sure if she was, but one thing he did know was, she believed it.

Back at camp Henry, Ray, Michael, and Claire had their morning prayer together. They did this every morning together, after which Ray would hold a devotional. As they finished, Ray and Claire began clearing the camp from the night's watches and getting breakfast ready.

"Ray, I'm so worried about Thomas," Claire said. "I know I haven't said much about it. I'm trying to be strong for Carl. He feels so responsible. He keeps telling me that if he hadn't run off, then maybe Thomas would still be here. He is convinced Thomas is dead. I keep telling him not to give up hope, but every day they come back without him, it becomes harder and harder to keep his spirit from crashing. I'm getting scared." A tear ran down her cheek.

Ray held her. "Claire, listen to me. In the last week, we've seen the most insane things we could ever imagine. The dead walking and evil flowing like a river. The evil one is busy these days. Right in the middle of it all has been Thomas. He hasn't been getting lucky, he has been blessed. God will not abandon us. He has chosen our champion, and it's Thomas. He'll be back. I have faith, and God has never let us down, and He is incapable of doing so. Carl will recover. This group will be whole again soon."

Billy, Carl, and James made up the second search party. They had been trying to locate where the vehicle that had taken Thomas had gone.

"Billy, we've been looking for tracks for days now. Maybe we ought to try looking in a different area."

"Do what you want, James. I'm sticking to this. That car, or whatever, went this way, and there has to be a trail. It went somewhere. I just need to find a clue."

"Billy, you've been out here for days. You've barely come back to camp and haven't eaten more than two meals. When was the last time you slept? I know what he means to you—hell, to the whole group! No one here knows more than I do what it means to not have him around, but keep this up and you'll be no good to him or anyone else. Please take a day to eat and get some rest."

Carl stayed quiet; he hadn't said much for days. Billy knew James was right. He was feeling the effects of fatigue, and his body was beginning to rebel from lack of nutrients. Billy was nearly ready to head back to camp. He only worried that, once there, would he have the strength to pull himself up and back out again? He hated to admit it even to himself, but he was beginning to lose hope.

The car driving down the road was coming fast. It stopped about a hundred yards from Billy and James, who watched as it stopped for several seconds before backing up and pulling away. It had left something on the side of the curb. Billy took his binoculars, looking down the road.

"O Lord, please no… no!" Billy took off running, and James followed behind.

* * * * *

Sera walked down the hall with Caleb. "Did you finish with the sheriff, Sera? Is he all set with the offspring?"

"I did one better, Caleb. I sent him off as a warning to his little band of rebels," she replied with a smile.

"Sera, you put too much effort into these humans. I thought the sheriff might give me the smallest amount of amusement. They're really not worth the time," Caleb said with very little interest.

* * * * *

Billy and James had loaded Thomas in the truck and were almost back to camp. Wayne and the others were on their way as well. James drove while Billy tried to stabilize Thomas; he was busted up badly, and Billy's medical experience was limited. They just had to keep him stable until they could get him back to camp. Carl was on the radio, preparing the camp for their arrival.

"It's going to be okay," Carl said. "My mom is there, and she's setting up a trauma unit with the supplies we got from the hospital."

"She knows what she's doing, right, Carl?" Billy asked.

"My mom was an ER nurse. That's how she met my dad, Billy. She knows what she's doing—he's going to be all right."

"Thank you God for workplace fraternization," Billy said, smiling at Carl.

They arrived at the campsite, and Claire moved quickly into action. It was just like her old days in the ER, and she hadn't missed a step. Billy had stabilized Thomas very well. Placing Thomas in a makeshift bed, they inserted an IV immediately into his arm. Claire needed to evaluate the extent of his injuries, so she cut his shirt and pants off. He had bruises over his whole body. Claire had hung blankets from wires they'd attached to trees and now closed the blankets together. She knew from the description Billy had radioed in that the kids didn't need to see this, and she had prepared for the situation.

She called Billy in to assist, and they began to attempt to save the one who had, at one time or another, saved them all.

Thomas had a fractured skull and ribs, multiple lacerations, and a broken jaw. He looked like he'd been hit by a bus.

"We have to get the swelling down so we can determine what his injuries are," Claire said.

Thomas was extremely dehydrated and malnourished. Claire's main concern was pneumothorax, a trapped air pocket outside the lung caused by the blunt trauma. This would prevent his lung from expanding, basically suffocating him over time and killing him. This was outside of Claire's area of expertise.

Please, God, she prayed, *help us.*

Wayne gathered himself, because dusk was coming fast. He had to get the group together and put the watch shifts in place. Seeing Thomas like this sent his head spinning, but he still had a job to do.

"Henry, Paul, get ready for your watches. Everyone else, gather everything together and load the trucks in case we have to make a quick exit. You all know the drill. Michael, make sure Claire and Billy have everything they need for Thomas."

Wayne sat down against a tree, bowed his head, and prayed. He couldn't remember the last time he'd done that. Ray sat down with him. Wayne raised his head.

Wayne asked, "You think he heard me?"

"Seek and you shall find. He heard you, Deputy."

"Do you think He'll answer me? I haven't exactly been a model Christian."

"He always answers. Sometimes we don't understand or even like His answer, but God won't turn His back on us."

"I don't know if it's my faith or fear that's turning me to God. Maybe He doesn't like last-minute desperation prayers."

"God will use many tools to get the attention of His children."

"You think this is His doing, Ray? The end of times?"

"I don't know, Deputy. I have been praying and reading the Scripture more these days than ever before. I don't have an answer yet. All will be revealed in His time, however. Have faith, brother.

We're counting on you, Deputy. You won't let us down." Ray went to prepare his area and left Wayne with his thoughts and his prayers.

Time passed in the camp. The group continued to gather supplies by day and take refuge in the forest by night. Thomas's condition continued to improve, and Claire never left his side.

"Claire…" Thomas finally opened his eyes after what felt like forever.

"Thomas! Take it easy. Don't try to move. You're still in a pretty bad shape, but you're stable."

He started, "The kids… ?"

"They're fine," she said.

"How long… how long have I been out?"

"Two weeks. It's been two weeks, Sheriff. You gave us all a real scare. It was touch-and-go for a while there. Wayne has done a great job taking care of us during your vacation, though," she said, smiling.

"I have to talk to Wayne and Billy. I have to tell them what happened," Thomas said.

Thomas was getting worked up; his heart rate was racing, and Claire was worried he might hurt himself further.

"Thomas, you have to calm down."

It was no use; he was incogitant.

Claire injected a sedative into his IV, and Thomas slipped into a restful sleep. Claire then sent for Wayne and Billy; the sedative was mild, and she wanted them there when he woke again. Thomas had said he had something important to tell them. She needed him calm, or he could reinjure himself—and he was still in a very fragile state.

Wayne and Billy sat close as Thomas regained consciousness. Claire sat by his side, making sure he didn't get too agitated.

"Take it nice and slow, Thomas," she cautioned.

"I'm okay, Claire. Thanks. Wayne, Billy, I have to tell you something. It may take you back a bit, or not, considering what we've seen," Thomas said. "The guy that did this—the Crawlers, the Spewers—beat me nearly to death…. He's not human."

Billy's face froze, just unsure how to register this information.

Wayne didn't seem fazed. "Yeah," he said. "Alien, I assume." Thomas nodded. "I can see that," Wayne added.

"Okay. How are we gonna help ET get his ass home?" Billy asked, shaking off his shock.

"We don't, Billy. We can't beat this thing. We stay hidden and survive," Thomas said.

Billy couldn't believe what he'd just heard. "Say again, Sheriff? I couldn't have heard you right! Quit? No, no. You didn't say that! You quit and we die! You spent the last few weeks showing us that we can do this. Don't break us now."

"Billy, you haven't seen this kind of evil or power. Before today, neither had I. It's not just his physical strength. He seems to be bored, like this is taking no effort. He's just doing enough to accomplish his end-game, and he could do so much more if we do something to get his attention. We go back to the woods in West Virginia. We know those woods like no one else. We can go deep, to the old Miller mines. Hide in the earth till this horror passes. I'm sorry, Billy, this is how it's gotta be."

Billy got up, heartbroken. He walked back into the camp.

Wayne looked at Thomas. "He's young, Sheriff. He doesn't understand what you're doing."

"Do you, Wayne?"

"Yes, I get it, but honestly, I don't like it either. I'll back your play 100 percent though, Sheriff."

Claire stepped in. "He needs to rest, Wayne, please."

Wayne got up and went back into the camp.

"God bless you, Thomas," Claire whispered as Thomas rolled over back into a troubled slumber.

CHAPTER 8

West Virginia
Four Months Later...

With Thomas's recovery, the group relocated and settled at their camp back in the Appalachian Mountains close to the Virginia border. The mine the camp was in ran down about a hundred meters into a cave, ending before a lift that led deeper down into the mountain. They had set up inside the cave and blocked the entrance with wood boards and rocks. Four new people had joined them during their trip back to West Virginia: Kenny Martin, who had led a small group out of a nearby town; Kenny's younger brother, Mark; Mark's wife, Rita; and Keylin, Mark's childhood friend and a recent Georgetown graduate majoring in electrical engineering. They mixed well and accepted Thomas's leadership. Kenny and Mark had spent their entire childhood hunting. Their father was an outdoor survivalist, and he'd taught them everything he knew. Kenny and Mark had taken Jessica under their wing and began teaching her survival tactics, including how to hunt and clean animals. Jessica used what she learned from the Martin brothers and, with her skill with a bow, had become the group's primary food supplier.

Billy had not accepted this surrender at heart but knew the group needed cohesiveness, so he gave in. He and Thomas had become distant. Thomas hoped it would pass, but he wouldn't risk the whole group for Billy's sake. Shirley and Charley had all but adopted Danny. Danny and Jimmy had become close and, with Jax, spent most of the time together.

Kenny had spent the day going through the camp's supplies. There was a problem. "Sheriff, I need to speak to you," he said, approaching Thomas.

"What's up, Kenny?"

"Well, with the camp set up primarily in the mine, we've been able to get by on small fires because the Spewers can't see the flames in the caves."

Keylin had set up a venting system to funnel the smoke from the fires out of the caves using a portable fan and tubing system. The smoke would vent out deeper in the cave system so it couldn't be detected from the outside.

"We've got enough weapons and ammunition. We'll need more food and water. Problem is, winter's coming and the mine is pretty close to the surface. That means the ground above us is going to freeze, turning the caves basically into freezers, and the small fires won't be enough to keep us alive. We've got two choices. We can find deeper mines, which will more than likely be inhabited by bears or, worse, Spewers. Second option: find a more effective source of heat. These mines are stripped off coal. That means a trip to a sporting goods and outdoor store. We know how the Spewers stay indoors during the day, and night travel isn't much of an option," Kenny continued.

"That's exactly what we're going to have to do, Kenny. I'll do some nighttime dry runs for the next few nights, see if I can pin down their movement patterns. I think a night run into what I'm hoping will be an empty store is our best bet. I'll put together a team and a plan after I gather as much information as I can."

"Sounds good, then, Sheriff."

Word of Thomas's nighttime run spread across camp, and as soon as she heard, Jessica rushed to talk to her dad. She found him talking with Kenny and Mark.

"Dad, can I talk to you?"

"Sure, Jessie, what's up?"

Jessica sat down with the three of them, but Kenny and Mark got up, about to give them some privacy.

"Can you guys stay?" Jessica asked. "I'd like you two to be part of this discussion."

Thomas nodded, and they sat.

"Okay, I've become a valuable part of this group, but I can do more. I've learned so much from Kenny and Mark in the last few months," Jessica said, looking at the brothers. Both nodded in agreement. Jessica continued, "I want to be part of this supply run. I've done hundreds of runs. I know what I'm doing. I'm not asking as your daughter, I'm asking as a member of this team."

The three sat in silence until Thomas spoke. "I respect what you've accomplished, Jessie, I really do. But this run will be at night. We've never done anything like this before. I'm gathering as much information from recon runs as I can and talking to the brothers here. After that, Wayne and I will work out a plan that honestly won't have a place for you. It's going to be too dangerous, so I'm sorry, but the answer's no."

"I knew that would be your answer. That's why I asked Kenny and Mark to stay. I'd like to hear their opinions," Jessica said defiantly.

Mark spoke up first. "She's the best shot I've ever seen with that bow, Sheriff. We don't have any silenced guns. With all due respect, we can't do what you do. We can't take those things on bare hands or, more than likely, even with a knife. If things go wrong, a silent ranged weapon may just save some lives, sir."

Kenny, not happy to be caught in the middle of this, answered, "Jess, your dad is in charge for a reason. I won't question his decisions—they're the reason we're alive. You are the best shot I've ever seen also, and I was raised with woodsmen, but the way you've put Mark and me on the spot and ambushed your dad like this shows too much immaturity for a mission like this. If this were a vote, which it is not, I'd say no also."

Jessica, feeling her cause lost, got up and went back into the camp. Thomas wanted desperately to go after her, but there was so much to do. This was a critical run, a difference between life and death.

Carl sat waiting for Jessica. "He said no, huh?" Carl said.

"Captain Obvious to the rescue," Jessica snapped.

"Relax, Jess, give him time."

"You didn't, Carl. You took the reins and got the job done. Don't be a hypocrite!"

"Hypocrite? Two men died because I didn't listen, Jess. If you think a day goes by when I don't think of that, you're wrong! You need to grow up."

"Really, Carl. This is the world now. People die! Maybe I'm not the one that needs to grow up."

Jimmy walked by with Jax. "If you two are done, Carl, your mom wants you and Jess to help with lunch."

"Yeah, I guess I'll go take my place in the kitchen," Jessica said, walking off.

* * * * *

Two days later, Thomas had collected all the information he felt he could gather. He called for Paul, Kenny, Mark, Henry, Billy, and James.

"Meet me in twenty minutes with your gear. I'll brief you all on what we're doing, and prepare to move tomorrow night." Thomas walked through the camp, past Jessica, who made an effort to avoid eye contact.

"Hmm, the cold shoulder? That's too bad. It'll be hard to explain what I need you to do on the run tomorrow night if we're not talking," Thomas said.

Jessica tried but failed not to smile.

Thomas changed his posture. "Now, you tell me you're not coming to me as my daughter. Fair enough. Now I'm coming to you as your commanding officer. I wasn't moved by your childish act, but Mark is right. You could save lives out there. Show me your bow." Jessica had a Dream Season Decree 29 compound bow. "What's the effective range, Jessie?"

"It's advertised at thirty to forty yards, but I've hit marks at almost sixty."

"Okay, good. You'll be on my team out there, Jessie, so stay close to me. By the way, Carl told me about your conversation. He said you were right... this is the world now," Thomas said. "You follow my every order. You're right, people do die. But trust me when I tell you, you don't want to be responsible for getting a person killed."

Jessica nodded; she understood.

The night of the run was clear, and the moon was high and bright. Thomas separated the group into three teams. Jessica and Kenny were with him. Paul with his sniper rifle, James his spotter, and Billy his ground security made up the over-watch team. Henry and Mark would provide the distraction.

Thomas, Kenny, and Jessica made their way to the tree line that surrounded the town, where they took cover. There were infected all around the store, simply walking around in an inactive state. Henry and Mark had set up a fire circle by the river. It would burn bright enough to pull in the infected around the store but would burn right into the river after about an hour—that would be time enough for Thomas to get in and get what they needed.

Thomas conducted a radio check, and after an all clear from Billy and Mark, he moved into position.

Thomas was preparing to give Mark the signal to light the fire when he noticed the infected became stimulated. What had happened? Thomas worried they'd noticed someone in the group. Then he heard a familiar terrifying howl he'd first heard months ago from what they'd now begun calling a Rager. It came out of the forest just barely thirty feet from where Thomas was hidden. It went right at two of the infected that were near where the Rager had come out of the woods. The Rager grabbed the closest one, picked it up by the neck, and twisted the infected's neck, breaking it. Almost at the same time, it pounced on the other one, taking it to the ground and pushing the infected's eyes in with its thumbs till it had crushed its skull. The Rager was so full of violent anger its face was twisted with venomous rage and reflected only madness and murder. The other infected attacked the Rager, about twenty to thirty of them. The fight was savagely fierce.

"Mark, come in, do not—I repeat, DO NOT—light the fire," Thomas said into his radio.

Thomas took advantage of the Rager's incursion. He signaled for his group to hold and ran across the parking lot into Sam's sporting goods store. His gamble paid off; the store was empty. Thomas ran directly to the portable propane heating units. They were big, and he needed at least two of them plus propane. He prayed for God to stay with him, because he didn't want to have to make two trips, and when that Rager fell, the infected would be all over him. Thomas grabbed two heating units and began dragging them toward the exit; they were too heavy and making too much noise. Thomas heard something in the aisle—there was definitely something over there. Had the infected finished the Rager and were now back in the store. Or worse, was the Rager?

"Thomas," a voice whispered. James came around the corner. "Figured you could use a hand. Give me one of those," he said, grabbing one of the units.

They moved quickly to the exit, but Thomas stopped short of the door. He looked out to see infected walking around the parking lot. The fight was over—the Rager's body was ripped to pieces, surrounded by what appeared to be about fifteen dead infected. Thomas counted about a dozen infected in between them and the tree line. At sunup, they would be making a beeline for the store. It was time for that distraction. Thomas radioed Mark, and the forest lit up in a blaze. The infected, stimulated by the fire, began running right toward it. James broke out of the store and to the propane tanks in the locker outside.

"James, no, wait!" Thomas whispered.

But it was too late.

Two of the infected noticed James and were running right at him. James grabbed the tanks, running to the trucks parked past the tree line. Thomas followed, grabbing more tanks. The infected were closing in on James—the unit and tanks slowed him too much. He wouldn't make it.

As the infected closed to within a few feet, Jessica's arrow brushed so close to James's head it felt like it had cut the air around it. It struck the infected dead on through the forehead, and it dropped cold. The second infected was too close for Jessica to reload and fire another arrow. The crack of Paul's rifle stopped Thomas momentarily in his tracks. The shot dropped the second infected. Already knowing what to expect, he turned to see the rest of the infected move frenziedly toward them. Already at the truck, James finished loading his haul and began running back to Thomas, who was still on the move toward the tree line. James had his assault rifle readied as he approached.

"Load the stuff and get out of here. They're too close, Sheriff. You'll never have time to load up and get away. Besides, can't take a chance of them following us back to camp. I'll hold them as long as I can," James said as he ran on, not waiting for Thomas to reply.

James ran into the infected, firing and dropping as many as he could. He had the attention of most of them, but one ran past him and continued after Thomas. An arrow through its eye ended the pursuit. James fired his weapon into the infected. Most fell but got right back up. As the weapon ran dry, James grabbed it by the barrel, swinging it at the infected, trying gravely to keep them busy for just a few more precious seconds.

Paulie, baby, I'm coming home to be with you, he thought.

Those were his last thoughts as an offspring crawled up his back and latched into his neck.

An arrow through his forehead ended James's suffering. *Our people don't become Spewers,* Jessica thought as she lowered her bow, trying hard to keep her tears at bay.

Thomas loaded the equipment and called for the group to withdraw as he, Jessie, and Kenny rode off back to camp.

* * * * *

During the next few days, Sera watched Thomas and the camp from the trees, undetected. She was impressed by the group's ability to survive. Caleb had gone too far; she hadn't signed up to cause the annihilation of an entire species. She had watched long enough; it was time to make introductions.

Paul sat in an old hunter's perch, on watch, when he saw someone in the woods walking toward the camp. He radioed Thomas. Sera walked into the camp and was met by Billy and Wayne's rifle barrels and Jessica's arrow, tensed and ready to fly. Sera wore a hooded raincoat with gloves, long cargo pants, sunglasses, and hiking boots.

She was covered head to toe, as Thomas's attacker had been. This didn't sit well with Thomas.

"One wrong move, and we see just what it takes to kill you," Thomas warned.

Sera responded, "Is this how you treat guests, especially a guest that comes bearing gifts?"

"Gifts?" Thomas asked. "What gifts?"

"Well, your lives, for one. Maybe your planet. If I wanted you dead, Sheriff, you know I could have done it. I may not be as strong as my male counterparts, but compared to Earth men, I might as well be your mythical strongman Hercules. You know this firsthand, Sheriff, do you not? I really am here to help, so please lower your weapons."

Billy stepped forward, retraining his rifle on Sera's head. "It may be strong, but I bet it ain't bulletproof, Sheriff!"

"My name is Sera, not *it*. No, I'm not bulletproof, not entirely, but I could take your weapon and kill you before I went down. This is information you will need if you're to have a chance against Caleb."

"Lower your weapons," Thomas said. "I've seen them heal. She's right, Billy."

Everyone lowered their weapons, everyone except Billy.

"You killed my wife, my friends… my town. Them other things out there, those Spewers, they're just animals, but you… you and your comrades are the handlers. Killing you would make it right." Billy's finger tightened on the trigger as a tear came down his cheek.

"Billy, we need her. Lower your weapon, Deputy… now!" Thomas ordered.

Billy held his position, and Thomas wasn't even sure he had heard him. But they needed Sera, so Thomas started to reach out to disarm him. Jessica gently put her hand on Billy's barrel, lowering the barrel and holding Billy. Sera felt the heat from his hatred as Jessica led him back into the camp.

"Okay, Sera, what now?" Thomas asked.

"First, we should find somewhere to sit. This will take a while."

They walked into the cave, and Sera began.

"We come from a planet very far from here called Usrafax Prime. It's about six thousand of your light-years away."

"Wait," Keylin interrupted, "no living thing can survive a trip of that length."

"Not with your current technology, no, of course not, although we age at a much slower rate than humans. We measure time in cycles instead of years. One of our cycles would equal about ten of your human years, and we live about ninety to one hundred cycles on average. Some much longer, like our council members. We only get stronger as we age, unlike your species. We can get to that later, young man. Please let me continue.

"Even with our technology, it was just a stroke of luck that we did find this planet. We were desperate, in dire need. Our planet is dying, and we need a very special and rare alloy called Theozin. Your planet has an abundant supply of it. Since the alloy is located close to the planet's core—approximately 4,800 kilometers deep within the Earth's inner core—and your species has only drilled about twelve kilometers into the Earth's crust, it's an alloy you would know nothing about.

"A group of my people came together to explore the known galaxies and find a solution. We selected one of my people to lead the expedition, who was Caleb. He was a lead scientist among our people. We've worked closely during the last forty of your Earth years. He is dark, and twisted. He wants the salvation of our people, but his means are more than I can bear. He has gone too far."

Thomas sat listening, measuring Sera. Could she be trusted? She seemed sincere, but could this be some kind of mind game?

"Sera, why don't you just take what you need without all this genocide?" he asked.

"Sheriff, we are a small group. We could never mine the alloy by ourselves, and there's no time to bring in enough of our own people to do it. We are only eight. After we found your planet, Caleb unveiled his plan on how to mine the Theozin from your inner core. He would develop an offspring that would enslave your planet, and we would use your people as a slave workforce. Originally, there were ten of us. Two of our group, Japon and his mate, Eldon, spoke against Caleb. They refused to destroy an entire species, even to save our own. Caleb told them the species didn't matter because taking the Theozin from your core would disrupt the planet's magnetic pull so that it would drift too close to the sun's radiation and kill every living thing on the planet within a year of our departure. Caleb called his offspring a mercy killing of the planet's inhabitants."

"This is insane!" Kenny said.

"I agree," Sera said. "So did Japon and Eldon. They spoke to the group and tried to convince them to find another way. They suggested negotiations, trade, or even threats if all else failed. We studied your people for many months before touching down on your surface. It was decided that you could not be trusted to keep a trade pact. Your species kills one another over useless things like oil or land, which your planet freely gives, has in large supply, and provides easy access to. You murder and maim one another in masses. It was also felt you would not be threatened. Even with your limited capabilities, your people's arrogance would make threats inapt. In the end, negotiations and threats would waste time that our people didn't have. Japon and Eldon took a shuttle and departed the group to try to find another option. I stayed silent and in place, hoping to discourage the others or, if necessary, sabotage this madness."

Billy was taking in everything, but the more he heard, the more disheartened he became. "Why?" he asked Sera. "Why betray your people, your family, for us?"

"Because, young Billy, I do not want to just see my family's faces again. I want to be able to look at them also."

"Okay," Thomas said. "No more sitting on the sidelines, hoping this will pass over us. It's no longer just about our survival, this is about our existence. Sera, how do we fight this? What can you tell us about the Spewers and Crawlers. Anything you can tell us?"

Sera sat, ready to help Thomas and his group in any way she could.

"You have to understand that this team… we are not soldiers or warriors. We're scientists and explorers. I have no kind of combat training. Our group is not warrior breed, and our people have not had conflict in many decades. Caleb is different—he has a taste for this violence. He sees we are stronger than your species and is acting like what you would call a schoolyard bully."

"Yeah, well, I ain't ever had much tolerance for bullies, no matter what planet they're from," Billy said.

"You said you're stronger than us, Sera. How much stronger?" Thomas asked.

"As a female, I am about twice as strong and fast as your typical human male. Caleb would be twice that, about four times stronger and faster than the average person. That is not your main concern, because our brains are capable of transmitting certain wavelengths. That is how Caleb controls the infected host through the offspring."

Thomas perked up immediately at the mention of this. "I knew they had uniform behavior, but how can he control so many at once?"

"It is not like that, Sheriff. In our weakened state, he can only program them. It is like how a human can teach a dog to sit but not drive a car. He programs them, and then it's like pointing them in a direction and they go from there."

"Sera, what do you mean weakened state? How are the Crawlers controlling the Spewers? And if Caleb can control them, can you also? And is it reversible?" Thomas began asking so many questions he had to slow himself down and take a breath.

Sera understood and was patient. "It's okay, Sheriff. I'll explain everything. The offspring, or Crawlers, as you call them, are the key. Caleb created them using our technology to splice his alien DNA with Earth insects, ants of some sort. Six offspring eggs are injected into the host. Gestation takes moments before the offspring hatch. Five attack and destroy major organs, namely the heart, liver, kidneys, intestines, and lungs, killing the host. They then prepare for regurgitation. The sixth, however, is very different. Think of it as the queen. It attaches to the brain stem and takes over the motor functions of the body. It produces another six offspring, which are continually regurgitated whenever the infected find a fresh host. The queen acts like a transmitter that receives Caleb's wavelengths. That's how he controls them. Our weakened state is from your sun. The UV radiation kills the infected because of the DNA from Caleb. They have some of our strengths, but all our weakness as well. The UV won't kill us, but it will weaken us. Without it, our physical strength will increase and our mental capabilities will exponentially expand, which is why Caleb plans to block out your sun."

Keylin jumped on this. "Wait, what? Block out the sun?"

"Yes. He is building a blackout tower that will generate a powerful beam that blocks UV radiation. It will reflect from the satellites that you have in orbit already, and half of your planet will lose sunlight. When that happens, Caleb will regain his full mental capabilities and be able to completely control the hosts, therefore allowing his workforce to begin mining the Theozin. I can't control them, because they are spliced with Caleb's DNA and they're akin to him and him alone. I can cause some mental static, if you will. In a tight situation, it might give you a few moments. As for reversing the effects, no, the host is already dead. I'm sorry."

"We've seen a different kind of infected. We call them Ragers. They seem to kill anything they see, including the other infected," Wayne said.

"Yes, Deputy, we've seen them too. This seems to be happening because the queen offspring loses contact with Caleb's wavelength instructions somehow. This is causing a malfunction, and the infected enters into a heightened state of agitation, causing it to lash out and attack. These Ragers are extremely powerful creatures. They do not follow Caleb's protocols to spread the infection. He sees them as a threat. They are very dangerous. They attack everything they see, including infected and even my comrades and me."

"Guess they ain't all bad, then," Billy said.

Thomas might not have shared Billy's feelings completely, but he did see the possibility of using this to their advantage.

"I have a question," Mark said, raising his hand. "Why don't the Air Force come in here with two hundred thousand Marines and waste this Caleb and his band of little green men?"

Sera, not understanding the little green men reference but getting the context, explained, "Phase 1 of Caleb's plan was to neutralize any prevalent opposition, namely your armed forces. It wasn't difficult. He sent half of us to multiple countries, your allies. They waited for confirmation from Caleb that the test run here had been a success. They then executed phase 1. They released their offspring into major cities and military facilities, especially air bases. By the time they knew they were under attack, it was too late. The ground forces were overrun in days, even hours sometimes. The air forces could not distinguish between friend or enemy, and they hesitated. Caleb relied on that. He depended on your humanity. With proper strikes, you might have been able to burn out the infection before it could take hold on your planet. It would have meant many hundreds of thousands dead, but now Caleb estimates his workforce at about six hundred million across the United States and Europe. The number increases daily."

"Over half a billion dead! Oh, sweet Jesus, help us," Claire said.

Mark held Rita as she cried. Some of the others, completely overcome, also held one another and cried. Billy got up and left the cave.

Thomas felt the despair come over the group. "This is bad, people, we know that. We're in a fight, and we're losing, but now we have a chance. Sera will provide information, and I will find a way to beat this evil bastard. I've been living with my head in the sand. I'm sorry for that. I was wrong. That ends now! He landed on the wrong planet and picked a fight with the wrong planet. Caleb's a walking corpse, the dumb son of a bitch jus' don't know it yet."

* * * * *

As the weeks went by and fall turned to winter, the group embedded themselves deep into the cave. Sera brought intel and supplies as often as she could without raising suspicion. Jessica and Kenny made frequent hunting trips, but the animals had been driven out or to ground by the cold. Billy made many runs into town, often alone, despite Thomas's explicit orders to the contrary. Each time, he went out farther and farther and came back with less and less.

The winter was taking its toll on the group. Thomas spent most of his time analyzing the information given to him by Sera. It was so much to take in, and the specs she supplied on the tower were overwhelming in particular. There were towers all over the world, but the blackout tower was the connection for them all. He knew that its completion meant death to him and all he knew, so bringing it down was his top priority. The tower was located in the city center in downtown DC. Caleb and some of his comrades had constructed a compound around it. Sera said he had stationed hundreds of Spewers in that compound. Getting in without waking them would be next to impossible—not to mention Caleb and whichever of his alien superfreaks were there with him. Sera said they rotated in and out of the station. Thomas examined the platform schematics and the infrastructure of the tower, looking for weak points. He had found the proper stress points, but getting in was a different story. He lacked the munitions and personnel to even attempt something like this. There had to be a way; he'd just keep moving forward until it presented itself.

Billy had pulled the last of whatever supplies weren't rotten, worthless, or looted he could out of Ghostwood. He'd also hit every town within a hundred-mile radius. There was another town about three hundred miles south in Virginia, near Salem, that seemed viable. It would mean an overnight trip, one he couldn't make alone. Billy would have to check in with Thomas and get a vehicle.

Billy arrived at camp and met with Thomas. Their relationship had gone from strained to broken with the arrival of Sera. Billy didn't trust her, and he didn't like the trust Thomas had put in her.

"Billy, I don't like you going so far out," Thomas said.

"You rather we starve, Sheriff? There's not much choice. Unless your extraterrestrial Benedict Arnold coughs up food and propane, I need to venture farther out."

"Don't forget she is selling out her own people and whom she's selling them out for, Deputy. We owe her a great deal."

"Really, Thomas, if it weren't for your new bestie and her people, Jackie and about a billion people would still be alive, and we wouldn't need her damn help! I hate them, Thomas, all of them. I always will."

"Get what you need, Billy. Take Paul. Get us what you can."

"That's what I wanted to talk to you about. Paul's great—he's a dead eye with that rifle, and I trust him completely. It's not Paul that hinders this run, it's the rifle. It's too loud, and it'll bring Spewers and Crawlers on us. Sheriff, I need quick and quiet. I need Jess and her bow."

Just hearing her name made Thomas swell up inside with a quick shot of anger.

"Have you lost your mind, Billy? Do you think I'd send my little girl out there with you without me? Take Paul and go. Don't push me on this, Deputy. You won't like where it goes," Thomas warned.

At that moment, Jessica came into the makeshift room where Thomas and Billy were. "How about me, Dad? Can I push it? Billy already talked to me. I knew this is how you'd react, but you said this is about the survival of the planet. Do you really think this is the time to play whose life is more important than another? This is the logical move. Billy's right. Dad, Kenny and I have tried everything—there is no more food here to hunt. I need to go farther south. Follow the warmth, and we'll find the food."

"It all makes sense, Jessie. You and Billy are right. I've given everything to lead this group, and I'll give all I am, but my price is, my children stay with me. I've earned this bad call. You're not going."

At that, Thomas walked out of the cave. Billy ran after him.

"Sheriff, I'll take Paul, and we'll do what you say. I just want you to remember that even though we are at odds over Sera, I'm still the same guy that's looked up to you since I was ten. You've been like a father to me, and I'd die before I let anything happen to her."

"I know, Billy. That's part of the problem."

Thomas left Billy to begin prepping for his trip.

A few hours later, Sera arrived at the camp with food, a couple of canisters of propane, and some more information Thomas had asked for. Thomas had come to trust Sera over the last two months—she was his only card and had proven reliable.

"Sheriff, I brought some supplies. I wish there were more I could do."

"Sera, you've done a great deal for me and my people. The information you've given us is invaluable, but without manpower and the proper resources, it's just a lot of paper. It's like having the answers to a test but not the actual test to take. Wayne and I have been over and over this—it just can't be done. Six months ago, with our infrastructure still in place, maybe, but now, alone..." Thomas trailed off. He'd compromised so much lately. With the lack of sleep and stress, Thomas was feeling the weight.

"You need to get out of this cave. Let's take a walk and get some air," Sera suggested.

They walked the camp. The air was cold and crisp. Thomas welcomed the fresh air. He had been in the cave too long, and the mountain air was doing him a world of good. Then he saw something that made his heart almost skip a beat.

"Paul, what the hell are you still doing here? Where's Billy?" Thomas asked.

"Jessica told me you wanted her with him. No skin off my teeth if you send the great white hunter with him. Something wrong, Sheriff?"

Thomas knew it was too late to go after them. It'd be dusk soon, and by now, Billy would be driving into the woods to set up camp.

Carl approached Thomas. "She told me to give you this when you came out of the cave," he said, handing Thomas a folded note. "She said not to disturb you, just to wait till you came out. After that, she and Billy loaded up and went on a supply run."

"Thank you, Carl," Thomas said, taking the note while still looking down the path Billy and Jessie had taken out of the camp.

"She's changed, Sheriff. She's capable in this world. I know she'll always be your little girl, but I spend most hours of every day with her. I watched it happen. She evolved into what she had to in this new place we live in now. Jess has always been strong, but now she's more than that—she's a survivor," Carl said as he and Sera walked back into the camp to give Thomas a moment.

Thomas opened the letter.

> *Dad,*
>
> *I won't bother telling you not to be upset or worry— of course you'll be both. You have such a big job now: you're literally trying to save the world. I have to do my part, and you have to do yours. I love you, but you're completely blind when it comes to James and me. We're always going to be your children, but I'm no longer a child. I have to do this. You can no longer afford to be the caretaker of a few of us; it's much*

bigger than that now. If you won't see that, then we've already lost, and that means everyone loses.

Billy and I will get what the group needs. I'm not naive, and I know the chances that I'm taking, but we all take them now. It's part of this new life as we know it. I know that I may not come back from this. If I don't, more than likely, Billy won't either. If he does, though, know this was my doing, not his. If I don't, know I love you and my little brother more than anything in the world.

That's why I'm doing this, because I love you both so much.

Jimmy needs food and supplies, and you need someone else to take even just some of the weight off your shoulders. To do that is worth any risk and any sacrifice. We're helping you even if we have to force you to let us. I don't know if I'm more worried for you or proud.

We will contact you tomorrow before we drive outside of radio contact.

I need you to know something: Mom's death was not your failure. I never blamed you because it was your fault; I blamed you because I knew you were strong enough to take it and you love me so much that you'd let me do it.

You've always been my rock, but now I need you to be the world's rock. I've never seen you fail.

I love you, Daddy.

Jessie

And a child shall lead us. Thomas felt Jessica's words. She had grown indeed, right under his nose. There was much to do still. He folded the letter, put it in his pocket, and went back to the cave. He still had no idea how he was going to get this done, but there was now a renewed spirit—it was going to happen!

CHAPTER 9

It was too cold to sleep outside, and Jessica and Billy knew they couldn't afford to build a fire in this foreign area. They had to take shifts sleeping, covered with blankets in the truck. They couldn't risk the sound of the truck's engine attracting any nearby infected, so the truck's heater was not an option either. Jessica lay under about four blankets in the front passenger seat of the truck, while Billy was outside, on watch duty. There was such loneliness to him that he wore it like clothing. The temperature outside seemed like nothing compared to the cold emptiness he must be feeling. She couldn't lie there any longer; Jessica got out of the truck and sat next to Billy.

"What are you doing out here? You should try to get some sleep, Jess."

"I can't sleep, Billy. It's too damn cold. I'm wrapped in, like, fifty layers. All you're wearing is that jacket. How are you not a copsicle?" She laughed.

"Wow, I didn't know you still did that," he said.

"Did what?"

"Smiled," he said.

"Not much to smile about anymore. You know that better than most."

"Guess I do."

Billy returned to focusing on watch. Jessica stayed next to him and wrapped her blanket around them. She put her head on his shoulder and was asleep before she knew it.

Jessica woke to the warmth of the morning sun, lying in Billy's lap.

"Why didn't you wake me for my watch?"

"You were out. It's okay. You can drive us into town. I'll grab some shut-eye. Hurry up, and let's get the truck warmed up. Turn the heat on full, Jess."

"Oh, what happened? I thought you were a tough-guy supercop that didn't feel the cold."

"I am. I meant for you," Billy replied with a wink.

They loaded up and were back on the road. The ride and the heat put him to sleep almost instantly. Billy normally suffered night terrors, but his rest was easy this time. In this dream, he wasn't killing his wife or having to hear her beg for help as she slipped further and further from him. This time, they were having a picnic on the beach. Billy's subconscious briefly struggled, trying to decipher if this memory was real or not, but in the end, he just lay back and enjoyed the rest.

He woke and realized they had stopped, and Jessica was not in the truck. Momentary panic took him till he saw her outside on the radio, presumably talking to her father. Not a conversation he envied her having, to say the least.

Jessica walked back to the truck and got in, rubbing her hands in front of the vent, soaking up as much heat as fast as she could. "It's freezing out there."

Billy sat like a prisoner awaiting sentencing. "Well, what did he say? Just how dead are we?"

"I told him you kidnapped me and this was all your idea," she said with a smile.

"Jess, come on…"

"He doesn't like it, but he's accepted it. He went over some quick tactics and told us to be careful. It'll be okay, Billy."

"What did he say about me?" said Billy, barely able to look up as he asked.

"Don't worry about that now, Billy. You two have been butting heads for months now. We'll get the job done, then I'll lock you both in a room till you work things out. For now, we've all got bigger things to fix besides you and dad's bromance."

"Well, he is an attractive man. He'd be difficult to get over."

They laughed and headed toward town. Jessica plugged her cell phone in the lighter socket to charge it. Billy looked at her with a small smile. "Why do you insist on keeping that thing charged? You can't make a call on it anymore."

"It still has its uses. The apps still work, including the compass app, which comes in handy. Besides, it reminds me of better times and that I'm still a teenager."

Billy nodded in agreement. They would be in town in about an hour. He knew they would need shelter; it would be too cold to sleep outside again.

* * * * *

Thomas was studying plans, trying to shape something that could take the tower down. Not only was nothing he could come up with feasible, but they also all ended with 100 percent group fatality.

Sera came into the room with a panicked look on her face.

"We have a very serious problem, Sheriff. Caleb has weaponized our Zperion Spore. I believe we are lost."

Thomas didn't understand what exactly she was talking about, but he understood there was a problem. He let Sera collect herself then asked her to explain.

"The Zperion Spore is a seed. We inject them with a special growth serum and plant them in the soil. They can grow up to seven hundred feet and weigh as much as fifty tons. We use them primarily for demolition as well as construction. The Zperion Spore is a semis-entient life-form, so we can use our wavelength to control it. Caleb has mutated the Spore, giving it capabilities it never had or was ever intended to have."

"How long before it's active?" Thomas asked.

"The Spore reaches maturity in days. Caleb has planted it already, and you cannot stop it, Sheriff. I'm sorry."

"We're not done. We just have to figure this out," Thomas said. "I need to think. I'm going for a walk," he added as he went outside.

God, Thomas thought, *if you were going to throw me a bone, sooner would be better than later.*

* * * * *

Ray, Michael, and Henry sat with Claire, finishing their morning devotional, as Paul walked in.

"Henry, I don't understand how you can sit there every day with the God squad. After everything that's happened, either He doesn't exist or He's left the building for good," Paul said.

"You know, I never really was into the whole religion thing, but after seeing what I've seen, well, let's just say He's got my attention. You know, Paul, maybe you should talk to Ray. This is some real fire-and-brimstone-type stuff going on."

"Yeah, maybe," Paul said.

Thomas came in. "Paul, grab your rifle. We got something."

"Well," Paul said, "duty calls."

Wayne, Thomas, Henry, Paul, and Sera sat inside at the table Thomas had put together, the plans for the compound laid out in the center. Thomas brought the group up to speed on the information Sera had provided.

"Sera said the Spore is as big as a seventy-story building, so it won't be easy to miss. We need hard intel on this, so we're going to use the trucks to charge up the camcorder. We'll use it to collect information, then we'll go from there. Paul and I will track into the woods and get as close as we can. Sera places about two hundred Spewers in the area, so Wayne and Henry will be our secondary extraction. You two stay clear unless we contact you."

Sera got up and began spreading markers on the map. "This route will place you close enough to gather the information that you'll need. It should also be the path of least resistance. I will accompany the sheriff. I may not be able to control Caleb's infected, but I sense his wavelength, so I'll know if they are close by. Like I said before, I can cause small amounts of interference that may afford you a window to escape should it become necessary."

Thomas got up. "Okay, people, ready to move in sixty."

Paul walked out with Thomas. "Guess we see just how trustworthy she is now. We're marching right into the mouth of the beast with her as our guide," Paul said.

"She could have brought Caleb and a hundred Spewers here while we slept anytime she wanted, Paul. She's good with me."

* * * * *

Billy and Jessica parked half a mile outside of town in the woods. Salem was about three times bigger than Ghostwood, but with a population of twenty-four thousand, it was still very much small-town USA. With it surrounded on both sides by mountainous terrain, the wilderness all but swallowed up the town. The walk into town would be laboring but manageable. They grabbed their bags and hiked the rest of the way. Maintaining covertness, they kept in the tree line as they circled the area to get a better layout.

"We need to split up so I can hunt, Billy. I brought a camouflage net Kenny and I made."

Jessica pulled out a mesh net stitched up with leaves and sticks and interlined with a thermoliner to give her some protection from the elements.

"Whoa, Jess, what's that smell?"

"Deer urine. We soaked this in it for three days. You get used to it." She laughed.

"Geez, who are you? Okay, Jess, meet back here in two hours no matter what."

Billy waited and watched Jessica melt into the forest. She had become so much so fast, he thought as he made his way into the town center. There were a lot of stores, but they were severely depleted; this town had already been run through. Spending most of the day going through buildings that he could get in and out of without venturing into dark areas and coming up empty, he was quickly becoming demoralized. He was about ready to start heading to the rendezvous point when he saw a promising haul. The propane cage was still locked—that was a good sign. Taking out some tools, he went to work on the lock.

After she had spent a good forty-five minutes under her camo tarp, a nice eight-point buck passed in Jessica's sights. Waiting until he finished his survey of his surroundings, she prepared to take her shot. Jessica had set up by a stream, and her gamble had paid off. The buck began to drink from the stream and was soon joined by three more deer. Jessica rose slowly from the ground, just high enough to position her bow. She held the bow sideways so she wouldn't reveal herself. She took aim at the buck—he wasn't just the biggest, but he was also the farthest from the group. With any luck, she could bag two of them. The bow was silent, but if the buck caused too much commotion when hit, the others would run off.

Jessica aimed for his heart; it should be quick and quiet. She released the arrow, and it flew, tearing into its target with deadly accuracy. With an almost-single motion, Jessica flipped the tarp back, grabbed another arrow, and rearming the bow, pulled and released just as the deer realized the danger they were in. Another arrow flew, hitting the second deer, just missing the heart, but still enough to drop it. As the final deer ran into the woods, Jessica walked past the already-dead buck to the deer that was still alive but barely moving.

"Sorry, I really meant to make this painless," she said as she drew her hunting knife from its sheath.

She bent low, putting her knee on its body, lifting its head and slitting its throat. Two in less than an hour—this area seemed very flush with wildlife still. There was still an hour before she needed to meet with Billy, so she began to gut and clean her prey.

Billy got the locks open; the locker had full tanks of propane in it. There was still a good six hours of daylight left, and with any luck, Jessica would have hunted down some food for the camp, and they could find somewhere to hold down for the night.

Billy walked back to the truck to meet Jessica. He saw her waiting with blood-smeared clothing, which meant she, in fact, had found food.

"What did you get, Jess?"

"Two big ones about a quarter mile that way."

"I found a locker full of propane tanks. We'll take the truck and pick up the deer then circle around and get the tanks."

"Sounds good."

Gathering her stuff, Jessica became fully alert as she heard the snap of twigs breaking under the weight of someone's foot. Billy was walking ahead. Taking a breath to warn him, she realized it was too late. Jessica pulled her camo tarp up and dropped to the ground under it. Turning around just in time to see three men come out of the tree line, Billy raised his weapon as they leveled their weapons at him.

"There are three of us, man, give it up!" one of the men yelled.

Billy lowered his weapon, in part because he was outgunned, but also because he realized Jessica was under the camouflage. She was all but invisible and safe, and that was all that mattered. Billy surrendered his weapon.

"Who else you out here with?" one of the men asked.

That was very good; that meant they had no idea about Jessica. "There are hundreds of us, so maybe you just give me my weapon back and let me be on my way."

"Funny guy, huh? He's alone. Let's get him back to camp, see if he's still funny after he meets the boss."

* * * * *

Thomas was readying his gear when his radio came to life. It was static and inaudible. Thomas grabbed the radio.

"Jessie, is that you? Come in. Over. Jessie, Jessie!"

It was no use; the signal was lost. Whoever it was was out of range, and without a repeater, he couldn't get a stronger signal.

Thomas, Sera, and Paul loaded up a truck. Wayne and Henry took another.

* * * * *

Kenny and Mark monitored the radio and coordinated operations as best as they could from base. The drive took about three and a half hours, and there was little to no talk. Thomas, as hard as he tried, couldn't stop thinking and worrying about Jessica. Thomas loved Billy, but he knew if anything happened to Jessie, there would be no forgiveness.

Arriving at the city limits, they parked the trucks. The rest of the trip would be on foot. They walked to the edge of town. Washington, once a symbol of freedom and inspiration, had become an empty, darkened image of its former self. The proud high-rises and buildings that housed people from the poor to the presidents now held only death and its agents. Vegetation overgrowth had begun to take a lot of the city. There was considerable damage from the futile law enforcement and military attacks on the infected. All they'd managed to do was destroy parts of the city with what looked like rocket, tank, and small-arms fire.

Thomas could see the Spore from where they were, but not good enough to get clear footage or see its capabilities. Paul separated from Thomas and Sera when he found a high building to set up an over-watch. Seeking high ground, he climbed the fire escape outside the building to the roof. Reaching his destination, he set up his rifle and followed Thomas and Sera through his scope.

The city was empty, a complete ghost town. Thomas wondered how Devon and his crew had fared through the winter or if they were even still alive. It was getting late, and Thomas knew they would be running out of sunlight before long. If they could get the footage and make it back into the woods or maybe hide out in an empty building, they could make it till sunrise.

As they moved closer, the Spore became clearer and more terrifying.

"How much farther till we get a clear vantage point?" Thomas asked.

"Not too much. Up ahead, about a mile, there's a building we can set up in. There should be no infected in it. Caleb summoned most of the infected in the immediate area to protect the compound. The rest just wander and patrol the street after sundown, looking for human hosts."

As they reached the building, Sera grabbed Thomas by the arm, gesturing for him to wait. She closed her eyes for a moment then opened them, and they moved on.

"So you were checking the building for Spewers?" Thomas asked.

"No. I can't sense them, but there are no wavelengths transmitting in this building, so there are no infected in here, at least no infected controlled by Caleb. These Ragers, as you call them, have no connection to Caleb, so there will be no wavelengths to sense."

"Well, that's great, Sera. So we just have to worry about the crazed rippers that may be walking around in here?"

"Yes, Sheriff, just them."

"If we do run into one of those things, do you think you would be able to handle it, Sera?"

"Like I told you, Sheriff, I am not a warrior. I really don't have a proper gauge on just how powerful they are, but from what I've seen… no, Sheriff, I don't believe I could incapacitate it alone."

"What about weapons, Sera? You don't have any kind of advanced weaponry?"

"This was an exploration mission. We have basic defensive capabilities, but nothing more than what you already have available here on your planet. This is why Caleb had to design and mutate from what we had on board. We never set out to conquer anyone."

"Seems you're well on your way to doing just that, anyway. Maybe you should take a page out of your colleague's playbook. Get together something from that ship of yours that will give us a leg up here."

Sera didn't understand the terminology Thomas used, but the context was clear enough.

They found a window on the second floor facing the compound. Setting up the recorder on a tripod, Thomas pulled the window open and began recording. The compound consisted of a city block protected by fifteen-foot-high concrete walls. The tower was being constructed by the Spore. The Spore was a giant plantlike creature and so much bigger than they'd thought. Its massive form dwarfed the surrounding buildings by comparison. The thousands of vine extensions that it used as arms were miles long and almost ten feet thick. The Spore worked with robotic efficiency.

"What are the offensive abilities of this thing, Sera?"

"That is hard to say, Sheriff. I am not sure what exactly Caleb did to the Spore. I do know that its natural passive state has been modified to an aggressive one. For example, if the Spore discovered any sentient life force during the demolition, it would cease all activity immediately. Now, the Spore not only continues operations despite the presence of human life, it will also act if threatened. The

Spore is designed to withdraw into a seedling if threatened, but not attack. Caleb has changed its instincts and patterns of behavior."

Thomas sat in awe of this breathtaking, deadly menace he would have to face while Sera became suddenly alert. "Sheriff, you have to hide now. There is danger."

* * * * *

Jessica followed Billy and his captors, using the camo tarp as cover, close enough to overhear them talking. Billy walked in between them blindfolded, with his hands tied behind him. Billy could tell these were mountain men. Two of them most likely related. The small one walked over to Billy.

"Boss goin' to have some questions for you, boy. Best you in a talkin' mood by time we get there. You don't wanna go making him mad. Boss ain't like the rest of us. He's real special like."

"Stop your jawboning, Clint. Simon will say what he got to say when we get back. He don't need no introductions," the other man said.

"That's my big brother, Roy. Don't pay him no mind," Clint said.

When they came to the camp, Jessica stopped following the group; she didn't want to trip any hidden traps or stumble across any patrols that might be out. Jessica went wide and flanked them. It would be dark soon, and Jessica knew better than to move around too much at night. She would have to brave another cold night. She took up a position that gave her the best view of the camp. She could still see Billy. Jessica took out a pen and whatever paper she could find and took notes of what she saw. She wrote down the number of armed people she saw, weapon types she recognized, and she sketched the basic layout of the camp.

Billy was led into a cave in the side of the hill. It looked like they had the same idea as her group: stick to the woods. Jessica counted twenty-two armed men so far. There were little to no guards or protection until the entrance to the opening in the hill. How far down did it go? Was it a cave or a mine shaft? She couldn't know these answers. The sun was setting, and the cold was mind-numbing. She wasn't prepared for this type of cold. She hadn't had time to grab extra gear before these people had led Billy away. But she would never have found them if she hadn't followed them back here. She was truly suffering. She had to keep rubbing and shifting to keep the blood flowing.

Hypothermia was her biggest worry. She decided that she couldn't maintain this and would take her chances making her way back to the truck. She would grab the deer meat also; the camp still needed the food and propane. Jessica scanned the area for Spewers or, worse, Ragers. She had seen the mayhem that was the Ragers, and she wanted no part of them; they terrified her to her core.

Jessica rose up and began moving as quickly and quietly as she could back the way she'd come. *I'll bring help, Billy. Please be okay,* she silently pleaded as she made her way through the woods.

* * * * *

They took Billy's blindfold off. They had a fire going, and there were men and women everywhere. Billy was taken into a tent. They tied Billy to a wooden stake they had driven into the ground.

"Is this really necessary? Look, my name's Billy, and I'm not a threat to anyone, Clint," Billy said, trying to humanize himself to his captor.

"Yeah, sorry, Billy, it's the rules. Now you behave and answer the boss's questions, and you'll be okay."

"Yeah," Roy said. "Act right, and maybe you won't end up in a cooking pot… Billy."

A very unassuming man came into the tent. Clean-cut, with glasses and a Richie Cunningham haircut. He reminded Billy of his tax accountant. He kneeled down next to his captive.

"Where did you come from? And how did you get here?" he asked, getting right down to business.

Billy knew that if they were asking how he got here, they hadn't found the truck, which meant Jessica could still escape. But he had to buy her some time.

"I walked in from the woods, but listen, this isn't necessary. If you give me a chance, you'll see I can be a valuable addition to your community," Billy said.

"You walked in from where?" he asked.

"I'm not really sure. I've been on my own and wandering for a while now. How is it you're able to have fires in the open? Aren't you worried the Spewers will see you?" Billy asked, half-trying to stall and half-curious.

His question was met with a back fist from his interrogator.

"You're stalling, Billy. I think it's because you're covering for someone else that's with you. This is bad, Billy boy. I gotta go to the boss with a bad report, and he won't be happy. Roy, get two men. Check around and see if he was alone."

Roy got up and began to walk toward the exit but then paused. "Cole, it's gonna be dark in less than an hour. If we get too far from the camp, what do we do about them?" he asked nervously.

Cole gave him a cold glare. "You wanna take your chances with them or Simon?"

Roy didn't answer; he just lowered his head like a whipped pup and walked outside the tent.

Billy felt a desperate rush come over him. "You're sending your men to their deaths for nothing. I'm telling you, there's nobody else out there."

"You best worry more about yourself, boy. Simon is coming, and when he gets here, you'll understand why. Can't say you didn't have your chance."

Cole left the room. Billy had a feeling Cole was right, but whatever happened, he would never give up the group or Jessica. He'd die first, a thousand times, slow and painful.

* * * * *

Thomas found an old desk, pushed it over, and hid behind it. "Come on, Sera, there's room for both of us."

"Don't worry about me, Sheriff. They won't touch me. It's only humans they're after."

Thomas took cover and drew his Ka-Bar knife from its sheath. Three infected entered the room where they hid. Sera's presence didn't stimulate them; they noticed her but just continued to wander without incident. One of the infected wandered out of the room, while the others stood in place. Thomas watched on as the two remaining infected stood looking out into nothing, their faces blank and void of expression.

I'd rather be dead than one of these blank slates, he thought.

Thomas knew he couldn't stay there long; the sun would be down soon. He didn't want to be boxed in, with no sunlight to retreat to. Sera looked at Thomas, and he signaled that they had to move. Sera was strong, but Thomas wasn't sure how effective she would be if this situation went bad. After all, like she'd said, she was no warrior.

Thomas couldn't wait any longer; the sun would be setting soon.

Sera, picking up on Thomas's urgency, walked in front of the infected, who turned and faced her, giving their backs to Thomas. Thomas's plan was to get to the window and scale down to the ground. They were only on the second floor, but Thomas couldn't afford a broken leg from crashing through the window and jumping down. One of the infected broke his gaze on Sera and wandered through the room, coming to a stop and blocking Thomas's path to the window. Thomas would have to take it out. He moved with utter silence toward the infected, praying the other one didn't turn around. He got behind the infected and thrust his blade into its brain stem. He caught its body and gently lowered it to the ground.

He'd walked to the open window and begun climbing out when the other infected turned and saw him. The infected immediately switched on and made a lightning-fast line toward Thomas. It was stopped short as Sera reached out, grabbing it under its chin and the back of its head, and with a quick motion, she snapped its neck. The body fell hard, crashing into a nearby cabinet and knocking it over.

"Come on, Sera, we have to move now!"

As Sera made her way toward the window, two more infected rushed into the room. Sera grabbed one of them and threw it against the wall. The other grabbed her from behind and threw her to the floor. Thomas was clear and could climb down to the ground; there was still enough sunlight to cover his escape. A third infected came crashing into the room. They stood over Sera, smashing blows down on her. Thomas climbed back into the room, and before they noticed him, he'd brought his blade down into the skull of one of the infected. The other turned and caught him with a vicious blow that sent him sailing over a desk. He was back to his feet in time to see the offspring come falling out of the infected's mouth. The other infected started walking over to assist, but Sera grabbed its leg, regaining its attention and its aggression as it again began pummeling her again.

Thomas moved toward the window. Standing in front of it, he waited, still wary of the offspring that was no doubt making its way after him. The infected recovered from spewing up the offspring and readied to attack Thomas again. Thomas had his hand on his gun but knew firing a shot would bring every infected in the area to him, and he had no way of knowing how many were in the building. With the infected charging him, Thomas had one shot at this. He grabbed the infected by the shoulders and side-stepped, rolled onto his back, pushed his knee into the infected's chest, and shoved it over him. Its own momentum sent it flying through the window into the deadly sunlight. Thomas spotted movement on the floor as the offspring crawled toward his hand to inflict its lethal bite. He reached over with his Ka-Bar, impaling it. Thomas rose to his feet, exhausted, his ribs feeling broken again.

The infected stood over Sera's unconscious body. It turned to face Thomas. There was no more strength for Thomas to call upon. As he drew his gun, the infected lunged forward, knocking the pistol from his hand. It grabbed Thomas's wrist with a vise-like grip, and he cried out in pain. The infected opened its mouth as the offspring came crawling out.

Thomas's radio chirped as the sound of Paul's voice came through. "Down!"

Thomas dropped to the floor as Paul's bullet tore through the offspring as it attempted to exit the infected's mouth. The round blew the back of the infected's head away, and its body flew backward onto the ground. Two more infected rushed into the room and were likewise met by two of Paul's long-range greetings. Thomas ran over, picked up Sera, and made his way out the window. They hit the ground, and Thomas laid Sera down to quickly evaluate her injuries.

As Sera regained consciousness, her cuts and bruises closed up and healed right before Thomas's eyes. She was on her feet and ready to move.

"Amazing," Thomas said.

"We must go, Sheriff."

Thomas got up, running toward the truck as he grabbed his radio. He instructed Paul to meet Wayne and Henry and go back to camp. There was no time for Paul to come to them; the sun was setting.

"This is not the way to your vehicle, Sheriff."

"I know. We're not going to make it to the truck. I think my ribs are broken, and I don't heal like you. We have to try to make it to a secure area, and I think I might know just the place," Thomas said. "What happened back there, Sera? I thought you said the building was clear."

"It was, Sheriff. When we entered the building, there were no infected in it. They must have entered after we were already inside."

"That's not possible, Sera. Ten seconds in the sunlight, and they turn to soup."

"Tunnels, Sheriff. Caleb must have integrated tunnels under the city so the infected could travel during the day. With the Spore, that would be a very simple task."

"This guy doesn't miss a trick," Thomas said.

The sun set as they tried to make their way into the nearby woods. Thomas knew they had no real cover; they would have to travel around the city on foot to their destination and hope they could find sanctuary with Devon and his people, if they were still there and still alive. It would take a couple of hours, then they would know for sure.

* * * * *

Billy sat tied as he awaited his fate. Simon entered the room. Billy saw him, but he wasn't sure what he was looking at. He was a beast of a man at six feet six inches, an easy 280 pounds, with little body fat. His left arm was missing from the forearm down and replaced with a metal covering where the arm had been amputated. He had one very bloodshot blue eye and one eye that was whited out, just like the infected. His skin was pale and perspired. He wore no shirt and was seemingly unaffected by the low-teen temperatures. For all intents and purposes, he was one of the infected. Until he spoke.

"I want three things from you, and I'll only ask once. Where did you come from, who was with you, and what do you have to offer in exchange for your life?"

Billy leaned forward. "I can be of great use to you and your group. I was with another group, but we had a falling-out a few months or so back. We split company, and I have no idea where they settled after that. I came in from Alexandria after the world went crazy. That's the truth—I got no reason to lie, and I got no one to protect."

Simon paused. He studied Billy, trying to measure his truth from his lies. "What did your group fight about to make you leave?"

Billy paused. Telling Simon the truth about the infection was a card he had to hold until he had nothing left to play. "They were weak. I suggested trimming a little fat for the sake of the group. I knew we couldn't save everyone, but our fearless leader couldn't make the tough, necessary decisions. I knew it would only be a matter of time until their luck ran out, and I didn't want to get caught up in what I'm sure by now has become their demise. I packed a few essentials and made my way on my own. Lucky for me, I ran into your guys." Billy hoped he had bought Jessica enough time to escape.

"I tell you what, Billy, call me a cynic, but I don't believe you. You met Cole, haven't you? He's my little brother. He saved my life. See, I got bit by one of them little ones, right on my hand. He didn't hesitate. He squashed that ugly little bastard and cut my arm off right here under the elbow. I guess whatever makes them things didn't get enough in me, so I'm only half-dead. Not all bad, though," Simon said as he reached up with his half-arm, bringing it down and smashing a concrete cylinder block like it was made of cardboard. "I got their strength, plus you can't kill me, not even with sunlight. Any cuts close right up before the blood hits the ground. Now, like I was saying. Cole, to be honest, he's been a mean cuss all his life about. This whole end-of-times thing ain't changed him. Matter a fact, I think he likes it. He gets to be himself. You and he gonna have a conversation. If you're lying, he will find out, then he'll kill ya. Good luck, though, Billy. I hope you make it. I kinda like ya."

Simon got up and walked out of the room as Cole came in with two men.

"Take him to the cold room, strip him down, and tie him to the chair."

They cut Billy from the pole and led him away. Billy knew he couldn't talk them down. He could see the hint of excitement on Cole's normally cold, expressionless face. This was going to happen because Cole wanted it to, probably needed it to. He was a sociopath; he would hurt Billy regardless of what Billy told him.

But Billy would keep Thomas and the others safe, even at the cost of his life. He kept telling himself that. He only prayed he would have the strength.

They took him into the makeshift interrogation room. There were bloodstains across the floor and a bloodstained metal chair bolted to the ground in the middle of the floor. A wave of momentary panic came over Billy, and he tried to pull away from his captors. They pulled him inside the room and slammed the door.

CHAPTER 10

Jessica gathered her things and swept her tracks like Kenny and Mark had taught her. She had to move fast to try to get ahead of the infected. As she moved through the tree line, she was careful not to catch the attention of the many infected that were now roaming town. She was losing much of the feeling throughout her hands and feet. *Just gotta keep moving,* she told herself.

Jessica saw the trail that led back to the truck. Her heart sank— the Spewers blocked the trail, so she would have to take cover and wait. She pulled the camo tarp up over her and lay down on the ground. She just had to hope they wandered away from the trail before she froze to death.

* * * * *

Roy, Clint, and Davis searched the camp perimeter. Davis was an experienced tracker; if there was a trail, he'd find it.

"Over here," Davis announced. "I got a trail. There was some-one here recently. They did a good job of trying to cover their tracks, but I got 'em, though. This way."

Roy and Clint followed Davis as they began their pursuit of Jessica. Clint and Roy walked a bit behind Davis, partly to give him room to work and partly because he just creeped them out.

"Roy, why we gotta go chasing some ghost, risking our necks for what might not be nothing?"

"'Cause, little brother, when Simon tells you to do something, you do it if you wanna keep breathing."

"Simon Says… always hated that game," Clint said.

161

"Yeah, well, I sure hate it now," Roy replied.

They walked down the trail, drawing closer to an unsuspecting Jessica.

* * * * *

Billy sat handcuffed to the metal chair, wearing nothing but his underwear and a T-shirt. He was freezing.

Cole came into the room. He looked different, happy, like a child that had just gotten the toy he'd always wanted. "Listen," Billy said, "I keep tellin' everyone this isn't necessary. I'm not a threat. I got nothing to offer you expect maybe an extra hand to help out around here."

Cole continued putting together his equipment as he glanced over at Billy. "We'll soon see." Cole walked over to Billy and put his hand on his shoulder. "Billy, I want to explain something to you. I'm not sure if you know this, but there are five basic principles of inter-rogation. Deprivation, blunt, hot, cold, and my favorite, sharp. Now, we will be fair. Right now, you're experiencing the simple ones. A little cold, hunger, thirst, some fatigue. That's deprivation. You'll get used to that though. It's not very effective. Then you'll graduate to blunt, another of the more enjoyable techniques. The key to blunt is control. You can't really tell me what I need if I beat you into oblivion now, can ya? Like I said, we will be fair. Cold and hot in this environ-ment are pretty much irrelevant, so if we get to that point, we'll jump right ahead to sharp. Any questions? No? Then let's begin, shall we?"

* * * * *

Thomas felt his ribs burning; breathing was becoming a chore. Sera was holding him up, but Thomas needed a break.

"Stop, Sera, I have to sit for a minute."

"Is that wise, Sheriff? If the infected discover us, I will not be able to protect you. They will overwhelm us this time."

"No, Sera, it's not wise, but necessary." Thomas took a drink out of his canteen and sat to catch his breath. "We're close to my friend Devon's hideaway, maybe a couple of hours out now. We need to get you something to hide your appearance. We don't need them seeing you're not exactly from around here. We'll get a wig and some sunglasses."

"Yes, I agree. That will not be a problem. I can walk to the town center and retrieve the items while you rest here for a while. The infected will not attack me as long as I do not provoke them. Stay here, Sheriff, I'll return soon."

Thomas sat against a tree and watched Sera walk out of the tree line into town. He was grateful for the break. He knew he needed medical attention and could taste blood building in his mouth as he spat out a thick, dark glob. Between that and his weakened state, he knew he had internal bleeding. He wouldn't last alone much longer.

* * * * *

Wayne, Paul, and Henry drove down the road back to camp. It was too dark, and they knew they had to get off the road before they attracted the infected's attention with the truck engine and lights. They had waited for Thomas despite his explicit instructions to the contrary, so they were way behind schedule and far away from the point they had set up to spend the night. They had no choice but to pull off the road into an unsecured and unprepared area.

"There, over there," Wayne said, pointing to a clearing where an old abandoned warehouse still stood.

Turning off the headlights, Henry parked the truck and they got out to unload their packs and weapons. They made their way to the edge of the woods to get a better vantage point.

"You think it's empty? They're normally out wandering about this time, right?" Paul asked.

"We're still about fifty miles from the nearest town, so we should be good," Henry replied.

Wayne got up and grabbed his weapon. "You guys stay put. I'll go check it out. Watch for my signal."

Paul and Henry both got up together. "We won't need a signal, Wayne, 'cause we'll be standing right beside you," Paul said.

"Yeah, Wayne, he's right. You know better. We'll do this together."

There was no arguing, plus the warehouse was pretty big. Wayne knew he'd need the help to clear it.

They made their way to the door. There wasn't any sign of infected, so they went inside. The building was big but long abandoned. It was a pretty open building, with some offices with broken glass windows. Good thing was, it was clear to see the building was empty. Downside was, any fire might easily be seen from the outside. It was freezing cold, and they would need a fire to survive the night.

"We won't live through the night without a fire," Paul said out loud what they all were thinking.

"We'll have to contain it, find a space we can use that isn't exposed," Wayne said.

"Tell me again why we can't just stay in the truck with the heat on?" Paul asked.

"You know why, Paul. The smallest sound from the engine or the heat from it will bring any Spewers or those damn Ragers down on us," Henry said.

"At least I'd die warm," Paul muttered.

Wayne found a spot in one office. It was walled up, and there was a large hole in the ceiling, but it was the best they had. They gathered broken wood and trash from around the building and started a fire.

"Easy, Paul. Keep it small, just enough to keep us from getting hypothermia," Henry warned. "I'll take first watch, Wayne. You and Paul get some rest. Not to be funny, but sharing a sleeping bag might make the difference between seeing sun in the morning and freezing to death tonight."

"I'd rather freeze," Paul said.

"Stop your crying, Paul, and get your sexy self in here," Wayne said, pulling the sleeping bag cover back.

"If my mom could only see me now," Paul said, climbing into the bag with Wayne.

"I'll try not to spoon, Paul."

Henry couldn't hold in his laughter anymore. It was contagious, and they shared a short laugh. It was nice to feel something other than fear and despair again, even if for a moment.

* * * * *

Jessica's body temperature was dangerously low. She had stopped shivering, which was a sign of worsening hypothermia. There were no other options, and she had to move now. She knew that her bow was all but useless—she could barely grip it. She slid her Glock out of its drop holster. The noise would bring them down on her. That was better than lying there freezing to death, and at least she would take some of them with her.

Her thoughts were of her dad and brother. *I'm so sorry, Dad. He's going to take this hard. At least I'll be with my mom again,* she thought as a tear streamed down her cheek.

Taking a deep breath, she gathered herself to her feet. Just as she was about to stand up, she noticed three men coming down the trail she had taken. She stayed down; they wouldn't notice her under the camo tarp, not right away, anyway. They must have tracked her from the camp. There might be a chance to use this, but it was risky. Jessica knew they were on her trail, and soon enough, they would discover her. Slowly moving up the trail, she put a little distance between them. When she was far enough ahead of them she stopped. She had to at least give them a chance. She had no misimpression; if she did this, it'd be the same as putting a gun to their heads and killing them herself.

* * * * *

Davis led Roy and Clint down a path, following Jessica's trail. The cold was blistering, and the infected were so close they could hear them groaning. They came over past a tree, and there they saw the sign impaled to the tree with a hunter's knife. It was written crudely and hurriedly on a piece of cardboard, but the meaning was clear.

TURN AROUND NOW AND LIVE. KEEP COMING,
AND I'LL END ALL THREE OF YOU!

"What the hell? How do they know we're following them?" Clint whispered.

"It ain't no they, it's one person. They're close by, and we're gonna finish this. Move out now!" Davis quietly shot back. They walked down the trail, careful as they moved forward.

"This is insane. We don't even know what we're looking for," Roy protested.

"Tell you what? You and your little brother go ahead and run back to camp. I'm sure Simon won't have any problem with you not finishing what he sent us to do. More than likely, he'll turn you over to Cole, and you know how he likes to play."

Roy knew that he didn't like his and Clint's chances out here, but Cole... there were some things worse than death and the infected.

They moved on.

* * * * *

Jessica was set. She saw the men continue to pursue her, though she'd prayed they'd turn back. They'd made their choice; may God have mercy on their souls, and may God forgive her.

* * * * *

Cole dumped a bucket of cold water on Billy, shocking him back to consciousness. "Come on, Billy, we're just getting started. You have to stay with me." Cole had beaten Billy for the last twenty minutes without even asking any questions. Simon was serving him up to Cole to satisfy Cole's psychopathic needs. Billy knew this. It didn't matter what he said or didn't say; Cole was going to play this out.

"Okay, Billy, I need you to give me something. Give me something to make all this ugliness just... go away."

Billy knew things were just going to get worse. "Cole," he started, "can I call ya Cole?"

Cole nodded slightly.

"Okay, then, Cole, how about we cut the crap? We both know you're a pathetic mama's boy with psychopathic tendencies. Your brother keeps you around to do his dirty work and because you have, or rather had, the same blood coursing through your veins. Who knows what that freak of a brother of yours has in that abomination he calls a body now since you lopped his arm off? So just get on with whatever you got planned in that sick, twisted head of yours."

"Okay, Billy, so be it."

Billy hoped Cole was now mad enough to either make a mistake he could exploit or, at the very least, make his death quick.

* * * * *

Henry sat on watch as Wayne and Paul slept. It was quiet, really quiet. Henry decided to walk the area and stretch his legs. The moon was high, and the night sky clear. The cold was still sharp, but take away the circumstances of this invasion, and it would be a beautiful winter's night. Henry had felt enough of the cold cutting through him. He turned to head back to the fire when he saw it, and it saw him! Outside in the street, the Rager looked in through the window, into Henry's eyes, and maybe into his soul.

Neither it nor Henry moved.

Henry stayed still in some hope that maybe it hadn't comprehended the fact he was there. But the Rager's screech was almost enough to make a heart stop in terror alone. The staring contest over, the Rager charged hard toward the building.

"Rager! Wayne, Paul, get to the truck now!" Henry yelled as he himself ran in the opposite direction from the truck.

Henry had to lead it away from the truck if they were to have any chance at all. Henry was a big man, built for power, not for speed. The Rager burst hard through the door. It was fast, Henry knew, too fast. He wouldn't gain any more distance. He raised his rifle and fired. His shots hit the Rager, knocking it back, but not down. Henry kept his aim on the Rager's center mass—it was the widest part of the body, and that was the only thing buying him the time Wayne and Paul needed to get away. Henry couldn't risk the headshot; one miss, and the Rager would be on him, finishing him and then his friends.

Wayne and Paul were at the door leading outside, and they could see Henry losing ground fast.

Wayne grabbed Paul's shoulder. "Don't miss. I'll get the truck!"

Paul was already in motion and set the Rager square in his sights. The Rager was right on top of Henry as Henry fired his last round. The familiar sound of Paul's rifle cracked through the air around them. As usual, Paul's aim was impeccable. The round struck true, hitting the Rager perfectly in the back of the head. Only this time, his target didn't go down; instead, the Rager turned, facing Paul. Paul met its eyes, and the name Rager no longer seemed adequate. The heat and rage made Paul go so numb he no longer felt the cold. It was just about to charge Paul when Henry's giant hands reached out and grabbed the Rager by the head, throwing it to the ground.

"Run, you stupid bastard!" Henry called out.

The Rager was on its feet before Henry could finish the sentence. It grabbed Henry and lifted him into the air, slamming him against the wall and then to the ground. Henry reached up, grabbing the Rager by the head and slamming it into a brick wall. Henry rolled over on top of the Rager and picked up a nearby slab of broken concrete, using his powerful arms to bring it down on the Rager's head with tremendous force. Paul had realigned his sights but couldn't get a clear shot past Henry.

Wayne ran back into the room. "What happened, Paul? Did you miss?"

Paul didn't reply, his focus 100 percent on getting the shot and saving his friend. Recovering from the blows, the Rager reached up and grabbed Henry by the neck. With tremendous force, it threw Henry off and regained the top position. It began savagely striking and ripping into him as he lay there helpless. The Rager's screech was so horrifying Paul lost his concentration. Running madly toward the Rager, Wayne fired his weapon into its head until it finally dropped. Paul rushed down to them, and they pulled the dead Rager off Henry. Blood covered Henry, and he was badly beaten. There was so much damage that if they hadn't known it was him, they wouldn't have recognized him.

"Henry, Henry! We got you, bud, it's okay," Wayne said.

Henry reached up, and Wayne took his hand. Henry struggled to speak. "Wayne is… are you guys o-okay? I can't see."

"Yea bud, me and Paul are fine. You saved us, man. Everything is ok now. Take it easy. Don't try to talk, Henry. We're going to get you out of here and back to camp. Claire's gonna fix you up good as new," Wayne said.

Henry pulled his hand away from Wayne. "No, no, I'm good right here, that... that was a lot of... shootin'. Too much noise. They'll come now... get outta here now! Go, leave! I'm at... I'm at peace. It's okay. Paul, not... not your fault... hit 'em right in the head, son of a bitch jus' wouldn't fa-fall. So tired, jus' gonna rest now."

Looking up at the stars through the broken ceiling, he smiled, as if hearing an inside joke. Henry took in a deep breath, let it out, closed his eyes, and died.

"He's right, Paul, we gotta move now! Help me get him in the truck."

They'd begun picking Henry up when Wayne caught a glimpse of something coming out of the woods. "Spewers! We have to go, Paul. We can't take him—there's no time!"

"No, Wayne, I can't leave him here like this!"

"We stay, we die, and Henry died for nothing. You want to take his sacrifice away from him? Okay, then, we stay," Wayne said, reloading his weapon.

Paul wiped the tears from his face, picking up his rifle, and they ran for the truck. They got in and had begun to drive away when an infected jumped in the bed of the pickup and smashed the rear window. Wayne swerved hard to the left, sending the infected flying out of the cab and into a tree. They were everywhere. Wayne hit two more that jumped in front of the truck. The infected were fast. One of them slammed his body into the side of the truck so hard it knocked the truck into a fishtail. Wayne regained control but had to go off road to avoid a nearby tree. He switched the truck over to four-wheel drive, and they drove through the forest, careful to avoid trees, until they came out of the woods into a clearing that led back to the road.

They had eluded the infected for now, but there were still a couple more hours until dawn. They decided to risk driving at night.

They didn't speak. Paul held his head down, crying for his lost friend. Wayne gave him his space and silently mourned Henry. It would be a long ride home, even after the sun had blessed them with its presence.

* * * * *

Jessica lay against a tree, covered and hidden by her camo tarp. She held her bow strung and arrow ready to fly. Her timing had to be right. The men came from around a tree Jessica had mentally marked as the point of no return. They were coming for her. They'd made their choice.

She let the arrow fly, but the cold had numbed her hands and her aim was off. She'd meant to graze the man's leg, but instead, she'd buried the arrow into his hip. Clint fell to the ground as the arrow slammed into him, fighting every instinct to yell out, knowing what that would bring. Roy and Davis immediately dropped to the ground, taking cover. Roy began to see to his brother.

"I told you we should have gone back!" Roy whispered angrily to Davis.

"Just tend to your brother, Roy. I saw where that arrow came from, and I got him now."

Davis had spotted Jessica's position. His weapon was silenced with a suppressor, so he would have no trouble shooting his target and still maintaining stealth. Davis took aim. *Clever camo tarp,* he thought to himself. He held his breath and prepared to squeeze the trigger. The blaring sound of Jessica's air horn alarm went off. She had hidden her cell phone under a bush at the designated spot where she had chosen to disable one of the men, setting the timer for ten minutes; it might as well be a dinner bell.

"What the hell is that? Where is it coming from? Turn it off! Turn it off!" Davis exclaimed, panicking.

Roy found the source and silenced the phone, much too late.

The infected shot through the parking lot right at the three men, including the ones blocking Jessica's path. Davis was on his feet and running full speed back into the woods.

"Wait, help me with my brother!" Roy pleaded.

His words fell on deaf ears as Davis ran past the brothers without even a second look.

"Roy, you have to go. You gotta leave me, brother. It's all right. Set me up against the tree and go. I'll cover you as long as I can."

"No, little brother. We do this together."

Roy propped Clint up against the tree, and the two men waited for the onslaught. They didn't wait long, and the infected rushed on them like a wave. Roy and Clint fired defiantly into the infected, refusing to go quietly. The brothers were expert shots, but in the end, there were just too many, and the brothers fell.

Jessica made her way to the truck, wiping the tears from her face. She felt for the men, but if this was what it took to protect her people, then she would do it a hundred times over. She loaded the propane tanks then made her way to the fallen deer she'd killed and covered. It felt almost impossible loading the deer into the truck by herself, even using a rope hoist, but she'd done it. Jessica had done many things she would have believed impossible before, but that girl was gone now, and this one could and would do what needed to be done.

* * * * *

Sera returned to find Thomas sound asleep in the same spot. Reaching down, she woke him up. He opened his eyes and barely recognized her. Simply wearing a blond wig and a hat had made her indistinguishable between human and Usraian. She had even found some contact lenses to hide her alien eyes. With her looking almost completely human, Thomas understood how the aliens had come to live among them without detection for so long.

"Sheriff, we must go now."

Thomas looked at his watch; he'd been out for about forty-five minutes. It had been much needed. Rested, he was ready to move. They came to the address Devon had given him. It was in an old neighborhood. The houses sat close together. They were almost identical, and it seemed completely abandoned. Because there was no light, at first, Thomas saw nothing. He began to believe that maybe it was too late and Devon and his crew had either moved on or, worse, been discovered by the infected. Moving along the perimeter, Thomas spotted a guard standing close to a window in a nearby house.

Thomas pointed to the man. "Look there, Sera, that's an overwatch. He's our ticket in. You stay here. I'm not sure if that's one of Devon's men. I'm going to find out."

Thomas flanked around and behind the guard. Even with Thomas's injuries, the guard never stood a chance. Thomas came up behind the man and applied a rear naked choke. The guard was unconscious and disarmed before he heard the first sound of Thomas's approach. With the guard taken care of, Thomas signaled for Sera to come to his position.

The man came to to find his weapon gone, his hands bound, and his mouth gagged. Thomas squatted next to the man.

"I know this looks bad, but I just couldn't take any chances. I know you know what's out there, and I didn't want you mistaking me for one of them. One shot, and they would be here in moments. All that being said, I am not your enemy. Do you know Devon?"

The man just looked at Thomas, a look as hard as Thomas had ever seen.

"Listen to me, just nod if you know him. He's a friend of mine. I don't mean him or any of you any harm. I need his help. He gave me this note with this address and told me I could come here if I ever needed him," Thomas said, showing the man the note.

The man nodded. Thomas took the gag off, and the man spoke. "Man, I don't know you. You come in here choking me like you some crazy fool. Now you got my gat and I'm all tied up. Yeah, I know Devon, but that don't mean nuthin'. I ain't taking you nowhere, white boy."

Thomas saw he'd need more convincing.

"Look, what's your name? I'm Thomas. This is Sera. My friend and I here need to talk to Devon. If you contact him or Marcus, they'll verify what I'm telling you is true, please."

"You know Marcus too? Okay, give me my radio. If you being straight up, then cool. If not, well, then, I think you know what's up."

Thomas held the radio to the man's mouth and held down the transmission button.

"Hey, this is Ron. I got some crazy white boy here say he know Devon and Marcus. Got a note sayin' he get a pass around here. He got me tied up and my gun."

A voice came back over the radio. "Hold up, Ron."

After a few minutes, a familiar voice came over the radio.

"He look like a run-down small-time cop?" Marcus asked.

"Yeah, kinda," Ron said.

"Bring him down in the morning. No movement before the sun comes up," Marcus said.

Thomas took the radio. "Marcus, I'm hurt, I need medical attention. I'm not sure I'll be around come sunup."

"Hold up, man," Marcus said. After a few minutes, he came back. "We'll come to you. Tell us what you need. We can't risk bringing you here while them things are running around."

"I understand, Marcus."

Thomas briefed Marcus on what his injuries were and what he needed. He untied Ron and gave him his weapon back. Thomas then lay back, and before he knew it, he was unconscious again.

He woke in a room on a bed, the sun shining in through a window and his ribs wrapped and his wounds treated. Sera sat in a chair by his bed. "You're awake. That's good."

"How long was I out? Who fixed me up? And how did I get here?"

"Well," Devon said as he walked in the door, "we carried you here this morning, so you only been out a few hours. Your friend here patched you up with the supplies we brought her. She a doctor or something? 'Cause she did some work on you."

"No, I am not a doctor, but I have studied human anatomy in my spare time over the last two years. Luckily, your physiological makeup is quite basic, so 'patching him up' was relatively simple."

"She always talk like that, bro?" Devon asked.

"That's a long story, Devon. I need you and Marcus to sit with me. I have a lot to fill you in on."

* * * * *

Cole's scalpel cut into Billy's arm, cutting pieces out of Billy as if carving up a turkey. Billy hated himself for yelling out and giving this twisted coward his satisfaction. Billy had been beaten, but he wouldn't be beat. He was bloodied but refused to break. This was beginning to infuriate Cole.

"What is it you're trying to prove? Who are you protecting, boy?" Cole yelled, almost in a rage.

Billy was weak and tired, barely conscious, but he managed a small laugh.

"Something funny, Billy boy?"

"Who am I protecting? You really want to know? You'll meet 'em, and when they come for me—and they will come for me—I promise you I'll be the very last thing you see before you die screaming like a coward. Your brother said you can tell when people are lying... do you believe me?"

Cole felt a chill run through him. This was not the reaction he expected yet somehow found that he craved. In the past, he had always needed a scared, screaming, and broken man to give him the bliss he desired so desperately.

"Okay, Billy boy, fine. You're going to make me work for it? I'll just have to up my game. The end result will be even better than I've ever experienced before. I'm going to make you my greatest creation. You'll be the story scary men tell to scare scary men! First, I'll get you all fixed up, though. I'll get our camp medic to come fix you up. Then I'll have you fed and bathed. I want you fresh and strong before I take you apart. Enjoy your time, because while you're healing up, I'm going to retreat to my quiet place and come up with the most unique, graphic, and frightening things that I can get dark enough to perform. It's a primal, animalistic concept I'm gonna shoot for. It'll take some real soul-searching and hard work, but with your help, I will be able to bring these thoughts to full fruition. Oh, Billy, I've been waiting for you my whole life."

* * * * *

"You have got to be shittin' me, man!" Marcus exclaimed.

"Marcus, calm down. I know this is a lot to take in, but every-thing I've told you is true," Thomas said.

"You expect me to believe that there's aliens running around, smokin' foos? Hell naw! D, you goin for this man?"

Devon looked at Thomas. "This is a bit much, Thomas," he answered.

"This chick is supposed to be one of 'em, huh?" Marcus said in disbelief.

"Okay," Thomas said, "how about a little test? She's what, five foot five, right about a hundred and twenty pounds, right, Marcus? You're six feet tall, about two hundred and ten, am I right?"

"Two fifteen, all muscle, cop," Marcus said, full of pride.

"Okay, then. How about something simple: you arm-wrestle her. If you win, you're right and I'm full of it. You lose, then you sit down, shut up, and listen."

Devon, clearly intrigued, added a little fuel to the fire. "Marc, you lose to this little woman, it'll be worse than when Tiny whooped ya ass in the fifth grade. Callin' him Tiny wasn't no play words either—he was, like, four feet tall, Thomas," Devon said as the two men shared a small laugh.

"That nigga snuck me. Anyway we ain't talking elementary school games here. No offense lady but to get through this crap the cop here is shoveling, Imma have to break your arm off," Marcus said, sitting down at the table and putting his arm up with his hand open.

Sera was confused. "Sheriff, there is no point in this. I do not understand why—"

Thomas cut her off. "Sera, do you trust me? Please, I'll explain later."

Sera did trust Thomas, so she sat in the chair across from Marcus. She was familiar with this human game; she had watched the movie *Over the Top* so she knew what to do. She placed her hand in Marcus's.

Devon called out, "Ready, set—"

"Wait!" Thomas said. "This isn't fair."

"I knew this cop was full of crap yo," Marcus said, claiming victory.

Thomas walked closer to the table. "Marcus, use two hands."

"What the... you crazy, cop?"

A surprised but fascinated expression came across Devon's face. He sat up straight in his chair as Thomas now had his full attention. He hadn't known Thomas long, but he knew him to be a man of no-nonsense.

"Do it, Marcus, now. Don't hold back either, I mean it!" Devon said, now very serious.

Marcus took his other hand and placed it over the top of Sera's hand to get a two-handed grip.

Sera looked at Marcus. "I understand your skepticism. I will try not to hurt you."

The room lit up with laughter, all but Thomas and Devon.

Devon began again. "Ready... set... go!"

Marcus pushed hard, as hard as he could, with both hands and his body weight behind him. Sera's hand did not budge. Marcus continued his useless struggle, his massive muscles bulging and straining. The vein in his forehead looked as if it might pop right out of his head, and sweat began running down Marcus's face.

Sera looked up at Thomas. "Sheriff, have you proven your point yet? Should I put his arm down now?"

"Yes, Sera, now."

With one swift motion, Sera shifted her body weight, pushing her arm down and slamming Marcus's hands into the table. "Do not feel discouraged. You are very strong, for a human."

The room was completely silent. Finally, Devon spoke. "What do you need us to do?"

Sera got up from the table. "Sheriff, I don't understand. Why not just have me remove my disguise? If I revealed my physical differences, would that not have been enough to convince them?"

"Sera, we live in a time when people have horns surgically attached to their heads. That's not the reason I had you put on that show, though. One, for guys like this, you have to earn their respect or they won't follow you. Also, I don't want them associating you with Caleb or his monstrosities. I want you to be as human as possible to them."

"Understood, Sheriff," she said.

Thomas walked outside to get a lay of the land, and Devon walked out with him.

"Alien invasion, Thomas? I knew it was some crazy stuff going on, but this? I'm blown away, man."

"Trust me, you're not alone. What we have to do is impossible, and I'm at a loss. If we don't take out that tower, we're all dead. If we attack with what we have now, we're all dead. No-win scenarios have never been part of my way, but this one… like I said, I'm lost."

"What can we do to help? I got sixty men, and not one of them is scared of a fight."

"That's just it, Devon. We could throw six hundred of the wrong men at this, and we'd still come out on the losing end. No, keep your men here, doing what you've been doing. Speaking of which, how do you keep this place going?"

"Well, if you look at this from the inside, it looks like a regular neighborhood. We use the surrounding hoods as cover. They look so abandoned no one would bother coming in this far to look. We used old abandoned cars and 18-wheelers to block all the incoming roads. We sit right smack in the middle of it. It surrounds us and makes us damn near invisible. We stick to strict rules on movements, like zero coming-and-going after dusk. We hide in plain sight."

Thomas was impressed as he took in all Devon was showing him.

The conversation was interrupted as Sera came running out with Thomas's radio. "Sheriff, you must take this. Your daughter is calling."

Thomas quickly took the radio. "Go ahead, Jessie, I'm here!"

Jessica told Thomas everything about what had happened. "Dad, I'm on my way back to the camp. We need to go get Billy."

"I'm not at the camp. Send me Billy's location, then you head back to camp and drop off the supplies. We'll get Billy and meet you there."

Jessica gave Thomas the location and all the information she had collected on the camp and the men and weapons in it.

"You did good, baby. We'll take it from here."

Devon looked at Thomas. "You gonna risk everything for one man?"

"I can't leave a man behind."

"I know you can't. Gonna get you killed one day."

There was no arguing that point. It was just the kind of character that made Devon respect Thomas to no end. He looked Thomas in the eye and gave a crooked smile.

"Looks like the apocalypse is on hold. What do you need from us? Let's go get your boy!"

CHAPTER 11

Davis arrived back at the camp exhausted, having managed to escape the infected mainly due to the two men he'd left behind to die. Davis couldn't believe how badly he'd been outmatched.

Apprehensively, he walked to Simon's room and knocked on the door.

"Come," Simon beckoned from the other side of the door.

The dimness of Simon's room gave Davis extra anxiety as he entered. Simon could see in the dark since being bitten, and he had become quite comfortable in the darkness.

"Well, Davis, report!"

Davis knew he couldn't tell Simon the truth. He hesitated; it was all or nothing. "Roy and Clint fell to them things out there, but not before we killed ole Billy boy's partner," Davis lied.

"That's a shame. The brothers were loyal. At least you made it out. Survival of the fittest, I guess. Okay, Davis, you can go. Tell the camp the brothers died doing something heroic. It's better for morale."

Davis left the room, thankful he was reporting to Simon. As screwed up as Simon was, he was ten times better than his brother. Cole was just plain evil.

* * * * *

Jessica arrived back at camp, and Claire met her as she drove in. She walked over as Jessica exited the truck, hugging Jessica and holding on.

"I'm so glad you're back safely, baby. We've been so worried!" Claire said.

The camp was down, dim even.

"What's happened?" Jessica asked.

"Henry, baby. He's gone. Wayne and Paul got back just a few hours ago. Where's Billy?" Claire answered.

Upset by the news of Henry's death, Jessica felt torn having to deliver more bad news. But they needed and deserved to know the truth.

"Get everyone together, and I'll explain everything," Jessica said. "Where's Jimmy?"

"He's with Danny and Jax by the creek, gathering water," Claire said.

"Okay, I'll get them and meet everyone inside the mine. I need a minute with my brother, and I'll be there," Jessica said.

"Okay, Jess. Carl will be happy to see you."

Jessica smiled. Their time as kids seemed like a distant memory that she just could no longer relate to. "Tell him I'll see him soon, Claire, 'kay?" Jessica said as she headed toward the creek.

Claire watched as Jessica walked down the hill and realized that she was no longer looking at the little girl she knew, but at a new woman. Whatever had happened out there had hardened that girl's heart.

This world is damned, Claire thought. *God has damned this world.*

* * * * *

Thomas, Sera, Devon, and Marcus sat in the dining room. Thomas had a map that he'd found in a gas station. "Got a plan, cop?" Marcus asked.

"Yeah, Marcus, I have a plan. I don't know how much time we have, so we have to move now. I'll fill everyone in en route. From Jessie's coordinates, their camp is only a two-hour drive from here," Thomas said.

"What? Easy, cop. It'll be dark soon. We don't move at night!" Marcus protested.

"I know the dangers, Marcus, but we need to come in at night. The Spewers have a pattern we can anticipate. The people in this camp will have safeguards in place that we'll have to observe, and that we have to do at night," Thomas explained.

"You know, last time we took a risk for you, we lost some good homeboys. Seems like you do the plannin', we do the dyin'," Marcus said.

Thomas grew irritated with Marcus's attitude, but he knew with him out there, Billy's chances were a lot better.

"I know, Marcus. We were right there with you, fighting right beside you. What you and your people are doing for us is probably something I'll never be able to repay. I'll tell you this, though, for what you've already done and what you're doing for us, I'd give my life for anyone of you. I consider you people part of my group, my family."

"What you mean by *you people*, white boy?" Marcus asked with a smile on his face. "Okay, cop, we got your back," he added.

Devon sat up in his chair. "Okay, now that you two are a happy couple again, can we get on with this? How many men are we going to need, Thomas?"

"No *we*, Devon. Sera and I, Marcus, and three good shooters. I've seen what you've accomplished. They need you here. If something goes wrong out there, I need you to go gather my people and bring them here. Please trust me on this."

Devon looked at Marcus.

"Cop's right for once, cousin. Nobody here would be here wasn't for you. Nobody else can hold it together either. This truce with the other neighborhood crews was fragile enough as it is. I'll look out for the boys out there."

Devon didn't like sitting out on the sidelines, but he understood they were right. "I think we should go 'head and bring your people in, anyway, Thomas. Be easier to watch out for everyone if they're under the same roof."

"Might be a tough sell. They're comfortable and won't want to move if unnecessary. Wait until you hear from me. Or don't hear from me," Thomas said.

"Coo', I gotcha," Devon said, shaking Thomas's hand.

Devon said his goodbyes to Marcus and his men as they walked out toward the vehicles.

"We'll need those also," Thomas said, pointing to two dirt bikes leaning against the building.

* * * * *

Billy sat tied to the chair and covered with a blanket. A fire burning in a fire pit warmed him further. His wounds were treated, and he'd even been fed. Cole was very serious about him regaining his strength. The sadistic bastard was the type of person to break something then fix it just for the pleasure of breaking it again. He reminded Billy of that kid Sid from the movie *Toy Story*.

Cole walked into the room. Billy tried to keep his composure despite the sinking feeling in the pit of his gut. "So, *Sid*, what's on the agenda for this evening?" he asked, trying his best to sound unafraid.

Cole was very much up for this game. "Well, Billy, I've been racking my brain to come up with ways to keep you entertained. This is what I've come up with."

Cole's eyes lit up with excitement and anticipation as he unrolled his tools in front of Billy. There were shaped and curved blades of many different varieties. Cole took a hooked blade with a wooden handle and walked over to an open fire that was burning in the room. Cole placed the blade in the fire.

"We'll leave that to marinate," Cole said and walked over to Billy. "You don't mind if I warm up a bit, do ya, Billy boy?" he said as he brought a smashing fist down across Billy's jaw.

He hit Billy again, this time with a hammering back fist that busted open Billy's inner gumline and causing his mouth to fill with blood. He spat the blood out and lifted his head, looking Cole directly in the eyes in defiance.

"You're a bully without a cause, Cole. I'll never give in to a wannabe punk like you. You're a small, little man. You were small before this virus hit, and now that your brother's some superhuman freak, you're even smaller now. Always the tagalong, huh, Cole?" Billy said, even managing a small smile.

"Okay, Billy, playtime's over, friend."

Cole walked over to the fire and took the now red-hot blade out. He walked over to Billy and placed the blade on Billy's chest. The metal seared his flesh, binding flesh and metal into one. Cole ripped the blade away, tearing skin that had integrated with the blade. Billy screamed, in contempt of himself. Cole took the blade and dug into his chest. The cut was deep, and he pulled out a piece of Billy's flesh. Billy yelled out, on the brink of unconsciousness. Cole made it a point to hold back until Billy had stabilized. He didn't want him losing consciousness during their time together. Cole put the hooked blade back in the fire and took out a similar blade and placed it on Billy's pinky finger.

"I'm going to ask you one last time before we begin the dismemberment phase of our interrogation. Tell me about your group."

Billy felt the pain and pressure and prayed again that he'd never betray them. "Do your worst."

So Cole began.

* * * * *

The night was still and cold but crisp. Thomas had stopped the vehicle. They left one man with the truck, and Thomas and the rest of his group traveled the remaining two miles on foot. Marcus and his boys were not happy about the current traveling conditions.

"It's colder than a muther out here," Ron complained.

"Well, you let the white boy sneak you. Had you all tied up like some S&M chick role-playin'. That why D got you out here, to learn something," Marcus shot back quickly. "It is cold, though," he added.

"We can't take the chance of the vehicles being heard or seen. We have to watch out for humans and Spewers alike," Thomas said.

They came to the edge of the camp. Jessica had done well; her description of the camp held true. Thomas found it hard to imagine his little girl up here cold and scared and trying to gather as much information as she had. The thought gave Thomas a heavy heart. There would be time to suffer old wounds later. For now, he had work to do.

Thomas gathered the group.

"Okay, we're going to split up. Sera and I will go east, you four head west. This is for intelligence-gathering only. Do not engage until we meet back up and put a plan together," Thomas instructed.

"Yes, sir, General, sir," Ron mocked.

They split off and were on their way.

Thomas counted twenty-six men in the camp, most armed with automatic weaponry. The attack had to remain stealthy. With the men he had, that could prove to be extremely difficult. These were good men, good fighters even, but with no shadow training, they were broadswords where scalpels were needed. *Unless...* Thomas thought. Maybe there was a way to make the most of their talents.

They regrouped, and Thomas laid out the plan for them.

"Risky," Marcus said.

"More like insane," said Ron.

Thomas heard the doubts in their voices, and he understood.

"We can't take this camp head-on. There are too many, and they're well-armed. This is the only way. Sera, you're phase 1, the heavy muscle. Will, Marcus, and I will be the secondary. Ron and Jay, you guys are the bread and butter of this plan. If you two fall through, we're all as good as dead," Thomas said.

"No pressure, though, huh."

Ron's sarcastic remark did little to deviate from the fact that his part was both critical and potentially deadly.

"If there were another way, believe me, Ron..."

They split up again and set the plan into motion.

* * * * *

Cole pressed the red-hot curved blade into Billy's shoulder. As he carved out a piece of flesh, Billy screamed in excruciating pain. Billy was cut up and bleeding. This couldn't end too early, so Cole was very careful not to stab or cut too deep. A true virtuoso, Cole knew you had to keep the body at the perfect level of pain and suffering. Too much pain and the body would activate its natural defense mechanisms. It would cause the person to lose consciousness or simply shut down the nervous system. Of course, not applying enough pain would cause the interrogation to lose its effectiveness. Cole had applied the appropriate amount of physical affliction. He had to let Billy level out, let him appreciate the fact that he wasn't, at the moment, suffering.

"I know you think I get pleasure from hurting you. I admit, it isn't the worst part of my day, but you're wrong about one thing. You believe that I'm more of the hunt instead of the kill kind of guy. The fact of the matter is, the end result is all I care about. Tell me what it is you're hiding. By the way, I spoke to my brother before I came back in. Your partner that was with you is dead."

Billy's heart sank.

Could it be true? Was Jessica dead? What had he done? He had no strength left, nothing left in him to fight with. Billy was hurt and bloodied, and now he felt it. Now he was broken.

Cole sensed it. He knew he had him, and it was time to press the assault.

"They said your partner suffered, cried out. Our men were merciful and put a bullet right in the back of his head."

Billy looked up right into Cole's eyes. "Say that again, Cole. Your men were what?"

"I said they showed your friend a great kindness and killed him quickly," he said. "I can do the same for you, Billy. I can stop your pain. This world has nothing for you any longer. Let me send you on your way with ease and swiftness. It's that, or I'll have to move on to more drastic measures. I've been heating this up, partly hoping you'd break before I had to use it, but mostly hoping you wouldn't," Cole said, holding up a thin straight piece of metal about twelve inches long.

Cole pulled the metal out of the fire. It was still orange, holding in the searing heat from the flames.

"See, Billy, I'm going to slide this into the corner of your eye. The heat will cause the tissue to cauterize to the blade. Then I'll simply take my time pulling it out slowly. Just fast enough to cause you unspeakable amounts of pain, but not so fast that it causes you to blackout."

Billy felt panic run through his body as Cole began to walk toward him with the metal rod in hand. With each step closer Cole took, Billy knew he was going to break. Tears began streaming down his face; he would give Cole everything he wanted. He'd won. Billy began praying for forgiveness.

"I'll talk, Cole. I'll tell you everything you want to know, just please, please don't."

"Oh, Billy, I know you'll talk. The thing is, you know when you have your mind set on strawberry ice cream? You know it's not good for you, but your mouth is already set for it. That's kinda how this is. I already have my mouth set for it. Hey, though, tell ya what? I'll only take the one," Cole said with a hellish smile on his face as he pushed the hot metal rod into Billy's eye socket.

Billy screamed, a horrifying, gut-wrenching scream that filled the camp.

* * * * *

Thomas heard the screams and knew the time had come to move. He tapped Sera's shoulder and said, "Now, Sera, go!"

Sera ran down the small hill. The man standing guard in the makeshift tower spotted her coming out of the tree line and raised his rifle to fire. Sera knew to expect him, and her speed was intense. The guard couldn't get a bead on her to fire. Sera jumped hard, using a rock to lift off from, and launched fifteen feet into the air. Landing in the tower, she grabbed the guard by his jacket, tossing him through the air and to the ground below, knocking him unconsciousness. She jumped from the tower and moved deeper into the compound. Sera kept hearing Thomas's instructions echoing in her head: *Ruthless aggression, Sera. Don't hold back. Don't be afraid to hurt them.*

This wasn't her way, but she understood the need for it.

Sera overtook two more guards, hard. She took them from behind before they knew she was on them. She took the first guard she came to by the back of his collar and threw him four feet through the air into a wall. With a powerful back fist, she knocked the other guard out cold.

This did not go unnoticed.

Two patrolling guards raised their weapons on Sera and fired.

* * * * *

The sounds of gunfire bellowing through the camp made Cole stop twisting the metal rod in Billy's eye.

"What the hell was that? You hold tight, Billy boy. I'll be right back."

He left Billy beaten and bloodied, the rod sticking out of his eye. Cole came out to find his men carrying a body covered with a blanket on a stretcher through the camp toward the medical tent.

"What's going on? Who is that?"

One of the men answered, "Some crazy woman. We had to shoot her. She was jumping the men. Strong little thing. Must be high on some kinda drug, that PCP maybe."

Cole pulled back the sheet to see a woman. She looked strange to him, but he couldn't quite put his finger on it. "Yeah, she looks like she's definitely on something. She looks strange," Cole said.

Simon came out of his tent. The men explained the situation to him as he looked at the body. It was strange to him too, but also strangely familiar.

"Take her to the medical room now," Simon commanded.

* * * * *

Thomas and Marcus had followed the sound of the screams to the cold room. Thomas had seen men battered, bloodied, dismembered, even dead, but it had never jolted him like it did when he saw Billy tied to that chair. Marcus held Billy up as Thomas cut him free.

"Damn, cop, they really messed yo boy up. What the hell is that poking out of his eye, man?"

"Don't touch anything. We'll get him medical attention back at camp. We have to stabilize him for the trip home. Taking it out now will only cause more damage," he said. "Billy, Billy, it's Thomas. We're getting you out of here. There are too many of them for us to walk out, so you're going out with Marcus and I'll catch up with you soon."

Billy was too weak to walk on his own. Thomas looked at the damage they'd done to his friend, and it made what he planned to do so much easier. They got Billy to his feet and walked him over to the door. Billy stopped, leaned close to Thomas, and with what strength he had left, whispered a single word into his ear.

"Cole."

Thomas had a name, and soon he'd have the rest.

"Okay, Marcus, you know what to do. Get him out of here and wait for the signal."

"I got you, cop. I'll take care of him."

They walked out of the room Billy had come to accept he would never leave. They split up, and Thomas circled to make sure Marcus got Billy to the tree line.

Once they were safely out of the camp, Thomas moved into position.

* * * * *

The men took Sera's body to the medical room and put her on the examination table. They put her down and waited for Simon and Cole.

"Well, Simon, I see you have this all in order. I've been rude to our other guest long enough," Cole said.

"Cole, don't play with your food too long. It's about time to finish it and move on. Don't worry, we'll get you a new plaything later," Simon said as he patted Cole's head, giving him a wink and a smile.

"Whatever you say, Simon. One more hour, then I'll put him down. Fair enough?"

"Fair enough," Simon replied.

Cole walked back to the cold room. He opened the door, only to find Thomas sitting in the chair Billy had been in.

"What in the hell!" Cole exclaimed.

"Cole, I presume. You and I have to have a conversation concerning a friend of mine."

"I don't know who you are, friend, but you've made a serious mistake," Cole said.

Thomas stood up and walked toward Cole. "One of us has... friend," he replied.

Grabbing a knife from his waist, Cole slashed at Thomas's throat. Thomas sidestepped and weaved back, easily dodging his attack. Thomas stepped in close, grabbing him by his wrist and pressing his thumb up into Cole's wrist right above the bone that connected the wrist and the hand. Thomas pushed and twisted, causing an involuntary muscle reaction that forced Cole's hand to open and drop the knife. While still holding his wrist, Thomas used his free hand to hit him in the throat, dropping him to the ground.

"You hurt my friend. I'm going to return the favor."

Thomas walked over to the table where the tools had been laid out. He picked up a straight very sharp blade and began walking toward Cole. Thomas readied the blade in his hand as the door opened and two of Cole's men came through the door, weapons ready.

"Drop the knife, now! Get on the ground!" they commanded.

Thomas dropped the knife and raised his hands.

Cole staggered to his feet. "Well, looks like we'll get better acquainted, after all. Hope you're as fun as your friend. Billy was a screamer. I really liked that about him," Cole said hoarsely.

"What's that? Couldn't quite understand you. Sore throat?" Thomas said, adding a wink for good measure.

The men took Thomas and led him out of the room.

"Time to introduce you to my brother. He's gonna love you. Then Simon will give you to me, and we'll play a little game. I'm going to enjoy cutting you up," Cole said. "Can you hear me now?"

Simon sat with his medic as he prepared to examine Sera's body. Cole came into the room with his prisoner.

"Simon, we got another one."

As they passed by Sera's body, Cole stopped and pulled the sheet from her face. "You know her?" Simon asked Thomas. "Do you know this woman?" he repeated, aggravated this time.

Thomas looked slowly at Simon. "What the hell are you?" he asked with genuine awe.

"Would you like to know?" Simon asked angrily as he grabbed Thomas by the throat, picking him off the ground one-handed with little effort. "Now I'll ask you once more. Who. Is. This. WOMAN?"

Simon was close to rage.

Every eye in the room was on Simon as the men watched him prepare to take the prisoner apart.

Thomas had pushed far enough—he had what he came for.

"Why. Don't. You. Ask. Her. Yourself?" Thomas mocked.

Simon turned to see Sera leap to her feet. Simon and Cole's men were completely frozen from the shock of seeing the woman they had just shot dead moving very quickly toward them. Sera had disarmed them and knocked them unconscious just as Cole unsheathed his knife and lunged at her. Cole was fast and caught Sera with a deep gash in her midsection. Sera stood, looked at her wound, and then eyed Cole.

The wound slowly closed and healed before his eyes.

Simon saw this and dropped Thomas. Sera's healing, strength, and speed matched his own. She would have the answers he so desperately desired. This changed Simon's priorities, and he charged toward Sera, giving Thomas a chance to get back to his feet. Searching desperately around, Thomas reached out and grabbed the first weapon within his reach, a metal pipe from the floor. Thomas chased after Simon.

Cole recovered from the revelation of Sera's recovery and attempted another attack. It was like he moved in slow motion; Sera grabbed Cole's arm and, with a quick, sharp twist, broke it. Cole yelled out and dropped to his knees just as Simon reached her and grabbed her by the arm, violently turning her toward him.

"What are you? Why am I like this?" he yelled in Sera's face.

Sera tried to pull away, but Simon was strong, very strong. Sera pushed against him with both hands and all her strength. This knocked him back and off balance. Taking advantage of Simon's vulnerability, Thomas put the metal bar across Simon's throat and pulled him to the ground. Simon was strong, too strong for Thomas to hold him down. Using all his strength, Simon was pulling the pipe away from his throat. Seeing this, Sera jumped on top of him, bringing down powerful blows to Simon's head. Cole saw his brother in trouble and moved toward one of the guns his men had dropped. Out of the corner of his eye, Thomas saw Cole pick up the assault rifle.

"Sera, watch out!" Thomas yelled.

Sera rolled to her side just as Cole opened fire. Seizing the opportunity to kill two birds with one maneuver, Thomas pushed Simon up into Cole's line of fire. The bullets ripped into Simon. Thomas pushed Simon's limp body off him as he threw the pipe, hitting Cole on the head and knocking him unconscious. Thomas got to his feet, and Sera regrouped and prepared for their quick egress.

"We have to get out of here, fast. Those shots won't go unnoticed."

They opened the door and had started moving toward the woods when a hail of bullets rained down on them. Thomas pushed Sera down into a wood pile just as the bullets began to come down around them. They weren't hit, but there was nowhere for them to go. Thomas couldn't pinpoint the origin of fire.

"There are too many of them. I can't tell where they're firing from."

"Thomas, I can draw their fire so you can escape. It's the only way."

"No, Sera, you can't take that much damage. Even if you can, you'll be down and out of commission. We came in here together, and believe me, we're getting out of here the same way."

The men continued to fire on their targets, Davis leading the charge. "Keep pourin' it down on them, boys. These bastards come into our house, they ain't walking out of here alive!" he blared over a bullhorn.

Thomas and Sera crawled from the wood pile to behind a building in the camp. They were still surrounded and taking fire. *Come on, Ron, where are you?* Thomas thought.

"Keep pounding on them, boys. Get ready to move into position, and let's finish these fools off!" Davis continued to yell into the speaker.

Simon came out of the medical tent, having recovered from the gunshot wounds.

"Davis, get Cole a medic. He's down in the medical tent!" Simon ordered. "Give me that bullhorn!" Simon, now speaking into the bullhorn, called to his uninvited guests.

"You two come on out. I just want to talk to the girl. I got some questions she has answers to. Nobody's gonna hurt you," Simon said.

Thomas sat up to be heard but still maintained his cover behind the building. "I've seen how you ask questions, Simon. We'll pass."

Simon's anger was becoming overwhelming. "Mister, your time is about up. I'm about to send every man I got at you. They'll shoot you on sight, and her, they'll take alive. Well, alive enough. Make a choice, mister. I'm really starting to get bored with this!" Simon yelled through the speaker.

"Well," Thomas yelled back, "good thing we brought some entertainment!"

The distant sounds of motorcycle engines had been drowned out by Simon's bullhorn, until now. Simon and his men looked around as they realized something was coming their way, fast.

"Be alert, men," Simon instructed. "Shoot the first thing you see that ain't us!"

Ron and his partner thrust out of the forest and into the camp. Simon's men trained their guns on the pair, ready to open fire, when they noticed. They weren't alone. As the two men rode out of the woods, a horde of infected that were feverishly tearing after them followed right behind. As Ron and Jay rode through the camp toward the rendezvous point, the infected refocused their attention on slower targets. The infected spread throughout the camp with blinding speed. The men in the camp fought back, firing wildly into the invaders but doing little to no damage. It was total and complete chaos. Thomas's plan was working perfectly so far, and now all they had to do was get out alive.

Ron and Jay were near the RV point when a shot hit Jay in the chest. "Dammit!" Ron cried out. One bike down, but Ron rode steadily to his destination.

Thomas watched as the infected and men in the camp tore at one another. It seemed everyone had all but forgotten about them. The infected and their offspring began to overtake the camp. Thomas ran forward, trying to focus on getting them through the anarchy that was everywhere. The chaos surrounded them. They had been lucky so far, until an infected jumped over a small ridge at Thomas.

"Sheriff, watch out!" Sera yelled.

Thomas turned to defend himself just as Sera leaped forward, grabbing the infected seconds before it reached him. She pulled it back and broke its neck, severing the brain stem and killing the infected. More infected saw the assault and gave chase to the pair.

Thomas and Sera made their way to the RV point moments before Ron arrived. "We have a problem. Jay din't make it. There's only one bike!" Ron said.

Thomas's plan was acutely dangerous, but the simplicity of it made it viable. Have Sera cause a distraction. Sneak in and get Billy out. Retrieve Sera. Have Ron and Jay bring in unlikely cavalry. Escape on the bikes before all hell broke loose. Admittedly, Thomas didn't and couldn't have taken Simon and his freakish condition into account, but they had dealt with that situation. The only hitch was, both bikes had to be there. One bike couldn't carry the three of them to safety; the weight would be too much to outrun the infected.

"Ron, get Sera and get out of here. I'll make my way out on my own," Thomas said, picking up a fallen rifle off the ground.

"I'll not leave you, Sheriff. I can handle the infected much more adequately than you can, even with your crude weapons."

A group of infected were on top of them. Thomas fired three shots, and three headshots later, the infected fell to the ground. "Not bad, for a crude weapon, I mean," Thomas said with a small smug half-smile.

"Nonetheless, you will run out of the ammunition that you require to fire the weapon. I've already attacked them, so they will target me now. I can buy you time while you escape. It is the most advisable solution."

Thomas raised his weapon, killing two more infected.

"One of you get on, or I'll leave you both," Ron said.

Thomas realized she wouldn't leave him, and even if he could knock her out, Ron couldn't carry an unconscious body on the bike. "Go, Ron, tell Devon to get my people! Go now!" Thomas shouted.

"You one crazy white boy. We gon' get your people and look out for them, that's my word."

Ron shook Thomas's hand and sped off. The camp was still in turmoil, but the infected and offspring were starting to overwhelm the men, and it wouldn't be long now.

Thomas and Sera started to make their way to the tree line then hoped they could melt into the woods. A few feet away from sweet sanctuary, they came around the corner of one of the buildings, and Thomas's heart sank. The infected were everywhere; they were trapped. No choice. They had to turn back and try to find another route. The infected had cut off any chance of retreat forward or back. They were truly trapped.

Ducking down behind a small pile of stacked wood, they would gain a few moments of concealment. Thomas's plan had begun to collapse on him. *At least we got Billy out,* he thought. Thomas picked up an extra magazine off the ground.

"Sera, I'm sorry."

"I also am sorry. I should have done more to stop this from ever happening. I am prepared to give my life for my failures. At least we got your comrade out, Sheriff," Sera said, echoing Thomas's thoughts.

He smiled at her and handed Sera his knife. "Get as many as you can. If you get the chance to escape, you take it. Don't worry about me. You will be more valuable to my people alive than dying trying to save me. Promise me, if you can, you get out."

She nodded.

"Well," Thomas said, taking Sera by the hand, "here we go."

* * * * *

Marcus carried Billy to a ridge above the camp. Billy was in and out of consciousness, and Marcus laid him down so he and Billy could rest. They needed to get back to Will, who was waiting with the truck. There was time. Will would not leave without them. Marcus looked down at the camp and watched the madness ensue below. There were infected everywhere. He watched as Ron and Jay rode through the camp. *What have we done?* he thought. It was a war zone down there.

Marcus watched as Jay was gunned down and knocked off his bike by a random shot. He saw Thomas and Sera get pinned down and surrounded by infected. He'd had serious reservations about Thomas's plan from the beginning, but now all his apprehensions were being played out in front of him like a reoccurring nightmare. The camp's floodlights were barely enough to give Marcus a clear view, but it was enough for him to make out the fact that Thomas and Sera had no way to escape the camp. They were completely closed in. It was still hours until sunrise, and they wouldn't last minutes.

He had always given Thomas a hard time. He wasn't used to cops like him. Marcus had always been at odds with the police, mostly because of his affiliation. They were cats and dogs predestined for animosity. But Thomas was different somehow. He felt the sorrow of losing a friend at the thought of Thomas's death.

He wouldn't let it be in vain, though; he would get Billy to safety.

Rest well, cop. You deserve it.

Billy was still unconscious. Marcus supported him up over his shoulder and began making his way through the woods to Will and their ride home.

CHAPTER 12

Simon fought the infected off with the viciousness of a wild animal, but he'd sustained severe injuries. The infected sensed that he was somehow unaffected by the offspring's bite and, therefore, was to be terminated instead of assimilated. He'd killed half a dozen infected before making it to the tree line and getting into the woods. He'd abandoned his men, his camp, and his brother. There were simply too many of them. He'd lost everything. Simon could see the camp clearly and spotted Thomas and Sera cornered. He wouldn't run until he watched the man that had caused all this die. He lowered himself behind some brush and settled in to see the coup de grâce.

* * * * *

Thomas fired his weapon, careful to take calm, precise shots. Sera used the knife with unexpected skill. They killed many infected, but Thomas understood it was only a matter of time. And he was right.

Two infected had finally coordinated their attack. One launched high in the air and came down hard with a two-fist attack as the other tackled Sera from behind. She went down hard, and there was a loud snap as her back fractured. Thomas fired fiercely on the infected attacking Sera, dropping one, but the sound of the dry click as he attempted to shoot the second signaled the end of his ammunition. Thomas turned his rifle around, grabbing the still-warm barrel and choking up on it. He held it like a baseball bat, ready to swing for the fences. By now, there were so many infected around him he felt like he was the last man alive in the camp.

Hope those two bastards got it bad, he thought of Simon and Cole. *It'd be nice to know I took them with me.*

The infected rushed him, fast, and locked on to a single target. The first two to reach him were greeted with the stock of his rifle. That was all he could manage. The third grabbed Thomas around the waist and threw him down to the ground so fiercely the air was taken out of his lungs. Thomas lay on the ground barely able to breathe and helpless. The infected held him down and bent over him. As it opened its mouth, the offspring began crawling up through the infected's chest and out of its mouth.

"No!" Thomas yelled out.

As the offspring became visible, the night sky lit up.

Daylight, Thomas thought, *that's impossible!*

One flare, then another, and another.

The infected's skin began to burn, the process that turned them into mush. They jumped to their feet and scattered into the woods with blinding speed. Soon the whole sky was filled with flares. Thomas could barely tell it was the middle of the night. Almost as fast as the infected had come, the camp was completely cleared of them.

Thomas made his way to his feet and ran over to Sera. She was barely conscious, not moving.

"Sera, talk to me. Are you okay? Will you heal from this?"

"Sheriff, I've never been this badly injured. I cannot say for sure. I'm very tired. I must rest."

"No, no, Sera, stay awake. Stay with me. Sera, Sera!"

It was no use, she was out.

* * * * *

Men in uniforms came running out of the woods. They were wearing dark goggles, and they were definitely military.

"Hands up! Lie on the ground. Do not move, or we will fire!" the commanding officer ordered.

Thomas did as he instructed, but he was worried about Sera.

"My friend needs a medic. Please, she's unique and requires very special care. Please let me help her," he pleaded.

The soldier kept his weapon trained on Thomas. "Don't move. We have a medic here. He'll help your friend," he said, signaling for the medic. "Over here, Doc. We have a live one!"

The medic came rushing over. He knelt over Sera and started examining her. "What the hell is this? She's not human!" the medic said.

Thomas couldn't see very well because of the flares, but he heard the voice of his old friend and almost jumped to his feet with excitement before he remembered the M4 barrel still trained on him.

"Tim! Tim, it's Thomas!"

Tim Winters turned and saw Thomas. "Soldier, let him up. He's with me."

The soldier hesitated.

Tim rose up and stood directly in the soldier's face. "Stand down! That is an order! Now, step aside."

The soldier did as he was ordered.

Thomas got up and hugged his friend. Tim gave him a spare pair of goggles. "Where are Carl and Claire? Are they all right? Please, for the mercy of God, tell me they're okay, Thomas."

"They're fine, Tim. We have a camp. They're there now. I'll explain later, but this woman is critical to what's going on, and if we don't save her, then everything that's happening is only the beginning."

"Okay, Thomas. Tell me what to do. We don't have much time. Those flares are very special. They are treated with high amounts of ultraviolet radiation, and they're the last of their kind that we have. They will keep the carriers and parasites at bay, but we don't have much time. Once the flares burn out, they'll come back. We have to move her into one of the empty buildings, where we can hold up until the sun comes up."

Thomas nodded.

"This way. They have a medical building set up right over there," Thomas said.

They took her and moved her into the medical building. As they walked in, Thomas saw a still-unconscious Cole. "Tie him up, Tim. That guy's very bad news."

Tim motioned to the soldiers to secure Cole. They set Sera on the exam table.

"How long until the flares fade, Tim?"

"Maybe ten more minutes. We can hold up here."

Eight soldiers entered the room and set up a perimeter. Thomas noticed they weren't soldiers—they weren't army at all, but Navy. US Navy SEALs, to be exact.

"Sir," one of the men said. "We have two incoming. Looks like walking wounded."

Thomas rushed to the window. It was Marcus and Billy. Billy barely able to walk, Marcus half-carrying him. "Those are my men, open the door," Thomas said.

They opened the door, and Thomas went to meet them.

"What happened? Why didn't you get out?" Thomas asked.

Marcus looked at Thomas for a few seconds, his face still with wonder. "How the hell are you still alive, cop?"

"I'm on my ninth life. Don't look so disappointed," Thomas joked. "What happened?" Thomas asked, getting back to business.

Marcus laid Billy down, and Tim went to work on him. "Well, we… I thought for sure you were dead. I didn't want to watch, so I started makin' it for the truck when the night lit up like it was noon or sumthin'. Them damn things started flyin' back into the woods faster than I coulda got your boy outta there. We doubled back here and saw them soldiers. I was just hopin' they wasn't none of them rednecks from the camp. Lucky us, huh. Boy, you harder to kill than the homie Tupac."

"Yeah, well," Thomas said, "remember how his story ended?"

"Real talk, homie. Still, though, you one crazy white boy."

"So I hear," Thomas said. He then walked over to Tim. "How is he? Will he be okay?"

"He suffered major trauma. I doubt we can save the eye. Who did this to him?"

Thomas looked over at Cole, who was now awake and sitting handcuffed on the ground. "How did you find us?"

"There's a government still, Thomas. Nothing like we knew, but functional. We were able to piggyback on one of the old weather satellites that's been out of commission since the mid-eighties. We've been tracking for any signs of survivors. A few days ago, we tracked some minor firearm activity in this area. We got there today, but whatever had happened was over. It looked like a couple of men holding off some carriers, but they didn't hold long. Next thing we know, our sensors lit up like Christmas trees. Major activity from this camp. The firefight between the people in this camp and the carriers brought us right to you," Tim responded. "Thomas, you'll have to excuse me. I have to focus on Billy. We'll catch up soon."

Thomas next went to the SEAL team commander. "Sir, my name is Lieutenant Thomas Pratt, former SEAL Team 10 commander. You came through and really pulled our butts out of the fire. Thank you." Thomas extended his hand, but it wasn't received by the commander.

"I'm Lieutenant Commander Steven Haul. I don't like this babysitting assignment, and I don't like risking the lives of my team in some backwoods skirmish. I don't care what you were, Lieutenant. It's what you are. From the looks of things, you, your crippled comrade, and the gangbanger here are liabilities. Stay out of our way."

Thomas lowered his hand. "Yeah, okay, Commander. Your show." Thomas walked over and sat with Marcus.

"Aw, look at you, cop, already making friends."

Marcus and Thomas laughed quietly.

"I'm going to try to get some sleep while I can," Thomas informed him.

First-Class Petty Officer Sites walked over to Haul. "Sir, I know that man. I worked with him on Operation Jubilee. We had a multinational task force with the Brits on a dual-task hostage rescue mission in Afghanistan. He was my team leader when I was with Team 10. He's a damn good SEAL. No offense, but the best I've ever worked with. He left the teams when his wife got sick, I heard. I'd transferred to 6 by then, though."

"Thanks, Sites. I hear you, man. I know who he is. But we have to stay frosty and on point. He's been out a while and stuck in civilian lifestyle. He's not up on our tactics. You know better than anyone that you can function with another SEAL team but not function on *this* SEAL team. The world's gone insane. We can't afford a rogue."

"Copy that, sir, I understand." Petty Officer Sites returned to his post.

The night wore on, and the infected had returned to the camp. They were no longer in a stimulated state and wandered around the camp like they had been prompted to come but forgotten why they came. The SEALs remained engaged at their posts, waiting, prepared to take action and drop hammers in an instant.

Tim worked steadily on Billy. The medical tent the camp had set up was surprisingly well-stocked, so Tim was able to give Billy effective care. Tim knew Billy to be a good man; he was young, and he always looked for positive and fair means by which to live his life. He was married to one of Tim's nurses, Jackie. Tim wondered what had become of her. Was she in the camp with Claire and Carl also?

* * * * *

Simon saw as Thomas managed to evade the infected. He watched as the soldiers saved this man he had come to loathe. He would get his payback, but it would have to wait. The infected had never come near his camp before. Simon believed it was because they feared him. His arrogance had been met with reality, and the results equaled disaster for him and his people. He wondered what had become of Cole. He wouldn't leave his brother to them, he decided. He would wait, and when the time was right, he would go in and get him out.

* * * * *

The sun came up as Tim was finishing up with Billy. He walked over and woke Thomas. "How's he doing, Tim?" Thomas asked, sitting up.

"I had to remove his eye. The rod they used was heated, so there's no infection in the socket. I'm treating him with antibiotics to be safe. The cuts and burns will heal. He'll have a lot of scars, inside and out. The slash on the side of his face that I stitched closed worries me the most because of a possible infection. We'll see by the end of the day. I wish we could let him rest, but time is a luxury we don't have." Tim sat down next to his old friend. "You know, Thomas, I went back to Ghostwood. I told them I needed research material, but really, I just had to go back for my family. When I saw the town and what had become of it, I thought the worst. I know they would have never made it without you. I owe you everything. I'll never forget what you gave me." Tim placed his hand on Thomas's shoulder.

Thomas just nodded, and the two friends sat together for a moment in silence.

Billy began to stir. He woke and opened his eye. He felt strange. Something was wrong, something was missing. His vision was blocked, so he reached up and felt the patch over his right eye. He was beginning to sit up when a hand gently pushed him back onto the bed. He was still very disoriented, and his vision was blurry. He couldn't quite make out who it was standing over him.

"Just relax," the man said. "We have a lot of work ahead of us. Still got unfinished business, Billy boy!"

* * * * *

As Cole leaned in quickly with a burning, hot piece of wire and thrust it into Billy's only remaining good eye, he woke from the nightmare with a terrible start.

Billy took in all that was around him. There were men loading and packing gear up, obviously preparing to move out. Thomas and Tim sat talking nearby, and Marcus was sleeping in a makeshift bed beside him. Then there was Cole sitting on the ground, handcuffed, his guard standing over him and barely taking notice of his prisoner. Billy looked at Cole. This man had hurt him, marred and maimed him, but worse than anything, he had broken him. He couldn't suffer the latter. He'd been willing to give up all he'd held sacred, all to end the torment Cole had subjected him to.

The words they'd exchanged earlier echoed loudly in Billy's head: "*I'll be the last thing you see before you die!*"

Billy needed this. Cole had to die, and at his hands. It was the only way to silence the deafening noise in his head. He struggled to his feet. Cole's knives were still on the table where he'd left them. Billy grabbed one as he stumbled by. He walked toward Cole. The guard had stepped away to help load the gurney that held Sera's still-unconscious body onto one of the transports. There was but one single thought in Billy's head right then: *This monster doesn't live to see the next five minutes of life.* As he got closer to the source of his suffering, just the thought of snuffing out this darkness brought him peace.

Billy had killed before. During his tours in Iraq, he'd been forced to take lives. In the defense of his life or the lives in his unit. This was different, and he refused to delude himself into trying to justify this as some kind of righteous kill. Although the knowledge that Cole would never hurt or kill anyone again was a viable reason for this, he knew this was a revenge killing, plain and simple.

Cole looked up and saw Billy approach. They stood for a moment, Cole staring into Billy's eye.

"Planning on something, Billy boy?"

Billy took the blade he had been hiding behind his leg out. "What you're seeing, Cole, is the last thing you'll ever see. Fair enough, though. Eye for an eye and all that," Billy said as he thrust the blade through Cole's eye and into his brain.

Cole screamed out, and the camp came to a halt. Stunned, they watched as Billy pushed and twisted the blade deep and hard into Cole's skull. Thomas was on his feet, running toward Billy. The guard raised his weapon and ordered Billy to get down on his knees.

"Don't shoot, don't shoot!" Thomas yelled. He reached Billy, pushing him to the ground. "Billy, what have you done!?"

"I killed a monster," he answered calmly. "It was the only way to quiet the noise in my head, Thomas."

The SEAL commander came behind Billy and placed handcuffs on him. "A magistrate will settle this back at base, Pratt. Stand down, we have this."

Thomas hated seeing his friend like this, but this was the way it had to be. Tim had been examining Cole; he looked up at Thomas and shook his head.

"Time of death: 10:22 a.m.," Tim said.

* * * * *

Simon watched as Billy shoved the knife into his brother's eye. The rage swelled up in him like an explosion. He began his descent down the hill toward the camp.

He would kill them all or die trying. He'd come around the ridge when he saw a figure standing between him and the camp.

"What are you?" Caleb asked with genuine curiosity as he looked upon Simon.

"Move aside, little man, or be another victim!" Simon growled.

"Be still now. Their weapons will cut you down, and I have so many questions for you. I need you in one piece to study, so you will come with me," Caleb said.

"Enough!" Simon yelled as he stepped toward Caleb.

Simon grabbed Caleb's jacket and brought a crushing blow with his other arm down at Caleb's head. Simon was astounded as Caleb simply reached out and caught Simon's metaled limb with his hand. Caleb grabbed Simon by the neck and slammed him down into the ground and held him there.

"Listen, it doesn't have to be this way. You cannot possibly defeat me, human. I need answers about your condition. I will have them either from you or from your remains. You choose."

Simon struggled but could gain no ground. Whoever or whatever he was, it was plain to see Simon could not match him.

"They killed my brother. I want their heads!"

"Yes, I saw that. Believe me, I could not care any less about them or whether or not you have their heads. As far as I'm concerned, you're all already dead. If you cooperate with me and my studies, I will make sure you have everything you need for your little revenge play, my friend."

Simon nodded, and Caleb released him.

"What are you called, human?"

"Simon. You are?"

"I am Caleb, but you will address me as master."

Simon felt the bad taste of submission fill his mouth, but he'd do anything for a chance to punish those he felt were responsible for Cole's death. He bent his head. "Yes... master."

"Come, Simon, we have much to do."

They made their way up the trail and back to Caleb's vehicle.

* * * * *

Tim and Thomas stood with Billy as they put him in the back of the SUV. "I'm riding back with him," Thomas said.

Haul stepped in front of him. "I don't think so, Pratt. This is a military transport. You and your partner ride in the other vehicle."

"Commander Haul, I've been more than accommodating with your blatant disrespect. If you try to keep me out of this vehicle, you and I will have a problem."

Thomas took a step past Haul and moved toward the Humvee. Haul grabbed his arm and pulled him away, and the fight was on. Haul was quick and skilled. He pulled Thomas off balance and attempted to sweep his feet out from under him. Thomas wasn't exactly ill-equipped for this situation either. Thomas anticipated the sweep and checked it, lifting his leg over Haul's. Thomas retaliated with an open palm to the center of his chest. The strike plate in Haul's body armor made the blow futile. Thomas knew Haul was too skilled and protected for any type of standing attack; he had to take this fight to the ground.

Tim looked toward Sites.

"You men gonna stop this madness or stand there and watch?" Tim protested.

"Pratt's a civilian. He doesn't fall under military jurisdiction. Besides, he was once one of us. Let them work it out frogman-style," Sites responded.

The others watched as the two men settled their disagreement. Thomas and Haul circled each other, looking for an opportunity. Feinting a high attack down and then shooting low, Thomas grabbed Haul in a double-leg takedown. As they fell to the ground, Haul pushed high on Thomas's shoulder and twisted his own upper body just enough so that when they hit the ground, he had enough leverage to grab Thomas around the neck. When they fell, he did just that. Thomas found himself in a furious guillotine choke hold. His hands placed around Thomas's neck with tremendous force; Haul's grip felt inescapable. The blood began to cease flowing to his brain, causing his vision to blur, and he knew he had less than a minute left before he lost consciousness. He had no choice. Haul was on his back, so Thomas pulled his feet in as close to his stomach as he could. He pulled Haul's hands apart just enough to put his fingers in between Haul's wrist and his throat. With one motion, Thomas pushed up and rolled forward, up and over Haul, causing him to lose his grip on Thomas's neck. Thomas rolled over and recovered a second before Haul. He lunged forward with a massive elbow smash across Haul's face. The blow was enough to daze him, and Thomas took full advantage. Gaining position behind Haul, he wrapped his legs around him, hooking his heels into Haul's thighs while, at the same time, sliding his arm under Haul's chin in an anaconda-tight rear naked choke. Thomas pushed his weight into Haul's back. Haul was completely defenseless. He reached up, barely conscious, and tapped Thomas's arm, signaling surrender.

Tim took a deep breath as Thomas released Haul. "If you two are done, I'd suggest getting a move on. Daylight's burning."

Thomas got up, sat in the vehicle next to Billy, and closed the door.

"Guess that's decided," Marcus said, barely holding in his smile. To Tim, he said, "Just drop me off about a mile north of here. My boy should be waitin' with my ride, Doc."

With that, everybody loaded up, and they were on the move.

* * * * *

After Marcus had been dropped off with Will back at their vehicle, Thomas and his group headed out to the camp. Tim was so excited to reunite with his family that he could hardly contain it. It was like something he only dared to fantasize about, seeing his family again. Tim turned from the front seat to talk to Thomas.

"Thomas, tell me about Carl. How did he do with all that's happening?"

"He's good, Tim. He's become his own man, that's for sure. You should be very proud. He's made and earned his own way."

"And Claire, how is she?"

"She's a rock that holds us together. She saved my life. I'd be dead after the beating Caleb gave me if it weren't for her. We're all very grateful for your family."

Tim did feel proud, but he knew Thomas was downplaying his role; if it weren't for him, Claire, Carl, and most likely everyone in that group would be dead. "Believe me, Thomas, my gratitude far outweighs any you may feel. Thank you again, my friend."

There were only about four hours left of sunlight. The plan to be in the camp at dusk had to be pushed back due to the situation with Billy, but they still had plans to be there before dark. No one wanted to spend another night exposed if they could avoid it. The group pushed on, and when the camp came into sight, Thomas signaled for them to stop so he could get out and show himself. The lookouts wouldn't recognize the vehicles, and the last thing they needed was for one of Paul's rounds to take someone out.

Paul sat in the makeshift perch, on watch. He spent most of his time up there now. With Henry gone, he didn't feel like there was anyone he could relate to. Ray was constantly trying to reach out to him, but Paul knew, as a padre, it was kind of an obligation. No, he would do his part watching over the group up high in his perch in voluntary isolation.

Paul picked up his radio. "Hicks, we got two—no, make that three vehicles approaching from the south. I don't recognize them. What do you want me to do, Wayne?"

"Stand by, Paul, I'm on my way."

Paul watched as the SUVs pulled up and a man got out. *Holy crap! Forget nine lives. This guy's gonna live forever!* he thought as he watched Thomas exit the vehicle.

Paul was about to key the radio and give Wayne the good news when someone else he recognized stepped out, causing him to just gasp.

"Ah, Wayne, you ain't gonna hardly believe this, but... guess who's back? And he brought company. You might wanna get Claire and Carl. Looks like Daddy's home."

Tim ran into the arms of his wife and son. The three of them held one another and cried and laughed and cried some more. Jessica and Jimmy ran to their dad, and they did much of the same. Jax jumped on his master, joining in on the excitement. Jessica and Jimmy held Tim and his family, and the two families held each other as one. It was a much-needed moment the whole camp shared. Even Mark, Kenny, Rita, and Keylin, who had never even met Tim, were lifted by the reunion.

Jessica looked and saw a handcuffed Billy being ushered from the back of the vehicle into one of the shelters. "What's going on, Dad? What are they doing to him?"

"I'll explain, Jessie, just give me a few moments. I need this, baby." Jessica gave her father the moment, and they just held one another.

"Claire," Tim said, "I'll need your help with my patients. Billy needs his bandages changed, and I need to attend to Sera. Can you see to Billy for me?"

"Yes, Doctor," she said, smiling.

Tim smiled at his wife and grabbed Carl by the shoulder. "You're with me, son." They parted and tended to the injured.

The family's reunion energized the group. Wayne and Thomas brought Tim and Commander Haul into the camp's staging tent, where they explained every detail they had learned. They explained the invasion of the aliens from Usrafax Prime, the Theozin they were willing to destroy the planet over, the blackout tower, and the more immediate threat of the Zperion Spore. Tim and Haul listened intently.

"That fills in so many gaps," Tim said. "We knew this was unprecedented, but the scale was completely alien to us!" he added, pun intended.

Haul took a breath. "Okay, the first priority is to take out that tower."

"I agree," Thomas said. "Do you have the resources for an operation of that magnitude?"

"That's not your concern, Pratt. You've done your part and given us invaluable intel. You're finished now. This is a military operation, and you're no longer cleared for operational status. As for the intel and your new alien girlfriend, they're both for the government to decide what to do with and how to handle."

Thomas stared at Haul with a deep seriousness. "Explain that last part, Haul. How is Sera a government issue?"

"Simple, Pratt. It came here with the intent of destroying not only the United States but also the entire planet. It is an enemy of not only the state but also of the world. A prisoner of war, plain and simple."

"First off, *her* name is Sera. She didn't come here to conquer us but to stop Caleb from destroying the planet. Haul, if I haven't already made it clear, I will do whatever I have to do to protect my people—all my people!"

"Is that a threat, Pratt?"

"Call it a warning!"

Tim stood up. "Enough of this nonsense. It's getting us nowhere. Haul, I have operational command here, so put away the rulers and zip your pants up, both of you. Thomas, you'll have to trust me. We can help you, but Sera will have to come back with us. We need her, and if you are right about her being here to help, then this is the best way."

"I'll talk to her when she wakes up. If she decides to come with us, then okay, but if not and any attempt is made to force her, my people and I will take that as an attack."

"Meaning?" Haul asked through his teeth.

"We'll respond," Thomas simply said as he got up and walked out of the meeting.

"You feel the same way, Hicks?" Haul asked Wayne.

"That's Deputy Hicks, Commander, and the sheriff was very clear. There is no division here. We've been through hell together, christened by fire. That man has led the way, every step of the way, and come out unsinged. It'd be best not to cross him. We're all only here because we've stuck together. All of us, Tim, Claire, and Carl too," Wayne added before following Thomas outside.

Tim turned to Haul. "Get the analog radio. We need to call in all the information we've gathered to the TOC, the tactical operations center. God forbid something happens before we reach base. We can't afford to lose this information."

Wayne walked outside, where Thomas was talking to Jessica. "Wayne, Jessie, come on. I have to talk to you two about Billy. It's ugly, but you need to know the truth."

They walked down by the river, and he explained what had befallen Billy.

Jaw clenched, Wayne tightened his fists as he listened. "Those bastards!" he quietly said.

Guilt flowed through Jessica. She'd left him, and the thought kept circling over and over in her head. Jessica processed her sorrow into anger, and her anger into restraint. There would be a time for retribution, but that time was not now. Her friend needed her more than ever, and she would be there for him. Ray joined them, and they not only prayed for Billy and Sera's recovery but also expressed gratefulness for the new hope.

As they finished their prayer and talk, Mark came down the hill. "Thomas, come quick! Sera's awake!"

Thomas ran to the shelter and found Sera sitting up on the gurney. "Sera, how are you? Are you okay?" he asked.

"Yes, Sheriff, I will recover. I am just a little weak still. The toll of my body healing itself has drained me. I need sustenance."

"Like what, Sera? What exactly is it you eat?"

"Oh, I assumed you knew. We eat people."

Thomas was taken aback, almost at a loss for words. "Wha-what?" It was the first time he'd seen her smile. Thomas felt silly. "Jokes... really? Oh, man, since when did you grow a sense of humor?"

"It was, as you say, 'easing tension.' You must have told them about Caleb and his plans, because I can sense the increased aggression in the soldiers. Their weapons are poised, and they are very tense."

Thomas noted the men at the ready. "Sera, no one is going to touch you or force you to do anything you don't want to do. Now, what can we get you to eat? Maybe Commander Haul?" he said, smiling.

"Amino acids and water. I need to hydrate."

Petty Officer Sites came forward. "Ma'am, this an MRE, meals ready to eat. It'll contain all the proteins and amino acids you'll need," he said, handing her the meal and a large bottle of water.

She looked at Thomas, who nodded in approval. Sera took the food and water. "Thank you, soldier."

"Sites, ma'am. My name is Sites, and you're welcome." As Petty Officer Sites walked away, he ordered the men to stand down and wait outside the tent.

Sera ate the food and earnestly drank the water. "What is the plan, Sheriff?"

"They want us to come with them. We have a fragmented government left, and they may be our last chance. I trust Tim, and he said we should go with them."

"Sheriff, you realize how they'll receive me. I am the enemy. You may not be able to protect me."

"You're right, and I know that is a possibility. We can give them all the information we have and strike out on our own. Whatever you feel, we'll all support it."

"That is appreciated, but the stakes are too high. I will go with them and cooperate. We will need all the help we can get, or all is lost."

Thomas nodded. "Then we leave at daybreak."

Thomas told Tim of their decision.

The entire camp packed up and got ready to move out at first light. They settled in and tried to get some rest. The excitement at the prospect of possibly ending this nightmare that had been their lives for the past eight months meant there was little sleep. Haul was briefing the team on movement. He allowed Thomas to sit in because despite all Haul's reservations, Thomas was still a trained, decorated SEAL. He had proven resourceful enough to stay alive without any military support. He would never tell Thomas this, of course. Haul might have secretly respected him, but respect and trust were two different things.

He believed with certainty that, given the choice between the mission and his group, Pratt would, in every case, choose his group.

That made him a liability. On this particular movement, Pratt would be nothing more than a gun, a tool for Haul to use as necessary.

Haul finished the briefing and pulled Thomas to the side. "Pratt, when we move, we will treat the alien as a POW. It'll be blindfolded and restrained. Before you go all *'I protect my people,'* hear me out. I know you have been in combat with it and you feel close. Maybe you're too close. We have everything to lose here. A major operation is located at our base. Maybe our last chance. The people and equipment there are a lot of all we have left. If, by some slim chance, you're wrong, we lose it all. You have to understand that. It's op-sec. You remember that, don't you? It's not personal."

"I understand operational security just fine, Haul. But she's an ally, not an enemy. We will treat her as such."

"Sheriff! I will comply with Commander Haul's request. Whatever we must do," Sera said from the doorway.

"So it's settled," Haul said. "We move at dawn."

"Sera, are you sure about this?" Thomas asked.

"The choices here have all but expired. This is what we must do."

"Okay, let's get some rest, then. Tomorrow's a big day."

CHAPTER 13

The night seemed to drag on like a snail on a salt trail, slow and agonizing, with the group desperate to get to the base. Commander Haul set his men in a perimeter watch pattern. Paul sat up on his perch alongside US Navy SEAL Petty Officer First-Class Darrel Skalny, team sniper.

"So, Navy man, that's a nice fancy long gun ya got there," Paul said, taking in the frogman's hardware.

"Well, this is an M110 semiautomatic sniper rifle. It's a 7.62-cal gas-operated bolt-action weapon. Range up to eight hundred meters. I got her fitted with a Vortex Viper PST rifle scope. With this baby, I could take the hair off a fly's ass at nine hundred yards," Skalny said, proudly boasting about his weapon.

"Well, this ole thing I got is just a lowly Remington 597. Scoped rimfire huntin' rifle. I ain't ever tried takin' no hair off no fly's ass, but I done sure as hell takin' heads damn near off some Spewers' shoulders!" he replied with a smirk and a wink.

"Good to know. I'm Skalny. My friends call me Rock."

"That 'cause you as smart as one?"

"'Cause my family's Polish. Skalny is Polish for *rock*, and that's easier to pronounce."

"Fair enough. Rock it is," Paul said.

They laughed and continued their watch together.

Thomas was still at odds with treating Sera like an enemy combatant. Although he'd only known her a few months, his sense of character was virtually impeccable. She had put herself at risk for his people and his planet time and again. She was a friend. He knew this in his heart and all the way into his soul. If Caleb was the devil, Sera was the angel God had sent to help them. Sera, however, seemed to have no problem with the arrangement.

"Sera, you didn't have to agree with Haul's condition."

"It was of no consequence. I must share something with you. Be still now." Sera reached up and touched the side of Thomas's head. "Close your eyes. Can you hear me? Now open your eyes." Sera lowered her hand. "Can you still hear me?"

Thomas heard her and noticed her mouth wasn't moving. "What the hell? You're in my head?"

"Yes. It appears, as my body shut down in a comatose state to heal, my mental ability also recovered. As I told you before, the ultraviolet radiation in Earth's atmosphere greatly limits most of our mental capabilities. This one, it seems, has recovered. We can speak telepathically. Also, I can, what we call, *peer* with you. What you see, I can see."

"Okay. For now, though, how about you get out of my head?" Thomas said out loud. "I know it may be different on Usrafax, but here you can't go into someone's head like this uninvited. It is the ultimate violation of our most private and sacred place. Don't do that again, and keep the fact that you can do it between us."

"If you think that is best, Sheriff."

As they walked on, Sera felt like a child that had accidentally and innocently said an offensive thing. She understood his logic, but this interaction would be necessary. This was a natural function on her world. The same as when humans talked to one another. Sera was in midthought when the sensation came over her.

"Infected, Sheriff. They are coming fast from the east! This is no random attack! He's pushing them to us!" Silence was not only pointless but a liability.

"How much time, Sera?"

"It is hard to gauge. From the strength of the signal, ten, twenty minutes maximum."

There was no time to waste. Thomas grabbed his radio and called Wayne. "Wayne, we have incoming from the east! Begin evacuation now! We have ten minutes till they're on top of us."

"Copy that."

Wayne had practiced and run through this procedure count-less of times, so they were ready. The group moved with swiftness and relative quiet. Henry and Mark, both automotive experts, and Keylin, an engineering graduate, all had the responsibility of convert-ing the armored truck James had brought to the camp. It was now the group's main mode of emergency escape. They had spent many daylight hours gathering and salvaging parts from junkyards and countless abandoned heavy-diesel engines. The result was the *Titan*, a modified, refitted six-cycle, eight-cylinder, five-hundred-horse-power engine with a cast-iron block and head. It had an elevated exhaust pipe to handle high water. The gunports had been bored out for better fields of fire, while keeping the edges jagged and razor-sharp. Any offspring trying to crawl inside through the ports would be cut to pieces. They had put four tires on each axle and wrapped them in spiked snow chains. If the outer tires were damaged, the truck could still move at near-optimum functionality. The two most impressive features of this treasure were the cone-shaped needlepoint aluminum front end and the chain flail system. Keylin had designed this six-foot piece of metal to be able to raise and lower six inches from the ground. It would divide any mass of infected to prevent the *Titan* from becoming stuck. The other feature, the chain flail system, had been taken from the mine flail design the army used to clear minefields. The device was attached to the very front of the *Titan*. It used heavy chains and fist-size metal balls attached to a horizontal rapidly rotating rotor held up by two metal arms. With the flip of a switch, the motor would begin spinning the chain and metal balls that would smash anything in their path. The inside was fitted with four seats bolted to the middle of the truck and benches alongside the walls. It could hold eight people securely, seat-belted in.

Thomas gathered Tim and Commander Haul. "We have a breach in the east perimeter. They're moving fast."

"I have men on that ridge, and they just checked in two min-utes ago. If there were incoming, I'd know about it," Haul snapped.

"Recall your men, Haul, now. There's no time. We move in less than ten."

The readiness in Thomas's stature commanded even Haul to respond.

Haul quickly radioed an all-personnel immediate recall and regroup. Haul knew himself to be intractable and stubborn, but he also knew when to listen. Although the mission would always be foremost, the lives of his men were vital to him. Losing men in combat was fated, but wasting the life of a single man was inexplicable. The SEALs moved with unequaled speed and efficiency. They set up a point and rear vehicle protection perimeter around the group to guide and protect the civilians. They were all ready to move within twelve minutes of Sera's warning.

Unfortunately, they weren't fast enough.

The first of the infected leaped out of the tree line, snatching Petty Officer Barnes from the cab of the pickup truck, where he was manning the vehicle's M-249 light machine gun. The reaction was second nature. There was zero panic, only urgency, in the SEALs communication.

"Contact left. The Saw is down. Rock, get on the Saw," Sites ordered.

Skalny slung his rifle over his shoulder and immediately jumped into the cab of the pickup to man the Saw. As the infected jumped from the tree line, Skalny put the light machine gun to work. His sniper skills shone bright as ever, even with the automatic machine gun. His rounds struck their targets as though he were using his scoped weapon. Infected dropped around the camp as rounds from the Saw tore their heads open like ripe melons.

Sites had already jumped from his vehicle in an attempt to locate and rescue his fallen teammate. Barnes was nowhere to be found, and Sites understood how the infected worked. He knew his teammate and friend was no longer himself by now. He remounted the rear vehicle.

"Commander Haul, we are RTM," Sites radioed. The ready-to-move command came over the radio.

Haul knew the fate of his fallen man. "Convoy, move out," he replied.

With that, they began driving out of the camp as the SEALs laid down covering fire.

Everyone else watched as the SEALs did what they did best. Thomas was at home with these familiar maneuvers, but for the rest of the group, it was like watching Da Vinci create the *Mona Lisa*. They were indeed artists, and this was how they created their masterpieces. Carl, in particular, watched with intense fascination. If the SEALs were frightened, their actions didn't betray them. They were calculated, controlled, and most importantly, deadly effective.

The infected continued their assault. Sera's forewarning, the group's preparation, and the SEALs' overwhelming firepower and pinpoint training made the infected's attack possible to escape. Moving at night was never good, but sometimes, as now, necessary. The sound of gunfire grew more infrequent as the convoy distanced themselves from the infected's onslaught. Soon it was all quiet, and the group settled a bit. Some even slept.

Jessica, Jimmy, and Danny rode in the vehicle with Thomas and Billy. Jax sat in the rear with Wayne as they both kept a watchful eye out. Senior Chief Miles, who was driving, reached back and handed Wayne a pair of NVGs (night vision goggles). "Here you go, Wayne. These will help you keep our rear in the clear," he said with a smile.

Thomas sat in the front seat next to the senior chief.

"So I hear you got a helluva story, Sheriff."

"No more than any of you guys, I'm sure, Senior. I've been lucky, or blessed, according to Pastor Ray. Depends on what you want to believe, I guess."

"As a black man from the South, you best believe I know who my Lord and Savior is, but the stuff I've seen makes me question most everything else I thought I believed in," Miles said.

"Yeah, me too. Since this thing started, all I've seen is turmoil, death, and despair, but now there's light. We have a chance, and where there's a chance, there's hope. That's something we've been in short supply of lately."

Jessica was sitting next to Billy. She put her hand on top of his, looking closely at him for the first time since they returned. He looked so different. Not just his scars or the bandage covering his ruined eye. Billy looked like a man who had felt the burn of hate and now would be content to watch the rest of the world feel it too.

"Billy, I'm so sorry I left you. I see what they did to you, and I know it's my fault. I tried, Billy, but it was so cold. I was weak, and they did this to you, and I don't know what else." The tears began to stream down her face.

Billy turned his head toward her. "Jess, this isn't your fault. Cole and Simon showed me a truth. Maybe not everyone's truth, but a truth. This world had monsters in it long before these freaks landed on our planet. We're blanketed by evil, and there will be few who will survive. Those who do will either be just as evil or be willing to become so. No one goes untouched in this."

Jessica wasn't sure how or why, but she understood exactly what he was saying, and she agreed. She looked at his handcuffs.

"Dad, can we please take these off him? I mean, where's he gonna go?"

"Senior?" Thomas asked.

"Commander Haul will have my butt if the prisoner arrives at the compound unrestrained, so please make sure they're back on before we arrive," Miles said, handing the key back to Jessica, who uncuffed him.

Billy rubbed his wrist. The freedom of movement felt better than he'd admit. He leaned his head against the window and went to sleep.

* * * * *

The warmth of the sunlight through the window woke Thomas. He looked around the vehicle. Jessica was sleeping with her head on Billy's chest. Billy was still sleeping with his head against the window. Jimmy and Danny also slept. Wayne sat still, alert, in the rear row of the SUV.

"Morning, Sheriff. We're getting ready to stop for a quick R&R in Fairfax," Miles said.

The vehicles pulled into the small town outside Arlington, where they stopped at a truck stop. The most direct route to the compound had been northeast, but considering the infected's attack came from that direction, they had to reroute and go directly east through Virginia. The reroute had cost fuel they hadn't planned on using, so this stop was more than a simple R&R. They wouldn't make the compound without refueling. As everyone got out of their respective vehicles, Thomas saw Haul and his team gathered near the pumps. Thomas walked over.

"Is everything okay, Commander?"

"Come over, Pratt. This affects you and your people. We have to get these pumps going, but obviously, there's no power. These small-town gas stations aren't going to help, but these big truck stops always have generators. We did a perimeter check, and it's not out here. But we did find a venting pipe."

"Let me guess. It's in the basement," Thomas suggested.

Haul nodded. "We'll send in a team. Hopefully, if there's resistance, it'll be mild. Senior Chief, assemble your men to search and clear the basement. Find and secure the generator, Hooyah?"

"Hooyah, Lieutenant. Sites, Rock, Lamer, Tillson, on me," Miles responded.

Thomas grabbed his elbow. "Senior, with the loss of Barnes, you're a man shy. Simple clearing hasn't changed since my days. Let me help."

"Not my call, Sheriff. Lieutenant?"

"You're my NCO, Miles. Your call. Just be sure."

"Suit up, Sheriff. Welcome back to the bigs."

Thomas geared up with weapons and spare equipment. It was just like riding a bike. Everything fit right into place. Sites saw Thomas's subtle enthusiasm.

"Lookin' right at home, *Lieutenant*," he said, only half-kidding. "Senior Chief wants me to go over some things with you. We had to modify some weaponry since all this happened. This is a UV burster. They're one great invention when you got a handful of... what did you call them? Spewers? Yeah, Spewers around you. Pull the pin just like a standard grenade. Toss, release the spoon, and you get about eight seconds of UV radiation. Not enough to kill them, but it'll buy you some precious seconds. The body armor is also lined with a UV emitter. It puts out small doses of UV radiation. We keep the dose low enough so it doesn't burn us up too, but it's a fine line. Pretty sure if we survive this, we'll end up with skin cancer, but you know, what can you do?"

"Okay, I got it. Anything else?"

"Everything else is pretty much by the numbers, Sheriff. You know the drill, I'm sure. We got briefing in ten by the *Titan*."

"Roger that."

Thomas found Sera. "Sera, are you picking up anything from the gas station?"

"There is a high volume of infected activity in the area, but I'm not sensing any in the gas station. You must exercise caution all the same. The infected may be able to move through the same tunnel system that allowed them to almost overwhelm us before," Sera said.

"That's why I want you on comms while we're in there. Anything changes, you give us the heads-up."

"Would it not be better if I simply accompanied you inside?"

"No, Sera, not this time." Thomas knew getting Haul to sign off on Sera actually being part of the breach team was a losing argument. There was no use in pushing that envelope.

The briefing wrapped up, and the team moved into place. The gas station had plenty of windows, so the first floor was clear. They stacked on both sides of the entrance. Two-, three-man single-file line formations. With silence being key, the man at the rear of the line placed his hand on the shoulder of the man in front of him. Squeezing the shoulder signaled readiness. The two men facing each other after receiving the shoulder squeeze gave a nod to each other, acknowledging the men were ready, and they made entry. They were precision made flesh. As each man moved into the gas station, they began going the opposite direction as the man across from him to clear the area. Moving in, they took control of each corner of the room. After securing the corners of the first room, each man signaled all clear, and the team moved on to the next doorway.

* * * * *

Sera sat on the tailgate of the pickup truck. She had an earpiece attached to her ear and a mic, ready to communicate with the team. A

You've got to move now!" Sites yelled in an uncharac-
nicked tone that told Thomas the intensity of the sit-
rabbed Miles and didn't even bother to look up at the
ve of what he knew was certain death. They made their
eps and out the door into the lifesaving sunlight as the
drew back down into darkness.

he hell happened? Why didn't you two use the body
ights?"

gger broke in the fall off the steps," Miles replied.

just forgot I had them," Thomas said.

t of the group rushed to help the men. They refueled
nd then were once again on the move. Next stop, the

* * * * *

udied Simon intently. He'd even gone so far as to dis-
Simon's rapid healing and his deadened nerve endings
sia or even IVs unnecessary. It was fascinating! The off-
ndeed injected larva into Simon's body, but Cole had
i's arm before the larva could attach to the vital organs.
en larva had managed to hit her mark. She had attached
column and secreted into Simon's body, giving him
nd healing. Without the other larva to shut down the
organs, he was able to remain functional. It was what
called dumb luck, a one-in-a-million chance. The odds
this anomaly, even with a vast control group analyzing
ducting experiments, were immeasurable.

my friend, you truly are one of a kind. That makes you
e. I'll have some use for you."

the people that killed my little brother. The sheriff, the
ed him, and that freak show witch. I want them dead.
o your own dirty work!"

sation came over Simon, very mildly at first. Then, as if
e ripping his fingernails out or smashing the tips of his
all-peen hammer, the pain rushed over him so quickly
ground into a fetal position.

---

sudden rush came over her, and she became dizzy and disorientated. Haul stood nearby and noticed her apparent distress. "Problem?" the commander asked.

"Something is wrong, Commander. There is a strange type of… psychic echo, for lack of a better word."

"Explain, ma'am. Are my men in danger?"

"I cannot be certain. It is as though someone is hitting a trash can lid with a metal stick in a large empty warehouse. I can sense infected activity in the area, but I cannot be sure as to their precise location. Perhaps we should pull your men and Sheriff Pratt out."

"Ma'am, we leave without fuel, and we might as well lie down and die right here. The men stay on mission. Still, all the same, let them know. Looks like they're on their own down there."

Sera passed the information on to the men. They took it as well as could be expected.

"Well, hell, thanks for pissing in my cornflakes, lady!" Tillson muttered.

"Stow that chatter, Till. We still track our mission, copy?" Miles replied.

"Roger that, Senior Chief."

The men moved from room to room, clearing them as they went. Their NVGs gave them the light they needed to move, but the uneasiness that came from losing Sera's psychic over-watch didn't go unnoticed.

"Anybody know the difference between Simba and O. J. Simpson?" Thomas asked.

Miles picked up on Thomas's attempt to put the men at ease. "Be advised, Sheriff, any jokes based on race, religion, gender, or sexual orientation are strictly prohibited by US Navy regulations… unless it's funny."

"Well," Thomas said, "one's an African lion, the other's just a lying African."

The seconds of silence were followed by steady, audible laughing. It had worked, and the men relaxed just enough.

"Bingo, Senior, I've got joy," Lamer radioed as he spotted the generator.

The generator was fully fueled. Lamer primed and started it.

"Okay, guys, let's form up and move it out of here. Skip the pleasantries, gentlemen, and let's get the fu—"

"Contact left!" Tillson shouted suddenly.

With machinelike precision, the team rotated their weapons left and faced the threat. The infected swarmed toward them like a wave of death. "Light 'em up!" Miles ordered, and the men replied with an awesome barrage of definitive firepower. The wave of infected fell almost as fast as they arrived.

Thomas knew better than to think the situation had reached a conclusion, as did the senior chief. "Form a line! Prepare to move out using fire maneuvers, three teams of two. Thomas, on me. On my command… move!" Miles's orders were clear, precise, and executed without flaw.

The six men lined up in a horizontal line. In pairs, they fell back toward the exit. The other four held fast to repel any resistance and defend the others' movement. Lamer and Tillson moved first. Once the men were in position, the next two would move, while the other two pairs stood fast to defend their forwarded position. This would provide a steady flow of suppressing fire. There would always be two moving and four covering them. Sites and Rock were next to move. As Senior Chief Miles and Thomas prepared to move, the second wave of infected arrived. The four men began firing as Miles and Thomas ran back.

"Crawlers!" Sites shouted over the gunfire.

The offspring were much smaller, faster, and harder to hit, even for the seasoned eye of a SEAL. The extra time it took to hone in on the Crawlers stifled the rapid movement of the team. It was apparent they were not going to be able to fall back fast enough for the team to escape.

"Frag out!" Miles shouted.

At the command, the SEALs simultaneously converted from the firearms to the UV bursters. Six modified grenades rolled into the approaching horde of infected and offspring. As they detonated, the infected retreated and Crawlers were either killed or injured too severely to continue their assault. The men retreated quickly, know-

ing this was only a temporary ⸻ to the sunlight.

"Break rank and fall back! ⸻

Tillson, Sites, and Lamer ⸻ Thomas followed. Miles turne⸻ recovered from the UV blast. O⸻ the air, grabbing him and kno⸻ off the side of the steps. The ⸻ closing quickly.

"Man down! Lay down su⸻ Thomas yelled out, assuming co⸻

The team reacted instinc⸻ infected on his back. He rolled,⸻ pushed with all his might, launch⸻ his weapon, but never leveled it,⸻ vise-grip squeeze with blinding ⸻ He could see them, but even wit⸻ enough shot to drop the infecte⸻ He jumped over what was left ⸻ and into the fight.

"What the hell are you doi⸻ too damn many!" Sites yelled to ⸻

"Your body armor UV light⸻

Sites's advice to Thomas w⸻ fire. Thomas moved toward Mil⸻ infected. Miles delivered a crushi⸻ it couldn't regurgitate the offspri⸻ infected. Sensing it could not p⸻ automatically reverted to its secon⸻ ilate, it would terminate. The inf⸻ With the infected's strength, it wo⸻ snap his neck, and it would take b⸻ faster, though. Finally gaining the ⸻ his round, striking the infected j⸻ dropping it to the ground.

"You see, Simon, you may think I cannot control you like I do the other hosts, but I do control the offspring attached to your spinal column, and as you can see, you can feel pain. I can give you massive amounts of pleasure or insurmountable pain. The choice is yours. So in essence, I very much do control you."

The pain eased as Caleb allowed Simon to recover. Simon slowly got back to his feet.

"Do we understand each other, Simon?"

"Yes… master," Simon answered hesitantly yet with a firmness that left no doubt Caleb was in charge.

"Now, as to your request. The sheriff and his lackey are of no concern to me. Do with them as you wish, but the *freak show witch*, as you put it, her name is Sera. She is on a special mission for me to help quash this little rebellion the humans think I know nothing about. You will not touch her or interfere with her progress in any way."

"Yes, master. Sera is your agent? She fights very passionately for this sheriff and his people. Are you sure she is still loyal to you?"

"Quite sure, Simon. We have no secrets from each other. We could not, even if we wanted to. You see, my dear Simon, Sera and I are linked. Our thoughts are intertwined. There is no possibility of betrayal. She is not some agent as you say. She is my sister."

CHAPTER 14

The convoy arrived at the gate of what Thomas assumed was the compound. The gate was unmanned and open, so the vehicles passed right through. It was a huge compound. There were several hangar bays that were old, run-down, and empty. Whatever aircraft had been housed here were long gone.

The lead vehicle containing Commander Haul led the convoy into one of the hangar bays and came to a stop. Haul took out a keypad controller and pushed in a series of combination codes. The ground in front of them lowered fifteen feet, making a ramp for the vehicles to drive down. As the last vehicle drove into the tunnel, the ramp rose, sealing the entrance. The vehicles then came to a giant twenty-foot blast door. Thomas noted two M45 .50-caliber machine gun quad mounts, one on both sides of the door. These weapons were modified to be fired either by remote or set to fire using proximity sensors. Four mounted .50-caliber machine guns on each mount. Nothing short of an Abrams tank was coming through here without permission. Commander Haul keyed in the proper codes, deactivated the weapon turrets, and opened the blast doors. The vehicles drove farther into the compound until they came to a massive industrial freight elevator. The elevator was large enough for the entire convoy.

Commander Haul made sure all the vehicles were loaded on and secured.

"Everybody can get out of the vehicles and stretch your legs. The way down is slow. We're going over thirty meters below the surface, and the lift moves slowly to compensate for the weight. We got a good twenty minutes till we get to the first level."

"You see, Simon, you may think I cannot control you like I do the other hosts, but I do control the offspring attached to your spinal column, and as you can see, you can feel pain. I can give you massive amounts of pleasure or insurmountable pain. The choice is yours. So in essence, I very much do control you."

The pain eased as Caleb allowed Simon to recover. Simon slowly got back to his feet.

"Do we understand each other, Simon?"

"Yes... master," Simon answered hesitantly yet with a firmness that left no doubt Caleb was in charge.

"Now, as to your request. The sheriff and his lackey are of no concern to me. Do with them as you wish, but the *freak show witch*, as you put it, her name is Sera. She is on a special mission for me to help quash this little rebellion the humans think I know nothing about. You will not touch her or interfere with her progress in any way."

"Yes, master. Sera is your agent? She fights very passionately for this sheriff and his people. Are you sure she is still loyal to you?"

"Quite sure, Simon. We have no secrets from each other. We could not, even if we wanted to. You see, my dear Simon, Sera and I are linked. Our thoughts are intertwined. There is no possibility of betrayal. She is not some agent as you say. She is my sister."

CHAPTER 14

The convoy arrived at the gate of what Thomas assumed was the compound. The gate was unmanned and open, so the vehicles passed right through. It was a huge compound. There were several hangar bays that were old, run-down, and empty. Whatever aircraft had been housed here were long gone.

The lead vehicle containing Commander Haul led the convoy into one of the hangar bays and came to a stop. Haul took out a keypad controller and pushed in a series of combination codes. The ground in front of them lowered fifteen feet, making a ramp for the vehicles to drive down. As the last vehicle drove into the tunnel, the ramp rose, sealing the entrance. The vehicles then came to a giant twenty-foot blast door. Thomas noted two M45 .50-caliber machine gun quad mounts, one on both sides of the door. These weapons were modified to be fired either by remote or set to fire using proximity sensors. Four mounted .50-caliber machine guns on each mount. Nothing short of an Abrams tank was coming through here without permission. Commander Haul keyed in the proper codes, deactivated the weapon turrets, and opened the blast doors. The vehicles drove farther into the compound until they came to a massive industrial freight elevator. The elevator was large enough for the entire convoy.

Commander Haul made sure all the vehicles were loaded on and secured.

"Everybody can get out of the vehicles and stretch your legs. The way down is slow. We're going over thirty meters below the surface, and the lift moves slowly to compensate for the weight. We got a good twenty minutes till we get to the first level."

ing this was only a temporary reprieve. They had to get upstairs and to the sunlight.

"Break rank and fall back!" Miles ordered.

Tillson, Sites, and Lamer reached the top of the stairs. Rock and Thomas followed. Miles turned to race up the steps as the infected recovered from the UV blast. One of them leaped thirty feet through the air, grabbing him and knocking him through the handrail and off the side of the steps. The other infected were right behind and closing quickly.

"Man down! Lay down suppressing fire and keep them back!" Thomas yelled out, assuming control of the team.

The team reacted instinctively. Miles hit the floor with the infected on his back. He rolled, got his feet under the infected, and pushed with all his might, launching the infected off him. Miles drew his weapon, but never leveled it, as the infected grabbed his wrist in a vise-grip squeeze with blinding speed. Thomas heard Miles yell out. He could see them, but even with his NVGs, he could not get a clear-enough shot to drop the infected. There was only one thing to do. He jumped over what was left of the handrail down onto the floor and into the fight.

"What the hell are you doing? We can't hold them! There are too damn many!" Sites yelled to Thomas.

"Your body armor UV lights, turn on your UV lights!"

Sites's advice to Thomas was overpowered by sounds of gunfire. Thomas moved toward Miles to try to get a clear shot at the infected. Miles delivered a crushing blow to the infected's larynx so it couldn't regurgitate the offspring. This did little to stave off the infected. Sensing it could not produce the offspring, the infected automatically reverted to its secondary instinct. If it could not assimilate, it would terminate. The infected grabbed Miles by the throat. With the infected's strength, it would take a small amount of force to snap his neck, and it would take but an instant. Thomas's bullet was faster, though. Finally gaining the position he needed, Thomas fired his round, striking the infected just centimeters above its ear and dropping it to the ground.

"Move! You've got to move now!" Sites yelled in an uncharacteristically panicked tone that told Thomas the intensity of the situation. He grabbed Miles and didn't even bother to look up at the incoming wave of what he knew was certain death. They made their way up the steps and out the door into the lifesaving sunlight as the infected withdrew back down into darkness.

"What the hell happened? Why didn't you two use the body armor's UV lights?"

"My trigger broke in the fall off the steps," Miles replied.

"Hell, I just forgot I had them," Thomas said.

The rest of the group rushed to help the men. They refueled the vehicles and then were once again on the move. Next stop, the compound.

* * * * *

Caleb studied Simon intently. He'd even gone so far as to dissect Simon. Simon's rapid healing and his deadened nerve endings made anesthesia or even IVs unnecessary. It was fascinating! The offspring had indeed injected larva into Simon's body, but Cole had cut off Simon's arm before the larva could attach to the vital organs. Only the queen larva had managed to hit her mark. She had attached to the spinal column and secreted into Simon's body, giving him his strength and healing. Without the other larva to shut down the host's major organs, he was able to remain functional. It was what the humans called dumb luck, a one-in-a-million chance. The odds of repeating this anomaly, even with a vast control group analyzing data and conducting experiments, were immeasurable.

"Simon, my friend, you truly are one of a kind. That makes you valuable to me. I'll have some use for you."

"I want the people that killed my little brother. The sheriff, the boy who killed him, and that freak show witch. I want them dead. Until then, do your own dirty work!"

The sensation came over Simon, very mildly at first. Then, as if someone were ripping his fingernails out or smashing the tips of his toes with a ball-peen hammer, the pain rushed over him so quickly he fell on the ground into a fetal position.

sudden rush came over her, and she became dizzy and disorientated. Haul stood nearby and noticed her apparent distress. "Problem?" the commander asked.

"Something is wrong, Commander. There is a strange type of… psychic echo, for lack of a better word."

"Explain, ma'am. Are my men in danger?"

"I cannot be certain. It is as though someone is hitting a trash can lid with a metal stick in a large empty warehouse. I can sense infected activity in the area, but I cannot be sure as to their precise location. Perhaps we should pull your men and Sheriff Pratt out."

"Ma'am, we leave without fuel, and we might as well lie down and die right here. The men stay on mission. Still, all the same, let them know. Looks like they're on their own down there."

Sera passed the information on to the men. They took it as well as could be expected.

"Well, hell, thanks for pissing in my cornflakes, lady!" Tillson muttered.

"Stow that chatter, Till. We still track our mission, copy?" Miles replied.

"Roger that, Senior Chief."

The men moved from room to room, clearing them as they went. Their NVGs gave them the light they needed to move, but the uneasiness that came from losing Sera's psychic over-watch didn't go unnoticed.

"Anybody know the difference between Simba and O. J. Simpson?" Thomas asked.

Miles picked up on Thomas's attempt to put the men at ease. "Be advised, Sheriff, any jokes based on race, religion, gender, or sexual orientation are strictly prohibited by US Navy regulations… unless it's funny."

"Well," Thomas said, "one's an African lion, the other's just a lying African."

The seconds of silence were followed by steady, audible laughing. It had worked, and the men relaxed just enough.

"Bingo, Senior, I've got joy," Lamer radioed as he spotted the generator.

The generator was fully fueled. Lamer primed and started it.

"Okay, guys, let's form up and move it out of here. Skip the pleasantries, gentlemen, and let's get the fu—"

"Contact left!" Tillson shouted suddenly.

With machinelike precision, the team rotated their weapons left and faced the threat. The infected swarmed toward them like a wave of death. "Light 'em up!" Miles ordered, and the men replied with an awesome barrage of definitive firepower. The wave of infected fell almost as fast as they arrived.

Thomas knew better than to think the situation had reached a conclusion, as did the senior chief. "Form a line! Prepare to move out using fire maneuvers, three teams of two. Thomas, on me. On my command… move!" Miles's orders were clear, precise, and executed without flaw.

The six men lined up in a horizontal line. In pairs, they fell back toward the exit. The other four held fast to repel any resistance and defend the others' movement. Lamer and Tillson moved first. Once the men were in position, the next two would move, while the other two pairs stood fast to defend their forwarded position. This would provide a steady flow of suppressing fire. There would always be two moving and four covering them. Sites and Rock were next to move. As Senior Chief Miles and Thomas prepared to move, the second wave of infected arrived. The four men began firing as Miles and Thomas ran back.

"Crawlers!" Sites shouted over the gunfire.

The offspring were much smaller, faster, and harder to hit, even for the seasoned eye of a SEAL. The extra time it took to hone in on the Crawlers stifled the rapid movement of the team. It was apparent they were not going to be able to fall back fast enough for the team to escape.

"Frag out!" Miles shouted.

At the command, the SEALs simultaneously converted from the firearms to the UV bursters. Six modified grenades rolled into the approaching horde of infected and offspring. As they detonated, the infected retreated and Crawlers were either killed or injured too severely to continue their assault. The men retreated quickly, know-

"Can we take the hood off Sera's head, please, Commander?" Thomas asked.

"Yeah, should be fine."

Thomas went over to Sera and removed the blackout hood. He moved to help Billy from the vehicle so he could stretch out.

"How about removing the handcuffs from Billy, Commander? Where's he gonna go?"

"Negative, Pratt. He remains cuffed until we get him into a holding cell and Admiral Tomlinson confers with acting president Martinez. They'll hear your case and decide a course of action."

"President Martinez? Secretary of State Felix Martinez is now the president?"

"President Johnson, Vice President Henderson, the speaker of the House, and the president pro tempore of the Senate were all killed during the initial attacks in Washington and New York. Therefore, Secretary Martinez became President Martinez, until such time as an election can be held."

What was the extent of the death and damage from this invasion? Just what was left of the world he knew? And could they even recover from this? There was so much to take in. Thomas was sitting in the vehicle, deep in thought, with the door open, when Tim came over to him. "Thomas, as soon as we reach the lower level, I want you to come to medical. I don't think your ribs are broken, but we do need to x-ray them and change your wrapping."

"Yeah, okay, sure thing, Tim. What can you tell us about the base?"

Tim began to fill the group in on the facility.

The platform reached the lower level, and the convoy proceeded to the garage. Designed in 1963 after the Cuban Missile Crisis, the compound had been continually upgraded over the last fifty years. Maximum capacity was set up to accommodate a thousand people. At last count, there was just under that. Totaling four levels, the compound was strategically separated. The lower level was for transport, equipment, and weapons storage. Generators and fueling stations were also located there. The ceiling of the lower level was supported by steel beams that ran from the floor along the walls, which were nothing more than the Arcadian earth the fortress was built under. The compound's lower-level garage was the size of three football fields. There were various vehicles there, including Humvees, armored SUVs, and even some civilian cars. Flickering lights made the garage dim, although lighting was sufficient. The floor above held offices, meeting rooms, the tactical operating center (TOC), and the holding facility. Secured bedrooms and living spaces for high-level staff and their assigned security details were also there. Much of this floor had keypad and keycard-protected doors, and security was very strict. The second level was general living quarters and facilities. The medical wing and research labs made up a large section of the east part of the second level. The top floor consists of the dining hall, kitchen, recreation center, library, and spare restrooms and showers. The top three levels of the compound had a very sterile feeling, with bright lighting and cream-colored title floors and walls.

The group unloaded their supplies and gathered together. Jessica stayed close to Billy.

Claire spoke to Thomas. "Honey, we'll take the kids to the dining room with Petty Officer Sites. A delicious meal will work wonders. We'll get them settled while you get situated. Thomas, no matter what, you saved and took care of over a dozen people in the most impossible situation in history. Thank you." She gave him a long hug and a soft kiss on his cheek. "God is with you, and you're doing His great work," she said in his ear before she took the kids and the others with Petty Officer Sites.

"End of the world or not, I don't normally let another man snuggle with my woman like that." Tim smiled. "Now, let's get you to medical. There is someone else I want you to meet."

Thomas watched as the compound police took Billy into custody from the SEAL team. Jessica gave Billy a hug as they prepared to move him to a holding cell. "I'll come see you as soon as I can, okay?" she said.

The officer took him by the arm to lead him away. "It'll be okay, ma'am. We'll get him medical attention, and then we'll get him some food. We got him. You can come see him in a few hours."

Jessica nodded and let him go.

* * * * *

Sera sat in a conference room at a large oval table. The room fit about twenty-five people, but for now, it was just her and the two police officers that had been assigned to her. She sat quietly with her thoughts and established her mental link.

"Caleb, are you there? Can you hear me?"

"Yes, sister, I am here. I have monitored your progress, and I am very pleased. You have their utmost trust. I have scanned their thoughts regularly. Apart from this Commander Haul, they trust you completely. He will have to be dealt with in time. Now that I have this location, I will swarm the hosts upon this facility and eliminate them once and for all."

"Is that wise, brother? The humans may serve to further our purpose still. Are there not still more of these pockets of Terran resistance? Would it not be logical that the factions be correlative? One would, in fact, lead to the others. It would be much more efficacious to dispense with the species in one fell stroke. It is time-efficient, and there is no benefit in lingering. We must do this for the survival of our planet and our people, but there is no reason not to be civilized."

"Yes, little sister. I will continue to monitor your progress. Find out what you can regarding the location of the other groups, and let us end this and go home."

Just then, the door to the conference room opened. A man entered, surrounded by an entourage of security and advisers. He was a younger man, maybe forty-five. He was Hispanic and had black hair with grayish streaks, more than likely brought on by recent events. He extended his hand out to her. "Sera, right? I'm President Martinez. I understand we owe you a great deal of gratitude. We have much to discuss, ma'am."

"Yes, Mr. President, we surely do, sir."

Sera had been among the humans and had grown quite fond of them, but her planet and her people would perish without this. She knew what she must do, and she would carry out the plan without hesitation or deviation. She was thoroughly convinced all other possible avenues had been explored and there were no other possibilities. Caleb had been her protector, big brother, and faithful guide all her life. His plan had been atrocious, and there was no choice now. Caleb had shown her that the cost of the destruction of a planet and its inhabitants was necessary for their planet's legacy. She had expressed this to her brother, and he was very pleased. They would celebrate her as a hero after this. She was no hero, but neither did she feel that she was a monster. The weight of this betrayal was not lost on her, but she would not be swayed, no matter the cost.

* * * * *

"Okay, Thomas, get your shirt off and have a seat up on the exam table. Julia will be with you shortly. She's just on her way up from examining Billy."

No sooner had Tim finished his sentence than Dr. Anderson walked into the room.

"Thomas, this is Dr. Julia Anderson. Doctor, Sheriff Thomas Pratt."

Thomas lightly shook Dr. Anderson's hand. He remembered her from the videos he had recovered from the lab at the university. She was even more beautiful in person, Thomas thought to himself.

"Okay, Thomas, first thing I need to do is check out those ribs. I understand you fell out of a building. How long ago was that?"

"Maybe a week or so ago. It's hard to keep track of time lately."

"I understand. Being so far underground, I don't know if it's day or night."

Dr. Anderson ran her hands across Thomas's ribs. Her cold hands and the pressure on his bruised ribs caused him to flinch mildly.

"Sorry, I know my hands are a little cold," she said.

"Trust me, Doc, this is the most action I've had from a pretty girl since even before all the fire and brimstone," Thomas said.

"Yeah, I bet you're a regular ladies' man, Sheriff."

"Only one lady, and she was one in a million."

"Okay, Sheriff. Nothing broken. You seem to be in one piece. A pretty bruised and battered piece, but one piece nonetheless."

"Can I get dressed now?"

"Sure. Uh, one more thing. I need to get some blood work on you really quick."

Julia drew his blood, and he put his shirt back on.

"Hmm, hey, Doc? I hear they serve a pretty mean meatloaf. Can I buy you dinner? It's the least I can do after the free checkup."

"Uh, free? You mean you don't have insurance? Great!" She smiled.

Thomas found himself returning to his high school *golly* smile, but he couldn't seem to stop. She decided to let him off the hook. "I've got some things to tie up here, and there are a lot of very important people anxiously waiting to talk to you. I doubt they would appreciate me hijacking their newfound golden boy. Tell you what? How about I finish up here and we meet for a late dinner afterward?"

"It's a deal, Doc."

"Please, call me Julie, Thomas."

Thomas left for his meetings with a feeling he thought for sure was long gone, anticipation. He'd forgotten what it felt like to look forward to something.

As Thomas closed the door to the medical room, Tim came out from the back room. "Did you get it, Julie?"

"Yes, I got it. Do you think there's a chance?"

"Well, with the blood sample I collected from Sera while she was unconscious, and if I'm right about Thomas, then yes, I think there's a very good chance. We don't have any time to spare. Begin the tests right away."

"Yes, Tim."

Tim hated keeping this from Thomas and the others, but if he was right, it wasn't something Thomas would need on his mind. He was doing this for Thomas's own good. That's what he told himself, anyway.

* * * * *

Caleb had been busy. He needed Simon to handle the task of eliminating the resistance. In all honesty, Caleb felt it would command too much of his attention. There were much more pressing issues he needed to attend to, and this was not worth his time and effort. Simon was more than sufficient, especially now that Caleb had equipped him with upgrades. Caleb had replaced Simon's missing limb with bionic cybernetics. It responded to Simon's offspring, allowing him to control it as he would any other part of his body. It added crushing power to his already-incredible strength. Caleb also modified Simon's offspring to greatly increase his sense of sight and sound. If Simon was going to clean up Caleb's human problem, then he would need help. Caleb's greatest gift, far above all the others, was the partial control he gave Simon over the infected. Through the offspring, Simon could now *point* the infected in the direction he needed them to attack. Simon was a fluke, but a fortuitous one, and Caleb would take full advantage of it.

* * * * *

Jessica took Billy his food and sat inside the holding cell with him as he ate. Billy hadn't had a solid meal in months, although he didn't feel he had an appetite. When Jessica brought down the hot rib eye steak, baked potato, and asparagus in a butter sauce, he dug in with a fierceness that was almost savage-like. Billy had to pull himself together and remember that he had company. He looked up at Jessica with butter sauce around his mouth and grease on his fingers. Following an awkward silent moment, the two of them burst out in an uncontrollable fit of laughter.

"I did the same thing. No hating here," she said, wiping away a tear.

Billy finished his meal with more bearing, and once he was done, the two friends sat and talked. The mood became somber.

"Billy, I know what they did to you, what they made you do to them. I'm so sorry I left you. I just needed to get my dad. With all the grief I've given him over what he does, I knew he'd come for you, and I knew he'd get you out. It would be hard, it would be bloody, and people would die, but he'd get you out. That used to scare me, knowing my dad dealt hand in hand with so much death. I used it to blame him for my mother's death. Now, though, I see him. I never saw him before. In this world infected with death, Thomas Bradley Pratt falls into place like a stroke of a great painter creating his masterpiece portrait of oblivion. He doesn't scare me anymore. He's a necessity, Billy. Without him, we all would already be dead. I know you may hate him, blame him for your situation, but I'm here to tell you something he's told me time and again. GROW UP! I couldn't hear that before because I couldn't see him, so I couldn't hear him. The world has opened my eyes in the most horrible way, worse than any man could imagine. Now we need each other in ways that could only be understood if the world turned on itself, and it has. I'm here, Billy. I left you before, but never again. We're family now, Billy Hall. For better or worse, we're what we got."

"I never told you this, but your mother used to babysit me. I was, like, ten or eleven. I remember the first time she came over. I had been protesting all evening, hell-bent on convincing my parents I was old enough to watch after myself. That was until Suzy rang the doorbell. I opened the door, and man, that was it. One hundred percent ten-year-old true love. She musta been about sixteen. She was, hands down, the prettiest girl in town, maybe the county. She was so sweet to me. Never treated me like the dumb, lovestruck kid I was. She was already dating your father by then. Thomas Pratt was it, too. He was a star halfback, one of the best in the country, and a state-ranked wrestler. He knew me and, well, every guy around had it bad for your mom. They both took me in under their wing like a little brother. Your dad always represented the highest levels of achievement to me. Things I could only wish for were second nature to him. From scoring touchdowns to winning state in two sports, marrying the perfect girl, and not just becoming a US Navy SEAL but commanding a team. Thomas Pratt could not fail. I came back home after the army and joined the department just to work with him. Jackie and I could have gone anywhere. I could've joined any big-city police department. I wanted to work with the best and learn. I still carried hope of becoming half the man my hero, your father, was… is. Then the sickness came to Ghostwood, took your mother. I don't think you know, but it took mine too. I was away during the bulk of it.

"I don't blame your father for what happened to me. I hated the fact that when he lay down and quit, I couldn't find a way to push forward on my own. I had put all my eggs into his basket, and when it broke, I was just some lost little puppy without him. I'll never be that attached again. Now we're supposed to be bedfellows with the same bottom-feeding parasites that caused all this, that killed our town, our friends, and family… my Jackie. He fell down. Falling down, I can forgive, but falling in… I'll die first."

They were silent for a while after that, and Jessica sat with him a while longer. She got up and hugged him.

"I'll be back tomorrow, okay? They said the steak was a special meal for our first day here, so don't expect too much. It'll probably be franks and beans," she said, smiling.

"I'll keep my expectations to a minimum," he said as Jessica walked out the cell.

* * * * *

Tim came back to his room, where his wife and son were waiting for him. Something was wrong. Claire had a look of panic on her face. That was something she rarely exhibited, even on the most stressful shifts she and Tim had worked together with in the ER. She and Carl sat on the bed, but she got up as Tim entered.

"Talk to your son," she simply stated and left the room.

Carl sat on the bed, his hands in his lap and his head slightly bowed.

Tim plopped down next to his son. He took a moment then spoke. "What's on your mind, son?"

"I never want to disappoint you two. I've been talking to Petty Officer Sites—they've modified the course for SEAL training. It's no longer BUD/S, or Basic Underwater Demolition/SEAL, it's now Modified Advanced SEAL Training. MAST. Makes sense, being a naval term. Anyway, Dad, I'm going to do this. Petty Officer Sites thinks, with my heavy wrestling background and being only eighteen, that I'll be able to handle the grueling physicality of it. I know, after all I've been through, I can handle the mental aspect. I've always been a thinker, and I know how to use what God has blessed me with. Sites seems to think I can handle it. So does Sheriff Pratt. I'll need a letter of recommendation from a SEAL. He said he'd write me one only with your blessing. I asked him before he headed into a meeting. This is what I'm meant for, Dad. It's what I'm meant for since everything became... this."

Tim sat and listened to his son. There was no confusion; Carl knew exactly what he was saying and what he wanted. This was going to happen.

"As a parent, I share all your mother's concern. These boys are dying, son. Every mission, they come home with fewer and fewer men. As a man, I couldn't be more proud. I ask a compromise. The training facility for the recruits is located in another undisclosed location. So I ask that you go through all the training and, after you've passed selection, you assign with my team. It would help your mother maintain her sanity, and I'd feel better having you close by."

"Okay Pop, deal."

"Okay, Carl. I have a meeting to get to myself. I'm proud of you, son."

By the time Tim got to the meeting, Thomas, Sera, the president, Commander Haul, and several other high-ranking staff members were seated and ready to begin. President Martinez stood up to start the proceedings.

"First, we'd like to welcome two people that have given us an invaluable outlook on what we're facing. Without them and their incredible will to survive under incalculable odds, we're facing a most certain doom. Ladies and gentlemen, Sheriff Thomas Pratt, former lieutenant commander US Navy SEALs. It is also my pleasure to introduce a very special lady. This is Sera Daxron of the Usraians from the planet Usrafax Prime."

The assembly became a stir. The members were startled by the revelation that there was not only other life in the universe, but now that life was also sitting in the room with them. The combined muttering and whispering among them was deafening.

President Martinez gave them a moment to take this in, then regained order.

"Settle down, people! I know this is a shock. I only found this information out recently. Other than myself, Sheriff Pratt and his people, Admiral Tomlinson, and Commander Haul and his men, only the people in this room are aware of this, and I want to keep it that way."

A man raised his hand and was recognized to speak. "I have a question. What do the aliens and the attacks have to do with one another?" he asked.

"I will explain everything to you all, but first, everyone calm down. What you are about to hear is difficult, to say the least. You must listen, and you must remain open-minded. Do not be quick to condemn and judge."

President Martinez told the members the situation as Thomas, Sera, and Commander Haul had reported it. When he finished, the members sat silently in dismay. A woman broke the silence.

"So… we're all lost? I knew things were bad. I assumed a plague or some other natural event, maybe even something biblical. I never dreamed it would be… intentional. You've come to exterminate us and take from us until even our world is obliterated. I, for one, cannot sit in the same room as this… thing!" As the woman got up to leave the room, the president motioned to one of the military police officers. The officer blocked the woman's path.

"I understand how you feel, but I must insist you stay," the president said as he stood up, took her gently by the shoulder, and escorted her back to her seat. "Everything we know is on the verge of annihilation, nothing less than absolute extinction. But we will come together. I brought you, staff members, here for a very specific reason. We have a plan. I've read so many reports and had more meetings over the last twelve hours than during most of my time as secretary of state."

"Perhaps a little less time on the golf course would have been prudent in hindsight, huh, Felix?" Admiral Tomlinson joked. The room lit up with light laughter.

"Yes, well, Admiral, if you saw my handicap, you wouldn't be complaining."

The room's mood was lightened, even if by a hair, but at least they weren't ready to riot.

"Thank you, Cliff," President Martinez quietly said to the admiral. "Now, everyone, we have a plan. It will be beyond dangerous, and it will involve using all our resources. We will be bringing in our battle group."

"Sir, with all due respect, should we be discussing this option with the alien present? She is still part of an enemy invasion!" Commander Haul said.

"Stand down, Commander, right now!" Admiral Tomlinson ordered sharply.

"Thank you, Admiral. To address the commander's, and I'm sure others', concerns, if it weren't for Sera's intel, we would have no idea what we are up against and this plan, which is our best chance to avoid the utter destruction of our planet, would not be possible. Therefore, I have the utmost confidence in her. Her information, partnered with Sheriff Pratt's inducement, is good enough for me. If it makes you feel better about her involvement, aside from her actions reported by others of her consistently saving human lives, know that we cannot do this without her assistance."

Sera sat quietly, listening as they prepared to lay out their final plan.

She would mentally relay the necessary information to Caleb and, with it, bring an end to it all. The humans had brought her into their sanctum. Their trust would bring pain and death to many of them, most likely to some in this very room. In the end, though, her actions would save a planet, and many more lives would be spared than lost. This brought her solace and reconfirmed the certainty in her actions. In the back of her mind, she wished she could have spared Thomas the hell she was preparing to put him through. It was highly unlikely he would survive, but without him, they would have never accepted her. He was necessary, a piece used to ensure the survival of a species. He was one of this planet's warriors; surely, he would understand sacrifice, she reasoned.

* * * * *

Jessica sat in her room, lost in thought. The rooms were dorm-like, with books, a TV, even a selection of DVDs that could be signed for at the compound's library. None of these things interested her.

It was almost time for bed, and she wanted to go check on Jimmy before then.

Jimmy and Danny were bunked up in a room down the hall. They had a video game console in their room, so the normalcy was such a breath of fresh air.

As Jessica opened her door to go down to the boys' room, she found Carl sitting on the floor in the hall. "What are you doing sitting outside my door, weirdo? Why didn't you come in?"

"I have to talk to you, and I just wanted to get the words right."

She slid down the wall next to him. "Okay, what's going on? Don't worry about the words. Just talk to me, like we always have."

"You're not going to like this, Jess."

"You're starting to freak me out, Carl, please." Jessica had already started to tear up. She didn't know what to think, but she was certain he was right—she wasn't going to like it.

He put his hand on hers. "I love you, Jessie."

There it was, *Jessie. This is going to be bad,* she thought.

"I have, since the sixth grade. I always thought we'd be in each other's lives forever, in one capacity or another."

"Carl… where are you going? And when are you leaving?" she interrupted, tears now streaming.

"I'm training to work with my dad as a SEAL. I'm gonna join the fight, Jess. I have to. I leave in the morning."

"Carl… no. They go out, and most times, not all of them come back. Please don't do this! I can't lose you! I can't."

Carl took his friend into his arms and held her. She already felt the loss. She had felt it before when her mom had died. It wasn't anything anyone would get used to, or should ever have to. She cried in his arms. He stroked her hair and used his sleeve to wipe her face. He hadn't seen her cry like this since her mom had passed. He had held her the same then as he did now.

"Jess, it's not that I'll never see you again. Besides, you are nowhere near that little girl that needed me to protect her anymore."

"What are you talking about? I used to kick your butt all the time in the park."

"We were, like, twelve, and I'd let you win. Every time you'd win, you would get so happy… and dance! Do you remember that stupid victory dance you used to do? You looked so serious."

"Don't hate on my moves. You know this white girl can get down."

They laughed and, for a moment, forgot. But only for a moment.

"I'm going to miss you, Carl. I don't know if I know how to be without you. You've been there for me more than a friend, more than a best friend, like a brother. I love you too, Carl, I always will."

They held each other.

"You better get going, Jess. I saw Jimmy and Danny raiding the vending machine and heading toward their room with a handful of video games from the library. Looks like an all-night junk food, game-night bender. Somebody's gotta maintain order."

"Super sis slash wet blanket to the rescue, I guess." Jessica wiped her face.

"Jess, I need to say my goodbyes now. I can't head out in the morning with this on my heart."

They hugged, and he kissed a tear off her cheek. They looked into each other's eyes, and he wiped away another tear. No more words were needed. He turned and walked down the hall, Jessica watching until he was out of sight. Then she turned, took a few steps, and found her legs like jelly. She leaned on the wall and slid to the floor, overtaken with grief and unable to hold back. She sobbed quietly but uncontrollably.

Carl had maintained himself as long as he could, but now with Jessica out of sight, his tears ran slowly down his face. Jessica loved him. *As a brother.* He'd never let her know the love he felt for her was not the love of a child or a sister. He was *in love* with her. And as much as he loved her, the world had become a place where love, even true love, was a comfort that was too expensive to afford.

* * * * *

President Martinez had brought a laptop for a PowerPoint presentation that was projected onto the wall.

"After all the attacks began, we started gathering data. Our initial loss estimations were grossly inaccurate. As of twenty-four hours ago, we are at an approximate loss of sixty million souls on the East Coast. Those figures are guesstimates, because our communications are all but nullified. The good news is, due to some very fast and lifesaving thinking by Admiral Tomlinson, Naval Battle Group 13 was rerouted to a secure, solitary location at sea. Admiral Tomlinson, via some very distinctive and *sui generis* Morse code, got an entire battle group to maintain radio silence. As we all know, we lost the vast majority of our military forces due to responding to calls for assistance. The brave men and women of our armed forces raced into the face of danger, as they always have, without regard or concern for their own welfare. That ultimately led to their demise. Battle Group 13 is standing by with its warships, air wing, ground force contingents, and if need be, special weapons. With all that said, we have lost all major satellite usage. Due to Sera's information, we now understand why, but that still doesn't help us solve the dilemma. Our main goal is taking down what has now been designated *Blackout Tower*.

"That being the case, we must, with a joint effort, use our SEAL team to mark the areas with a laser guidance system. Our subs can then use their Tomahawk missiles to take out the target. The battle group's air wing can use the A-6 bombers to back the subs up as a contingency."

The room seemed at odds. "Mr. President, it cannot be that simple, sir."

With that, President Martinez introduced Commander Haul. Haul got up and took control of the meeting.

"Ladies, gentlemen, in fact, no, it will not be easy at all. In order for us to, what we call, *paint* the target, we will have to be within fifty yards. There will be a vast number of enemy combatants in close proximity. These enemy combatants, as you know, are highly versatile, strong, fast, focused, and extremely difficult to kill. We've been able to tap into an old weather satellite, and early scans read approximately sixteen hundred of the enemy in the area. So no, ma'am, there will be nothing easy about this mission. We will infiltrate at first light to reduce the chances of enemy contact due to the deadly effect the sun has on them. Two teams, Alpha and Bravo Teams. Each team's equipped with SARHs, *semiactive laser homing* devices. The teams will deploy to mark two different targets. Alpha Team will move on the Spore itself. The Spore is the Blackout Tower's main defense. Any aerial attack will be ineffective as long as the Spore is still in play. Alpha Team will HALO jump, high-altitude, low-open-ing, into the area. Our intel, Ms. Daxron, tells us the only way to take down the Spore is with a direct hit at the base of the target. The thermobaric warhead on our Tomahawk missiles will burn away the protective layers of the Spore, and the neurotoxin she helped our sci-entists develop will take it out. It will take the force of the blast and the toxin to kill the Spore. At which point, Bravo Team will move in and paint the tower—our missiles will do the rest. In the end, we will paint the targets, stand fast to confirm the targets' destruction, then track our way back to base. Are there any questions?"

"I have one," one of the members said. "Will both teams be jumping in?"

"Good question. The answer is no. We will not risk putting both teams together. In the unlikely event one team in neutralized, the other will take up both tasks."

"One more question. Who will lead these teams?"

"I will lead Alpha Team, assisted by 2IC Petty Officer Sites. Bravo Team will be led by… Lieutenant Commander Thomas Pratt, assisted by 2IC former Senior Command Chief Darren Miles. I say *former* because as of 0700 hours this morning, President Martinez and Admiral Tomlinson have promoted him to command master chief of the US Navy, the highest rank an enlisted man can achieve. Hooyah!"

"Hooyah!" Thomas and a couple of former naval men in the room echoed.

The meeting wrapped up. Everyone had all the information they could hope to have. Haul walked over to Thomas. "A word, Sheriff? President Martinez needs to swear you in and reinstate your commission. I know I went past you and dropped this on you, but I know it's precisely where you need to be. You can refuse, but know Master Chief requested you. I don't like you, but damn, you're a

SEAL, not by name, but by nature. I can't refute that fact. We need you. Make a choice. We're waiting."

Haul walked over to the president and the admiral and stood with them. Thomas knew what he needed to do. He walked over to them, retook his oath, and it was done. US Navy SEAL Lieutenant Commander Thomas Pratt once again. This mission would define not only him but also the history of his planet. No pressure, though.

CHAPTER 15

Professor Julia Anderson was the top in her field and among the top in many others. She had studied the toxin and effects of the offspring as compared to countless other insects known to man. She had drawn many conclusions, but nothing like what she uncovered since gaining the blood sample Dr. Winters had gathered from the alien. It was a revelation. So many blanks filled in. So many questions answered. She was on the brink of discovery. The greatest discovery since Penicillin, only this had the capacity to not only rewrite human history but, in fact, also save it. She had taken blood from Sera and Thomas and broken the samples down to their essentials.

She and Tim had been working on something they felt would stem the tide. If they could find a cure to the bite of the offspring, maybe there would be a chance. Unfortunately, the bite caused almost immediate results. There wasn't a plausible solution for this. So they had instead shifted their thinking. They had tried reverse-engineering the offspring's toxin to maybe find how to isolate the gene that gave the infected their strength and abilities. If possible, perhaps create an advanced, progressive-type soldier in order to fight this threat. The result had been dismal at best. Men had volunteered by the masses, fully informed, to no avail. There had been many deaths.

But the alien's blood was a game changer. Tim and Julia had found that the blood worked as a bonding agent. Extraterrestrial blood had bonded with the offspring, though it wasn't Sera's blood. Still, her alien blood provided the missing bonding agent that was now in Julia's possession. Professor Anderson had taken the blood of Sera and Thomas and created what she hoped and prayed would create the missing link needed to bring salvation to Earth. There was no time for testing; this was not sanctioned or authorized. She had listened to what Tim had said about this man and read the reports concerning his actions in the field. He was a top-tier operator, physically able, even gifted. If ever there was a candidate for this serum, it was Thomas Pratt. Months of engineering, multitudes of deaths, and much sacrifice. Many might call her a mad scientist or even a heretic playing God, but she knew her heart and would not be oscillated. She was meeting Thomas for dinner soon and would do what must be done. There was no turning back now.

* * * * *

Jessica sat in Billy's cell. She hadn't been able to bring steak, but by the usual standard of their meals before arriving, it was still very much an upgrade. She seemed distracted, and Billy took notice.

"You know, even with only one good eye, I can still see something is eating at you, Jess. Come on, spill."

"Carl left this morning. He's going off to train with the military. He's going to be a soldier, or sailor, or… whatever. I don't think I'll ever see him again. My dad spent the night out with this doctor. Not sure where that's heading. Jimmy and Danny are inseparable. At least I know you're not going anywhere, all locked down and all. Looks like you're stuck with me," she said, giving him a playful punch in the arm.

"Yeah, well, maybe. Your dad came down early this morning. He's having them arrange a tribunal. They're in the middle of planning some kind of mission, so he's moving them as fast as he can. He said as soon as they hear my case, he's confident they will chalk it up to temporary insanity. Due to the torture inflicted on me, I was not in my right mind, therefore, I didn't know what I was doing."

"That's great news, Billy. I want you out of this cell. You don't deserve to be in here."

"I'm not going to do it, Jess. They want me to say that what I did was wrong. In this world we live in, is it insane to destroy evil, regardless of its species? I wasn't out of my mind. I knew exactly what I was doing. I won't say otherwise. I don't know if I'm crazy, or if maybe insanity is the new normal. Things have changed, and if we don't change with them, we'll be swept away."

"Billy, if we don't maintain our humanity, then they already won. I'm not saying I don't understand what and why you did what you did, but that can't be our norm. You can't beat evil by becoming it. You have to be above it. We kill to defend ourselves and our loved ones. Once we do it for any other reason, we become less than human and more like Spewers. That's not us, Billy."

"I don't know what I am, then. If given the opportunity to kill Cole, Simon, Caleb, or any of them, I wouldn't hesitate, not for one second!"

"At what cost, Billy? What would you trade for it? Your life or compassion? My life? Where do you draw the line? The problem is, after a while, you'll no longer see the line."

"I won't say what I did was wrong, Jess. I can't make you understand. You have no idea what malicious things he did. More than the physical torture, he stripped away my resolution. He made me give up all that I held sacred. If your father hadn't shown up when he did, I was ready to give him everything I knew about the camp, you guys, everything. I don't think I'll ever be sure of myself again. He took that from me, Jess."

"I'm here, Billy. No matter what, I'm here, and we will get through this together."

* * * * *

Caleb sat studying two of the failed hosts the humans had labeled Ragers. He and Sera had managed to capture them, but it had not been an easy task. They were very strong, much stronger than the controlled infected hosts. It had taken Caleb and Sera's combined strength to capture them one at a time. Caleb had used Usraian bonds and powerful electromagnetic locks to restrain them. He had concluded that the Rager's queen offspring had not correctly attached to the host's spinal column. As a result, the offspring became unable to create the necessary bond with the host brain. The signal sent by the offspring fried the host brain, in essence, rendering it useless and causing abrupt and absolute madness. The increase in strength was caused by the absence of Caleb's influence controlling the influx of adrenaline and epinephrine from the offspring into the host body. Without his control, the offspring would unleash a plethora of the enzymes, similar to a baby rattlesnake unable to control the venom it unleashed. This would cause rapid burnout and deterioration. Caleb conjectured the life span of these failed hosts would likely be four to five weeks. After he completed the reconditioning of his human laborers, the Ragers would need to be his next primary task. They would cause an abeyance in the workforce, and that could not be allowed.

* * * * *

Sera had relayed the humans' complete plan to Caleb, but there were a few modifications he would need her to make, which he did next.

"Sera, are you there?"

"Yes, Caleb."

"When the Bravo Team comes to destroy the Blackout Tower, I want you to persuade them to use the east tunnels. I will have a welcome party waiting for them. I want the sheriff taken alive. Bring him to me. The others are inconsequential. You may add them to the labor force."

"The Alpha Team will be attempting to destroy the Spore. We cannot allow that."

"I have studied the weapon system they plan on using, and it will be ineffective against the Spore. Once the missiles have been fired from their battle groups at sea, I will be able to pinpoint their exact location and have them dealt with. All possibilities have been accounted for, Sera. Their end will be swift and facile."

* * * * *

Thomas sat in his room, completing a final equipment check and reviewing the mission briefing. A knock came on the door. "It's open," he yelled out.

Tim came in and sat down in a chair.

"What's up, Tim?"

"Thomas, you've saved my family's life, and I'll always owe you. There's something I have to tell you. With you heading out tonight on this mission, I feel like I have to tell you now. I have struggled with this since we found out. I know what you have ahead of you, the difficult mission ahead of you. I hope you can get past this and function, Thomas."

"What is it, Tim?"

"We finished a massive study in the short time we've had Sera's blood. It has opened many doors for our studies, and we've had a very disturbing discovery. The illness that took Sue and those other eleven poor souls appears to have been derived from Usraian DNA. It seems Caleb was using Ghostwood as a testing ground to find the right strand of virus to use in his parasites. That's why we were never able to isolate the strand, because he kept mutating it. He was trying to find one that wouldn't kill us before the host had a chance to take control of the body, since he needs us to make up his planet of slaves, but there were casualties."

"He killed my wife?" Thomas asked, almost under his breath.

"Yes, Thomas, he did. I'm so sorry."

"Don't be. This mission has an execution order attached to it. Caleb has been deemed too dangerous to allow to live. Sue's death was untimely and unfair, but I've always had to accept it as the nature of life. Now you've given me someone to blame… something to kill!" he said then paused, as if thinking. "Excuse me, my kids are waiting for me."

Thomas walked out of the room, leaving Tim sitting in the chair. That wasn't all Tim had planned to tell Thomas. He needed to tell him about the serum and all its possibilities. The serum would be bonded with Thomas's DNA so any effects would occur to him and him alone. Tim still had many tests to run on it. Thomas would make it back. *He always comes back,* he thought to himself. It could wait for his return; he had enough on his mind.

Thomas, Jessica, Jimmy, and Jax sat in the now-empty dining facility. They gathered close and held one another. "When are you coming back, Dad?" Jimmy asked, eyes full of tears.

"I'm going to do my best to fix this mess, Jimmy. It's okay, I'll be back. In the meantime, you listen to your sister and take care of Jax."

Thomas held his son tightly. He'd been on many missions, and he tried to maintain that this was just another one of them. He tried not to hold on to the fact that this was literally a mission to save the world. It sounded like such a trite statement even when he just said it in his head. He also tried to convince himself that this wasn't a personal vendetta. Caleb had killed his wife. Did Sera know about the testing? She couldn't have known Sue was killed as part of his twisted experiment. Thomas wouldn't let himself believe that.

He let Jimmy go and took Jessica by the hand. "Walk with me, Jessie." They walked to the other side of the hall.

"Dad, are you coming back? You don't have to lie to me. It'll be better if I know what to expect. I need the truth, Dad. Is this mission worth never seeing us again?" Jessica looked at her dad and bravely waited for his answer.

"Jessie, I love you. You're my world, the best thing I've ever done. Without you and Jimmy, I have no purpose. You two *are* my mission! I'll come back to you. I'll finish this for you, Jimmy, and your mother. We will always be a family, and I'll always be with you no matter what. They will pay for what they've done, all of it. There will be a reckoning—I promise you that!"

Jessica had never seen such resolve before. It scared her, seeing her father like this. She leaned in and held him. She hadn't held him like this since she was a little girl. She hadn't realized how much she had missed it, or needed it. Holding her just as tight, Thomas hadn't noticed the tears slowly coming down his cheek. He hadn't cried in so long he'd almost forgotten what it felt like. For the first time since Sue died, he had his little girl back.

The door opened to the dining facility, and Wayne walked in.

"Thomas, can I have a word with you, in here?" he said as he opened a door to an adjoining room.

They walked in, and all his family was there: Tim, Claire, Ray, Paul, Michael, Martha, Charley, Danny. Two military police officers entered the room, and Billy walked in with them. They uncuffed him and told him and Thomas they had ten minutes. Mark, Kenny, Rita, and Keylin came in and stood with the others. Surprised, Thomas felt his heart warm at this much-needed reunion. As every eye in the room dampened, they all took turns embracing Thomas. They held hands as Ray prayed for the group and Thomas's safety and success. He gave thanks for the ark of protection God provided them and asked God to take care of those who had perished.

At the end of the prayer, Shirley took Thomas by the arm. "Sheriff, sit with an old lady, will you?"

"You find me an old lady, and I'd be happy to," he said, smiling as they sat.

"I remember when you first won the election. I didn't know what to expect. You were always such a willful boy when you were young. Your mother used to worry because you kept your feelings so private. I think she used to take that personal. You had everything going for you, football hero, prettiest girl in town… you shouldn't have had a care in the world. But you always seemed discontented, you always seemed to be searching for something more. Your mother, God rest her soul, thought she wasn't mother enough for you. Your father was so proud of you I don't think he ever noticed how she felt."

"I know, Shirley. We had a good, long talk before she passed."

"Thomas, I say that to say this. I may not have known what to expect at first, but you have come to be like a son to me. You're more than anyone could have ever expected, and I thank God for you, Thomas Pratt. Come back to us, son."

They held each other as the tears soaked their shirts. Charley came over, put his hand on Thomas's shoulder, took his wife by the hand, and held her as they walked away.

Thomas got up and took Wayne and Billy aside.

"Wayne, you have been my right hand since long before this madness. You are my brother. I have a favor to ask. I have every intention of coming out of this alive, but if, for some reason, something happens—"

Wayne put his hand on Thomas's shoulder and stopped him short. "Like they were my own, Thomas." The two friends hugged.

Thomas turned to Billy. "Billy, you've always been like a little brother to me. I've known you most of your life. You will be okay.

You'll heal from this. Your soul will heal from this. I love you, man, and I need you. Take care of the group. Look out for my son. Take him under your wing the way Sue and I did for you. Be there for my son the way I was there for you, until I get back."

"I will, Thomas. I'm sorry… I'm so sorry for what I've become, for the hate that has come to consume me." Billy couldn't hold the pain inside for another minute. The dam burst, and Thomas held him as he cried out the anguish.

"Billy, it's okay. I'm proud of you—you survived! I'm just sorry for what you went through. You stay strong. You'll be out soon, and when you are, remember your promise and take care of Jimmy."

The police took Billy, cuffed him, and led him to the door. "Give 'em hell, Thomas! Rain it down on the bastards' heads!"

Thomas smiled at his friend. *I fully intend to,* he thought. *I'm going to burn them all!*

Thomas looked around the room at his family and all the people who had become his family.

Paul walked over to him. "Well, hero, off you go, big S on your chest. Not sure I like your odds without me watching your back, Sheriff."

"Me neither, but the group needs you more than I do this time. It took literally an apocalypse for me to like you," Thomas said, smiling. "I misjudged you, Paul. When metal met meat, you were one of the best I've ever had the honor to serve with. You've saved my life more than a few times over the last nine months. If you will allow me, men and women… ATTENTION!" Thomas yelled loud and sharp.

Everyone in the dining facility, including the police officers and the military staff members who had made their way in, rose to their feet and stood tall, most with their hands at their sides.

"Mr. Paul Daniel Singer, I recognize you as a man of valor. A man courageous in the face of adversity, who stands fast in the midst of the storm. Sir, we salute you!"

Paul looked around at the hands held high against temples in his honor. Being the town drunk and troublemaker, he never would have imagined this. He was overwhelmed, and as everyone slowly lowered their hands on Thomas's command, Paul had to wipe a tear from his eye.

Thomas put his hand on Paul's shoulder. "You're a good man, Paul. Thank you."

"Aw, hell, Sheriff, now I really do feel bad I didn't vote for ya," Paul said with a smile.

"Ain't like they let felons vote, anyway, Paul," Wayne heckled from the back.

The room filled with laughter. Eyeing the room, Thomas saw Julie standing in the back. Shaking Paul's hand one last time, he made his way over to her.

"Hey, you. I was going to come by and see you before I left."

"I don't doubt that, Sheriff. Let's take a walk, okay?"

They made their way outside and down the hall toward the vehicle bay. She reached down and took his hand.

"Julie, I jus' want you to know that last night meant more than just a final-night-before-I-go-off-to-war-type thing. It meant more than you know. You're the first since—"

"I understand, Thomas. I don't want to be the lady in waiting, hoping her fella comes home from the fight. So we'll just see what happens, okay, Commander?"

"Sounds good."

"There is one thing you could do for me. Do you trust me?"

"What are you getting at, Julie? Just tell me."

"I want you to let me administer a shot to you. I can't tell you much, because there's simply no time. Just know that I've put every bit of everything that I am into this one thing. If Tim knew I was asking this of you, he'd lose it."

"Julie, I need more than that. What is it?"

"The future, Thomas, and not just yours. To be honest, my first thought was to just give you the shot as part of your premedical workup for your reinstatement to the teams. After meeting you, I couldn't do that, so please trust me."

Thomas had always relied on his instincts, and they told him to trust her. "Lead the way, Doc. Guess our future's in your hands."

They walked, still hand in hand, to the medical bay. She managed the weight of humanity in her hands without the slightest doubt. It would work, not because it had to, but because every road leads somewhere. Most people quit when the road becomes too long and dark to follow, but Julia Anderson was no such person; she had followed this long, hard road. Through trails, failure, even death. It had been dark and sometimes even teetered on the border of beastly, but she'd ridden the ride all the way to the end. The end had led here, and there was no other destination. She had been completely thorough; she'd left nothing up to fate or luck. Once Thomas proved what she already knew, she would mass-produce this miracle and the human race would never need to fear this type of event ever again.

Every ounce of hope she felt emptied from her and into Thomas as the last drop of the serum left the syringe into his bloodstream.

"What should I expect from this serum?"

"An increase of strength, stamina, and endurance. You should witness accelerated healing of minor wounds. You won't feel anything right away. It should trigger, and I can't tell you when or how. Thomas, if there were more time to run the proper tests, I could tell you more. I've worked every possible theory and hypothesis, so I'm not shooting blind here. The only thing I can't account for is the extent of potential. It could either make you slightly improved or exceptional. What I do know is that this opportunity for a field test is too valuable to pass up. There is too much at stake here."

"I trust you, and I understand. At this point, we need any and every chance we can get our hands on."

* * * * *

As the sun began to rise and crest the horizon, Thomas met his team in the vehicle bay. Bravo Team consisted of Master Chief Miles, Petty Officer Tills, and Lamer, whom he already knew. Petty Officer Barnes, who had been killed in action back at the camp, had been replaced by SEAL sniper Petty Officer Ryan. Thomas met Ryan, and they shook hands and introduced themselves. Ryan had been fully briefed and was 100 percent operationally ready. Haul and Alpha Team came through the vehicle bay en route to the awaiting helicopter. The helicopter would take them to the C-130 that they would jump from into the AO (area of operation). Sites and Rock, Thomas already knew, and Haul introduced the members of his team that he hadn't met yet.

"Commander Pratt, these are Petty Officers Shaw and Canberra."

The two men stood at attention and saluted Thomas. He returned their salutes then shook their hands.

"It's a pleasure, sir. I heard a lot about you. The things I've read in the after-action report about you… truly amazing, sir," Petty Officer Shaw said.

"Damn, Shaw… fanboy much?"

"Maybe the commander would like a chocolate placed on his pillow in the morning."

"Back rub might be nice." The guys gave Shaw some playful shoves.

"That's enough!" Haul ordered. "Let's move out! Shaw, gotta little something on your… ," Haul said, gesturing to the corner of his mouth.

The laughter filled the bay as the men moved out to the final staging positions, saying their last goodbyes.

Thomas felt a surge shoot through his body. The rush nearly buckled his knees.

"You okay, Top?" Miles asked.

"Yeah, just getting my sea legs back, I guess," he lied.

Thomas knew it was the serum. Was it taking effect? He knew there was no time for questions. He would keep it to himself. The mission was priority.

Sera joined them in the bay. "Sorry I'm late, Sheriff. I had last-minute preparations to attend to. I have found a more efficient route to get us to the tower." Sera showed him the diagrams and maps she'd put together.

Thomas looked the plans over. "Sera, are you sure about this? Is this the only way?"

"It's the best way for us to achieve our goal. I believe Caleb will not expect us to take the eastern tunnels. He would think the threat of a heavy presence of infected would dissuade any incursion."

"Yeah, well, pardon me, ma'am, but doesn't it?" Petty Officer Tills said.

"It would, warrior, or do you prefer soldier?"

"Actually, I'm a United States sailor, HM2 Tills, ma'am. US Navy SEAL, United States Navy. You can call me Doc, though, or Tilly, or just plain Tills," he said with a large, proud, but sincere grin.

"Okay, well… Till. Yes, the tunnels would be a very dangerous and nonviable option, but not in this case. You see, I can, for lack of a better word, redirect them. I will simply plant an image of humans in their heads, which will lead them out of the tunnels. Thus clearing the way to give us a straight route to the target."

"Wow, you can do that?" Lamer said.

"Yeah, Sera, you can do that?" Thomas added with skepticism.

"Sheriff, I've explained that since my reawakening, some of my dormant abilities have been reacquired."

"Okay, Sera. Guys, we're gonna reroute for new entry point, east tunnels. Equipment check in five. I want UV lights in the armor fully charged, UV bursters taped and ready, UV stream lights attached to rifles. Check and double-check. We move in thirty."

CHAPTER 16

Dr. Anderson had taken a sample of Thomas's blood since giving him the serum. There was little change, but the serum was overtaking the white blood cells. It wasn't killing them, and the transformation didn't seem hostile. The white blood cells were not attacking the foreign substance as they would any other invader. Instead, it seemed to blend with it to become more adaptable. This was a very good sign. The B-lymphocytes, or B cells, combined partially well with the serum. This was expected. This was what she attributed to the alien DNA's healing ability. Thomas would never get so much as a common cold again. The blood plasma also acclimated with the serum at an unprecedented rate. The mutated proteins would form platelets in the plasma, causing wounds to clot and heal with uncanny acceleration.

As she studied the blood, Dr. Anderson found a potentially problematic drawback: the blood contained an alarmingly low level of glucose. Increased sugar intake or insulin should correct this situation. *Great,* she thought, *I've helped create the world's first superhuman diabetic.* When Thomas returned from his mission, she would be able to correct this oversight.

* * * * *

Haul's team sat ready as the plane approached the LZ. Dropping twelve klicks from the target, they would make the rest of the trip on foot. The C-130 would parachute two J8 Chrysler light patrol military vehicles down to the landing zone. The vehicles would be stocked with reloads, supplies, and a mounted M240 Bravo heavy machine gun. The team would not use these vehicles to approach the target; they couldn't risk the noise, even during the day. The vehicles were to be used for egress only. Upon touchdown, the team would make the approximate seven-and-a-half-mile journey with great haste. It was stealth over force, which was the way of the SEAL. Although highly trained, equipped, and motivated, any frogman will tell you it is better to be in, out, and have the top back on the jar before anyone even knows the cookies are gone; after all, they don't make movies about successful SEAL missions, only the ones that go wrong.

The men lined up as the rear hatch opened. Sites released the two vehicles from the cargo hold of the aircraft and watched as they traveled down toward the Earth. The men waited thirty seconds and then deployed themselves and, with a terminal velocity, raced toward destiny.

* * * * *

The Spore had reached complete maturity and was as big as a seven-story building. Its true capabilities were in its roots, which stretched for hundreds, even a thousand miles, thus creating the tunnels the infected could use to move about during the day. The roots also could emerge from the ground and act as weapons. Its regeneration rate was unmatched. A severed part, if it was worthless or torn away, would regrow within minutes. Superficial damage would not be enough to have an effect. The hit would have to be perfect at the root base, the destruction complete.

Thomas's team moved through the city. The buildings in the area had been long abandoned, and the Spore had generated so much overgrowth that the city had taken on a jungle-like appearance. They had driven within eight klicks of the tower then went the rest of the way on foot. Sera reassured the team the area was cleared of infected. That made perfect sense to Thomas. Caleb would have all the infected in the area guarding the compound. His biggest concern were random Ragers. They were not subject to Caleb's commands and were a very dangerous wild card.

Bravo Team were spread in a fire line, their movement flawless. Their approach patterns and angles of attack were completely in sync, always keeping a line of sight on one another. They had comms, but hand signals would be their standard mode of communication. With their proficiency, they could relay a message almost as fast as it could be spoken. They moved to the edge of the designated hold point outside the tower's perimeter, using abandoned vehicles as cover. Thomas used the binoculars to see what they would be up against. The base of the tower sat within a fenced-in area. The fence was nothing more than flimsy chain-link, with a broken post barely supporting the half-open door on the gate. Getting in was not an obstacle; the conundrum was getting to the target and staying alive long enough to bring it down. Without the Spore's destruction, that wouldn't be possible. So they would wait and pray Haul would send the go-ahead so they could move in.

Sera moved with Thomas. It was simple. When he moved, she moved; when he stopped, so did she. Thomas touched her hand and pointed to his temple. She understood.

"I'm here, Commander. What is it?" Sera said inside his head.

"The east tunnels? Are you sure that's the best way?"

"It's the only way, Commander. I know the risks are monumental, but if you are to save your planet, you must trust me."

"Is everything still clear? Are they free of Spewers?"

"Yes, we are clear. We may proceed."

Thomas waved his hand in the air in a back-and-forth motion, signaling the men into a single-file formation. The men attached suppressors to their weapons and began stacking for breach. They lined up along the wall on the east tunnel. At the last minute, Thomas broke formation.

"Master Chief, we're splitting units. You, Tills, Lamar, and Ryan hold fast. I need a team to take up position and stand by. Sera and I will make our way down the tunnel and observe the target. If we're not back by dusk, have the team take out the target."

"Top, I don't understand. Are you sure—"

"Master Chief, you have your orders. Fall out, and stand fast."

"Roger that."

Sera didn't expect the switch, but having fewer men to deal with was a welcome change.

Thomas motioned Sera to his side, and they headed into the tunnel.

* * * * *

Billy and Jessica sat eating breakfast in his cell, as they'd done every day for the last two weeks since arriving.

"I talked to Wayne. He told me he talked to one of the senior staff members about your case. They say if we lose our ability to govern one another, then we've lost this war," Jessica said.

Billy nodded. "Spoken like a person who has never been outside these walls."

"Billy, I'll get you out. I'll wait and see if they will do the most sensible thing and free you. Should they not, though, I've made other plans."

"Jess, what the hell are you up to?"

"I don't just bring you meals every day. I've made sure to bring both our trays at the same time on many occasions. My police escort is way too much of a gentleman to let a poor, defenseless young girl carry two trays. So the last couple of times, I had a *particularly* hard time not dropping them when your guard was entering the access code to your cell. My escort took the trays for me as the guard entered the code and set them on the table behind us. That gave me the chance to get a look at the code. He entered the same code both times. Now I plan on getting another look on Monday to make sure they don't change it weekly. I'm getting you out Billy, one way or another."

* * * * *

Haul and his team regrouped, gathered their equipment, and began their trek to the target. As they got closer to the target Haul's heart sank. A quarter of a mile ahead, the city was as dark as night even though the sun was high overhead. The Spore had blossomed thick vines and wide leaves over and throughout the city, completely blocking out the sun.

"Sites, we have a problem," Haul said, his eyes still trained ahead.

"I guess we'll have enemy contact after all, sir," Sites stated.

"Looks like it's about four miles to our target. We should expect heavy resistance. Brief the men."

"Yes, sir," Sites responded, trying to push down the unease he was feeling.

The team utilized an early-detection prototype Dr. Anderson developed. This was the first field test they had performed, a baptism by fire. They moved swiftly and silently through the city and into the dark.

* * * * *

Thomas and Sera moved down into the tunnel. The slight sound Master Chief Miles made as he closed on their location was enough to alert Thomas. Thomas brought his weapon around level to the threat.

"Easy, Commander, you don't wanna take out the only person left on Earth with Mrs. Miles's secret peach cobbler recipe," Miles said.

Thomas was not amused. "Master Chief, I told you to back me up and take out the damn target should we fail. What part didn't you understand?"

"Actually, your orders were to have a secondary team on standby should you fail. That team is on standby under Petty Officer Tills's command. Should we fall, he will complete his assignment."

"You were to lead that team!"

"We can argue semantics all night, or we can finish this mission. I'm with you, Top. Requesting permission to finish the mission."

There was no time for this, so Thomas had no choice. "Granted, Master Chief. Let's move out." The three of them moved farther into the tunnel.

"There's an opening up ahead, Commander," Sera said. "We will be able to move more freely through the city up there."

Miles grabbed Thomas by the arm. "Sir, with all due respect, I don't recommend taking that path. We'll be completely exposed, giving up cover and concealment."

Thomas gently removed his hand. "Just follow my lead, copy?"

"Roger that, sir."

They came out of the tunnel, where they saw heavy overgrowth above the city had blocked the sun. Making their way across the street, Thomas caught movement in his peripheral vision. They were fast and on them almost before he could react. Miles caught it too.

"Contact!" he called out.

Thomas and Miles began firing muffled shots from their weapons, and the infected fell around them. "What the hell! Where did they come from?" Miles asked. "Sera, why didn't you pick them up? How many are you detecting in the area?"

Thomas looked around, took a deep breath, and lowered his head. Miles saw the despair drape across Thomas's face.

"Sir, what are your orders? We can't hold here!"

"Drop your weapon, Master Chief. We've been outmaneuvered," Thomas said as Simon came around the corner of one of the buildings followed by hundreds of infected.

The infected stayed in a loose formation behind and alongside Simon. They weren't like soldiers, but more like obedient dogs awaiting their master's behest to attack.

Simon came forward as Thomas and Miles lowered and then dropped their weapons. Simon looked at Sera. "Good job, Sera. I guess Caleb was right about you."

Sera turned and handed a piece of paper to Simon. "Simon, before I forget. They have three men standing by at this location. Send some of your infected to assimilate them. They are heavily armed and well-trained, so make sure you send a big-enough force to end it quickly."

Simon studied the paper, putting the image in his head and then in the heads of several dozen infected. He mentally pointed them in the direction of the men and signaled for them to attack as soon as the sun went down. The infected bolted off on their mission.

Thomas looked at her. "Sera, why? I treated you like family! I would have died for you!"

Simon laughed. "Don't worry, Sheriff, I'm sure you'll still get the chance to. Now, Caleb said I had to bring you back alive, but he didn't say anything about your black butler here."

Sera stepped forward and walked past Simon. "There is no need for undue suffering. Just kill him and let's get moving."

Thomas drew his sidearm from his drop holster and pointed it at his own head. "Aye, lapdogs!" he shouted to Simon and Sera. "Your boss wants me alive? Anything happens to the master chief, and I disappoint your master. Something tells me he'll be a bit vexed! How does that work out for you two?"

"This is of little use to you, Commander, but if his prolonged suffering means that much to you, so be it. Let him live, Simon. Bring him along. I guarantee you, Commander, Caleb will make you regret it. By the way, he's not my master, he's my brother. Enough talking. Let's go! There is much to be done, and the distraction of this little rebellion has gone on long enough."

"First chance I get, sir, I'm going to kill that bitch! I don't care what it costs!"

Thomas just looked ahead. His face held a broken, distant, thousand-mile stare.

They moved along toward the stronghold. They passed hundreds, maybe thousands of infected along the way. Caleb had brought them in to guard the compound. This was an impassable force, and on top of it all, Sera had been a plant. Guiding them right into a trap. Worst of all, she knew the location of the compound, the location of his children and mankind's best possible chance of survival. She had this information thanks to him. She had played him perfectly.

Simon took great pleasure in seeing the man that had taken part in the death of his brother so completely fractured. "Sheriff, this is only the beginning. Caleb has promised me your little friend Billy. I'm going to finish what my brother started with him. Then I'm going to start on little Jessica and Jimmy! Yeah, I know all about them too. Sera has given us every bit of info on you, your plans, even your family. Not that she could have kept anything from Caleb, anyway. The man can see into your heads as easily as reading a child's book. You never had a chance."

The thought of his children in this monster's hands further pushed Thomas down into the anguish he had brought on himself.

* * * * *

Haul and his men made it to the target without incident and set up the SARH device, and Sites radioed the sub that was offshore with the prepared missiles. Sites painted the Spore. The blinking red LED display TARGET UNREADABLE made his heart skip a beat.

"Reboot it and try again. Maybe something jarred during the jump and just needs to recalibrate. Let's hope that's all it is."

The device rebooted, and Sites tried again to paint the target: TARGET UNREADABLE. Sites tried painting several nearby targets. The same disheartening message continued to show.

"Sir, what are your orders?" Sites asked.

"Get HQ on the line. Advise them we have a situation. In the meantime, run a full diagnostic check on that damn machine. Maybe we get lucky and it's something we can fix. If not, then God help us."

What else could go wrong? Haul wondered.

* * * * *

Thomas and Miles were brought into Caleb's lab. He was still examining the Ragers strapped to his tables. They were still livid, although fixed in place and unable to move. Simon pushed Thomas to the ground, then Miles.

"On your knees!" he demanded.

Caleb brought a crooked smile to his face as he looked at Thomas. "Sheriff! How good to see you. Last time, we had such a good time that I just couldn't wait to see you again!" Caleb said. He walked past them and greeted Sera. "Sister, all is well?"

"Of course, brother."

"Sheriff, I see you've uncovered my little secret. Sera here is, of course, my sister and would never turn against me. In fact, after our first meeting, I would have just assumed killing you and being done, but this whole scheme was actually her idea. She is a great tactician, it seems. Now I have everything I need to finish this and get back to the job at hand. I could not have done this without you, Sheriff. Your people would never have accepted her if not for you. Thank you for that. I now have their location and the means to crush them. Speaking of which, Simon, take your forces to their compound and kill everything in sight."

Simon looked at Thomas and smiled. "Cheer up, Sheriff, you'll be havin' a nice family reunion very soon." Simon took his infected and led them out of the room to prepare for his assault.

Caleb looked at Thomas and Miles. "He will take around three thousand of my children and break down the doors of your great hall. It will be over soon. But I bet you're wondering why I brought you here. I want you to see just how insignificant you and your people are. I need you here to witness. This other human will be added to my workforce, but not you, Sheriff.

"You have the audacity to think you can challenge me or even stand up to me. You are your people's best hope, yet to me you are but a mere speck. I will kill or convert everything you hold dear. If you are lucky, maybe I will take you with us when we leave—you may yet live as my pet. Your alternative is to stay behind as your rock of a world spins into your sun. After all you've lost, what choice does a broken human have?"

* * * * *

"Commander Haul, we have HQ on the line," Canberra said.

Haul grabbed the radio and explained the situation. He listened intently as he received his instructions. Haul ended the transmission. "Sites, send the signal for the sub to send its first battery of missiles."

"Sir, spray and pray? Without the laser locked on, those missiles could land anywhere, and we need a direct hit to the base of this damn thing."

"I know that, Sites. Don't you think I know that? We have our orders, and we will follow them. Send the signal, now!"

It wouldn't be long now. Fifty long-range Tomahawk missiles were blindly on their way at almost Mach 1 speed. Trying to hit a needle in a stack of needles. Things couldn't get any worse, until they did.

"Sir, the infected detector, it just lit up. We have incoming!"

* * * * *

Simon and his horde were on their way to the airfield to breach the compound. He had a detailed description of the layout from Sera, or rather the images Caleb had drawn from her memories. Caleb had given him a very special package to deal with the heavy steel door Sera had told him about. There were already hundreds of infected in the area that he had directed to the perimeter of the compound. He gave the mental command for them to begin the barrage. They ripped through the airfield and found the hatch leading to the freight elevator. With their great numbers, inhuman speed and strength, and Simon's cognizance directing them, Caleb had his perfect army. They tore through the elevator hatch and were making their way down to the compound. It wouldn't be long now.

* * * * *

The breach alarm blared suddenly and loudly. Jessica jumped to her feet and ran to Jimmy's room. Wayne was already there, gathering Jimmy and Danny. "What's going on, Wayne? What is that?" she asked, feeling a wave of panic.

"Spewers, they've found us. We have to move! They're evacuating the base. We're meeting the rest of the group in the vehicle bay and then boarding an evac tube they've built into the mountain. It'll take us to the planes that will take us out to the naval fleet. There is a US carrier equipped and ready for this exact situation. Everything is going to be okay, but we have to move now."

"What about Billy?"

"They'll bring him. Now, let's go, Jess!"

They ran toward the vehicle bay. Jessica couldn't help feeling the same feeling of abandonment she'd felt the first time she left Billy behind. She couldn't go through that again; she couldn't take that chance.

"Wayne, get the boys to the bay. I'll be right behind you."

"Jessica, no! Your father left you guys in my care. I can't risk it!"

"I wasn't asking. Jimmy, go with Wayne. I'll be right back."

"You're lying, Jess. Come with us, Jess, I need you… please, Jess," he pleaded.

"Right back, little brother. I love you." With that, she turned and ran back down the hall.

Jessica ran to her room and grabbed her bow and quiver of arrows. She burst out of the room, almost running into people who were going the opposite direction toward the bay. She headed down the stairs to the holding cell. The guard was gone. Had they already left and taken Billy with them? She prayed they hadn't changed the access code to the cells. She punched in the code, and the screen lit up with green lights, opening the door. She made her way back to Billy's cell, where he stood by the door.

"What's going on, Jess?"

"They're here, Billy. We have to get out of here now! Everyone is meeting in the bay, and there's an evacuation plan. Where's the guard? I need the key to the cell!"

"They left, Jess. They ran out of here when the alarm sounded. You have to go too. It's okay, I'll get myself out and meet you guys in the bay."

"How? Can you pick the lock? How are you going to get out?"

"Jess, I got it! You can't be here when those bastards get in. Go, now!"

"Billy, I can't leave you again! I can't! I'll—"

"Jessica, trust me, I'll be okay. I just can't focus on getting me out if I have to worry about you. Get out of here now. You being here is going to get me killed! Get the hell out of here now! Stop acting like a child and listen!"

She looked at him, tears streaming down her face. "Billy…"

"Go," he said softly.

Jessica turned and slowly backed to the door. "I'm so sorry, Billy, I'm sorry." She turned and left.

Billy stood by the cell door for a moment, then he turned and sat on the bed. He would wait. He knew what was coming. He'd seen it plenty of times. He was tired. Maybe it was better this way.

* * * * *

Thomas kneeled in Caleb's lab. He'd listened to this lunatic rant on and on. Now it was his turn.

"You thought we would roll over and die, Caleb? You don't know us, not a thing about us! You can't beat us, 'cause we'll never quit fighting you. Me or those like me will always rise up. We will keep pressing and pressing until we break you! Another would-be autocrat named Bin Laden tried this same thing. He made the mistake of uniting the people and the government together as one. He unified us as a nation, and you've unified us as a species. He killed a few thousand of us, and we erased his entire way of life. You've killed countless millions… what do you think we're going to do to you?"

"Really, Sheriff? I must have missed something. Your little team trying to destroy my Spore will find their laser guidance weapon inept. My Spore simply secreted an enzyme everywhere within range that absorbs the light the homing device projects. Your weapon is rendered useless, and your missiles are ineffective. I've researched the destructive capabilities of your Tomahawk missiles, and without a very direct—I mean *precise*—hit at the Spore's base, they will do no damage. The Spore will regenerate faster than you destroy it. Your plan to destroy my tower was also futile. I have already had my colleagues construct dozens of them around the world. The destruction of one would be no more than a minor inconvenience. I control all of them from here. You've seen the sheer number of hosts that surround this structure. Any ground force you could possibly muster would be converted or killed before they got within a thousand yards."

Miles had sat silently and was startled when Caleb spoke to him. "Master Chief Miles! I can hear your thoughts as though you were yelling out loud. You're wondering why you are not restrained. You're thinking the two of you should just rush us and try to get to your weapons and equipment," Caleb said, pointing to all of Thomas's and Miles's gear. It was sitting in a pile where Simon had dropped it. "Well, Master Chief," he mocked, "I'll tell you what. I'll give you three seconds to reach your weapons. After that—"

Caleb didn't finish his sentence before Miles was on his feet and racing toward his gear.

"Miles, no!" Thomas shouted.

"Well, I'm not often surprised, but..."

Caleb, true to his word, counted aloud to three. Caleb finished his morbid death count and began to move toward Miles. Thomas watched as certain death rushed at his friend. He felt a sudden rush as his adrenaline began spiking wildly. His heart felt as though it would burst from his chest. Thomas felt cold sweat pressing his shirt to his body; the room went completely silent, and he felt as if he could barely breathe. Thomas watched as Miles ran to the equipment and Caleb ran toward Miles. Something was amiss. Everything slowed down. Thomas knew of Caleb's supernatural speed, but when Thomas watched Caleb and Miles, they both looked like they were running in slow motion. There was no time to try to figure it out; Caleb was right on top of Miles. Thomas leaped to his feet and headed toward them. As soon as Thomas stood up, he ran toward Miles with what felt like average forward momentum. He had covered forty yards in less than two seconds.

Caleb brought down what was meant to be a crushing blow to the back of Miles's neck, but Thomas reached out and grabbed his punch. Swinging Caleb around by the wrist and using the momentum, he spun around and sent Caleb twenty feet across the room into the wall.

The serum Julie had given him. *Thank you, baby,* Thomas thought.

It happened so fast Miles barely noticed. Wasting no time, Miles ran and grabbed his M4 assault rifle. He fired at Sera, who used her speed to avoid the shots and ran into the control room next door.

"No, focus on Caleb!"

"Roger that, but after we burn this bastard, you got a lot of explaining to do, sir!"

Caleb was back on his feet.

"So, Sheriff, it appears there is more to you. That's okay. I can't wait to open you up and find out exactly what that is."

* * * * *

Haul ordered his men to set and hold a perimeter. "Sites, how much time do we have?" Haul asked.

"Twenty-two hundred meters. At their speed, five minutes tops."

"Roger that. Keep a tight pattern. We don't move till we see that damn tower come down, hooyah!"

"Hooyah!" the men said in unison.

The first battery of Tomahawks rocketed above their heads. With no indicators, the missiles crashed into buildings, cars, bridges. Everything except the target. When one of the Tomahawks did sway too close to the Spore, its limbs knocked them off course, causing even more damage to the city. Without laser guidance, the warheads had no chance to lock onto the Spore or avoid its limbs. They were shooting blind. Haul knew the mission was a scrub unless something changed, and fast.

"Contact left!" Rock called out as the first wave of the infected arrived.

He fired into them, his hands steady and aim forthright. His M-110 sniper rifle had always been a true and reliable companion through every encounter. This one would be no different. The infected fell and became part of Rock's art as he composed a graceful symphony.

"Contact right!" Shaw called out.

"They're coming from both sides now. UV lights on, frag out UV bursters. Don't let them close us in!" Haul ordered.

"They're too fast, Top!" Sites shouted.

"Ow, dammit!" Shaw yelled as he smashed the offspring attached to his leg. "I'm bit, Top. Give 'em hell, fellas!" Shaw shouted as he drew his Glock from his drop holster, put the barrel to his head, and pulled the trigger.

"Close the formation and watch the ground for those sneaky bastards!" Haul ordered, knowing this wasn't the time to mourn his fallen comrade.

As the missiles continued to fly in and destroy the city and the infected closed in more and more on Haul's position, the small sliver of light that was once their brightest chance for survival was quickly fading to black.

* * * * *

Simon arrived at the compound, meeting the heavily fortified and well-protected entrance. The .50 cal-machine guns rained down into the infected! The narrowness of the tunnel negated their mass numbers and forced them into a tight fatal funnel. The ones that managed to get through were still trapped against the enormous steel doors. Their numbers were too few to force their way through the doors. Simon ordered the infected to withdraw; it was time for him to deliver Caleb's package.

He couldn't command the infected to do anything strategic or specific, like use tools. They were simple beasts. Without the Blackout Towers operational, Caleb's control over the infected was limited, but with them, Caleb would have absolute control. Simon had to get inside to take out the human threat. That was his master's plan. Simon had a more self-serving agenda. He knew in what was left of his heart that young Billy was inside this compound, and he would tear this door down with his bare hands if it meant getting to the man who'd killed his little brother.

However, that wouldn't be necessary.

Simon took the device out of his satchel. It wasn't very big, a box maybe the size of a microwave oven. Caleb had been very particular on the operation of the device. He needed to attach it to the door. The machine guns would make that difficult, but he had to get close enough to attach it, program the activation sequence, and then get clear before it detonated. It was strange Sera had not mentioned the machine guns in her report. Perhaps she had; she could withhold nothing from Caleb even if she wanted to. It could be Caleb's way of getting rid of Simon and the base in one fell swoop. Simon knew Caleb was a master planner. He would put nothing past him.

Simon salvaged some plate metal from the scrapyard on the surface. He pushed an old transport vehicle from the abandoned airfield down toward the huge steel doors. The machine guns blasted away at the reinforced truck, with Simon safely pushing it from behind. He got to the doors and placed the device. Once the sequence began, he jumped in the back of the vehicle, counting on the reinforced steel plates to protect him from the blast. Balling up and covering his head with his arms, he waited until a high-pitch shrill began. It was almost overwhelming for Simon, due to his acute hearing. Although the infected seem to not even notice the noise. He braced for impact, but the truck only shook with a mild tremor. He looked outside the truck to see the front end of another truck closer to the compound doors was completely gone. A hole the size of a small car was burnt through it.

They were in.

Simon held his infected outside the range of the still-active machine guns. He jumped from the truck, went through the hole, and tore apart the mechanism that controlled the guns. The machine guns went down. There was nothing between his army and the compound now, and they flowed inside like waves of death. The siege had begun.

* * * * *

Billy sat in his cell. He hadn't wanted to give up, but he saw no way out. He wouldn't become one of them, though. He tied his bedsheet up around the pipes on the ceiling and formed a noose on the other end. It wasn't the way he'd ever planned to go out, but the other option was out of the question. At least he'd see Jackie again. He would wait until the last possible moment. When he heard them come through the outside door, he would finish it. Billy kneeled beside his bed. He would talk to God and hope He heard him.

He prayed for forgiveness and for His grace and understanding. Billy had fought with his all till there was no fight left in him. God would understand that. Billy felt an unwavering feeling of peace and security cover him like a warm blanket on a cold morning. Everything would be okay. This must be God telling him his race was over, that it was time to come home.

Billy heard the outside door slam open. Billy's heart was beating like a rabbit's. A cold sweat streamed down his face. He wouldn't lose his nerve at the last minute, though; he would see this through.

They had burst through. He prayed Jessica and the rest of the group would find safety and, someday, peace. Billy hung the noose around his neck. He whispered one last prayer as he climbed on top of his bedpost. He wouldn't let them take him. He couldn't. The inner door sprung open, and they were in. Now or never, he thought.

Billy Hall closed his eyes and took in a deep breath. He was sure now. He had peace. The lights flickered and went out.

"I'm comin' home, Jackie…"

He wanted his last words to be of his beloved. He took the step and fell from the bedpost.

CHAPTER 17

Haul and his team now fired indiscriminately as the infected were now on their every side. They had used all the UV bursters they had.

"They have us enclosed, sir. We have no exit," Sites said with a calmness that showed acceptance but not surrender.

"Noted, Petty Officer. Your orders still stand. We fight till we can't," Haul replied.

"Roger that, Commander. Expect no less."

The men had the UV emitters that were built into their body armor on. This would slow the incoming droves of infected, but it wouldn't stop them.

"Surrounded? That just means I can shoot in any direction!" Canberra shouted.

"What the hell, Can, how long you been waiting to use that line?" Rock said.

The men laughed. Haul couldn't be prouder.

"Long gun's empty. Switching to sidearm!" Canberra yelled.

"Strip Shaw's weapon and ammo, Can, now!" Haul yelled.

"Already on it, Top!" Sites hollered as he took the last of the ammunition off his fallen teammate. "See you soon, brother. Godspeed," Sites whispered as he handed Canberra the extra magazines and returned to sending rounds into the infected.

Haul fired, hitting infected and offspring alike. He reached into his carrier and took out his last magazine. They would deplete all ammunition within a matter of minutes.

"Men, when you run dry, edged weapons and prepare for hand-to-hand. We'll take as many of these bastards with us as we can.

Make it a pyrrhic victory. Make them remember this day! It has been an honor leading you, men!"

The men retained their training, and the infected drew closer and closer but still fell in droves.

"I'm out!" Rock yelled as he drew his knife and drove it into the skull of the nearest infected to him.

Another rose behind him and leaped toward him. Canberra fired a round into its head. "That's me, brother. I'm out," he said as he, too, drew his knife and went back-to-back with Rock.

Haul and Sites were on their last magazines of their handguns. They would be out of bullets very soon also. They stayed with their backs to each other and Rock and Canberra in between them. The infected closed in fast, but suddenly, a deflected Tomahawk missile shot down into the infected. It blew them apart and created a large hole in the infected's line. The blast was close to Haul and his men. Although the defected missile knocked them to the ground, it gave them much-needed minutes. They slowly got to their feet.

"Sir, we have an opening—we can get clear before they regain the advantage!" Sites stated.

Haul looked around; the blast had knocked the infected back and had indeed created the opening the SEALs needed to escape. Haul's mission was not complete, though. He couldn't paint the target, that much was clear, but he had another idea, one last-ditch plan.

"Sites, get the men back to base. I have a plan! I'm gonna burn this damn thing to the ground."

"Sir, we're with you together, one way or another."

"Follow your orders, Petty Officer, now!"

There was no time for discussion. Sites understood this. "Men, on me. Fall back now!"

The men complied without hesitation. They began to make their way back to the LZ, where the egress vehicles were waiting. Sites tossed his sidearm to Haul.

"You got thirteen rounds in there still. Give 'em hell, sir!"

"Expect no less, Petty Officer."

They exchanged one final look before Sites and the remaining men fell back, heading out of the city, and towards the egress vehicles. Picking up the SARH, Haul set the autolock beam onto the base of the Spore. But TARGET UNREADABLE continued to flash across the screen. Racing out toward the Spore as the infected were regaining their momentum, Haul focused in on his objective. The infected were closing in around him as he reached the base of the Spore, sat, and leaned against it. Frenzied, the infected jumped at him, offspring crawling over debris to get to him. Haul held a weapon in each hand. He collectively fired the handguns into the infected, dropping them. The weapons ran dry. He drew his knife and drove it into the skull of the closest infected. He rolled over into the beam from the SARH, and as it locked onto his body, the LED changed from red TARGET UNREADABLE to green TARGET LOCKED!

"USS *Alabama*, fire all batteries on my SARH lock now!" he shouted into his radio.

Haul continued to fight the infected. He looked up and saw the Tomahawks bearing down on his location. "Have a fine Navy day you sons a bitc...."

"No!" Caleb yelled. He felt the Spore die. This was impossible. These miserable humans... they had gone from insignificant to aggravating "I have had enough of you people!"

"You people?" Miles said.

"Yeah, Cal, they don't really like that phrase," Thomas added, hoping to frustrate Caleb and keep him off balance. Thomas needed Caleb angry and sloppy; the madder he was, the more mistakes he was likely to make.

"Miles, he's too fast for a headshot. Let me wear him down, then take the shot when you get it."

"Roger that."

Caleb dashed right at Thomas. Thomas didn't know the extent of his newfound strength, but it was time he found out. Rushing out to meet him, Thomas felt a rush of power. With the combination of strength and his training, he hoped to match Caleb, but the beating he'd received before was still with him. It would take more mind than muscle. Thomas sidestepped him as they met. Caleb threw a punch that Thomas quickly blocked and countered. Striking Caleb in the chest, Thomas knocked him off his feet. He then delivered a jaw-breaking knee to the side of Caleb's face. Caleb rolled over. Bending down and grabbing Caleb by his shirt, Thomas lifted him off the floor and spun him around, using the momentum to throw him across the room into a wall. The force of the blow shook Caleb, and he was down. Thomas began to walk toward him.

"Not so fun from the other end of a beating, huh? I'm not going to kill you, although I should. You're going to fix this mess you created," he said. "Oh, and by the wa—"

Thomas stopped midsentence. He was sweating profusely, his vision blurred, his body began to tingle, and he was beginning to shake. A sharp pain in his chest dropped him to his knees.

Miles saw him in trouble and moved in. "He may not kill you, but I'm sure as hell going to." Miles raised his weapon and fired at Caleb.

Caleb had recovered and managed to move past the master chief's deadly fire. Miles fired again and again but could not get a headshot. Caleb jumped with tremendous force at Miles, knocking him down. Lying on the ground, Miles watched as the shots he had managed to land on Caleb closed and healed as if they had never been there. Caleb walked to him, picked him up into the air by the neck, and slowly began choking the life out of him. Thomas was in full diabetic attack; he lay helpless, watching this monster kill his friend.

"S-s-s-stop, Caleb. Don't, wait. I'm not... I'm not done yet. Ser... Sera..."

"Leave my sister out of this! There is no help for you! It's over, Sheriff, you are over!"

But Caleb was distracted just enough. Miles felt himself blacking out, but he held on to Caleb's wrist and brought his knee up to Caleb's jaw with a bone-crushing blow. It was enough to break Caleb's grip and cause him to drop Miles. Miles hit the floor, desperately gasping for air. Caleb walked over to finish him, and Miles put his hand up.

"Wait, no more, no more! You win. I can't take any more. This is what you want. Here, take it!"

Caleb picked the master chief up by his shirt. Miles reached out with a closed fist and put something in Caleb's hands. "Hooyah!" Miles said softly. Caleb looked into his hand with utter confusion. He did not recognize the pins from the two grenades Miles had managed to pick up when he'd grabbed his weapon. The blast sent Caleb across the room, the explosion ripping into his body.

Thomas watched as his friend died bravely, delivering what should have been a death blow. With any other enemy, it would have been. Caleb was very badly hurt, but he was healing already and would be back on his feet soon.

Thomas tried to regain his own footing. He couldn't get up and fell back down to the ground. He began pulling himself over to his fallen friend. *Dammit, Miles, you should have listened and waited for me with the men,* Thomas thought to himself. He held Miles's body, bidding him a last farewell.

"This is how you will always fare against me, Sheriff," Caleb said, already back on his feet.

He was standing but still having trouble moving. His body was still healing itself. Thomas lay with his back against the wall, still holding his friend's body.

"I knew I couldn't beat you, Caleb. I knew taking out the tower was not a viable option. I knew forcing my way in here was not possible."

"Then why try, Sheriff? I mean, I'm glad you did. I don't know what gave you temporary feat of strength, but I will find out. I will cut you open and find out all that you have to offer. Soon after that, I'll regrow another Spore. Without the human resistance, I'll be back on track, and I'll recycle this trash pit you call a planet! You've accomplished nothing!"

"No, Caleb, you won't. I thought there may have been a way to take you alive, maybe have you help fix my world. You don't fix—you only break, kill, and destroy. You're evil, and I'm going to watch you die!"

Caleb managed laughter; it was deep and bellowed. He had regained the use of his legs and was almost recovered. "You will watch me die? Sheriff, I believe your condition is far worse than I thought. You've become delusional!"

"You've killed millions, but among them, you killed one in particular with your virus. You ask why I try. Why won't I give up? Her name was Susan Marie Pratt. You killed my wife! You'll pay for that now."

"How's that, Sheriff? How will I pay for killing a lab rat?"

"I told you I wasn't done with you yet. You mentioned earlier Sera was an excellent tactician. Finally, something we can agree on. Sera, now! Enjoy the show, you bastard!"

"Japon, Eldon, release the veil," Sera said mentally.

In what was an instant, a flash of thoughts and memories rushed into Caleb's head. He saw Japon and Eldon, the other two Usraians who had been part of his team and had disagreed with his methods. Caleb saw as they met with Sera. They had never left the planet, as Caleb had thought, and blocked his mental probes of their meetings. He watched as Sera came up with a plan to stop her beloved brother. Her scheme to trap the humans had been a recruitment plan to find those who would fight all along. He saw as she secretly met with the sheriff a week before and told him everything. Japon veiled her thoughts from Caleb as Eldon shielded Thomas's. He saw the pain Thomas went through not being able to tell anyone else of his true plan. Anyone and everyone else's thoughts were open to Caleb and would reveal any resistance. Japon and Eldon could protect only two, and because of Sera's biological connection to Caleb, hiding her or any human's thoughts from him was impossible without Japon's masking. He watched as she explained to Thomas that the destruction of the one tower would be useless. Caleb saw Thomas come up with a plan to get past all of Caleb's infected and get inside the impenetrable building. He would have Caleb bring them and the gear they needed inside for them under the guise of surrender. Caleb was stunned.

"Sera, you will die for this! Sheriff, this changes nothing! You can barely stand. How do you plan on stopping me?"

"I don't, but I bet a couple of your houseguests would like to have a word with you."

Sera sat behind a thick glass panel in the control room.

"I am sorry for this, brother, but you have left me no choice. We cannot do this. I told you the destruction of a planet was a risk I was willing to take, I just never told you it was our planet I was willing to risk. I cannot allow you to destroy an entire species, seven billion life-forms. No, Caleb, I cannot trade one civilization for another. Not even if it is ours. I have to stop this. I have to stop you."

Tears streamed down her cheeks as she reached down and pressed the release buttons on the electric locks that held the Ragers. It had taken the combined strength of both him and Sera to subdue just one.

"You think this is over, Sera? I notified home command and sent an anchor point. When I don't report in, Kilian will send Jacob and his acolytes! He will make what I've done here look like the mercy I told you it was. The council will not lose this source of Theozin. All you've done is prolong their misery!"

The Ragers jumped off the table, confused by their release. Once they saw Caleb, the one who had tormented them over and over, they had one focus. Caleb turned and tried to run, but the Ragers were on him before he got five feet. They were savage and relentless. Caleb fought back, but they were too strong. They punched and ripped at him even as he lay motionless. Sera came out of the room and picked Thomas up. She gave him a shot.

"This will help you recover. This shot will stabilize you for now. Take this one for later. We have to move before they notice us."

"Wait, my backpack. Get the radio and the SARH!"

She did as he asked. Thomas autolocked the SARH on the panel in the lab that controlled the towers. He now stood on his own power. Whatever she had given him had afforded him a full recovery. They ran out the door and headed to the stairwell. Thomas called into the radio.

"USS *Alabama*, this is Commander Pratt. New target acquired, full-battery launch. Authorization, Martinez. Authentication code, Greenlight 25893." He turned to Sera. "Sera, we have three minutes. Can you get us out of here?"

"Yes, but we have to go upstairs."

They ran up three flights of stairs, out the exit, and onto the roof.

"We have to jump to the next building, Sheriff. It's an eighty-foot jump, but with your new gifts, you should be able to make it. Go! I'm right behind you."

Thomas gauged the distance. It looked completely impossible. But the past year had shown that word really no longer existed. Besides, there was no choice. Thomas took a deep breath and shot off in a dead run. He planted his lead foot hard and, with everything he had, leaped off the roof and soared through the air, barely catching the ledge of the other building's roof. He pulled himself up.

"Okay, Sera, your turn. Come on," he said to her mentally.

"Thomas, I am sorry I lied to you. You have surpassed me and my abilities. I cannot make that jump. We don't have much time, so listen very carefully. Caleb has sent an anchor point, and Jacob is on his way. It will not take him as long to get here as it took us. The anchor point is a direct route they can use to what we call star-jump. After Caleb fails to report in, you will have one year, two at the most. He is warrior breed. Kilian is our warrior supreme, and Jacob is his finest, deadliest, and cruelest disciple. I am truly sorry. I will try to find another way down, but I fear my time has run out."

The missiles were inbound. Thomas watched as she ran back inside the building.

"Sera!"

The missiles hit the tower as Thomas ran for cover. The missiles ripped the tower to pieces. The impact and heat caused the building to collapse in on itself. The destruction was complete. There was no way she could have survived. The only good thing was, if the Ragers hadn't finished Caleb, the explosion definitely would. What was coming, though? Sera had mentioned Jacob and his acolytes. She said they were warrior breed. Caleb was just a scientist with no tactical or military training, and they could barely stand against him. What chance would they have against battle-tested soldiers? They were coming; that was for sure. Thomas didn't know how, but he would be ready. He looked over the city. The missiles had caused so much destruction.

Thomas stood atop the high-rise building at the edge of the city. The city was burning. Fire was everywhere. And almost the entire city was destroyed. He watched as it burned, and wondered, Did it work? Was it worth it? He'd lost so much, sacrificed so many. It was all so chaotic. Choices so *impossible*. He was tired. The city was so still after all that had happened. Calm and quiet. As if the city decided to die in peace and go quietly into the night.

The placidity of the city gave him a brief moment of solace that had been foreign to him in what had become his world now. Before, stillness meant death.

The surreal, almost-tranquil state of the city made him relax too much. There was movement behind him. He reached for his weapon, but it was too late. It hit him with the force of a small truck. Pain, darkness. His mistake. Stillness meant death. That hadn't changed.

The infected that attacked him was different now somehow. It was no longer trying to convert Thomas; it was simply trying to kill him. This further convinced him of Caleb's death—the infected were no longer following his programming. Thomas caught his breath and recovered. He pulled the infected down off him. He knew how they worked now, and he had the strength to put them down. He punched through the infected's back, grabbed the queen offspring from its spine, and crushed it in his hand. The infected fell to the ground and began to spasm. It seized up and died.

There was a battle coming. This was far from over. Even in death, Caleb created havoc. Thomas had to prepare. Time was short, and he had very little idea where to start. What he knew was that he had to get back to the compound. Sera didn't think Simon would be able to get past the compound's walls and guns, but she'd been wrong. Thomas still had his team on standby; Sera had given Simon incorrect coordinates for his men. If only Miles had stayed with them. There was no time for that now. Simon had a head start, and Thomas had much ground to make up.

* * * * *

Jessica ran down the hallway. She had to get to Jimmy. *Where are you, Dad?* she thought. The lights in the base went out, and the emergency red lights kicked on. She came to the end of the hallway that led to the vehicle bay. The infected were swarming the bay.

"God, no, please. Let my family have made it out," she prayed softly out loud.

The bay was no longer a way out. She backtracked and ran down the passageway. It was pandemonium. People were running wildly through the base. The infected were everywhere. Somehow, they no longer seemed concerned with infecting people and now were more like Ragers. Jessica hid around a corner as the infected ripped into people. The mauled and mangled bodies littered the hallway. The metallic smell of blood filled her nose, and the smears on the walls painted a portrait of the carnage playing out in the compound.

A familiar voice called out to her. "Jessica! Jessica!" She turned and saw Mark, Rita, and Keylin.

"Jessica, have you seen Kenny?" Mark asked desperately.

"No, I'm sorry."

"We have to get to the bay!" Rita said.

"No! I just came from there. It's no good. They're everywhere!"

"What are we going to do?" Rita asked.

"The *Titan*! It's still down in the elevator bay. It was too bulky to put in the vehicle bay, remember?" Keylin said.

"Yeah, but they put the keys in the lockbox in the armory."

"Then that's where we go, the *Titan*," Jessica said.

"You guys go get the keys. I have to look for Kenny. We'll meet you at the *Titan*," Mark said.

"Mark, baby, please. I know you feel you have to do this, but would he really want you going back in there?" Rita asked. Her voice was shaky and pleading, her eyes tearing up. It was impossible for Mark.

"He's my brother. He'd do it for me. I'll meet you, I promise, baby."

"I'm the only one here with a weapon. I'll go with you," Jessica said.

"No, Jess. Protect the group, protect my wife. It's what your father would have done."

Jessica nodded; he was right. "We have to move, now!' Jessica said.

Mark ran back into the chaos, frantic to find his brother, as Jessica led Keylin and Rita toward the *Titan*.

* * * * *

Simon walked through the bay. The infected were murderous. They still followed his commands of where and what to attack, but now, instead of spreading the infection, they were killing and ripping people apart. He couldn't stop it, nor did he want to. The facility's soldiers were no match for the onslaught and easily dispatched. The infected killed without mercy or hesitation. Simon grabbed a security officer before the infected tore him apart.

"Where is the man who was brought here in custody—young Billy? Where is he?" Simon demanded as he squeezed the man's neck.

"Lockup… it's on the lower levels," he managed before Simon snapped his neck.

Simon made his way to the holding cells. And he found Billy. "So you've managed to escape me, after all." He ripped Billy's body down from the pole where he hung and slung him over his shoulder. "Just because you're dead doesn't mean I can't decorate my camp with the pieces of your body."

"No, Simon, that's exactly what it means. You're going to die here today, but how you put my friend's body down determines how much you scream doing it!"

Simon turned to see Thomas standing in the doorway of the holding cells. There were four dead infected lying at his feet. He pulled the queen offspring out of the back of another he was holding up, and it fell dead next to the other four.

"Sheriff, you've… changed. You know, I can't feel Caleb anymore. Did you actually manage to kill him? I'm impressed. I'm free from him. I can't hear him in my head anymore!"

"Free? Oh, don't worry, Simon, you'll *hear* him again real soon."

Simon knew that if Thomas had killed Caleb, then he would not stand a chance against the sheriff.

"You want this corpse? Take it." Simon threw Billy's body at Thomas. As Thomas caught it, Simon quickly closed himself inside one of the open holding cells.

"Sheriff, I'm sure you could rip these bars open to get to me, but know this: I've called every infected at my command. All the infected that were linked to me when Caleb died are now mine alone to command. That's around three thousand. Think you can take that many?" Simon said.

Tearing through those bars and beating that debauched smile off his face was almost worth it. But there was a war coming, and his family was still out there. Thomas took Billy and headed to the surface. He came out into the hallway, and the infected stood in force, blocking his path. There were too many to count. He would make a stand, his last. He gently lay Billy's body against the wall and kissed his friend's forehead.

"I'm so sorry, Billy. I failed you."

Thomas stood up; he was starting to feel the shortness of breath, and his vision began to blur. He took out the shot Sera had given him. He would need all his strength. He pressed the needle gun to his arm and injected himself. He felt the effects right away.

Simon walked out into the hallway.

"Seems you weren't quite fast enough, after all. Oh, well, it's for the best. I would have found you eventually. Now I'll have my prize back *and* get to watch you die. You were part of Cole's death. Just so you know, this doesn't end with you. I'll find your family and peel their skin away. They will die slowly, Sheriff."

Jessica squatted low on the balcony with Keylin and Rita, watching her dad in the lower level below her. She could see Billy lying against the wall, and she knew her friend was dead. Her sorrow was crushing, but she swallowed it. This wasn't the time for despondency.

"You two head to the armory and get the keys to the *Titan*. Get out of here!" she whispered.

Keylin and Rita looked at her. There was no time, and they couldn't afford to make the noise arguing with her. They went on toward the armory.

Jessica looked at Simon; he seemed to control the infected that now surrounded her dad. She would take that bastard out, no matter what. She loaded an arrow and pulled the bowstring back. She rested the arrow against her cheek. She breathed in and out, in and out, in, then held it. This shot would be perfect. If he held still a moment longer, it would tear right through his left eye. She was ready. She released! The slight whistling sound of the arrow cutting through the air caught the attention of Simon's enhanced senses. He turned his head and, with one blindingly fast move, caught the arrow only centimeters from his eye.

"And it's not even my birthday." Simon laughed as he looked up and saw Jessica on the balcony. "Sorry, Sheriff, there's no middle command here. My dogs don't fetch. There's only *stay* and... *kill*." The infected took the command and rushed up toward the balcony.

"NO!" Thomas yelled out.

He ran and jumped twenty-five feet into the air, grabbing the rail of the stairway. He pulled himself over and cut off the wave of infected. On the steps, he had a chance. Their numbers worked against them due to the narrow space. Thomas fought them with a savagery and fierceness only a parent of any species protecting their child would understand. There were no boundaries. Nothing was off-limits. This was not a fight of honor; he would not fight with dignity. It was horrifying. He had become a Rager!

Jessica fired into the infected, all headshots. She saw her father tearing into them. The rage, the breaking of bones and cartilage, the tearing and slashing of flesh did not so much as startle her. Thomas ripped, broke, killed anything he could get his hands on. The blood covered him, and he would not stop. He didn't want to. The infected jumped to the railing behind Jessica, and Thomas couldn't hold both sides. Arrow after arrow launched into the infected until she fired her last. They closed in from the other side of her. Thomas ran up the steps, picked her up, and jumped to the level below. But they were still cornered. He put her down behind him; they had landed right where Billy's body lay.

"Stay behind me, baby." She wasn't sure how he was standing against them with his bare hands. If this was the end, she was in the right place, with the right people. She sat next to Billy and held him. There were too many.

Simon walked in front of his infected. "This has been entertaining, Sheriff, but it's time now, time for you to die. I seem to recall a certain promise to skin your little lamb. I can try to keep her alive, but if you fight, my children will kill you both without a doubt. Would you rather give her a chance and have her walk over to me while I hold them at bay, or watch them tear her apart?"

Thomas said nothing. He had nothing. If Simon tortured her, at least she'd be alive, with the chance that his people would come for her. Of course, he could never do that. He was fast; he could take her quickly without pain, before they got to them. She would never know what happened. *Sue,* he thought, *I'm sending our baby girl home. I'm coming right behind her.*

"Okay, Simon, you win. You can have her. Let me kiss her goodbye, then she's yours," Thomas said, stalling. He walked over to Jessica. "Jessie, I'm doing this for you, baby. I can't fight them all. Mommy's waiting for you, honey, and I'll be there soon. I love you. I love you so much!"

Jessica understood. She put her head to her father's chest and held him. Thomas held her close also. Slowly he moved his hands under her chin. With a swift movement, he would pull her chin up and out, fast and hard, breaking her neck. She would feel no pain. After, he would make a direct line for Simon, fast, hard! The infected would no doubt kill him, and he was okay with that. He prayed for God to give him strength to finish this. Thomas took a deep breath and held it. He tensed and began to pull his little girl's neck.

The trembling and shaking of the room made Thomas pause.

The wall just next to them ruptured, and the debris knocked Simon and the nearby infected back. The *Titan's* flail system burst through as the balls and chains shredded the wall. The back door opened, and Petty Officers Till, Lamer, and Ryan burst out of the back of the truck, laying down heavy suppressing fire. The infected fell, and Simon retreated for cover.

Jessica ran and jumped into the back of the *Titan.*

"Hope you don't mind we picked up a few stragglers," Keylin said of the SEALs that were now on board the *Titan*. Mark, Kenny, and Rita pulled Jessica into the back of the truck. Thomas went to get Billy's body, but Till grabbed his arm.

"There are too many. We have to go now!" He was right.

Thomas took one last look at his friend then leaped into the back of the *Titan*. The SEALs continued to fire as they jumped back inside. Keylin drove forward. The flail system and the vehicle's pointed nose pushed through the infected and up the ramp toward the surface. The *Titan* burst through the doors and into the surrounding woods. The warmth of the sun brought soothing relief to them.

Thomas looked out the windows and saw the helicopters taking off en route to the waiting naval carriers. He prayed his group, his family, was aboard the helos.

"Dad!" Jessica said, her heart heavy and eyes full of tears as she held her father.

She thought about Billy and leaving his body behind like that. She felt she would never let go of her anguish.

"It's okay, baby."

"Sir, what happened out there? Master Chief Miles?" Tills asked.

"No, son, he's gone," he said. "But our fight isn't over. Someone's coming, someone worse. We have to prepare, prepare for what's coming."

They rode in silence. Not knowing what lay ahead. Afraid but willing to do what they must in spite of it.

ABOUT THE AUTHOR

Lamont Chatman is a first-time novelist. He loves to keep his readers on the edge of their favorite reading chair. He refuses to cheat them with fast fixes and impracticable solutions to the characters' situations. He is a great storyteller and loves taking the readers on a roller-coaster ride.